Praise for My Paperback Cape: The Unlikely Odyssey of a Bookworm

"This is a fabulous story about a young woman facing up to all of the simple and not-so-simple challenges in a modern girl's life. I loved watching Jackie's character stretch and grow and mature – we were there right along with her. I couldn't put this well-written, touching page-turner down. Teens will love all of the characters, situations and the language of this book — and grownups will too! A must-read."

"Wow! Loved this book. What a page-turner from the start. It was a joy and privilege to follow the development of the main character, Jacqueline. Every parent of teenagers should read this. Every teenage girl and boy NEED to read this. Its hilarious and shocking at the same time."

"I couldn't put it down! Wish this was part of school curriculum. It might not make it past censors but it deals honestly with many everyday things."

Also by Lynn Rankin-Esquer

The Unmooring of Mrs. Mango

The Tangerine Dress: An Order Out of

Chaos Mystery (Book 1)

My Paperback Cape: The Unlikely Odyssey

of a Bookworm

Lynn Rankin-Esquer

XandL Press
California

Dedicated to my heroes, Dave, Elle, and

Xavier

Chapter One

The Myth of Barbie

You want to know what the biggest pile of bullshit is? Barbie dolls.

When I was younger I loved my Barbie dolls. I played with them for hours, dressing them and arranging them and making their lives work out perfectly. They had boyfriends who adored them, families who were loving and successful. Their jobs were glamorous, their friends plentiful, their beauty indisputable. I really believed these little plays I put on were a preview of my life to come. When I pictured myself grown-up it was with platinum hair and a Barbie body.

Imagine my disappointment, at age fourteen, to have no hips, no chest to speak of, plain brown hair and zero boyfriends (and that's a *lifetime* stat). As for the loving and successful family, does one out of two count? After all, we *did* recently move into a mansion. Too bad the amazing house didn't come with the warm, fuzzy feelings our family seems to be lacking. Must need to purchase those separately. Or maybe we are more plastic than I thought.

"Mimi!" Mom cooed, stopping her empty grocery cart by a mass of cut flowers stacked in a pyramid of shiny black containers. We hadn't made it ten feet into the store before Mom saw someone she knew.

"Marion, how *are* you?" Mimi could have been a poster mom for the Kentley Heights Country Club. Her blond highlights were cut in a chic mom-bob, and she wore custom-fitted jeans with a sleek suede jacket over a green cashmere sweater. I'd bet she had a standing eyebrow appointment to get that perfect arch. Just another one of the fifteen or so BFF's that Mom had met within days of moving to Kentley Heights. I guess it pays to be a tennis stud. Not that I have any of that talent, even though Mom says I *should* be great with my extra long arms. I love those kinds of comments. As if it's a compliment that you have ape arms.

And like I said before, it's not like those ape arms are on a Barbie body. I wouldn't go so far as to say I'm ugly, but no one's stopped me on the street to offer me a modeling contract either. No, I had to get lucky in the brain department. I'm not exactly complaining about it, but if I had a choice, I would trade some of those brains for boobs. Equal out the endowments so to speak. So I wouldn't have skipped second grade. Big deal. Being younger just means my body looks even more immature next to the other girls in my grade.

"Parker, stop that! I told you, if you grab one more thing, no cookie!" Mimi manhandled her toddler's arms back into the cart and looked at Mom. "Hey are you playing Friday?"

Mom nodded. "And Lindsey's coming too. It'll be fabulous!"

How could these women so endlessly enthuse about tennis and the latest appetizer recipe? It was like they had no souls, just computer chips loaded with the latest in housewife apps.

I stared around the upscale store where Mimi clones bustled around, piling their carts with organic bananas and green cleansers. The whole green and trendy vibe didn't exactly match the Barry Manilow music playing through the sound system, but then again, it didn't match the parking lot full of gas-sucking SUV's either. Despite the crappy music the store was packed with people grabbing dinner. Why cook when you can get fresh sushi or hot enchilada pie? Throw a little money at it and the dinner problem goes away. Money solved a lot around here. For the millionth time in the six months since we moved I thought longingly of our old home in Michigan.

Mimi bent down toward my five-year-old brother Davy who was crouched in the back of our cart sticking his fingers through the grid and making shooting noises. "Hi there big guy!" Mimi said in that goofy, cutesy voice that moms use for babies.

"Bang!" said Davy, pointing his finger straight at her face.

"Davy! Say hello to Mrs. Vonn," Mom said through her clenched, over-whitened teeth.

"Pow!" Davy said, pointing at Parker, who burst into tears and grabbed at his mother.

"Now Davy, that's not polite," Mom said forcing her voice to be cheery, but I could hear the anger underneath. Any show of bad manners is humiliating to Mom. Davy would pay for that one.

"Hey girls!" rasped another one of Mom's friends. Cece pushed her cart alongside ours and faux hugged Mom, the stench of cigarettes floating around her like Pigpen's dirt cloud.

Cece's daughter Madeleine hung back behind her mother, looking around the store at everything except me. Madeleine's long dark hair was carelessly pulled into a ponytail and her dark rimmed eyes flicked around in the universal sign of extreme boredom. Like "why am I here and why do I have to put up with this?" Her Ipod earbuds effectively protected her from any conversation. Which was fine with me. Madeleine was in my grade, but had never acknowledged my existence. Not that Madeleine would have been high on my friend wish list. Madeleine smoked a lot of something more powerful than her mother's cigarettes.

"Maddy, say hi," Cece said, poking at her daughter. Madeleine didn't respond. Cece rolled her eyes and plucked out the white cords snaking into Madeleine's ears. "I *said*, say hi."

Madeleine tilted her chin up a millimeter and mumbled "hey" towards Mom. Her eyes stayed focused on something about a mile away.

"Jock-leen, say hello to Maddy," Mom said brightly, pushing at my shoulder in Madeleine's direction. Mom looked at Madeleine, "Jock-leen doesn't have any friends yet, really. You'll have to come over. I'll bet you two could be BFF's!"

Thanks for announcing my loser-ness Mom. In case Madeleine hadn't noticed.

Madeleine continued staring off into space. Nice strategy, maybe I'd try it myself.

Cece laid her hand along Madeleine's back. "Maddy, Mrs. Carson was speaking to you." Cece shook her head, looking towards Mom. "Of course that would be lovely, we'll have to set something up for the girls."

Really? My very own teenage playdate?

"Maybe Maddy could introduce Jock-leen around," Mom chirped, prolonging my social hell. "I know she's a year behind for her grade and looks a little, *young*, you know," Mom gestured up and down around her chest. "But she's smart, and I think she'd be a loyal friend."

Oh my God, she didn't just say all that. Thanks for pimping me out Mom.

I heard a snort from Madeleine's direction. So all it took to get her attention was embarrassing the crap out of someone. Good to know.

"Oh sure," said Cece. "Maddy has just *tons* of friends!"

Yeah, if you count pot-heads, drug dealers and zoners.

I stared at the ground, wishing I could disappear through the crack in the linoleum. My face and neck felt hot and I was sweating inside my ski jacket. I switched my stare sideways, at the flowers. Maybe I could disappear into them, like a bee.

"I told her to join the swim team or tennis team or *something*," Mom continued, oblivious to the fact I was seconds away from melting into a puddle of shame. "Some people are just, shall we say. . ."

"Shy?" Mimi jumped in.

"I was going to say 'slow,' slow at that sort of thing," Mom finished.

Too bad none of the flowers was a sword. I could have stabbed her right now in full view of all the shoppers. I'd rather rot in Juvie than stand here for one more second.

Mom is an idiot. All I do is get straight A's, help around the house and read a lot. And she's so desperate for me to be "social" that she'd rather I was hanging out with the druggies.

Not that it really mattered, but I wondered, as I stared at the flowers, whether my mom wished a social life on me for my sake or for hers. You know, the whole appearance of having a normal daughter thing.

She just wouldn't quit. "Maybe Maddy could introduce Jock-leen to some boys!" Mom said brightly. "Help her out in the boyfriend department."

More snorts from Madeleine's direction.

I could kill her. I really could.

"Pow pow! Take that you bum!" Davy hissed, as if he heard my thoughts. I glanced sideways and saw he was gesturing at Parker who cowered behind an enormous box of Cheerios. Davy watched a lot of TV.

"Davy! Stop it," Mom said. "We better get moving, this little guy is just losing it!" Mom said gaily, maneuvering the cart out of the little circle they had formed.

Lots of peppy "Bye bye!'s" and I was free. Free to follow Mom up and down every aisle staring at the checkered linoleum floor until my flush finally faded and I was sure we weren't going to run into Madeleine again. Free to obsess about my loser-ness. About my Mom's cluelessness. About the fact I didn't even mention that I actually do have a friend. A real BFF. Wait 'til Emily heard how Mom embarrassed me.

By the time we left the grocery store the lights were on in the parking lot. Although it was only about six o' clock, the dark chill of a Pennsylvania fall night made it seem closer to ten. I zipped my jacket up to my neck and grabbed Davy's hand as we started toward the car.

"Oh shit," Mom said. She shoved the cart and car keys at me. "Take these to the car, and put Davy in. I left my latte on the checkout counter."

Before I could answer she turned and hurried back into the store.

"Mama said a bad word!" said Davy.

"I know," I said. "Don't you say that, okay?"

One more of the "do as I say, not as I do" deals. Parents are full of them.

As I maneuvered Davy and the cart through the parking lot, Davy suddenly yanked his hand out of mine and ran for our car, several spots away. The red glow of rear back up lights headed toward him from the other side of the lane.

"Davy, stop!" I yelled, letting go of the cart to chase him. A flood of fear propelled me to his side in less than a second as the car stopped backing up inches away from his little head. I grabbed his jacket and pulled him out of the range of the car. I bent down and put my face in his.

"Don't ever do that again! You ran right behind that car!"

My heart was pounding so loudly it felt like it was coming out of my ears. What if something happened to Davy? How could I have let go of him that easily? All of a sudden he seemed incredibly precious. Sometimes he just had too much boy energy, karate chopping around the house, yelling and banging around corners knocking me down, telling infinite poop jokes, but mostly he was a good kid. And in this moment all I could see was Davy's soft brown eyes and the way they crinkled into dimples on the side when he smiled. And the way he had of cracking me up with lines from TV. Just yesterday he strolled in the door after a play date and announced "Davy's in the *house*," like a rapper about to throw down. Funny how that could all happen in a second.

"Hey," a voice said behind me. That casual, chocolate rich, smirking voice could only be Alex Madigan. Yikes.

I held onto Davy and turned around. Yep, it was Alex, pushing our cart. My adrenaline went up another notch.

"Need some help, Jock-*leen*?" he asked, managing to mock Mom and me at the same time. I didn't even think he knew who I was, but he must have heard Mom call me that at the country club. My name is Jacqueline and everyone else pronounces it "Jack-lin." Mom likes to pretend she is fancy and French when she is really just from here in the good old Pittsburgh area. It's not a bad place, but no one would confuse it with Paris. Alex didn't belong to the club, but Tommy Thornton had brought him to the pool a number of times last summer. Who knew Alex had noticed the new girl, the ape-armed, shy girl huddled in the far corner lawn chair? He rumbled the cart toward us, smiling with teeth so bright they lit up the dark parking lot.

Alex was fifteen and the top of every girl's wish list (probably some women's too). The rumors about Alex flashed through my head. He had, you know, *slept,* with a bunch of different girls. He had been arrested. He imbibed all sorts of non-performance enhancing substances. He had tattoos. I'd seen the tattoos but had no evidence of the rest of it. Not that any of it was hard to believe. My best friend Emily said that Alex was so hot she couldn't even look directly at his face, like he was a solar eclipse or something. He looked at a person as if he could see directly into your brain and right through your clothes. And like he was thinking of doing something to you when he got those clothes off.

He was looking at me that way right now.

Predictably, I froze. What good are all those IQ points if your brain freezes up when you need it?

"That's our food!" Davy said, pointing at the cart.

"Yeah," said Alex pushing it up beside us. "Where's your car?"

Davy pointed to the next car over, and I hit the remote, beeping up the back door.

I pulled on the cart and managed to mumble, "Thanks."

Alex seemed in no hurry to leave, and I felt the flush starting up my neck again. Just standing near him did weird things to my body. I didn't like it at all. Well, maybe one percent of me liked it. The adventuresome part. The rest of me wished he would go away.

I hauled Davy up into the back and nudged him towards his booster seat.

Alex started unloading the groceries into the back of the SUV, and I felt idiotic because I couldn't think of one thing to say. I had used up my entire repertoire with "thanks."

"So, you're out here by yourself?" Alex said, casually running a hand through his wavy dark hair. His bulky jacket made his already broad shoulders seem even wider. Even seen through peripheral vision his body was hot. "Driving without a license, huh? I like that in a girl." Still laughing at me.

I couldn't speak. It was like my tongue and mouth had forgotten how to form words.

Alex loaded the last bag into the car. "I'll take this back," he said, grabbing the cart. He gave me a wave, as if we had actually had a conversation. As if I had actually spoken more than one coherent word.

I barely even nodded. I just stood there watching his fine butt walk away with the cart.

Sometimes I really hate myself.

Chapter Two

Nowhere to Run

I ran my fingers over the book in my lap. I was re-reading *From the Mixed-up Files of Mrs. Basil E. Frankweiler* for about the twentieth time. Claudia wouldn't have stood there mute in front of Alex. Claudia would have had something to say. She wouldn't have been flooded with fear. Claudia wouldn't have been afraid to be herself. Not to mention that Claudia managed to escape from her clueless mother. Wish I could do that. I'd take Claudia's twelve-year-old confidence over my fourteen-year-old wimpiness any day. Ever since I first read the book years ago, I'd always imagined Claudia as aging along with me. An older version of Claudia would be kicking *ass* by now. Claudia wouldn't just think witty and profound thoughts, she'd actually manage to say them out loud. At the right moment. Unlike pathetic me.

I was startled out of Claudia's exploration of the Metropolitan Museum of Art by a snort from Mom. Unfortunately I was still in my life, sitting in the passenger seat while Mom drove home.

"Did you see Mimi's sweater?" Mom snarked. "That green was just not in her color wheel. It made her look ghastly."

"Hm-mm," I agreed, sneaking a glance at my phone.

"What do you think of *my* outfit?" Mom asked.

Ugh. Time for a PATT (Praise All The Time). Mom needed a constant stream of adoration.

"Perfect," I said. "You are *right* in your color wheel."

Whatever that means.

I tried to use her words whenever possible. She loved it and I'm lazy.

Mom glanced down at her bright pink sweater, crisp white collar peeking out and delicate silver chains overlying the whole set up. "Yes," she sighed. "Pink is good for me." She shot me a sideways glance, "But it's not too pink, right?"

How could she go from self-praise to uncertainty so fast? Whiplash.

"No, it's just right," I said. My script is very clear. Agree, praise, agree, praise.

Finally I heard the ping of my phone. Emily, replying to my "Alex Madigan talked to me!" text.

OMG! OMG!
R U JK?
U must b lying.
tell me every
deet. what was
he wearing? what
are you wearing?
where were you?
OMG, OMG, OMG
Em

Thank *God* for Emily. Almost six months here in Kentley Heights and she's still my only friend. In Michigan I had three best friends that I had known since fourth grade and a tolerable spot in the social hierarchy. I wasn't wildly popular, but I wasn't a nobody. Aside from not attracting any boys life was okay. Then thanks to good old dad's big promotion I was suddenly plopped down in Pennsylvania, stuck at the Kentley Heights Country Club for the summer. I swear we were the only new members in like forty years because everyone there had known each other from birth. And FYI: kids who have hung out together at the same country club since they could crawl can smell new money from miles away. They do that subtle nose wrinkle, like "I just caught a whiff of skunk but I'm too well bred to actually fully scrunch my nose."

I know I'm on the unnoticeable side but before last summer I'd never actually felt so ugly that people turned their eyes away from me. Every day I begged my mom to let me stay home, and every day she dragged me there and dumped me at the pool while she played tennis. Every day I sat there with a book, watching Davy splash in the pee pool and trying not to notice how intently the kids my age were ignoring me.

Mom grew up in a whole different kind of suburb of Pittsburgh. Norwick was only thirty minutes away from Kentley but several income brackets below. It sounded like a good childhood to me but Mom's itch to move back to the Pittsburgh area had a grander plan than row houses and a city pool. Now she acted like her family had lived in Kentley Heights for five generations and were the founders of the country club. Although to be fair, after what happened in Norwick five years ago I can understand why she avoids going there. I just wish it wasn't such an off limits topic in our family. I'd like to know why it all happened. I'd like to know it won't happen again.

Aside from being a tennis stud, Mom can pick up on the local fashions and mimic them immediately without looking like an idiot. Like, all the ladies at KHCC wear visors when they play tennis so Mom bought one in every color. I guess she thought a new look would make me fit in just as easily because she went out and bought me Ugg boots like the whole KHCC swim team wore. Yeah, that's all it takes to fit in, wear freaking fur boots in the summer time. You see me in Ugg boots you don't see a post-work-out-cold-and-weary-but-toned-and-athletic swimmer, you see a Dr. Suess character. Tall, geeky, shapeless.

And every day she'd pester me. "Go talk to all those cute boys and girls! Make some friends!" Like making friends was as easy as making cookies. Mom has a lot of issues, but shy isn't one of them. So she totally doesn't get it that it makes me feel all squid-like inside to even *think* of talking to someone new. She doesn't understand that I have a million cool, witty things going on in my head but none of them actually come out of my mouth. I don't think she's even noticed that I stand silent whenever anyone new speaks to me. Not that anyone at the country club was speaking to me.

Finally Emily had shown up at the club. She was fifteen, but since I had skipped second grade we were both going to be sophomores when school started up again. Emily had been hired to watch two of the Zabroski's five kids splash in the pee pool. Mom made me watch Davy for free. Emily kind of reminded me of a cute beagle, with big brown friendly eyes and a goofy kind of smile. Her dark blond hair was cut into a funny looking page boy that flipped up on one side and under on the other. She was tiny but looked strong, like those gymnasts you see on TV who look eight-years-old and turn out to be eighteen instead. No one talked to Emily either. So a couple of days into her employment I gathered up my courage and sat down beside her at the pee pool.

Sitting in the dark car all these months later I wondered if Emily had any longing to be different, like Claudia. Like me.

he came up to me!
he knew my name!
i stood there like an idiot.

I hit "send" as we swung around the last curve of our long driveway and looked up at our house looming large in the dark. A legitimate mansion. Wouldn't most girls be excited to live here? Then again, I doubt that her Dream House or Malibu Beach house made Barbie that happy either. Doesn't matter how fancy the accessories, in the end she was still just a brainless, plastic doll.

"Unload the groceries, would you Jock-leen?" Mom said after pulling into the garage and slipping out of the car. "I've got to get dinner on the table," she added, opening Davy's door and helping him out of his seat. "Dad will be home any minute."

Yeah, good luck with that. Dad rarely got home before ten these days. I guess practically running the entire steel industry is more than a nine-to-five job.

It wasn't worth the fight so I did what she asked. Just like usual.

Robo-daughter.

As I dumped bananas into the fruit bowl on the counter Mom punched the play button on the answering machine and Dad's voice echoed across the expanse of granite counters.

"Hey guys, go ahead and have dinner without me, I'm going to be late."

Big surprise.

"Dammit!" said Mom, slamming her purse onto the chair beside the kitchen mom-desk.

I felt my insides tighten up.

Here we go again.

"What is wrong with that man?" Mom said, turning to face me, eyes narrowing like it was somehow my fault.

I shrugged. My insides tightened even more.

"No respect. That's what he has for me. No respect." Mom kicked off her shoes and violently slid her feet into her in-the-house flats. It didn't matter how angry she was, the Perfect House Rules were never violated. Shoes worn outside were not to be worn inside. Number 47 of the 300 or so rules for beautiful living that Mom followed.

Mom shook her head and gave a big sigh. "I'm just so tired of all this."

Yes, living in a mansion is really draining.

I stacked the boxes of pasta in the pasta cupboard and then moved on to sorting the vegetables into their proper bins in the refrigerator. I'm well trained. Plus, not that I'd ever admit it to Martha Stewart over there, it is soothing to me to put things in order. I aligned the asparagus with the cucumbers, all pointing sideways in the drawer. At least I have control over the vegetables.

"A family dinner is very important. How many times do I have to tell him that? It's like he doesn't even care about us." Mom slammed the lid of the crockpot down after tasting the contents.

Yes, it is definitely more important that Dad get home and taste your slow cooker coq a vin than, say, do his job well. Seeing as it pays for this house and all.

Davy streaked through the kitchen waving a plastic airplane from side to side. "Veeeeeerrrr, whrrrrrrr," he yelled and disappeared into the family room.

"Don't roll that on the floor!" Mom yelled after him. "Those wheels will scratch the hardwood!" Davy lived in a constant stream of "don't do that" commands. Like he was just a constant annoyance to Mom.

Mom leaned over onto the center island, her shoulders slumping. "Jock-leen, what am I going to do?"

Uh oh, here comes Clingy Weepy Barbie.

I lingered over the vegetables, not wanting to look at her. Freeze like a deer and maybe I'd blend into the soft white of the kitchen.

"Stop putting those stupid things away and look at me," Mom said, her voice cracking at the end.

The air in the room closed in on my chest. It was like we had been transported to a planet with fifty times the gravity of earth. Like the whole atmosphere was pressing down on our bodies.

I slowly stood up and closed the refrigerator door. Finally, there was nothing to do but turn around. I dragged my eyes up towards her face. Mom's brown eyes tipped up just a smidge on the outside and her cheekbones were high, a combination that often had people asking if she had modeled in the past. Nothing pleased her more than being asked if she modeled, unless it was getting carded at the grocery store. Like she didn't know the checkout boy was just playing with her. I mean *really,* did she honestly think she looked younger than 21? Right now her eyes were scrunched up in a failed attempt to hold back tears, and her face didn't look like she could model anything except the need for antidepressants.

"He doesn't love me," she whispered. "I can't take it, I don't know what to do."

I stood, rooted to the spot, helpless. I had no idea of what to say or do. There are a thousand topics I have very clear ideas about (not that I ever actually manage to express those ideas) but this wasn't one of them. I felt like I was falling through space, endless space. With no oxygen.

Mom gave a little sob. "Tell me it will be all right," she begged. Her eyes looked wild and scared, like a petrified hamster facing the gaping mouth of a snake.

My insides were twisted tight. My throat felt closed. Could I even make a sound? I looked at the desperation in Mom's eyes. "It will be fine," I choked out. "I'm sure Daddy loves you. Everything will be fine."

"Do you really think so?" Mom cried, hope fighting against desperation in her trembling voice.

NO! I only said that because you told me to say that. Jesus Christ.

Mom walked around the island to me and put her arms around me. "Do you really think it will be okay?" she asked, her head buried in my shoulder.

No! What do I know?

I knew I didn't want her to end up like Aunt Helen. "Yes," I said forcing cheer into my voice. "I'm sure everything is just fine."

Without lifting her head from my shoulder Mom reached for my arms and placed them around her back.

I imagined that a fourteen-year-old Claudia would have told Mom to just deal. Claudia wouldn't stand here spouting big lies to keep Mom in denial-land. Claudia might even have raised the possibility that the reason Dad was staying at work longer and longer was because Mom was nagging him to death. I felt rush of jealousy that Claudia had been courageous enough to run away.

Jealous of a fictional twelve-year-old. Life is good.

I gave an inward sigh and squeezed Mom. "All fine!" I said. "Really."

Mom gave off a little sob as the phone rang. She looked at the caller ID and then punched the on button. "Hello?" she said, her voice bright as a brand new pre-school teacher.

Mom waved me away and continued talking in the "Mom Fake" voice I'd heard a thousand times. Tears and drama and then, boom, the phone rings and she picks it up and talks to a friend or a repairman or whoever as if she's the happiest woman on earth.

I knew which one was the real Mom, and it wasn't the one on the phone.

Chapter Three

Queen Bee Mean Girl Barbie

It was the day after the Alex encounter, and I was headed towards Emily's locker. We were going to walk to the gym together to see the posting of the newly chosen Poms. Alex walked by on the other side of the hall, and I slid a glance at him. Looking at Alex sucked out all of my brain so of course I walked right into a girl in front of me.

"Oops, sorry," I mumbled and then panicked as Cassidy Dubroski turned around and gave me her supercharged mean girl glare.

Of all the people to run into. What kind of idiot am I?

"Did you just *touch* me?" Cassidy sneered, wiping at her shoulder as if I were an open petri dish of E coli. "Uh, *walk* much?" Two Cassidy clones on either side of her laughed.

In my short time at my new school I had privately named Cassidy "Queen Bee Mean Girl Barbie." QBMG Barbie came with a Playboy body, long shiny blond hair, a stunning face and a viper's personality. QBMG Barbie was short on brains and programmed to hate anyone who wasn't a Pom. So far she had not noticed me, and I was kicking myself for managing to work myself onto her radar. Cassidy had yet to put it together that I was the daughter of Mike Carson. The very Mike Carson who came into United Steel and took the job Cassidy's dad thought he was being promoted to. And according to my dad, meanness ran in the Dubroski family.

I bent my head down and said, "sorry" again and tried to slide past Cassidy.

She pushed my shoulder with her perfectly manicured hands. "Where do you think you're going?"

Far away from your contaminating radioactive bitchiness.

"Back to the short bus?" one of the clones jeered.

Cassidy laughed, "Good one!" She turned to walk away but first flipped her long platinum hair over her shoulder, looking back at me. "See you, loser. Better yet, hope I don't see you."

Likewise, Queen Plastic.

I shook my head at my clutziness the rest of the way to Emily's locker. That was close. Cassidy might have actually figured out my name if that had lasted any longer. Good thing I was such an Unnoticeable to her. Not even worth putting a name to. I might think of clever comebacks, but they never make it to my mouth.

Don't you just love those stories where someone moves to a new town, goes to school and is instantly surrounded by friendly, welcoming students? I guess kids at Kentley High never saw those movies. It was more of a *Mean Girls* kind of school. I was lucky to have found Emily and mostly just took the head-down-get-through-the-next-four-years approach.

I shivered, thinking about Cassidy's latest casualty, Annabeth Spinzel. Annabeth did nothing except develop a nice set of breasts over the summer. Shawn Mellner posted a FaceSpace comment rating Annabeth's body as better than Cassidy's, and Cassidy swung her team of airheaded followers into action. They posted nasty comments about Annabeth, they pushed her around in the halls, and they spread vicious lies about Annabeth performing sexual acts on the football team in their locker room. Pretty soon Annabeth was a shaky mess and then she stopped showing up at school altogether. One rumor was that she had moved. Another rumor was that she moved and then killed herself. I would have thought there would have been more in the news if she had killed herself, but who knew? The point being, stay out of Cassidy's line of vision.

As Emily and I walked to the gym I mentioned re-reading *The Mixed-up Files* .

"Oh yeah, I liked that book," Emily said. "I read it when I was, like, nine . . ."

The implication being it was a baby book. I'd take Claudia over that sourpuss Bella Swan any day. Of course Edward and Jacob were a whole different story.

"Yeah, I keep re-reading it, I just like Claudia I guess," I said. "In fact, I wouldn't mind being more like Claudia."

"Yeah," Emily said, but she didn't really seem to be listening. She was looking down the hall, and when I looked the same direction I could see a horde of girls all bunched up around the bulletin board. Emily had actually tried out to be a Pom, which I found amazing. Not in a million years could I do that. First of all I'm a complete klutz. And second of all, I'm totally lacking the coolness gene. The thought of getting up in front of people and doing *anything* turned my insides to liquid, but the thought of getting up and *dancing?* Not even a date with the boy band hottie of the moment could convince me to try that. Not to mention that I am totally lacking the fanatical school spirit gene that the Dance team girls all seem blessed with. Emily has been taking dance for years so it wasn't actually an impossible dream for her. Except that secretly I thought she wasn't cool enough either.

The regular Pom tryouts had been held last spring, before I had even moved to Kentley Heights. Emily said she had gotten as far as the sign-ups but chickened out at the last minute. Then two weeks ago Mrs. Valari announced she would be holding a special tryout to replace two Poms who had spectacularly misjudged their spacing and managed to knock each other out for the year. One had two pins in her ankle and the other ripped up the ACL in her knee. Who knew dance was such a contact sport? Maybe it was my encouragement (what was I thinking? I was thinking she had no chance, that's what I was thinking), but this time Emily had actually gone through with the tryout.

So we pushed our way through the crowd and there it was on the wall.

> **New Dance Squad Members:**
> **Emily Channing**
> **Melinda Barnes**
> **Congratulations!**

Emily screamed and dropped her books and started hugging me. "ohmygod ohmygod ohmygod!" she yelled, grabbing my shoulders and looking at me with wild eyes as she jumped up and down. "I can't believe it, I'm a *Pom!*"

"That's awesome!" I said putting on a big fake smile for her as she almost pulled my arms out of their sockets.

Great. Bye bye Emily.

I was an awful friend. I knew how badly she wanted to do this, but all I could think of was that my only friend was about to disappear. Gene or no gene, Emily was now immediately cool. She was now part of *Cassidy Dubroski's* group for god's sake. Big breasts couldn't be far behind.

Even though we were standing less than a foot apart, I felt like a canyon just opened up between us. She was in a whole new world now. We were like a Venn diagram whose circles just moved apart. Overlap disappearing in front of my eyes.

I heard another happy squeal behind me as Melinda Barnes grabbed Emily and started jumping up and down. The gym doors flew open and a pod of Poms (minus the injured) poured out and surrounded Melinda and Emily. Mean Girl Queen Bee Barbie herself was leading the charge. Cassidy threw her arms around Emily and Melinda and as one amorphous beast they moved up and down. The squealing echoed off the hall walls, the sounds amplifying until I could feel my ear-drums vibrating. It sounded like pigs being slaughtered. The jumping and screaming group bumped me to the side of the hall.

Bye Emily, I thought as I walked away.

Alone.

Alone.

Alone.

By the time I was on the bus home I had worked myself into a complete funk. It was as if Emily never showed up at the pee pool. No, it was worse because God apparently was teasing me. Toss me a friend and then take her away. "Hey look! Everything's going to work out fine. *Psych!* Just kidding. You are a loser."

I hated my dad for making me move. I hated my mom for the easy way that she immediately made a new set of friends here. I hated Poms. I hated teenagers. I hated everyone in the whole world, most especially my own pathetic self.

Chapter Four

You Give Love a Bad Name

"Jock-leen, keep an eye on Davy while I run over to Cece's." Mom's head was sticking through the family room door, where I was slumped on the couch channel surfing. Nothing on TV could distract me from my lonely loser-ness, but I was trying all the same. Wasn't TV supposed to ruin your brain? I couldn't ruin mine fast enough. Unfortunately the loser thoughts kept streaming in at full volume.

"Did you hear me?" Mom's voice notched up in intensity and irritation.

Of course I heard you. Dogs three counties away heard you. Your voice could cut glass.

I didn't answer so she stalked into the room and stood between me and the TV. "Hello? I said, you need to watch your brother while I run these pans over to Cece's."

Ah yes, here I am, your built-in babysitter. Always home and always will be now that I have no freaking friends.

I shrugged. "Whatever." I looked up at Mom to see if there was a chance she had actually noticed that I was depressed. Weren't moms supposed to have some kind of special kid-radar to notice that kind of stuff?

Mom started towards the door. "Don't let him eat anything, we'll have dinner when I get back."

When I didn't answer she said, "Did you hear me? What's going on with you?"

Ah, there it is. Finally.

"Well, you know, I kind of had a hard day at school today." Even as the words left my mouth I wanted them back. What a wimp I am. Even twelve-year-old Claudia wouldn't have bothered trying to get attention from her mother. I'm a loser on every front.

Mom rolled her eyes. "Hey, *lots* of us have hard days. You wouldn't believe the shit *I* had to put up with today. So keep that little brother of yours from messing up the house, okay?" She swished out the door.

Mother of the Year.

A few minutes later I heard a crash from upstairs. I waited to hear crying but didn't and decided if he was really hurt Davy would call for me.

I flipped through the soap operas. No thanks, I've got my own real dramas. I stopped on the latest talk show, again a big no. I really didn't need to hear about protecting your children from perverts. Wasn't there anything funny or uplifting on TV?

I could read something. Return to Claudia's world. I was too lazy to even get off the couch to go find the book.

Only one thing left to do. I switched the Source button over to "Game" and picked up a Wii guitar.

Five songs later, my brain happily mellowed out by Guitar Hero 5, I shook out my hand. You'd think after all the hours I've spent playing Guitar Hero and Rock Band my wrist would be strong enough not to get all spazzy. A sore wrist was a small price to pay for forcing all my beastly thoughts back into their caves. Ah, sweet blank brain. In the break in the music I heard cabinets opening and closing in the kitchen.

"Don't eat anything," I yelled to Davy. "Mom says we're having dinner in a few minutes."

No answer.

I dragged myself off the couch and schlepped to the kitchen. Davy was sitting on the floor with his hand buried in a bag of cheese puffs, fluorescent orange cheese all over his face. He smiled at me and grabbed a puff, licked it, and stuck in back in the bag.

"Jackie, you should try these things! They're awesome."

I grabbed at the bag. "Mom said no snacks before dinner."

"I'm not eating them! I'm just licking the cheese off."

Like there's anything resembling cheese in those things.

As I stuffed the bag back in the cabinet I heard the garage door go up. "Hurry up! Wash your face," I said, pushing Davy towards the sink hoping it was Dad coming through the garage door, not Mom. Dad wouldn't notice if Davy's pants were made of cheese puffs.

Unfortunately it was Mom and Davy's face wasn't clean yet.

Bam! She slammed her purse down on the counter and charged at Davy.

"I told you not to eat anything!" she screamed.

Bitchy Barbie appears. Can you say "over reaction?"

"It was my fault," I said, "I didn't tell him."

Mom glared at me. "I *told* you to keep him from eating! Now dinner is just *ruined*."

Ruined by some fake cheese powder? He didn't even eat the actual puffs.

"I'm sorry," I said, as contrite as I could sound. Didn't need a fight.

Mom yanked at Davy, pulling him back from the sink and sticking her face down in his face. "Look at your face! Did you even get any in your mouth?"

Davy was cringing back, shrinking as small as he could get.

Scared of his own mother. Poor kid. Next act: kick a puppy.

I stepped closer and grabbed a paper towel. "Here, let me clean you up," I said to Davy, trying to slide between him and Mom.

Mom let go of Davy's shirt and stepped back. "What is wrong with you people? Can anyone follow a simple direction for Christ's sake?"

Mom opened a drawer and slammed it. "Look at this place! It's a mess!"

I looked around. Two dishes in the sink, a book and a notebook on the counter, and a pile of papers at the other end of the counter. Hmm. Hardly time to call *Hoarders*.

I wiped Davy's face. "Let's go, uh, straighten up the family room," I said to him, putting my hand on his back to push him along with me.

I don't know if it was a boy thing, or a kid thing, or just Mom's general moodiness these days, but she wasn't very nice to Davy. You'd think if you went to all the trouble of having a baby, and I know she did, you might actually show that kid some affection at times. I gave him a few hugs on the way to the family room and whispered, "Don't worry, that wasn't your fault. She's just in a bad mood."

We zipped around putting Wii remotes back in the charger, the guitar in it's cupboard, straightening magazines and pillows.

Right as we finished and had settled in to watch the Cartoon network, Davy snuggled in against my side, the garage door went up again.

Dad came in a moment later. If they made a Corporate Ken doll it would look like Dad. Dark cashmere overcoat, sleek leather briefcase and handsome fortysomething-year-old face with a little blue-tooth clipped to his ear. Just enough five o'clock shadow on his jaw to look manly, not so much that he looked like a lumberjack. Over six three so I knew where I got my height from. He was talking as he dropped his briefcase and stripped off his coat, tossing it over the side of the couch. I jumped up to grab it and hang it up. Didn't need more yelling from Mom.

"No, no, I can do 7:30. Just tell Gloria to move the eight o'clock back. Hmm hmmm, yeah, see you then."

Dad unclipped the blue-tooth off his ear and smiled in our general direction. "Hey guys, what's up?"

Mom is in Super Bitch mode. Davy just mainlined fake cheese. I lost my one friend in the state of Pennsylvania.

I almost opened my mouth to say those things, but Dad was already making a drink and not really looking at me. Funny how questions like "what's up?" are so often not really questions. More of a "hey I'm home and you're home and I need to acknowledge your presence but not really actually interact." Parents pulled that shit a lot, asking questions that they really didn't want to know the answers to. "How was school today?" being a prime example.

Maybe that was part of why I so identified with Claudia in *The Mixed-up Files*. Claudia knew that parents are full of it. Just like me, Claudia's mom didn't understand her, and didn't even seem to try. How could moms forget so easily? They were kids once, teenagers once. How could they travel so far into adulthood that they forgot what it is like? The difference between me and Claudia, though, is that Claudia didn't sit around obsessing about why her mother didn't understand her. She just made a plan and left.

Chapter Five

Inhabiting Claudia

You know the thing about Barbies? No one ever has just one. Somewhere I had a whole bin of them, clothes and cars and houses and nine or ten perfectly shaped plastic examples of what I was never going to look like. When I played with them they were always arranged *with each other*. Skipper and Barbie have lunch. Barbie and Kelley and Staci in the convertible on the way to the beach. Professional Barbie in a tailored suit at the head of a conference table full of other Barbies and a couple of Kens. In my Barbie plays I never once set up Barbie by herself in a lunch-room. Never stuck her in a loud miserable cafeteria at a back table with a big shining light over her head broadcasting her loner loser-ness to the rest of the packs of students sharing their lunch with each other.

But of course, that's where I was sitting, two days after the new Pom coronation, my head down, acting like I was so fascinated with my yogurt I couldn't be bothered to look up. I was sitting there alone because my one friend in the whole state of Pennsylvania was practicing her shake-your-ass routines during lunch period. Not much time to catch up with the rest of the Poms.

"How about here?" I heard a girl's voice near my table and saw a tray slide onto the opposite end from where I sat. I looked up to see a group of four or five girls standing by the table looking around.

"Ah, no, this table is no good," sniped a short girl with a high spout of a ponytail and a thick swipe of blue eye shadow over each eye. "It's already contaminated by a *loser*."

The rest of the group giggled and looked at me. I dropped my head and wished I could tell them all to get lost, but my mouth refused to open. I cursed at the hot feeling flooding my face, knowing they'd see me blushing and know I cared what they thought. Which I totally didn't, but my face didn't know that.

Ponytail number two, pink faced and piggish, chimed in, "Yeah, it's probably contagious. If we sit here we'll end up flat as a board with a horse face!"

The rest of the group cackled.

Or I'd end up with a nose like a pig and an ass to match.

Why couldn't I choke those words out? Why could I only *think* clever comebacks?

In my heart of hearts I knew they'd leave me alone if I could just look straight at them and tell them to fuck off. These girls weren't Pom material. They weren't even Color Guard material, but all crap runs downhill and they were abusing me like the more popular girls abused them. I just couldn't get my head to lift or my mouth to open.

As I stared at the crack between the laminate table-top and the gray lip around its edge, a vision of my hideous future floated before me. Every day I was going to have to sit here alone. Every day lunch period was going to feel like it was about six hours long, and I was going to sit in my loserness while every other single person on the planet walked around in a group of friends. And those groups of friends would stop by and bully me until I felt like a piece of roadkill, flattened and pecked to shreds by vultures. The only thing that stopped me from bursting into tears was knowing it would bring all the assholes more joy to see me crying. One of the girls bumped hard into my back as they walked away. Another reached over and flicked my yogurt container on its side, splattering pink drops onto my shirt.

I looked down at *the Mixed-up Files* and dove back in desperate to escape my shitty life. I was getting close to the end of the book, and as I read, thankfully, the magic of reading blessedly arrived. As my eyes scanned the conversation between Claudia and Mrs. Frankweiler after Claudia and Jamie first arrive at Mrs. F's house, I started to feel like I was in Farmington Connecticut, not Kentley Heights, Pennsylvania. My heart rate slowed down, and my breathing went back to something close to normal. My shoulders unhinged themselves from my ears. The lunch room faded. My brain began to send messages to my body that we were in Mrs. Frankweiler's dining room. I felt Claudia's confidence and command of speech. My own pathetic self disappeared, and now I *was* Claudia, confidently negotiating with Mrs. F. I convinced the crotchety old Mrs. F to let us look through her files to find the answer to the art mystery. It was *me* having that cunning conversation, *me* that had the audacity and presence of mind to negotiate so coolly. It felt great. It felt like the exact opposite of cowering before C list bitches.

I lost track of time and then something flickered in my peripheral vision. I was so immersed in being Claudia it seemed for a moment it must be Mrs. F's servant bringing our next lunch course. I looked up to see Alex Madigan sliding into the seat across from me, a big smirk on his face.

"Hey *Jock-leen*," he said, leaning forward onto his elbows, his flawless face so close I could see gold flecks in his brown eyes. I had never noticed how long his eyelashes were. You'd think it would look girly, but it just added to his hotness.

My normal Loser Barbie reaction would have been to freeze, all circuits offline so to speak. But somehow I hadn't left Connecticut and inhabiting Claudia. It was like I was still in conversation with Mrs. Frankweiler, and all of a sudden, it was Claudia talking to Alex.

"Oh, hi Alex. Wassup?" I could hear my voice, I could feel my lips moving, but it really wasn't me. Claudia, with all of her confidence and cool thinking, was streaming through me.

Alex raised his eyebrows, probably not expecting me to actually speak or look at him. Claudia-me felt bolder. It was almost like I was looking out through her eyes, like I could feel, for a second, what it must be like to have someone else's confidence. I don't know where I thought I was, but it wasn't at the loser table at Kentley High. I leaned forward looking straight into Alex's irresistible face.

"Hey, thanks for helping with the groceries the other night. Who knew you were such a boy scout?" I said, and if I didn't know better I'd almost say there was a flirtiness to my voice. Looking in his eyes sent a buzz through my body. A very pleasant kind of buzz that hit some of the more grown-up parts.

Alex laughed and this time there was no mocking quality to it. I laughed with him. "Oh yeah, that's me," said Alex. He pointed at the barbed wire tattoo circling his left wrist. "Got all my badges." He tilted his head and squinted his eyes at me. "And here I was thinking you didn't have a voice."

I shrugged, like who-cares-what-you-think? "Maybe I'm just, uh, selective," I said. I swear it almost sounded like I was purring. This was amazing.

Alex nodded. "Smart. I like that in a girl."

"Whatever," I replied. Like I couldn't really get excited to know what he liked in a girl.

The bell ending lunch period rang. Oh sure, now that I'm enjoying myself time goes at warp speed.

I stood up, pulling my stuff together. I shook my head to toss my hair back over my shoulders. Where did *that* move come from?

Alex gave me an intense stare, the one meant to weaken my knees and make me drool right in front of him.

"Catch you later," my not-me voice said easily, as if I talked to handsome get-you-into-trouble kinds of boys several times an hour.

"Yeah, later," Alex said with a last little grin.

As I watched him walk away I wondered when the Claudia magic would wear off. Was I like Cinderella at the ball, escaping before the spell disappeared?

I walked to my next class in a daze. What just happened? It was like my brain forgot to return me to reality, like I stayed in the book instead of coming back to my normal life. Lots of times I have fallen into books and had trouble finding my way back to reality, but the return usually left me speechless, not powerful. I never actually stayed in the character's mind like that, as much as I might have wanted to.

How had Claudia actually entered my mind, my whole body really, just when I needed her?

I felt a bubbling through my body, something swirling around in my veins in a way that threatened to escape my mouth as a giggle that might never stop. I just carried on a very cool conversation with Alex Madigan!

Books have always been my comfort, my entertainment, my own place to hide. Is it possible they can be more? If I can pretend to be Claudia and actually talk to Alex Madigan without sounding like a complete idiot, what else was possible? Or was it a fluke, would I not be able to summon that magic again?

I hadn't lost touch with reality. I knew that Claudia was a fictional character. I knew that she lived only in the pages of a book. And yet, having spent so much time in that world with her, I felt like she was a real person. And just now, I had felt what it might be like to *be* her, or at least have her kind of confidence and bravery, if only for a moment.

Forget Barbie, I wanted to be like *Claudia*.

Sitting on the bus on the way home I kept running my hands over *The Mixed-up Files*, like touching it conferred some sort of magic on me. I wondered what Claudia would do if she was fourteen now and her best friend became a Dance Drone. I wondered what fourteen-year-old Claudia would say to lunch room bee-atches. I wondered if I could summon Claudia-me again. I closed my eyes and tried to remember how it had felt to be Claudia when I talked to Alex. The memory brought back a little tingle to my body, and when I opened my eyes Claudia's spirit surged through me. "*Who cares about the stupid Poms?*" she seemed to be saying. It was like I was looking out at the world through her eyes again. Staring around the bus I felt Claudia say that most of the kids around me were idiots. What did they know about anything?

Much better.

That's it. I was going to pretend to be Claudia. Claudia-me decided that all this spirit shit was really pretty silly and nothing to be concerned about. After all, there is a very interesting and sophisticated world out there and dance may be fun, but it isn't exactly curing cancer.

The boy beside me flicked the ear of the boy in front of him, and I pulled myself up against the window to get away from their wrestling. Not to mention his obviously-didn't-shower-after-PE body odor.

What morons! Claudia-me thought, looking at the boys. *I'm not like these people. I need to think of a worthwhile way to spend my time. I need to enrich my life with things that matter. Things like art and music and reading. And maybe I should expand my friendships, since Emily is basically gone. Enrich and Expand. "E and E."*

Yes, that felt planful, like Claudia was planful. She had figured out all the details of running away, from the money, to where they could live in comfort, to how they would get there. I needed that kind of planfulness. I needed to map out my life. As pathetic as it was, it was all I had.

B.O. boy beside me banged into me again.

"Knock it off, dickwad," Claudia-me said. No one was more shocked than me at those words. Well, maybe the boy. He ducked his head down and mumbled an apology.

I opened my mouth!

Wow. It was back, the magic was back. That time with Alex wasn't just a fluke. I felt like I'd just slipped into Superman's cape.

Maybe I could *make another friend. Maybe I could do* anything.

I looked around the bus and smiled, feeling secretly powerful. The power of Claudia was with me. I even caught the eye of B.O. boy next to me and smiled at him to let him know there were no hard feelings. He seemed even more scared by the smile. Or maybe it was the smile coming so soon after the dickwad comment.

Delicious.

Chapter Six

Ebb and Flow

I floated up the driveway. I could feel something swelling up inside me, just like Mrs. Frankweiler had described to Claudia. Something good and strong, something I hadn't known was ever even in there. And yet, I knew, I just *knew*, it was real. And it was *me*. Maybe I wasn't a complete loser. I still couldn't believe that actual words, in a coherent order, had come out of my mouth today with Alex. I slipped through the garage and into the kitchen, almost tripping over a bunch of big heavy boxes stacked by the mom-desk.

There were dirty dishes on the table and on the counters. It looked like the leftovers from lunch and maybe even breakfast. Odd. Perfect Housewife Barbie never left dishes like this.

I headed in the direction of the family room, hearing the faint sound of the TV. I found Davy sprawled on the couch, watching a rerun of *The Hills*. Scattered around him were the remains of just about every junk food invented. I saw ice cream bar wrappers and smashed fish crackers and a half full sleeve of cookies. A blue energy drink had spilled on the coffee table, mixing with a squeezed yogurt tube.

"What are you doing?" I said, grabbing the remote and flipping off the TV. He didn't need to be watching *The Hills*.

"Watching TV," Davy said. "Turn it back on!"

"You can't watch that show, where's mom?"

"FINE! Put on Nickelodeon then. Or the Cartoon Network," Davy answered.

"Where's mom?" I said again. Obviously she hadn't been in this room for a while.

"Upstairs. Sleeping I think," Davy said, craning his neck to see around me. "Put the TV on!" he demanded again.

I held the remote up as a threat. "What happened today?"

"Nothing. We went and got a bunch of Grandma's old books and then mom said she was tired."

I flipped the TV back on, found Nickelodeon and headed upstairs feeling uneasy. What was going on? Dirty dishes and an unsupervised kid?

Mom's room was dark, the curtains pulled shut. I could make out a lump in the bed and went closer.

"Shut the door," Mom mumbled, throwing her hand up over her eyes.

"Are you sick? What's going on?" I said.

"Tired. Leave me alone," Mom said, rolling over and burying her face in the pillow.

I didn't know what to do. I tried not to think about Aunt Helen.

"Go away," came a muffled voice from the pillow. "I just want a nap."

I went.

They had gone to Norwick. Mom hadn't gone there for a while, I couldn't even remember how long it had been. Then again, a mom could just be tired, right? Just need a nap once in a while? It didn't have to mean anything. And yet, I wondered. How did it all start with Aunt Helen? Did she start sleeping in the middle of the afternoon for no reason? Did she start leaving her normally spotless house a mess? What were the signs that apparently everybody, including her twin sister, missed?

I went back to the kitchen and opened one of the boxes. Just a bunch of books. Then I remembered that when mom complained that she didn't have enough books to fill up the shelves in our new fancy library, Grandma had told mom to take the boxes of books in storage that were leftover from when they downsized houses. I couldn't imagine books had anything to do with her weirdness. Maybe something happened with Grandma?

I picked up the phone to call Dad and then put it down. What would I say? Mom is napping? It sounded so stupid, and yet I knew by the squeezing in my chest that something was off. Plus Dad had left for a business trip. Nope, I was on my own with this one. Whatever it was.

By dinnertime Mom still hadn't come out of her room. I had finished my homework, all the while straining to hear sounds of Mom's door opening. Finally I went back in.

"Mom, are you sick?" I said. She'd already said no, but I didn't know what else to say. She was lying on her back, staring up at the ceiling.

"Just tired," she said, not breaking her stare. Her makeup had worn off and her hair was messed up. *So* not the mom I was used to seeing. She looked *imperfect*. That was perhaps the part that was scaring me the most. This was the woman who put on a full face of makeup before she went to the hospital to give birth to Davy.

"Um, do you want dinner? Should I start it?" I said.

"I don't care. Go ahead and make something for you and Davy. I'm not hungry," she mumbled.

"Did something happen? Are you okay?" I asked. I had to know. What caused this?

Finally she turned to look at me, a tear slipping out of her eye. "I'm just so tired. It's just all so hard. I work and work and work, and get nothing for it."

I had no idea what she was talking about. What was she expecting to get?

"I'm just worn out. Order a pizza if you want. And if you have a chance, start putting those boxes of books away in the library. But for now, just let me sleep." She turned her back to me and pulled the comforter up around her neck.

I left her room more disturbed than ever. And yet I still felt like I couldn't call Dad. They were fighting so much these days I didn't want to add to it.

"Hey Davy, we get to order pizza!" I said brightly, my voice as fake as Mom's can be. Davy was fooled by it.

"Awesome!" he yelled. How he could still be hungry was beyond me.

While we waited for the pizza I made him help me clean up the family room. Then I did the dishes in the kitchen.

I've had to babysit Davy so much you'd think it would have felt normal to be sitting there, just the two of us, eating pizza. But something still felt all wrong in the house. Dad not home yet and Mom, not really home either. I didn't like it.

The happy fizzy feeling from school was gone. It seemed like a hundred years ago.

I was sitting in my window seat, staring out into the dark night. My head was leaning against the cool window and I held *The Mixed-up Files* in my lap.

I felt the magic of inhabiting Claudia slipping away from me. I wanted it back so badly. I couldn't just keep re-reading the book over and over again, but I had to escape the worry over Mom, so I re-read the last two chapters. I let myself disappear into Claudia's world again. I felt a small return of her confidence. Nothing like earlier today, but it was enough to think I might actually be able to fall asleep tonight. I got ready for bed, squirmed around in my sheets to warm them up and tried to imagine I was Claudia.

I started off in Claudia's world. First I ordered my little brother Jamie around a bit, just to warm up. Then I imagined sneaking around to my hiding places in the Metropolitan Museum of Art. Then I imagined looking through Mrs. Frankweiler's files and finding the answer to the mystery of the Angel statue. Finally, after really feeling like I was in Claudia's skin, I imagined taking that confidence back into my world. I saw myself talking to Alex again. I felt the witty words just flowing out of me. Mmmm, delicious. Temporarily distant from my worry about Mom I fell asleep.

Chapter Seven

Too Close to the Sun

I woke up to the smell of coffee. Boy was I happy for that because unless he they were teaching new skills at preschool it wasn't Davy down there making coffee. When I went into the kitchen Mom was up, if by up you mean out of bed. No make-up and still in her nightgown, which made exactly two times that I've seen Mom in the morning without her face on. The other time being the day after Davy was born. Davy munched happily away at his cereal, seemingly oblivious to Mom's condition.

"How are you feeling?" I asked her.

"Fine," Mom said, frowning at me like I just said something confusing.

"Well, you were so tired yesterday . . ."

Mom rolled her eyes. "I'm fine. I don't know what you are talking about."

Okey dokey. So we are going with denial.

"After school, I want you to put those books away," Mom said nodding towards the boxes I had failed to move last night. "And do the boxes already in the library, I never did get to them," she added.

Excitement over boxes of books fought with worry over Mom. The worry won, and I left the house unable to shake a feeling of unease. I'm sure lots of moms appeared in the kitchen first thing in the morning in their pajamas. Just not mine.

Emily and I were walking to chemistry.

"I still can't believe it!" said Emily. "I can't sleep. Nothing like this has ever happened to me!"

"Yeah," I said. "It's amazing." I wondered how much time I had left with Emily. She was walking right beside me, but I felt all quivery inside with the knowledge that it wouldn't last. Our friendship felt very precious, like one of us was dying of some awful disease. Come to think of it, one of us kind of was. Death by dance squad.

"Hi, Emily!" Jennifer Walker called out as she bounced up to Emily, ignoring my presence. "You look awesome!" Jennifer gave Emily an enthusiastic hug. "I'm so glad you're on the team with us!"

Jennifer looked like she stepped off a Southern California reality show. Her tanning salon dark skin contrasted with her flat-ironed bleach blond hair. Her heavily made-up green eyes were enhanced by long eyelashes curled so tightly they banged into her eyelids every time she blinked, and her stomach was flatter than her hair. Jennifer hugged Emily and continued her Tigger-bounce down the hall. Emily had on her normal outfit of Sketchers, jeans and stretchy T-shirt. She looked the same as she always looked and no one had ever, not once, gotten so excited about her appearance. Was I missing something?

Several more people greeted Emily enthusiastically before we made it to chemistry. None of them said hello to me. In fact, I don't think any of them even saw me. It was as if Emily was walking by herself.

In chemistry, as we headed toward our normal front-row seats, Cassidy pranced up to Emily.

"Hey! I didn't know you were in this class!" Cassidy said.

I can see your confusion, Cassidy. We've only been in this class a couple of months.

"We *have* to sit together," Cassidy continued, putting her arm around Emily's shoulder. We're Poms!"

"Oh, definitely," said Emily sliding a star struck look at me. Those eyes said "Cassidy Dubroski knows me! She touched me! She wants me to sit with her!" I started to sit down in my normal front of the class seat but Emily grabbed my arm, pulling me along with them to the back row.

Cassidy turned around and gestured at a seat for Emily. Finally she noticed me and narrowed her eyes. "What are *you* doing, the loser section is over there." She waved towards the front of the room as she gave me a little shove.

Ah, yes if by loser you mean the brains, the ones who might actually pass this class the first time around.

Emily was already sitting in the seat indicated by Cassidy and stared at me with panicked eyes. Poor Emily, stuck between her friendly past and her popular future.

"Hey, Jock-*leen*," I heard from the left. Crap! By coming to the back of the class, I had entered Alex Madigan territory. My heart doubled its beats in a split second. I could barely bring myself to turn toward him.

Cassidy snapped her head towards Alex. Was Alex Madigan talking to an Unnoticeable?

"Hey," I managed to whisper, bending my head down so my hair would fall forward and hide the blush flooding across my face. *Where are you Claudia?*

Alex gestured towards the empty seat beside him. "Have a seat, *Jock-leen*."

I saw him flick a glance at Cassidy, clearly amused by getting me to sit near her.

I slid into the seat and busied myself with my books. What was I doing? How did I end up sitting back here? I could feel Cassidy's evil glare. She was almost vibrating with anger. I heard Cassidy snort and slam herself into a seat.

I stared at my books waiting for my brain to recover from its paralysis.

"You slumming, coming back here?" Alex asked, poking my arm in a friendly way.

I flashed back to my fantasy last night.

Be Claudia. Be Claudia.

"Hmm, hmm," I agreed looking up at him, feeling the burn of his touch even though he had moved his hand away. "Thought you brainiacs might need some help."

Alex threw back his head and laughed. "You can tutor me anytime."

My Claudia confidence grew, and I looked boldly at Cassidy. She had morphed into Satanic Barbie, her eyes narrowed and practically shooting a red glare at me. If her hands had sprouted daggers on the end of every finger I wouldn't be surprised.

I turned and smiled at Alex. "I'm sure you're good at tutoring too."

"Oh yeah, a whole different kind of chemistry," he said, winking.

Without even looking at her, I could feel Satanic Barbie's outraged anger. How dare an Unnoticeable talk to Alex Madigan?

Being so close to Alex made my whole body tingle, and the waves of Cassidy's hatred spilling over me filled me with fear. I faced forward, but I wasn't going to hear a word of class.

As class started, I slid a sideways look at Emily. She was looking at me with horror.

With Mr. Redmond lecturing, I was spared the need to talk to Alex, but it was hard to ignore the force field around him. Even the smell of him scrambled the neurons in my brain. There was the faintest odor of soap or maybe one of those body washes. The scent was mixed with, could it be shaving cream? And maybe there was a little dash of something earthy in his smell, finished with just a hint of boy hormone. It was a smell that made me want to get closer. And start touching him. I'd start with his hair, run my fingers through the waves that could turn into curls if they were longer. . .

Stop!

I was reminded of the myth of, what was his name? Icarus, the guy who made wings and managed to learn how to fly and then his son flew too close to the sun and boom. The wings melted and he fell to his death in the sea. I didn't belong back here near the sun. I stared down at my desk and reminded myself I was Claudia, and I had just solved the mystery of the Angel statue. I let the delicious feeling of the secret swirl around in me until I could feel Claudia's bravery and confidence again. As soon as the bell rang I broke free of the Alex force field and hurried out the door.

Emily caught up to me and grabbed my shoulder, turning me toward her.

"What are you doing?" Emily demanded.

"What do you mean?"

"Flirting with *Alex Madigan*!" Emily hissed, looking back over her shoulder as she tugged me down the hall. "*In front of Cassidy!* Cassidy's crushing on him! She's going to rip your eyeballs out. She's going to drive you out of school."

"He talked to me first," I said. "Plus, she has a boyfriend already."

"I don't care. Don't speak to him. Don't look at him. Don't even *think* about him. Maybe you should drop the class."

"What? That's crazy," I said, even as fear flooded through me, trampling the budding Claudia confidence.

"Hel*lo*? Does the name Annabeth Spinzel mean nothing to you?" Emily said, looking back over her shoulder again.

I didn't like feeling scared again. The Claudia bravery felt way better. "Well you're best buds with Cassidy now, just tell her to lay off me."

Emily looked at me unhappily. She didn't say it but we both knew that Cassidy's first move would be to make Emily choose between being a Pom and staying friends with me.

All through math Emily shot me worried looks, like she could hear the battle going on in my head. I liked pretending to be Claudia. I liked how it felt to actually *say* something for once. I liked talking to Alex. On the other hand, I liked being friends with Emily. Even though she was a Dance Drone now she was still my only friend. Maybe I should back off this Confidence thing. Maybe I should go back to silence and, you know, not getting beat up. Maybe it was better to stay off Mean Girl Queen Bee Barbie's radar.

Yes, that's what I would do. Stay away from Alex, keep my head down around Cassidy and give Emily her chance to survive as a Pom. Even as I thought it I could feel the Claudia-me part of my brain protesting.

No, Claudia was saying in my brain. I'm not going back to being a scaredy cat. I'm keeping the Confidence, and I'll talk to Alex if that's what I feel like doing and Cassidy will just have to deal. Easy for Emily to say don't talk to Alex, she had a whole new pack of friends. One of whom hated me.

Yes, no, yes, no, my brain was a war zone.

I glanced at my phone and saw a text from Emily, how had she managed that during class? When Mrs. Buttondale turned to write a long equation on the board I read it.

> pls don't annoy
> 37assidy! Pls.
> my life will be

ruined. Pls.
Em

I guess Emily didn't care about annoying *me*. Her text had the opposite effect of what she wanted. Who is going to tell me I can't talk to a cute boy?

I had wanted to be a *quiet* hero, like Claudia, but getting involved with Cassidy was going to have nothing to do with quiet. It felt too late to go back but too scary to go on.

The life of a high school girl is never easy.

Chapter Eight

Book Rich

I was standing in the library drinking a soda and staring at the stacks of boxes. I still couldn't believe our house had its own library. Three of the walls were shiny, dark wood shelves from the floor up to the high ceiling and the fourth had windows almost as high looking out onto the back lawn. There were two overstuffed leather chairs with a reading light between them for furniture, but I don't think anyone had actually ever read in here. Maybe because it was one of the few rooms mom hadn't finished decorating yet. I guess she hadn't gotten around to finding a website that sells books by the yard for the recently rich.

I ripped open a couple of the boxes, surprised by how many books fit in each. This was going to take a while. I looked at the shelves surrounding the room. Mom had filled exactly one shelf before abandoning the boxes that we had brought from Michigan. It kind of surprised me that she hadn't really put them in any kind of order, given how perfectly organized the rest of the house was. I guess she didn't really care if she could find *The Seven Habits of Highly Effective People* at a moment's notice. Mom got her advice from Oprah.

Okay. Definitely needed to divide up non-fiction into its own area. And Dad seemed to have a number of business advice books, those would get their own section. I found some gardening books, those would go together. Reference books over here. And then I started digging through the books from Grandma's house.

Looking around at the books and the empty shelves I felt a rush of pleasant anticipation.

A bunch of ancient looking decorating books, I didn't think Mom would use them but they would pad the how-to section. Some dusty kids' books, Davy would like those. Some health books, probably outdated, but Mom didn't care, she just wanted the shelves filled up. And then I opened a box with the entire set of Nancy Drew. And the Hardy Boys. And then a bunch of books I hadn't heard of and some I had, but all were kid or teen types of books.

School problems seemed like a distant dream, fading by the second. Books, books, books. I felt like the Pleasure Fairy just swooped down and sprinkled happy dust all over my brain. I sat down and opened another box, pulling out and stacking books like I was running my hands through gold coins. I felt a tickle running up and down the middle of my body. Books I hadn't read yet! In my hands, in piles surrounding my body, was escape. Was fantasy. Was knowledge and friendship. Ali Baba's treasure couldn't have excited me more.

I had burned through every book for my age and older. I had read about star crossed vampire lovers, wizard orphans and unsuspecting demi-gods. I had lived in post-apocalyptic America. I had A Listed 'til my brain turned into wet cotton candy. I was ready for some good, old fashioned books for a change and here they were!

Oh the delicious decision, which to read first?

The door flew open.

"Are you putting anything *away?*" Mom barked, looking around. "It looks like all you've done is make a mess."

"I'm organizing," I said, jumping up guiltily. Although it was true I had set out with the idea of organizing, I had been reading back covers and dipping into the first pages and skimming more than I was actually putting anything away.

Mom looked at the books surrounding me. "Wow, I remember those," she said, her voice softening. She picked up a Nancy Drew. "*The Hidden Staircase.* I always liked these books." She ran her hand over the cover. "They look so out of date now, don't they?"

Funny, that's what I like about them.

"I read them all you know," Mom said, waving her hand at the stack of yellow books. "I was quite a reader. I think my mom thought I might turn out to be a librarian I read so much!"

Mom looked down at the book in her hand, her face relaxing into a faraway look. Seeing her with the Nancy Drew book in her hand made me wonder what she had been like at my age, made me wonder if she had fallen as deeply into books as I do. These days she barely managed to finish one book a month for book club. I wonder what had happened. I couldn't imagine not reading several books a week for the rest of my life. Nothing would stop me, I was sure.

"For a while there I think I wanted to be a detective," Mom smiled at herself.

My insides thrummed. She *was* like me.

Mom laughed, a harsh note entering her voice. "How silly! A detective. I mean really."

The thrumming stopped. Fantasy over.

I tried one more time. "What was your favorite book?"

Mom stared at me. "I don't remember."

"Well, did you like *A Little Princess*?" I asked, thinking of how magical that book was to me.

"Eh, it was alright," Mom said, shrugging. She tossed the Nancy Drew book back in the pile. "These'll look good on the shelves."

As she slipped out the door, I picked up the book she had tossed down. On the inside cover it read "Bennett," her maiden name, in neat block lettering. Which was the real mom? The one with the faraway eyes, who I'm sure wanted to be Nancy Drew, or the bitter mom who laughed at the dreams of childhood?

I wondered about that the whole time I sorted and shelved. It made a nice change from worrying about the whole Cassidy and Emily thing. I wondered how it was possible that someone could be unmoved by *A Little Princess*. The rational part of me knew not everyone loved every book or even reading at all, but deep down I was mystified that books didn't possess other people like spirits, mesmerize their very being, enchant their lives the way they did with me. It seemed like those people were missing a crucial part, like a heart or a soul.

Gradually I even forgot to worry about mom or abandoned childhood dreams or anything. Touching the books, helping each one to its proper spot, placing it next to kin was hypnotic, smoothing out the jagged corners of my brain like so many pieces of sea glass.

Pat the Bunny down here with the children's books, on the right with the shorter board books. Plato's *Republic*? It had Dad's name inside the cover, probably left over from college. Should I start a new shelf for philosophy, or was the *Republic* politics? In our family one shelf would do for both. Another stray Nancy Drew, *The Sign of the Twisted Candles*, reunited with her sisters in a section I had designated all for me.

Then a whole box that I guessed were Dad's college books. The box was so old and dusty I doubted whether it had even been opened when Mom and Dad moved to Michigan. I suspected it just got put in the basement and then transferred here without ever seeing the light of day. Dad's books were an odd mix, not surprising since he had double majored in Econ and English. I sat down by the box to sort them and for the first time that combination of majors struck me as kind of weird. The two don't really seem to go together and most people I knew who liked English were girls. And not many girls even, at least, not at Kentley High. I started a stack of Econ books, no temptation there. Picked up *The Portrait of a Lady*, by Henry James. *The Idiot. King Lear.* I thought about the Dad I knew reading and enjoying these books. All I heard from him was business-speak and I can't remember the last time I saw him reading a book. I wondered if that was from lack of interest or lack of time. If he had liked English enough to major in it I suspected it was from lack of time. The thought made me sad. I guess Mom wasn't the only one far from childhood.

Eventually, my back hurting and my eyes gritty, I looked at the jumble of boxes spilling books and those not even opened yet and realized that this was going to take more than a couple of hours. More like a couple of weeks. Time for bed.

Teeth brushed, face washed, nightshirt on, I climbed into my window seat, pulled the blanket around me and opened my journal. It was hard for me to leave a book behind. I always felt sad at the end of a book, even as I raced for the finish to see how it all came out. Sometimes I turned right back to the first page and dove back in. Delay leaving that world, at least for a couple of days. It was time to say goodbye to *From the Mixed-up Files of Mrs. Basil E. Frankweiler.* Sad, but the task was made easier by the stack of books I had brought up to my room from the library. I had something to look forward to.

Dear Diary,

Even as I wrote that I knew I couldn't be a quiet heroine. Not with Cassidy around. But I would definitely keep quiet about pretending to be Claudia. People would think I was a whack job if they knew.

I stared at the stack of books I had brought upstairs from the library and thought of all the boxes I still had not unpacked. It was in there, somewhere, I was sure. The answers, though I might have to dig for them, were surely there. The way to get through school, the way to manage Cassidy and Alex and Emily. Sitting warm and secure at home it seemed easy to decide I would continue to be the Confident Claudia. It seemed easy to believe it would all work out.

I picked up a book from the top of the stack, *West With the Night*. Within pages I couldn't put it down. Beryl Markham was a real person and moved to British East Africa when she was four where she lived a wildly exciting life, hunting wild animals, learning to fly airplanes, training racehorses.

As I read I wished with all my heart for many reasons that I was Beryl Markham. Not the least of which was because she was in *Africa*. What I wouldn't give to be that far away. And to have even a fraction of her bravery. And it was hard to imagine what it would be like to never be bored. Saved again by a book. And this one was *true*. I could feel it, she was going to give me something as good as Claudia had.

I stared out at the dark beyond my window, nothing visible beyond, but what I really saw, and felt, was the hot dry winds of Africa. I was the true life hero Beryl Markham, hunting wild pigs, training racehorses, flying a plane scouting for elephants.

My heart raced as I tried to land my plane without hitting a zebra, or a wildebeest or a giraffe. I felt the admiration and gratitude of the men on the ground as I managed to get the plane down and deliver the oxygen for the sick miner.

I crawled into bed and imagined I was in a tent, in an uncharted area of Africa, resting before my flight back to civilization. I squirmed down under my covers, hearing the sounds of the crackling fire outside my tent, the murmurs of the men's voices, the far off sound of a lion roaring in the bush. I felt Beryl's bravery, as steady as the pumping of my heart.

Chapter Nine

Flying Solo

In the morning I climbed off the bus at school pretending I was Beryl climbing down from her plane. I had made it to my destination even with a map that had large areas marked "Unsurveyed." Everyone was excited to see me, excited by the supplies I brought that would help them survive, amazed by my incredible skill with an airplane. The fact that no one actually looked at me did not spoil the fantasy. My hero status lasted clear to my locker.

Emily was nervously flitting around my locker. As I approached she ran up to me while looking side-to-side, as if she was afraid to be seen talking to me.

"Jackie, I, uh, I," she paused, not looking me in the eye.

With my brain still in Africa she reminded me of a spooked gazelle, skittery and about to dart away.

Emily thrust a folded-up piece of paper into my hand and fled. Yep, just like a gazelle.

> *Jackie,*
> *I'm so sorry. I don't know what to do. Cassidy doesn't want me to hang out with you anymore. I don't know what to do! She says if I keep talking to you she'll make sure I'm thrown off the Poms. She can do it, I know she can. I cried all night. You're my best friend and I can't choose. I can't! Help me. Tell me what I should do!*
> *Em*

Well that came sooner than I had expected. In a haze I dumped stuff in my locker and stumbled to my first class.

Alone.

Alone.

Alone.

I looked around the class. No one seemed to notice my existence. No one smiled or even made eye contact. I felt invisible. I felt like people could just walk right through me, like I was a ghost or something. My one friend in the whole world was gone.

And she was gone, no doubt of that. She wanted to be friends with me but she was desperate to be a Pom. I couldn't compete with that.

Queen Bee Mean Girl Barbie strikes again.

I sat down and clutched *WWTN*. What would Beryl do? She was fearless. She conquered a country. She did stuff women didn't even do, and then she wrote such a beautiful book about it that even Ernest Hemingway called it a "bloody wonderful book." I felt a mean rush of envy because Beryl seemed to have fairly successfully avoided school. Okay, so let's pretend Beryl did get stuck going to school, and in fact, she got sentenced to school at the very KH where I was currently sitting. What would she do? Beryl-me would put up with this school business and then go out and fly my plane and hunt elephant from the air and sit around the campfire in the dark night telling everyone about my adventures. I would not think about the betrayal of weak-minded friends because, as Beryl, I didn't have those kinds of friends.

Well, hadn't I actually made the decision yesterday anyway? A part of me knew Emily would do exactly this and leave me on my own. It was just official now. I was on my own.

I would be Confident like Claudia.

I would be Brave like Beryl.

I would think of Cassidy like a hyena, annoying but not dangerous like a lion is dangerous. I would not give Cassidy lion status.

Class ended and I started toward my locker. I made my way around a clump of people and was almost past when I heard a whimper. I peeked through the clump and saw poor Jeff Brice pressed against a locker.

"Hey SpEd! What's it like to be a *re*-tard!?" a boy with a plaid flannel shirt taunted, poking at Jeff's shoulder. SpEd, as in Special Ed. It was true that Jeff was retarded, not to mention so short he looked about six years old from the back. His parents insisted on mainstreaming him for at least part of the day. Little did they know.

Why does school have to be such a weak-versus-strong battlefield? Why couldn't those boys just let Jeff wander through his days alone? I mean really, what was it to them? With my brain still half in Africa I felt like I was watching a pack of hyenas tear into a helpless little baby zebra. Not even a zebra, because that would have been kind of the natural order. More like a defenseless puppy that had strayed too far from the farm. I wanted to crush those boys.

The old me would have slid by the group, praying they didn't notice me and turn their pimply-faced venom on me next. The new me, with Claudia and Beryl swirling around in my head, felt full of anger. I wanted to stab those boys with a spear. I wanted to stab Cassidy, and the Poms and Emily and everyone who divided the world into Winners and Losers.

Fuck the bullies.

This was it. I was done being a Loser Wimp.

I shoved through the edge of the group and put my face down into Plaid Shirt's face. "What's your problem?!" Beryl-me said, bitchier than a starving model with a plate of brownies waving in her face.

There was a stunned silence. I don't think anyone expected a girl to come to Jeff's defense.

Plaid Shirt found his voice. "What's it to you? Nothing wrong here."

"Really? So you are just hanging here with your best friend Jeff?"

Plaid Shirt didn't know what to say to that. If he said yes his friends would laugh at him. If he said no he'd prove my point, that he'd been teasing him.

"Yeah, uh, hey, what's it to you?" Plaid Shirt said, trying for some bravado. The guy wasn't much bigger than Jeff.

"I get it, Jeff is the only person who can't beat you up, is that it?" I said making a point to look down at him because Plaid Shirt was shorter than me.

The group laughed.

Plaid Shirt looked like he didn't want to be there anymore. I guess the fun was gone.

"SpEd lover!" he jeered at me and walked away.

The group scattered and Jeff scurried off. The Beryl-me rush of adrenaline faded, and I found it hard to even stand up. I leaned against the locker recently vacated by Jeff and looked down at the floor to collect myself.

When I looked up, I noticed Alex propped against the wall opposite me, staring intently at me. He didn't say anything but he locked eyes then walked away. Talk about melting.

By study hall I had recovered but was still thinking about the reckless impulse that made me step into that group. I was nervous but if I was going to be brave I had to press on. I had hoped to manage some bravery for myself. I hadn't counted on becoming protector of the misfits.

I started to giggle just thinking about myself as anyone's protector. *Me.* It made me think about Darwin and his whole survival of the fittest theory and how seriously out-of-date *that* is. It had to be, otherwise there could be no explanation for why I was still alive (me or all the other weakling nerds). Oh sure, I was superior in the brain department, but the brain takes *years* to develop. Meanwhile, physically, well let's just say that if we lived on the African plains, I'd have been the first wildebeest eaten. *No* speed. No coordination. No physical skills at all. And apparently no survival instincts. My God, I just walked into a group of teenage boys whacked out of their minds on oppression and testosterone. So theoretically my genes shouldn't be in the pool anymore.

I felt all warm and fizzy, like for a moment I had a little heroine in me too. I felt shaky too, thinking of how many enemies I had managed to collect recently. Claudia and Beryl, don't abandon me. I'm going to need every bit of your confidence and courage. Not to mention that you're my only friends now.

For the rest of the day every time I got breathless with fear I took my mind back to that look on Alex's face when I was recovering against the locker. Mmmmm, that *look*. Like there was something in me worth looking at.

Chapter Ten

Strangled by a Shirt

"Jock-leen! Come here!"

How did Mom hear me come in? I swear the garage door is a mile away from her bedroom.

I dropped my backpack on the kitchen counter and rummaged in the snack cupboard for a bag of chips before making my way upstairs. I couldn't ignore the call, but I could delay my reaction.

As I rounded the corner at the base of the stairs I heard a howl and saw something come flying at me.

I yanked myself backwards and barely missed getting tackled by a ninja. Davy landed at the bottom of the stairs and rolled. He jumped up and swung a plastic sword at me. He was outfitted from top to bottom in black, including a hood which left only a small opening for his eyes.

"You will die, scum alien!" Davy yelled, crouching sideway and slashing his arms around in my direction.

"Davy! You nearly knocked me down," I said. "Cut it out. I'm not playing."

"Oh! You are a secret agent I see," Davy said in an accent that sounded like a cross between Russian and Spanish.

"Jock-leen!" Mom called again, only a couple of decibels lower than an airplane engine.

"Coming," I yelled. Davy poked me in the back with his sword as I started up the stairs. Five-year-old boys just had way too much *energy*.

"I'm here," I said as I walked into her room, or should I say, suite. The bedroom part was large enough for a king-sized bed and a whole sitting area with a couch and chairs and a fireplace. On either side were his and hers bathrooms and dressing rooms and closets big enough that they could have been used as bedrooms.

The whole thing was decorated in soft colors, variations of whites and beiges and accented with pale turquoise. It would have been very soothing if Mom hadn't been in there.

Mom was standing in her dressing room in front of the full-length three way mirror she'd had installed. I don't know why she did it, now she just obsessed in 3-D.

"Do these pants make me look fat?" Mom asked, looking over her shoulder at the reflection of her butt in the mirror.

A rippled fun house mirror couldn't make my mom look fat. You actually have to have more than one gram of body fat to look fat. Not that my Mom was lollipop head skinny, she just was slim and really toned from tennis.

"Of course not," I said. "You don't have any fat."

"Look at this!" Mom said grabbing her leg and pinching it.

"That's muscle. And possibly bone," I said.

Mom spun around and looked at herself from the front. She turned side-to-side with her eyes glued on the mirror. I thought she looked good. Okay the jeans she was so carefully assessing probably came from Forever21, but they fit her well. And I couldn't wait to sneak in and try them on myself. They'd probably look better on me. You know, more my age. Although the truth was that Mom would put them together into a great outfit in a way I could never manage. She would find just the right top and a couple of cool bracelets and some killer shoes and she'd have a *look*. I'd just have on a pair of jeans.

Mom spun backwards again. "Honestly, what do you think? Does my butt look big?"

Her butt looked non-existent. Amazing how the low pocket placement could make your butt look smaller, but there it was. Genius.

"No, it looks perfect," I said. Calling anything about Mom perfect seemed to speed the conversation toward the end.

"They were on sale for nineteen dollars!" Mom enthused. The only thing she liked more than getting a bargain on her stylish clothes was being praised for getting a bargain on her stylish clothes. She lived for the moment when one of her friends would compliment her outfit and then she could say "Oh I got this shirt for fifteen dollars" and the friend would go wild with disbelief.

I dipped my hand into the chip bag.

Mom cut her eyes toward me. "Not too many of those."

I nodded. It wasn't about ruining my dinner, it was about ruining my (non-existent) figure. My gains in height were always ahead of my gains in weight, but Mom stayed constantly vigilant. The same way she stayed vigilant for herself, even though she barely even put on weight when she was pregnant with Davy. "Your metabolism can change overnight, Jockleen, *overnight*," she had said. "I've seen it happen to people. One day they're eating third servings from the buffet with no problem and the next day they smell a Cinnabon and put on ten pounds."

Mom ran her eyes up and down my body. "Hey, maybe we should go shopping!" she said. "You could use some new clothes. You know, spiff you up a bit."

"I'm fine," I said. Mom's idea of spiffing me up would have nothing in common with my idea of spiffing me up. I actually think I am already spiffed enough.

Mom stepped closer to me and fiddled with my hair. "No, really, you should be wearing pink. You look fabulous in pink. And some bright colors too!" She pulled my hair back from my face. "And you definitely should wear your hair off your face. Show off this nice bone structure!"

Puke.

"Nice bone structure?" I said. That was the best she could do?

"Some day your face is going to be really pretty," Mom said, as if she could read my mind.

Gee thanks for the encouragement. Another one of those comments that is supposed to sound like a compliment but is really a slam.

Mom darted to the side of her closet and plucked a shirt off the rack. "Here! I'm giving you this. You'd look great in it." She held the shirt out to me.

It was a pale pink, gauzy shirt with little pearl buttons halfway down the front. It had little rows of vertical ruffles on either side of the buttons. It looked like something from the Glinda the Good Witch collection.

"Ah, yeah, but no thanks," I said. This was new ground for me, turning Mom down, but hadn't I just today dispersed an entire pack of bullies? Didn't I have the Bravery of Beryl and the

Confidence of Claudia with me? Even so, a spurt of nervous something or other shot from my stomach up to my throat.

Mom raised her perfectly plucked eye-brows. That wasn't in the script. My part was to say, "Oh thanks Mom! Are you sure? It's beautiful!" This would let her feel generous, and then I would take the shirt and forget it even existed. We could both continue to live in a world where the illusion of a warm and loving mother-daughter relationship existed.

The eyebrows came together in a frown. "What do you mean 'no thanks'? This shirt is beautiful! And it cost over a hundred dollars! This is a designer shirt! Oh, I see, you might actually look like a *girl* in it. Enough of your boyish clothes!"

Hmmm. Time to choose. Revert to known script or continue bold independent stand?

"Ahhhh," I said, furiously trying to ignore the poison that seemed to have immediately filled the air. No one refuses Mom. No one disagrees with Mom. It just isn't done.

Mom's frown started to involve more of the muscles in her face. She wouldn't appreciate that, the wrinkling thing. She was still holding the shirt out toward me and she shook it in a "take it" move.

I felt my hand rising toward the shirt. What was the big deal anyway? Just take the shirt and bury it. And yet, my arm stopped part way up.

"Do you not like this shirt?!" Mom said, her voice getting hysterical. "I have worn this shirt a bunch! And you always said I looked nice. And LOTS of people have complimented this shirt!"

I never said you looked nice in that shirt. It's a goofy looking shirt.

"It's fine. It looks great on you," I said. Through my anxiety I somehow choked out, "Maybe it's just not for me."

"That's ridiculous," said Mom, grabbing my arm and draping the shirt over it. "If it looks good on me, it will look good on you."

Ah yes, I forgot, if you like something, then by definition that something is God's gift to the world. Yes, yes, I forgot.

Now Claudia and Beryl seemed to take over my brain, and the message they were sending was that a girl should be able to say she doesn't like a shitty shirt. I felt the little buzz through my body that meant I was turning into a braver version of me.

I held up the shirt to Mom. "Thanks Mom, but I'm going to pass on this one."

Mom's eyes got wide and took on the crazy glint she usually reserved for Dad. Her hands stayed at her sides but her neck stretched out and her face came at me all ET-like. "What do you mean?!" she yelled. "That is a *perfectly* good shirt!"

Now I was getting mad too. She sounded just as mean and irrational as Cassidy or Plaid Shirt. Wimps of the world unite. "I just don't want it!" I threw the shirt down at her feet and walked out.

All the way to my room my uneasiness grew, like Christopher Columbus must have felt as he sailed toward what most people thought was the edge of the world. Don't you think he had some moments of wondering if he was wrong and the world was flat and that some night while he was asleep his ship might just drop into the sky?

Dialogue That Would Happen if I Could Actually Speak the Truth Around Here:

> *Mom: You must like this shirt! It is the greatest shirt ever created on the earth. Do you know how I know that? Because I picked it!*
> *Me: It's a piece of shit that no one under the age of forty would be caught dead in. Maybe under fifty.*
> *Mom: No, it's quite fashionable.*
> *Me: Yeah, if it were still the eighteen hundreds.*
> *Mom: You must like this shirt! I like it and therefore you must like it. You must not ever question my opinion.*
> *Me: Yes, I understand that if I disagree with you, you might melt like the Witch of the West.*
> *Mom: I'm telling you! You __must__ like this shirt or my ego will be crushed forever, and I'll never recover.*
> *Me: Go for it!*

I stopped writing.

My insides tightened. What had I done? The last thing any of us needed was for Mom to be upset. The specter of Aunt Helen was always there, staring out from dark corners. I started to breathe faster. I panicked, what if I couldn't get enough oxygen in? My lungs felt frozen, like they could barely move. I was trapped. I was dying.

What have I done?

I got a few breaths into my lungs. I made sure my door was locked and went back to writing in my diary.

The Real Truth:
I hate her. I hate Mom. I hate Aunt Helen. There. I said it! She ruined our family. How could she do this to us? Why did she do this to Mom?

I knew Aunt Helen had killed herself. I didn't know why. I mean, obviously she must have been depressed. Duh. But no one would talk about *why*. It was crazy. I know Mom and Aunt Helen hadn't been that close for a while, but still, it was her *twin*. Everyone just acted like life went on, but Mom had never been the same. I mean how could you, your identical twin killing herself? The efforts we all made to not upset Mom right after Aunt Helen's death had turned into a habit that none of us had ever thought to break. Until now. I couldn't take it anymore. It's been five years. Find a way to deal. She was suffocating me. I can't even pick my own clothes? At fourteen?

I should have worked on my homework, but I pulled out *West with the Night* instead and disappeared.

It didn't take me long to feel like I was the one riding Balmy, watching the irreverent little race horse coax a zebra away from his mother. And it was my room the zebra came into every morning, looking for its bottle of milk. And it was me, flying through the night as an adult, thinking back in time to my thirteenth year when the zebra left its clan and followed Balmy home.

Sweet, sweet relief.

Chapter Eleven

The Lion on Your Back

I was feeling very Beryl-like in the morning. I woke up
ready to train my race horse right after I speared a few wild boars. I
mean, this was a girl who survived a lion attack. Which is to say I
had renewed my sense of Beryl's bravery. This did not play as well
in suburban Pennsylvania as I might have hoped. Just like Beryl, I
didn't see the lion racing up behind me until it landed on my back.

The pink shirt was hanging off of a stuffed satin hangar
hooked on the back of my chair at the kitchen table.

"What's this?" I asked, not seeing the lion lying in wait.

"Your shirt," Mom said, eyes never leaving my face, leaning
back on the bench at the end of the table, coffee cup in hand.

"I said I didn't want it," I said. Oh, if only my brain had re-
engaged with my real life, not my book life.

Mom stared at me hard, reminding me of Cassidy. Is there a
secret school where Mean Girls go to learn that stare? "I see no
reason for you to refuse that shirt," she said in a clipped voice.
"That is a perfectly beautiful shirt and we are not wasting it. You
will wear it."

I laughed.

This is ridiculous.

Mom's eyes got very squinty. "You think that's funny? You
will not disobey me on this."

"Mom, you can't *make* me wear a shirt! Don't I have any say
in what I wear?!"

"Not while I'm paying for it."

Okay, technically Dad *is paying for my clothes.*

I thought about Beryl, about how she hunted and flew and
ran around half of Africa barefoot. I thought about the bullies who
had scattered when I used my Brave Confident self. I thought
about flirting with Alex and how Dickwad had backed down so

quickly on the bus. I felt like I was looking right out of the picture of Beryl from the front of the book, my cap and goggles snug around my head. My face felt like it had morphed into her calm stare.

"Well I'm not wearing it," Beryl-me said.

Mom slammed her coffee cup down so hard the coffee slopped out all over the table. "How can you be so ungrateful!" she screamed, jumping up. "How can you stand there and be such a mean little *shit*?!"

Guess Mom is not used to the Brave Beryl.

Mom stalked around the table and grabbed the shirt, shaking it at me. "This is *quality!* This is something *I* picked and I can't believe you can't see how beautiful it is. What is wrong with you?!" By this time Mom's face was inches from mine, her eyes snapping, her mouth drawn back in a snarl.

I shrank back.

It's just a freaking shirt. What is wrong with her?

Mom stepped back and broke into tears. "I don't understand you! Why can't we be close? Why can't we share clothes? Why don't you ever tell me anything? I thought we'd be best of friends but you treat me like *dirt!*"

Mom threw the shirt at my feet and ran out of the kitchen crying.

WTF?

Although being Beryl hadn't worked so great at home, I dove right back into WWTN on the bus. I thought about how lucky Beryl was. No mother around to mess up her life. I thought about the part where Beryl leaves the farm at Njoro, the place where she grew up. Her father lost the farm because it didn't rain. Talk about not having any control over your life. Beryl's father decided to move to Peru to train race horses and Beryl wanted to stay in Africa. So Beryl got on her horse Pegasus and rode it over the hills to start a new life.

By herself.

At seventeen.

Only three years older than me.

Beryl started training racehorses on her own. She found herself a place to live and a job and she was successful at it. *At seventeen.*

I ran my fingers over the book and stared out at the colorless morning flying by. I felt like a little baby compared to Beryl. How could I become as independent as her? How could I become that self-sufficient? Imagine, not relying on a mother or father. What a dream life Beryl had. I imagined myself as Brave as Beryl.

Good thing. Because my day didn't get any easier.

I thought I couldn't hate PE more, but it turned out that I could. Because Emily looked at me mournfully, then slipped to a different side of the locker room to change. No Poms in the class but I guess Cassidy had spies everywhere. What a wimp. So she'd rather be a dance drone than friends with me. How mature.

I hunched over my gym bag and changed my shirt as fast as I could. I *hated* taking my clothes off in front of the other girls. At least I was finally wearing a bra (which was more of a "wear it and they will come" gesture than an actual necessity). I didn't need to ever go through something as embarrassing as begging Mom for a bra again. Was there some kind of handbook that required parents to humiliate their children a certain number of times? Mom discussed it at the *dinner table*. With my *Dad*. He was as mortified as I was.

I dragged myself out into the gym. Great, the volleyball nets were up. Another day, another failure.

I get the whole kids-in-America-are-too-fat thing, and I understand how PE is supposed to counteract that. But does it always have to be such a humiliating experience? I can't kick, hit, spike or head a ball. I can't run fast. I can't climb a rope or push myself on a scooter board. I'm not even good at *stretching*.

Mr. Donovan whistled the group into line and strutted back and forth in front of us. Normally Emily and I would roll our eyes at each other behind his back but even that small pleasure was gone. Mr. Donovan was in his mid-twenties and thought he was God's gift to teenage girls. He wore tight dry-fit shirts and warm-up pants and found a million ways to casually flex his muscles. Like standing with his arms crossed you could tell he was trying to make his biceps bulge. And he didn't do a very good job of hiding his stares at the more developed girls.

The silver lining to being an A cup. Actually a nothing cup.

We stumbled through PE, and then I headed off to English. Emily had a different class so at least I was spared the sight of my best friend ignoring me. Even so, I had a hard time concentrating, although I normally love English. I can't believe I get class credit to do my very favorite thing in the whole world. But today, I kept thinking about Emily and about Mom's crazy obsession with the pink shirt.

Time for a distraction. Time to start the Enrich and Expand idea I had the other day. Perfect time to look for a new friend. In fact, I was overdue.

My next class was keyboarding. I summoned up the spirit of Claudia, and after the first timed exercise, I forced myself to turn to the girl next to me, a shy red head named Melody. "How many words did you get?" I asked.

Melody didn't answer right away. She looked down at her keyboard and fluttered her hands around the screen. "Let me see," she started and then paused. "I guess, mmm, thirty-five."

Whoa! I typed seventy words in the same amount of time. Did she have glue on her fingers? Melody looked as embarrassed as I felt, which was not what I meant to happen.

"Thirty-five! Oh my God, that's pathetic," a snotty girl behind Melody said in a loud nasal voice.

Melody sat stiff and still, like a lizard frozen on a rock. It was sort of the if-I-don't-move-you-can't-see-me strategy. Her head stayed down, eyes fixed on the keyboard. I could see a red flush spreading up the sides of her neck underneath her ponytail. Yep, she'd be invisible if the walls were painted pale red. There were more giggles from the girls around us as the others heard the snotty girl's words. I heard a couple of other girls repeat "thirty-five!" and laugh.

Melody didn't ask me how many words I had typed. In fact, Melody didn't look up from the computer again the entire class.

Well aren't I just spreading goodness and cheer, I thought as I walked to my next class. So much for being the protector of the misfits. Why did I have to ask that question? Why didn't I say something different, I could have said I liked her shirt or something. I am an idiot.

Plaid Shirt (wearing another plaid shirt) came at me from the opposite direction in the hall and punched at my arm. "Retard!" he hissed as he passed.

My thoughts exactly.

I walked into chemistry only to be pushed backwards by Alex's mojo. My obsession with Melody made me forget about what I was going to do about Emily in this class.

Where was I supposed to sit? The front seats where I used to park myself were all taken. My heart was beating so hard my ears were pounding with the rhythm. What happened to the good-old-days when classes were boring? I scanned the class and noticed a seat in the very back on the opposite side of the room from Cassidy. That would have to do.

I couldn't help glancing over. Cassidy was leaning over Alex's desk, laughing and swinging her hair around.

"God, class is about to start," said Cassidy, wiggling her whole body at Alex. "Could it *be* any more boring?" I guess I'd be bored too if I was so dumb I was repeating half my classes. Then again, Cassidy believed that everything about school was boring except for dancing. I think Cassidy even thought the actual games she danced at were boring too. But the outfit and slinking around in the outfit, now those were great.

"Yeah," said Alex, not seeming to really be listening to her. I could relate. Cassidy had one of those silly little girlie voices that could cause epileptic fits if you actually listened for too long.

I snuck another sideways glance at him. Alex's ears may have been ignoring Cassidy, but his eyes were fully focused on the pair of D's she was dangling in front of him. I wanted to dislike him for it; then again, they were inches from his face and, to be honest, quite hypnotic in their swaying.

From the look on his face he was going to have as much trouble concentrating in class as I was.

What a hypocrite. Not only was Cassidy MGQB Barbie, she was also "Abstinence Barbie." She paraded around school promoting abstinence (WAIT Training!), but while her mouth was saying that stuff, her body was saying something entirely different. Like somehow the act of saying she wouldn't have sex made it safe to act seductive to everyone from Mr. Redmond to Jeff Brice. Someone was going to take her up on it one of these days.

Midway through class I noticed Emily and Cassidy giggling together. Cassidy whispered something to Emily, and Emily looked uncomfortably at me and then gave a half laugh, dropping her eyes.

I was never going to pass this class. My mind ping ponged from thinking about Mom's craziness to trying to ignore Emily and Cassidy to feeling awful for embarrassing Melody. Okay, that one I could do something about.

It took me two class changes scanning the halls to find Melody. Finally I saw her coming and planted myself in her path. My brain said this was a good idea, but my rapidly beating heart said I was scared. Between Mom, Cassidy, Emily, Alex and the Enrich and Expand program my heart was never going to slow down to a normal rhythm. Great, now I had to worry about having a heart attack.

I was anxious enough that I almost turned around and left, but Beryl wouldn't let me move my feet. No doubt Beryl was scared when the lion landed on her back or when her dog was gored by a warthog. She didn't run home and hide under her bed. *Say it anyway*, Beryl said in my head. What a novel idea, that you could continue a course of action *despite* being scared. I imagined I was staring out of Beryl's face, felt her calm confidence start to seep in.

Melody looked away and slowed her steps, but before she could actually turn around and leave, I walked up to her.

"Melody, hey, I'm sorry about keyboarding this morning. I just…" I got more anxious and stopped speaking for a second. "I just wanted to say hi, but instead I said that stupid thing about number of words. And the thing is," I started talking faster thinking she was going to run away. "The thing is, sometimes I can type a lot of words, but they all have mistakes in them so who cares anyway? And what about all the two finger typers? They must take an hour to write a sentence."

Melody's eyes were darting right and left as if she was looking for an escape.

"And what about the people who only text?" I added. "They are all going to end up with huge thumbs."

At that Melody lifted her head and gave me a faint smile.

"Imagine the kind of job you can get with big thumbs!" I said, trying to keep her attention. "Hitchhiker, you could do that. Or maybe there will be a game show to see who can type 'LOL' the fastest."

Melody laughed. My heart moved out of my throat and back into my chest.

"Hey, where is your next class?" I said.

Melody's class was only a short distance from her locker, but she let me walk with her.

On the way we passed Snotty-girl from keyboarding and she hissed at Melody, "Dumbass!" Her wicked giggle lasted down the hall.

Melody's stare hit the ground and stayed there until we parted.

"Don't let the bee-atches get you down," I said as Melody slid through the classroom door. The only sign that she heard me was an up and down motion of her shoulders.

Great, make a new friend by setting her up as a target for the mean girls. Well done, Jackie.

Chapter Twelve

Strangling Silence

As I dragged myself through the dead leaves scattered on our long driveway, I could hear the smoky roar of bus nineteen fading down the road behind me.

See you tomorrow Dickwad.

I looked up at our house. It was big and white and reminded me of a hotel we stayed in once on Cape Cod with its gray-shingled roof dormer windows. It was a place you could imagine the Kennedy family (all of them) living in. When I first saw it I was amazed, then excited, then embarrassed. Because in Michigan people would have teased me and looked at me funny and treated me different if they saw me living in such a huge place. But in Kentley Heights this was a middle-of-the-pack kind of house. It was respectable but nothing worth slowing down to look at. I thought about all the places Beryl camped, all the luxuries she often did without. I wondered what she would have thought of this house. Not that Beryl seemed uncomfortable in civilized places, it was just that she seemed able to move effortlessly between the tamed and untamed places of the world. Could I ever be like that?

I was in no rush to actually arrive at the house. I didn't know what kind of mood Mom would be in. There was a chance she had gone back to denial-land and was pretending we had never fought. Or at this very moment she could be moving my belongings to the basement, who knew? The woman was way hard to predict.

The house was completely silent when I came in. No TV noises, no loud boy slamming, nothing. I had walked past Mom's car in the garage so she must be here. I grabbed a handful of grapes from the refrigerator and went upstairs.

Still quiet. I headed into my room and then I saw it.

On the bed, arranged ever so neatly, was the freaking pink shirt.

What was *wrong* with that woman?

I picked up the shirt and threw it in my garbage can, pleased to think that Mom would find it the next time she emptied the garbage.

I slumped down at my desk to do my homework. The desk was arranged against the wall between two dormer windows that were set deep into the side of the sloping ceiling and had window seats built in. Normally it was the window seats calling to me that made it hard to do homework, but today it was the garbage can that kept grabbing my attention. That stupid pink shirt was in there beating like the Tell-Tale Heart.

Hadn't she invaded my life enough? Now she had to ruin the one place I found any peace at all, my room. It was like Mom herself was hiding in my garbage can, a soul-sucking vampire salivating over the last few drops of true Jacqueline blood still running through my body. I swear, one more incident, one more invasion of my brain, and I'd have no identity left whatsoever.

I pulled my diary out and opened it over my geometry notebook.

I have done my best. I really have. I agree with everything she says. I do everything I can to not upset her. I hug her every time she asks me to. But now I have to even dress like her?
Help! I have a soul-eating virus and it's eating me alive from the inside.

I sat up straight with a sudden flash of memory.

Strangler fig!

In seventh grade we were supposed to do reports on the countries of the world. I wanted France but someone had already taken it so I took Australia. While I was doing my research, I came across a description of strangler figs which grow in the Australian tropics. They are these vine-like things that are dropped as seeds into crevices in trees. They grow both upwards and downwards, winding around the trunk and branches, until they eventually surround the entire tree. The vines merge into each other, forming a cover to the tree, in some cases causing the tree inside to disintegrate. The sick part is that the form of the tree is still there, it's just dead inside. They *strangle* the tree. I had found this image disturbing in a horror movie kind of way, and I did not include anything about strangler figs in my report.

Now I knew why it was so scary. Now I saw that a *mother* could be a strangler fig. That she could slowly kill off your insides while at the same time gathering herself around your outsides so that no one actually ever noticed that you were gone. Draping herself around you in a way that looked like you but was *so* not you. Wear this beautiful shirt. Pull your hair back from your face. Don't you dare have an opinion different than mine. Do everything I want or I will make your life miserable. *Other people* could be strangler figs. The mean girls, the magazines, all the words floating around in the air about how you are 'supposed' to be. All of it sucking out anything that is unique, anything that is about *you*.

Mom tries the same stuff on Dad. I can tell, he goes out of his way to keep her calm too. He wears the stupid designer jeans she got him instead of his favorite old Levi's. He goes to the stupid wine tasting parties even though he's an Iron City beer man. He even goes to her hair salon instead of the twenty-dollar-a-cut barbershop that he prefers.

And we both do it because we can't stand the thought of what might happen if we don't.

I looked at my backpack lying on the floor, knowing I should start my homework, but I felt too churned up inside. Who cares about homework when you feel like you are being strangled to death?

I should have heard noises in the house by now. The silence was starting to bother me. I got up and went searching for Davy and Mom.

No Davy in his room or the playroom. I peeked in Mom's room, it was completely dark.

Hmmm.

It was so dark and her body so small in the big bed that I almost missed the fact that Mom was there. I walked closer.

"Mom?" I whispered. I didn't want to wake her if she was really tired, but yet, there was always the whole Aunt Helen thing. Would that ever be gone from my head?

No answer.

Then, as my eyes adjusted to the dark in the small sliver of light coming from the hallway, I saw an open bottle of pills by the bed. I grabbed it and turned on the bedside lamp. The label said "Ambien." What was she doing taking sleeping pills in the middle of the day? And where was Davy?

"Mom!" I said, shaking her.

No response.

I panicked, stuck my head down near hers to see if I could hear breathing. I couldn't tell.

I shook her some more, fear flooding my body.

"Mom! Mom! Wake up!" I yelled. I fumbled the light on and stared at her.

Nothing.

I stuck my hand over her chest, I could feel a heartbeat. I thought she seemed to be breathing, but I wasn't completely sure.

Shit, shit, shit. What do I do?

I shook her even harder and yelled right in her ear.

Still nothing.

I grabbed the phone off of her dresser and dialed my dad, hands shaking.

He barely got out "Hello?"

"Dad! Mom took Ambien pills and she's not waking up!" I was almost hyperventilating at this point and wasn't sure he even understood what I was saying.

"Oh my god," he said. "Are you sure? Is there a bottle there?"

"Yes! And I don't know how many are gone!" I shook the bottle. There were some left, but it wasn't full.

"Hang up and call 911," Dad said. "I'm on my way."

Shit, shit, shit.

My hands were shaking so badly I could barely dial "911" but I managed.

I told the operator what I had just told my dad. She said to stay calm and that the paramedics were on their way.

I shook Mom some more, but she still didn't wake up.

It seemed like forever until I heard the siren in the driveway. I ran downstairs and opened the front door, then ran ahead of the paramedics to show them where Mom was.

There were two of them, a wide-shouldered crew-cutted man and a slim, no-nonsense looking woman. They went straight to work, listening to her heart, checking her breathing, asking questions.

I told them what I knew and showed them the bottle.

"She mostly just seems to be deeply asleep, but we'll take her in to be sure," Crew cut said. He smiled at me. "Her vitals are good, she should be okay."

I burst into tears.

I don't think I had even let myself think about what it might have meant until I knew she was all right. Now I couldn't stop crying. What if she did this on purpose? I felt like I might faint and fought away the thoughts.

"Oh my god, I still don't know where my brother is," I said. I ran out of the room and flew around the house yelling for Davy. I couldn't find him anywhere. Please god let him be on a playdate somewhere. Please.

Dad called while they were loading mom in the ambulance. I told him what was happening and where we were going. Then, "And Dad, I can't find Davy!" I started crying again. "Should I go with Mom or stay home in case Davy is here somewhere?

"You better stay home. I'll meet her at the hospital." Dad's voice was in crisis control mode. He sounded calm and in control. I wished with all my heart he was standing here with me.

As they were securing her stretcher thingy mom started to stir. "Whass going on?" she said in a thick voice, her eye opening but not focused.

"Ma'am, I am Ken, a paramedic. Your daughter called because she couldn't wake you up. How many pills do you remember taking?"

"Huh?" Mom was still struggling to focus. She let her eyes close again.

"Ma'am, how many pills did you take?"

"Hmmm," Mom said.

Ken closed the ambulance door and they headed down the driveway.

I walked back into the house, unable to stop crying. What was going on? Where was Davy? Why did I have to be here all alone?

I retraced my path through the house, checking every room for Davy. I checked the basement and closets. I checked the backyard and the attic. He was nowhere to be found. I didn't know if that was good news or bad.

Finally it occurred to me to call some of his friends' houses. I found Mom's neatly typed list of phone numbers, in its plastic cover, in her mom desk drawer. On the third try I found him and had to work hard not to start sobbing all over again.

"No, Mrs. Harper, everything's fine," I said, sure that Mom would be mortified if I told anyone what had happened. "Mom's out and I just didn't know if, I, uh, was supposed to be babysitting him."

"Mom's out" was an understatement.

Turns out he was going to be dropped off in an hour.

Great, I had at least an hour by myself to worry and obsess. And decide what to tell Davy.

I kept thinking back to this morning. And how angry and upset Mom was at me. And how she had run out of the kitchen crying. And how the pink shirt was waiting for me on my bed when I got home. And how I didn't even go looking for Mom for, like, an hour.

I climbed the stairs slowly to my room. I pulled the pink shirt out of the waste basket and smoothed it out on my bed.

I felt sick and heavy inside.

What have I done?

Chapter Thirteen

No Place to Hide

I was sitting in the kitchen picking at the edges of my uneaten sandwich when I heard the garage door go up. My heartbeat went up with it. Mom came through the door from the garage ahead of Dad and lunged at me.

"What is *wrong* with you!" she screamed. "I was *sleeping*. And you are so crazy you call the paramedics?"

She was towering over me in a flash and before I knew it, had slapped me across the face. Beryl was right about the speed of a lion. She was on me before I could blink.

"Marion, calm down," Dad said, running up behind her and grabbing her arms. "I told Jackie to do that. She couldn't wake you up."

Mom spun at Dad. "That was an asinine thing to do. I feel like a big idiot! Do you know how many people I know who work at the hospital? I'm sure all of Kentley Heights knows by now!"

"Marion, she couldn't wake you," Dad said again, his voice calm and soft. The picture of reason. He held her by the shoulders as if to comfort her, but I knew it was to keep her off of me.

"She should have tried harder!"

"Well I'm still waiting to hear, why were you taking sleeping pills in the middle of the day? And how many did you take?"

Mom shoved Dad's arms away, her face directed towards him instead of me.

"I *took* them because Davy was on a playdate, and Miss Evil here was so awful to me this morning I just wanted to sleep and feel better. So talk to *her!*" Mom poked an angry finger at me.

"How many?" Dad said.

"What do you mean?" Mom said. Then her eyebrows went up. "You think I was trying to, you know, do something??! Jesus Christ! I just wanted a goddamn *nap*."

Dad and I looked at each other. It wasn't a crazy question to ask. Given the family history and all.

Mom shook her head violently. "I'm tired of both of you. I'm going to my room." She took two steps and then turned around. "To *read.*"

Dad and I stared at each other some more after she was gone.

I held my hand over my cheek. It stung, but more from the thought of being hit than the actual force of it.

"Dad she was really out of it. I mean, I could barely tell if she was breathing!" I felt tears forming again.

Dad hugged me. "I believe you. Hey, I'm glad it turned out to not be, you know, a bad thing, but you've got to call for help. You've got to assume the worst and take the actions for help until you know any differently. You were right. My god, I was the one who told you to call."

"And she *hit* me!" I cried. "That is so not right."

Dad nodded. "She can't do that. She really can't."

"She's so mad at me now," I sobbed, burying my face in his chest. "And she was so mad at me this morning. Over a stupid shirt."

"She's just embarrassed. She'll be calmer tomorrow."

Yeah, right.

In my room I was unable to settle down with my math homework so I pulled out *The Old Man and the Sea,* our next English assigned reading. I was still reading *West With the Night* but at least I could feel like I was getting homework done while I tried to escape my crap life. I settled into the pillows on my bed and as I turned pages I was relieved to find the book magic was still there; even with my chest still aching I felt myself being pulled into the old man's world. I could hear the gulls screeching and the rasp and clunk of an old boat. I could smell the salty ocean and feel the hot sun burning through my threadbare clothes. And even warmer, the boy's love for the old man, the way he eased the old man's loneliness.

Before I knew it, the fish was hooked and the battle was on. I decided to stop and read the rest tomorrow. It was comforting to be with someone else in the middle of a battle.

As I drifted off to sleep I couldn't help but think about my mother, and how she never did answer the question of how many pills she took.

Chapter Fourteen

The Perfect Daughter

In the morning Mom was up and dressed and feeding Davy when I came into the kitchen. She refused to look at me and she spoke to me only through Davy.

"Here you go sweetheart!" Mom said to Davy in a saccharine voice as she set a bowl of oatmeal in front of him. "See how fine I am?! I'm awake and serving my loving family breakfast. Just like a normal happy mom! A mom who needs no sleep!"

Ha ha.

I wasn't hungry anyway.

On the bus I read some more of *The Old Man and the Sea.* Santiago had been fighting the fish for almost two days and he never gave up. He kept finding more strength, and then when he thought he had none left he just kept going. He seemed so calm about it, just kept giving more and more. What would you even call that? I thought for a while and then came up with "endurance." When you are strong for a long time, longer than you think possible, that is endurance. I could use a little of that myself. Or a lot.

I pulled out a notebook and started a new page with the title: Desired Personality Characteristics.

Confident – like Claudia
Planful – like Claudia
Brave – like Beryl
Self-sufficient – like Beryl
Endurance – like Santiago

I thought about adding Courageous but decided that Brave covered it.

How would I ever be as Self-sufficient as Beryl? It seemed like years before I could live on my own. I didn't even think I could get a job yet. Maybe babysitting?

Then it occurred to me that there are other ways to be Self-sufficient besides earning a living. Because what I really really really wanted was to not rely on my mother. For anything. And maybe I could do that right now. I would do the Kentley Heights version of Self-sufficiency. I would need her for *nothing*.

The problem was, what if *she* needed *me* for something? You know, like staying alive.

And Endurance. How could I know what sort of endurance I had? Maybe I didn't have any. No, I would be like Santiago. I would not be the one who gave up this battle. I would not.

I stared across the locker room at Emily as she showed off her new routines for a couple of Unnoticeables. I could hear her twittery voice clear across the room. She was completely ignoring me, but I know she knew I was watching.

"Practice was *so* fun, you know?" Emily said, all happy and peppy. "We do like this triangle formation, and I'm the smallest so I'm in the front!" Emily posed with her right leg pointed out to the side, her left arm arched above her head, her shoulders twisted. She shook her hands as if they had pom poms and then slid her pointing leg back into her body. She suddenly spun in a quick circle, landing perfectly posed again and gave her audience a big smile.

Emily sighed and closed her eyes, an ecstatic look on her face. "And I got my pom-poms! My very own!"

You get pom poms and I get an overdosing Mom. The world is so *fair.*

Melody wasn't in keyboarding so I had no one to talk to. Not one person.

Aren't I just living a fabulous life?

I lingered in the bathroom stall, reluctant to go to the lunchroom. Gee, hard to believe I wasn't in a rush to sit alone, a target of Poms and Unnoticeables alike.

Finally I made myself push open the stall door. As I walked towards the sinks Madeleine Vonn came charging into the bathroom, fumbling in her pocket, whispering "shit shit shit" to herself. She jetted past me into a stall, flushed the toilet, then ran back to join me at the sinks.

The door flew open and Mrs. Brink, the meanest woman on the planet masquerading as a math teacher, came busting through.

"Madeleine don't move!" she barked, pointing at Madeleine.

Madeleine stood still, hands palms up in a "what do you got on me?" move.

Mrs. Brink strode over to her and searched Madeleine's pockets and then her purse. She whirled to face me.

I hadn't moved, stunned by the rapid events and the very good chance Madeleine had just flushed drugs down the toilet.

"What just happened in here?" Mrs. Brink snapped at me.

I shook my head. "Nothing. I don't know."

"Don't either of you move!" Mrs. Brink said. She darted into each stall and then came back to stand in front of me. "Let me check your pockets."

Oh, she thought maybe Madeleine passed the drugs to me. Haha.

I shrugged and held out my arms. "Go ahead."

She felt around and then turned to the garbage can and dug around in it.

Eeew.

Mrs. Brink turned back towards me and gave me a hard stare. "Did she come in here and flush something down the toilet?"

I couldn't look at Madeleine. I felt like Beryl, out on the African plain, facing a charging rhino. I looked straight at Mrs. Brink with my best goody two shoes face. "No ma'am."

"What did she do?"

"She just came in and stood in front of the mirror."

Mrs. Brink narrowed her eyes at me. "Really?"

I nodded.

She looked back and forth between me and Madeleine and seemed to conclude that we couldn't be friends. You know, given my nerdy look compared with her Goth eyeliner, torn up jeans and black nail polish. Not to mention the line of piercings going down her ears compared with my single little gold posts, one in each ear.

"Hmph," Mrs. Brink said and left, disappointed but beaten.

Madeleine took a deep breath and exhaled, putting her hands on the sink and leaning over. "Wow. That was close."

I nodded. I didn't know what to say. How would Claudia or Beryl handle this?

Madeleine looked at me, her eyes actually focused for once. "That was cool of you. Thanks."

I shrugged. Really, did she think I was one of those dorky kids who can't wait to get other kids in trouble?

"Let me know if you need anything," Madeleine said staring at me meaningfully. "I can hook you up."

"Yeah, sure," I said, belatedly adding, "thanks."

Just what I need in my already awful life, a drug habit.

"Catch you later," Madeleine said and left.

Would Mom count this as making a friend?

Later, as I waited in the clump of kids lined up for the buses, I finally lost the battle I'd been waging all day to not think about Mom. To not feel the crushing guilt that I was the one who caused her take too many sleeping pills. To not think about how Mom's identical twin had killed herself. To not wonder if there was something genetic that Aunt Helen and Mom shared that could destroy our lives.

Part of me really wanted to believe that she did just take one sleeping pill so she could get a good nap. Maybe it was no more than that. Or maybe that's how things started with Aunt Helen. And when Aunt Helen denied that anything was wrong everyone believed her. And look how that turned out. I couldn't do it. I couldn't live in denial-land with my mom. The consequences of being wrong were too severe. Like Dad said, I had to act as if the worst could happen.

Bus nineteen pulled up, and as I found a seat, I noticed that Dickwad waited until I sat down and then sat far away from me. A brief flash of satisfaction at that, and then the worry took over again.

How to keep mom from going over the edge?

It seemed ridiculously obvious, don't upset her anymore. None of this Brave or Confident business with her. I couldn't live with myself if it was a fight with me that . . . I couldn't even think it. No, with Mom I would be Subservient, Obedient, all those "ient" words.

Actually, it wasn't that I couldn't be Brave, I was going to have to be brave. I just couldn't be brave in standing up to Mom. I would be secretly brave. I would be Stealth Brave.

Yes, that was it. On the inside I would stay Brave and Confident, like Claudia and Beryl. On the outside I would be as stealthy as Claudia. And I would Endure it as long as necessary. I would be the perfect daughter.

Chapter Fifteen

Fake it to make it

Before I even had a snack I hunted through the house until
found Mom. I found her in her "workroom," the contents of her
wrapping closet pulled out and strewn around the big room. Mom
had been so excited when she set this room up for all her projects.
It was huge, with a pale yellow couch in front of a fireplace and
various work stations around the perimeter of the muted patterned
rug. A sewing area, a craft table, and a desk with a computer were
interspersed between the white trimmed diamond paned windows.
And of course the entire closet devoted to stuff just for wrapping
gifts. Martha Stewart would have wet herself for this room.

Mom was on her hands and knees, butt sticking out of the
closet.

"Hey Mom," I said to get her attention.

Grunt.

"Umm, can I help you with that?" I asked.

At that she pulled herself out and spun around.

"Oh now you're going to be all nice and helpful? What do
you want? Money? Some special privilege? To what do I owe this
honor?"

Stealth. Hold it together. Be nice to her.

"Well, I just, uh, actually, wanted to apologize," I said,
scuffing my shoe along the edge of the area rug. Was the shoe
scuffing overdoing it? Not for Miss Drama.

Mom sat back, propped her arms on her knees and said,
"continue."

I took a deep breath. No use doing it halfway. "I don't
know what I was thinking the other day. You are right, I've always
loved the way you dress and your fashion knowledge. I would be
stupid not to listen to you."

Mom nodded once. "Uh-huh?" she prompted, expecting
more groveling.

"I mean, you always look great. And you always have good ideas for me. And I'm sorry I was so snotty."

Mom was still staring at me, her expression a mix of pleasure and irritation. Like she enjoyed what I was saying, but I *still* hadn't said enough. "Do you know how much you hurt me?" Mom asked.

I looked down at the floor.

Geez, grow up! Get over it Mom.

Without looking up I nodded. "I'm so sorry. That was very thoughtless of me. I truly am sorry."

Sorry that I have such a screwed up mother.

"And I'm really sorry about, you know, calling 911."

"I can't even think about it!" Mom's voice got angry. "I mean, what if people are talking about me, right now?!"

"I'm sure they're not. And if they are, just tell them how dumb your daughter is. That I can't even tell when someone is . . . sleeping."

"Sleeping" being code for "comatose."

Mom's voice gave a little catch, "Oh Jockleen, I need you so much! Everything is just so hard, and I can't stand for you to be all, you know, teenagerish."

I looked up at Mom's face and saw a tear slipping out.

No! I'm supposed to be making her feel better.

Mom gave me a "come here" hand gesture.

I dragged myself over and got down on the floor in front of her. She leaned over and hugged me, pulling me into her knees.

"Oh Jock-leen, please be kind to me," Mom cried softly. "I don't know what I'd do without you."

Yeah, what would you do without a smartass teenager who is so upsetting you have to take sleeping pills to escape your life?

I patted Mom's back. "You're so strong, you'll be fine. We'll all be fine," I said, not believing anything I was saying but knowing it was what Mom wanted to hear.

After a few more rounds of my reassurance, Mom popped up and started picking up rolls of wrapping paper. "Okay! I'm just going get this all back in there. I can't stand to work out of a messy wrapping closet!"

Peppy fake Mom is back.

Better fake and peppy than depressed and real I guess.

Lie to mom? Check.

Make sure she doesn't hurt herself? That might be harder. With a last peek to make sure she was well involved in her project room, I slipped into Mom's bedroom and found the bottle of Ambien. Straining my ears for sounds that she might be coming, I dumped out the contents and counted the pills left. Seven.

Heart pounding at the idea of getting caught, I hurriedly replaced the pills and ran into her bathroom to find the rest of her drug stash. I came up with six Vicodin with a prescription date that matched Davy's birth, and an unopened bottle of twenty-four Tylenol PM.

Back in my room I scribbled the list of numbers in case I forgot. I'd have to keep a check on the bottles.

<u>More Dialogue That Would Happen if People Spoke the Truth Around Here:</u>
Me: Hey mom, any thoughts of overdosing today?
Mom: Nope, doing fine! But last night I considered it for about four hours. Thanks for checking.
Me: oh and by the way, why exactly did Aunt Helen kill herself?
Mom:

Now I was stuck. You know, having no idea of the actual answer to that question. I really really really wish I knew why Aunt Helen did what she did. Because then I could know whether to be worried about Mom.

What would Claudia or Beryl do?

Didn't Claudia actually solve a mystery? And wasn't that what I would call Aunt Helen's death? Claudia gathered clues and asked questions and finagled Mrs. Frankweiler into helping her find the answer. Maybe I could try the same thing.

Claudia would pursue answers and Beryl would have added bravery and a belief that she could do anything she set her mind to.

I thought about how much of Beryl's adventures were undertaken on her own. How absolutely alone she was at some very difficult times. And it didn't seem to bother her. And Santiago. It was all just him and the fish. And then the sharks. But he was alone, out there in the sea and he wasn't scared. I would be like that. I pulled out my diary and reviewed my list of <u>Desired Personality Characteristics</u>:

Confident.

Planful.

Brave.

Self-sufficient.

Endurance.

Stealthy.

It would be a two part plan. Part one: keep mom happy and alive until Part two: I solve the mystery of Aunt Helen's death.

If Beryl Markham could fly a plane across parts of Africa not even shown on maps, I could be nice to my mother.

If Claudia could solve an art mystery hundreds of years old, I could find out why Aunt Helen went off the deep end.

If Santiago could hold onto the fishing lines for days, his hands cut and bleeding, his shoulders stiffened, knowing he had to keep the *fish* calm, I could keep Mom calm.

For extra courage I went back to *The Old Man and the Sea.* Just when I thought the battle couldn't go any longer, the old man's patience is finally, finally, rewarded and he wins the battle. Or so he thinks. As he sailed home, a piece of my heart broke off with every piece of the fish ripped off by the sharks. And still, I kind of held it together until the boy appeared and his kindness broke off the last piece of my heart. I cried myself to sleep, but finally I was crying about something that felt clean.

Chapter Sixteen

Anger and Shame

I woke up with crusty eyes, and for a moment felt like I was Santiago, still tired and stiff after a full night's sleep. Like I had been the one holding onto an eighteen foot fish for over two days. I thought about the beauty of that book, about how Hemingway could take a simple story, a sad story, and make it so beautiful. How did he know how to twist my whole body into caring? The way Hemingway wrote *The Old Man and the Sea* made me feel like there was something noble about the simplest life. Then I thought about Beryl Markham's book and how she made her life seem so interesting and significant. Maybe that is what good authors do, they take the stuff of life and they make it seem meaningful, admirable even. They give you a blueprint for how to act.

And then I got lost in wondering about Hemingway and Markham. It sounded like they had met and I could imagine them together, on safari, in Africa. I could almost hear the roar of not-so-far-away lions in the night and moved closer to our campfire. I felt the excitement of danger lurking in the bushes and the confidence deep inside that I was up to any challenge. My alarm went off, startling me back to reality.

"Well don't you look adorable?" Mom cooed as I walked into the kitchen for breakfast. I was wearing the freaking pink shirt and feeling like I might suffocate on the spot. Not to mention all that lace was itchy. No doubt I would have a rash by lunch.

Brave. Stealthy. Keep her happy.

"Thank you," I managed.

Show the lion you are fearless. It is the only way.

"You look like Mommy!" Davy giggled.

Joy. Just what every fourteen-year-old hopes to hear, that she looks like a forty-two-year old housewife.

"I hope so!" I said, fakey fakey. "Everyone knows how pretty Mom is."

Mom gave me a huge smile. How could she not tell how fake this was? Was she really that desperate?

I gave her a big phony smile back. Anything was better than finding her comatose again. And the crying last night had, in an odd way, made me feel better. I could do this.

At school I covered the pink shirt with a gray hoodie, but not before Alex appeared at my locker.

He squinted at me. "Hmm, looking, uh, different there," he said, his eyes running all over my shirt.

He leaned in and played with one of the pearl buttons on the front. "Kinda pretty."

The shock of his touch was like being thrown in cold water, an absence of feeling for a few long moments and then an overload of feeling, everywhere.

It was a delicious kind of shock, but it was hard to speak when he was this close. I shoved my arms in the sleeves of the sweatshirt and zipped it up, pulling backwards from him. "What's the big deal?" I asked, all full of flirty innocence. I had returned to reading WWTN on the way to school, and while my body burned with a raging heat and a fluttering heart, my brain stayed Beryl-cool.

Alex leaned in again and bumped his shoulder against mine. "Can't a guy compliment a hot girl?"

He thinks I'm hot? He should feel the sweat in my pits right now.

"Anytime," I said, shrugging but smiling at the same time, like I get called hot on an hourly basis.

How is this stuff coming out of my mouth?!

Alex stared meaningfully at me, playing with the lacy collar sticking out of my sweatshirt. "I'll bet you wear lacy underwear too. Under those plain shirts and jeans."

I might not ever feel cool again.

"Well *I'm* not saying," I said, still flirty voiced, thinking of my faded Jockeys a thin layer away from his vision. "Gotta run," I added, feeling like Cinderella at the ball, like my magic could disappear any moment and I better go while the going was still good. Or before he got my clothes off, right here in the hallway of Kentley High.

Life was unfair. Here I was flirting with Alex Madigan and no one to tell. Melody was missing from keyboarding again.

"Hey, do you know Melody, the one with the red hair?" I whispered to the girl who sat near us in Keyboarding. Irina had a long thin face with a long thin nose down the middle of it. She also had a faint Russian accent and clothes that seemed the same as everybody else's but that got put together in weird ways.

"Yes!" Irina said. "Is she doing okay? Have you heard anything?"

"What do you mean?" I said.

"She got hit by a car the other day, walking home from school!"

"Oh my God," I said, feeling my chest tighten. "What happened? Is she, you know, really hurt? Is she in the hospital? Oh my God."

Mrs. Mitchum gave us a "shut up" look.

"She's in the hospital, a broken leg I think, and I don't know what else," whispered Irina. "I guess she was walking home from school and someone was teasing her and she ran away and a car hit her. I think it was Monday."

"Girls . . ." said Mrs. Mitchum looking at us.

I couldn't take it. I waited until Mrs. Mitchum turned around and leaned over to Irina. "Who was teasing her?"

Irina looked at Kelly Munson across the room and nodded and then at Sandra Bonita and nodded again.

"Them?"

"They were yelling at her that her IQ was thirty-five," Irina whispered back and then put her head studiously down at her keyboard, seeing Mrs. Mitchum glaring at us again.

I couldn't move, and I'm sure my face was completely pale because it felt like no blood was moving through my body at all. Oh good God, it was my fault. Thirty-five was the number of words she had typed. *Why* did I ask Melody that stupid question? I couldn't have felt worse if I had run the car right into Melody myself. So much for being tough.

What was wrong with me?

I was causing chaos everywhere. First Mom takes too many pills and now Melody is in the hospital. Maybe I shouldn't try to make any new friends. Maybe that wasn't a kind thing to do.

Maybe I should just spare everyone my disastrous presence and hide away forever. I could homeschool myself. Haha.

83

Chapter Seventeen

A Lonely Courage

I was on the family room couch brooding about how to find a way to check on Melody. Call her house? Yes, that would be pleasant. "Hi, this is Jackie, I'm the one who caused your daughter's accident. Say, how is she doing?"

No. That wouldn't work. Maybe I could call the hospital. With a lot of sweating and mumbling I discovered they wouldn't give out information to a non-family member.

My brain wouldn't stop, like a dog chasing two balls at once it ran from Mom to Melody back to Mom back to Melody.

A half hour of Guitar Hero stopped the chasing brain. Nothing like a little Smashing Pumpkins to smooth out the jarred neurons.

As I was unhooking the remote from the guitar and returning it to the charger, Mom came into the family room.

"How's it going with the books?" she asked, eyebrows raised, staring pointedly at the guitar in my hand.

I'm sorry, Master, please forgive me for doing something I enjoyed. I will go right back to being your slave.

"Just about to go work on them," I said.

Who needs to do homework?

"And just call me when you want some help with dinner," I added, giving her the fake smile.

I got a big smile back. "Will do!" Mom said.

Princess Fakey and her Mother, Queen Fakey.

Barf.

In the library I gave myself a little lecture. No wasting time on looking through books I wanted to read, I just needed to get these things put away. I diligently stacked and arranged for about a half hour while I considered the options for my two plans.

As I put the Nancy Drew books in numerical order, number one *The Secret of the Old Clock,* number two, *The Hidden Staircase,* it occurred to me that I could be like Nancy and investigate Aunt Helen's death. Nancy would have poked around, asked questions, put together the story of what happened. Number three, *The Bungalow Mystery.* Then she would have found an answer, an actual solution.

I finished the box with the Nancy Drew books in it, grabbed the first three in the series and headed up to my room. Nancy was my next mentor.

Door locked, I pulled out my diary.

Plan 1: Unraveling the Mystery of Aunt Helen
- *talk to Dad*
- *talk to Aunt Ruth*
- *call Uncle Wes*

No way was I going to ask Mom anything about it. History showed she wouldn't say anything anyway and it would only upset her. Plus she'd know it was because of the whole Ambien thing and be super pissed. Dad was the person to start with. Just as soon as he got home.

Plan 2: Melody

That one was more difficult. I felt sick all over again just thinking about it. Was Melody mangled beyond recognition? Was she near death? I couldn't take it. I had to know. I couldn't call one of her friends because I had never seen her with a friend. I just couldn't call her house. That left one thing.

- *find a way to visit the hospital and investigate Melody's condition*

Tomorrow was Saturday. Maybe I could come up with a reason to go to the hospital. It would have to be a fake reason because there was no way I was telling Mom or Dad I had caused someone to get hit by a car. I could barely think it. Then again, I was getting good at fake.

"Jackie!" I could hear Mom yelling from downstairs. She never did realize the ancient intercom system still worked. "Come and help me!"

Must keep her happy. I've damaged enough lives this week.

It was later Friday night, and I was sitting in my dark room, up on the window seat, by the dark window, the only light a small reading light attached to the book.

I was re-reading the scene where Beryl followed her dog Buller when he chased after a warthog. The Murani she was hunting with was injured and couldn't help her, and when she finally caught up to Buller she found him ripped to shreds by the warthog. Beryl plunged her spear into the warthog's heart and cradled her almost dead dog in her arms, far away from any help. She waited until Arab Maina found her, sitting in the dark, and helped her take Buller home.

I shivered, imagining it was me sitting there listening to the hyenas and hoping my dog could survive. Hoping someone would find us and help us home. I closed my eyes and tried to feel Beryl's concern only for the dog and not the far off roar of a lion. What kind of courage is that? To spear a wild animal, hold your dog that is ripped open along one whole side of his body, and not worry for yourself? It seems like I *only* worry about myself. I wonder if my recent little flashes of bravery could ever grow into something like Beryl's fearlessness. I wondered if I'd ever feel as comfortable in the world as she seemed to. Or if I'd ever feel as comfortable in my real world as I did in the fictional ones.

When I read *WWTN* I felt like I *was* Beryl. I believed that if I were suddenly transported through the pages into her world, into her body, that I would behave exactly as she had. It seemed so clear. And when I read *From the Mixed-up Files of Mrs. Basil E. Frankweiler* I felt like I was Claudia, that in her place I would behave the same way. In *The Old Man and the Sea,* I was the old man. I could feel that with every book I read. It was the real world that seemed so uncertain. And as soon as I finished WWTN I was going to become Nancy Drew.

I thought about the part where Beryl talked about not knowing yourself, about striving against loneliness. In trying on these different personality characteristics was I just trying to avoid myself? Was pretending to be someone else taking me away from my real self? It was hard to know. I definitely felt alone, no doubt there. And when I pretended to be brave or confident, I felt better. I couldn't help but worry. What if I was just avoiding loneliness with my Desired Personality Characteristics?

Enough worrying, enough delay, I turned to the last chapter of *West With the Night*. I let myself soak in the excitement of making the transatlantic flight. I felt the frenzy surrounding Beryl-me in New York City, the press interviewing me, the telegrams and letters celebrating my accomplishment. I let myself feel farther and farther from my own life. I imagined I was Beryl, sitting on the deck of the freighter sailing back to Africa, reliving her flight in her mind. I felt the heat of the sun, heard the lap of the waves as the ship chugged slowly home. I felt the swelling in my chest that meant the end of a book. It was a combination of gratitude and loss, a homesickness for the world I was about to leave. I grabbed my diary.

> *Dear Beryl,*
> *Thank you. Thank you. Thank you for your bravery, your self-sufficiency, your beautiful way with words. Thank you for entering my body and helping me be brave too. Please feel free to stick around. I think I'm going to need you.*

I let the diary fall into my lap, turned off the one little light beside me and stared out into the dark night. With no light inside I could make out the shapes of the trees and the sticks that would be bushes again in the spring. I didn't want to let go of Beryl, but I also needed to be in a book. I need to be in the world of a book at all times, especially these days. Tomorrow I'd find a new one, Nancy Drew maybe. I would pretend Beryl was right outside, circling in her plane above me until I needed her again. Feeling silly I gave a little wave up to the sky and then climbed into bed.

Chapter Eighteen

Secrets and Kisses

In the morning I woke up early and couldn't fall back asleep, even though it was a Saturday. I hate when that happens. Finally I could sleep as long as I wanted and boom, wide awake. I felt restless without a book world to live in, so I sorted around through my bookshelf. Nothing jumped out and said "read me!" so I went down to the library. Within minutes I was lost in the jumble of books in the boxes that were still waiting to be shelved. I opened all the boxes, found the one that had Mom's old Nancy Drew books and started looking through that. There were lots of books I recognized, the Hardy boys, *The Prince and the Pauper*, a couple of Oz books, and then even more books I didn't recognize. Those were the ones giving me a little thrill and I ended up with a stack of nine or ten that I didn't know but that looked interesting. I decided to come back to Nancy later and try one of the unknowns.

I opened *A Wrinkle in Time* and disappeared. It was delicious. I was Meg, wrapped in my quilt, worried about the wild wind and shaking house, thinking about my misery at school. Gee, that sounded familiar. Here was a girl like me. Worried, not fitting in, family tension going on all around. And then the magic started. Not just the magic of reading, the magic in the story.

An hour later, feeling like I had slept an extra ten hours, I woke up from book trance to the smell of bacon. Back to my life, at least for a moment. What to do about Melody? I squirmed deeper into the already deep leather chair and my eyes fell onto the stack of mom's old Nancy Drews. Even without re-reading them, I could remember enough of Nancy's investigative powers that I came up with the idea to tell my mother I was going to a meeting for prospective volunteers. Mom was a Candy Striper growing up and thought it was the greatest thing ever. I put it more in the yuck category myself. I hated hospitals.

Even better I could ask Dad to give me a ride. He came home so late last night I wasn't able to ask him about Aunt Helen. I ran to the kitchen to catch Dad before he left again. He worked most Saturdays and could give me a ride to the hospital.

I found him in the kitchen, filling his travel mug with coffee. Mom was sitting puffy eyed at the kitchen table, staring down at a newspaper.

"Jackie, that's a great idea," Dad said when I asked, throwing his arm around my shoulder. "Marion, did you hear that? She's going to follow in your footsteps."

Mom looked up from the paper. "Oh Jackie, that's so wonderful! I loved being a Candy Striper." Her eyes glazed over as her head tilted to the side. "So fulfilling, all those sick people and *me* being able to help them."

Yes, you and Jonas Salk, curing the world.

I loved riding in Dad's car. It was so clean and silent. No Mom, no whining Davy, no action figures all over the floor.

"I thought you hated hospitals," Dad said, giving me a sideways smile as we wove our way down the driveway.

Score one for Dad for remembering.

"Yeah, well, just going to get some information, that's all," I said, trying to figure out how to switch the topic to Aunt Helen.

I couldn't come up with a good transition so I just said it. "Dad, uh, you know, no one in the family ever talks about Aunt Helen."

"Is that why you are going to the hospital?" Dad asked, puzzled.

No that is an entirely separate area of failure in my life.

"No, no. I just, you know, have always wondered, like, why did Aunt Helen, you know," I was fumbling. This was harder than I had thought it would be.

Dad wasn't helping. "Hmm, well, that's kind of in the past."

"I know, but, I just want to know. Was she depressed?" That sounded stupid. Obviously if someone kills themselves they must be depressed, right?

"Hmm, I guess," Dad said. "I don't know much."

"Why not?" I asked. "Don't you want to know?"

Dad shrugged.

"Aren't you, um, scared?" I said.

We slid to a stop at a light, and then pulled away when it turned green.

Dad shrugged again. "Jackie some things are just better left in the past."

"But I want to know," I said.

"You don't need to worry about her," Dad said, making a right into the hospital driveway. "And for God's sake, don't talk about her around your mother, she's still sensitive about it."

Duh.

As I climbed out of the car Dad gave me a smile. "Enjoy the hospital," he said, and then added, "and forget about that other thing. Really, just not something you need to dwell on."

Wasn't Dad scared like me? Why was he so reluctant to talk about Aunt Helen?

Why are adults so willing to live in denial?

****

I walked nervously through the big automatic doors at the front of the hospital. I felt a wave of anxiety; what was I doing? What kind of stupid plan was this? I saw an empty bench in the lobby and sat down, surprised at how shaky I felt. That weird hospital odor, that mix of cleansers and antiseptic and old floors went past my nose and got stuck in my mouth. I wished I had a piece of gum to get rid of that taste.

Maybe I should just wait for Mom to come get me.

I saw Jennifer Walker swish by pushing a cart full of boxes. She had a volunteer pin and name tag on her chest. Not that you could see it very well under the neon yellow hair. I dropped my head so she wouldn't notice me.

Poms everywhere. Couldn't a person get a break?

I tried not to think about all the gross stuff going on at that very moment in the hospital. Things like people getting cut open, and people with weird things coming out of their bodies, and people *dying* for crying out loud. How could the doctors and nurses walk around talking about Caesar salads or their new Prius with all that bad Juju around us? I shivered.

Okay, that's not helping.

I stared straight ahead and breathed in and out. I repeated *Brave, Confident, Self-sufficient* over and over. I didn't feel any of those, but of course Brave was the most relevant here. Could I find some bravery? What would Beryl do? This was a woman who flew by herself over wild animals, not even knowing if there would be a place to land her plane, not knowing if she'd T-bone a zebra when she did bring the plane down. I don't think she would have even paused when walking through the front door. And Claudia would have marched right up to the information desk as if she owned the hospital. Nancy Drew would have just gracefully walked up and asked for help. After five minutes of imagining I was a combination of Beryl, Claudia and Nancy, I felt Brave enough and stood up.

I found a pleasant man at the information desk and who gave me a visitor tag and directed me to the fourth floor. Easy.

I found the elevator. Easy.

I found the fourth floor and my heart started pounding. No more easy.

I walked slowly down the halls glancing right and left, trying to look casual but also trying to find Melody's room. Some rooms had the doors closed, and others had curtains pulled around the beds. I didn't actually want to see what was going on in those rooms. The hospital smell was choking me. I was starting to sweat. I had just decided go back downstairs to wait for Mom when I heard a voice behind me.

"Jacqueline?"

I turned around to see Melody pushing herself down the hall in a wheelchair. Her left leg was in a cast and was sticking straight out, propped up by a metal shelf-like thing.

Panic-guilt-fear-relief rushed through me. She saw me (panic). She was injured (guilt). She might yell at me (fear). She was conscious and otherwise seemed okay (relief).

"Hi," I managed to say.

"What are you doing here?" said Melody, in a friendly, curious way.

"Oh, ah . . ." I said, and then couldn't get anything more out.

"Are you visiting someone?" she asked. Melody seemed to be in a good mood, not at all what I would have expected. And

Melody was more talkative than I had ever seen. At school Melody never initiated conversations and never spoke in a voice this friendly.

"Yeah," I said, not able to figure out what was going on. Wasn't Melody mad at me?

"Did you hear I got hit by a car?" Melody said. "It was really scary! I was walking home from school and this car came out of nowhere! This big Cadillac came up on the sidewalk right at me, and I tried to jump out of the way but it caught my leg."

I was even more confused. Didn't Emily say that Melody ran in front of a car?

"Yeah, this old guy was driving and he had a heart attack and lost control of the car and it ran right into me! How lame is *that*?"

Could it be . . . ? Could it be . . . ?

"And then he crashed into a tree. By the time they got him to the hospital, he was *dead*. How sick is that?"

I finally managed to speak. "Wow, I can't believe it!"

"I know," Melody nodded. "It's amazing, huh? I feel so lucky to be alive."

I sent up a silent thank-you to God. I mean, I felt bad for the old man, but I didn't even know him. I was giddy with relief — it wasn't my fault!

"Oh my God, I'm so glad you are okay!" I babbled. "I can't believe it, I just can't believe it."

"I know, it's a crazy story, isn't it?" Melody said, obviously not understanding what I couldn't believe.

I felt compelled to come completely clean. "I can't believe it because, well, I heard that, um, I heard that you ran in front of a car! I heard that Sandra and Kelly were teasing you, you know, about that stupid thirty-five thing in keyboarding and . . ." I couldn't say anymore.

"Oh no," said Melody. "I mean they did tease me, but that was way before the car thing. And you know what? Who cares what they think? I mean, I almost just *died*, I can't worry about stupid girls like them."

The relief kept bubbling through me. "Oh, I'm just so glad you're okay!"

Melody nodded, "Yep." Then she half smiled, half grimaced. "We could probably sue his family."

I had forty-five minutes before Mom was due, so Melody and I decided we'd go to the cafeteria. On the way there we saw five different girls from our school all wearing volunteer pins and name tags like Jennifer Walker. The candy striped outfits were gone but volunteer jobs lived on. Who knew?

"I can't believe they are all giving up their Saturday!" I said after we passed Melinda Barnes. Melinda was scurrying after a cute, white-coated guy and didn't even flick her eyes toward us. Well, maybe I could see why she was working here on a Saturday.

"Don't get too impressed," said Melody looking back over her shoulder at me as I pushed. "It's the only way to get into college. You've got to do some kind of community service, and play on a sports team, and get great grades."

Well I was one for three. Unless wheeling Melody around counted for community service. Sports and I had parted company many years ago. I can't imagine how many injuries had been prevented by *that* split.

After we had chips and a soda, we started back to Melody's room.

"Oh, wait, there's a bathroom, could you push me in there?" Melody said, pointing to one of those individual bathrooms with pictures of both a man and a woman on the door.

I turned the handle and pushed the door open, angling Melody's chair in before the door swung closed.

There was a squeal, and I saw that we had interrupted some serious making out. A tall boy had a girl pressed against the wall with his head buried between her breasts. Her shirt was up around her shoulders, and he got caught in it as he jerked his head up.

Time stopped as Alex Madigan managed to free his head and turn and look at us, his hands still around Jennifer Walker's waist. His face was flushed and his pupils were large and dark. Jennifer's straight blond hair was a mess and her mouth was red and puffy.

This scene was especially interesting seeing as Jennifer was going out with David Lewis and Alex was rumored to be with Shelly Tavole these days. Not to mention the fact that Cassidy was totally after Alex and wouldn't take kindly to another Pom poaching on her territory. No matter that she already had a boyfriend.

Jennifer gasped again and tried to get her hands up to her shirt but got stuck under Alex's arms.

"Sorry!" I said, whipping Melody's chair out the door. I zoomed down the hall and around a corner, at which point we broke into hysterics.

"Omigod, did you *see* that?!" Melody said.

I was laughing too hard to answer.

"Did you see Jennifer's face? Good thing she was in the bathroom because I guarantee you she just wet herself!" There were tears coming out of Melody's eyes she was laughing so hard.

Finally I managed to catch my breath. "Haven't they heard about *locks?* Oh my God."

That night I was too tired to read. I had gone from despair to relief to hysteria in less than twenty-four hours, and let me tell you wildly swinging emotions were *exhausting*.

Chapter Nineteen

Who's Your Hero?

It was Sunday night and I was in my room reading *A Wrinkle in Time*. I was stopped short by the line, *"You're going to have to do something about yourself. Nobody can do it for you."* I thought about how maybe I should start taking care of things. Nobody was going to do it for me, that was for sure. I pulled out my diary and stared at my plan.

> *UPDATE on Plan 1: Unraveling the Mystery of Aunt Helen*
> - *talked to Dad – Not much data.*
> - *talk to Aunt Ruth*
> - *call Uncle Wes*

Looking at the "talk to Aunt Ruth" goal, I thought back to my conversation with Aunt Ruth earlier tonight. Mom's younger sister had come over to borrow Dad's old lap top and ended up staying for dinner. I loved having Aunt Ruth around, but we barely saw her anymore. Mom said graduate school had taken over her life, but it seemed to me that living in Kentley Heights was what was setting us apart from Mom's family. Telling Aunt Ruth I wanted to show her the library, I managed to get her alone to ask her about Aunt Helen.

I figured I better start off easy. "Hey look, I've been finding books you guys used to read when you were young," I said, gesturing to the row of Nancy Drew books I had finally manage to arrange on the "teen section" shelf.

Aunt Ruth smiled. "That was more your mom and Helen. They thought they were going to be detectives."

"What did you like to read?"

"Oh, more non-fiction, some science kinds of stuff. I remember loving *The Wind in the Door,* though. That one's fiction. So good."

"I'm reading her other one, *A Wrinkle in Time!*" I said. "I love it already." But back to Mom and Helen. "What about Mom and Helen, did they include you in stuff?" I asked. "Like, as the younger sister did they ignore you or what?"

"Oh those two, they had their own little world," Aunt Ruth said picking up *Anne of Green Gables* and then putting it back on the shelf. "It was more than just ignoring the younger sister. It was that they did everything together, everything the same. If one of them got a chocolate cone, the other had to as well. They even dressed alike until they were, like, fourteen or so. Same hobbies, same college even."

I had heard that kind of stuff before, but it was starting to puzzle me. I didn't remember Aunt Helen being around much or even talking on the phone much with Mom.

"Was Aunt Helen mad when we moved to Michigan? Is that why we didn't see her much?"

"Hmm, I guess so," Aunt Ruth said turning away and staring out the window into the dark night. "I guess once you are married and living in different states . . . it is just harder to stay in touch." She turned towards the books, walking along the shelves, staring into the rows.

Worried that I was running out of time, I forced myself to ask the real question. "Aunt Ruth, what happened? I mean, you know, why did she, um, do what she did?"

Aunt Ruth turned from examining the wall of books and stared at me. Her eyes were crinkled as if she was debating how much to tell me. Aunt Ruth was the intellectual of the family and her stare was full of intelligence.

"Aunt Ruth, I'm fourteen!" I pleaded. "No one tells me anything. It's not fair."

Aunt Ruth nodded, her shoulder-length brown hair bouncing with her movement. She gave me a kind smile. "Yes, I always hated that. As the baby of the family no one ever told me anything either."

Mom always acted like her younger sister was the crackpot in the family. So she didn't match her shoes to her purse or have ecstatic fits over granite kitchen counters. So she didn't wear make-up or do fancy things with her hair. So she was a Democrat. That made her crazy?

Ruth was in graduate school at the University of Pittsburgh. I thought it was super cool that she was going to be a marine biologist. Mom thought it was a waste of time. How could it be a waste of time to get a job where you got paid to go to the *beach*?

"I just wondered, you know," I fumbled for words. "I mean, all I know is that she, you know, killed herself."

Aunt Ruth nodded, her face sad.

"No one said how, no one said why," I added. "I just want to know. How did she do it?"

So I can make sure it doesn't happen to Mom.

"Well, you were, what, nine, at the time? A nine-year-old doesn't need those kinds of details."

"But I can understand more now, and Mom and Dad won't say a thing."

Aunt Ruth sunk into one of the leather chairs and steepled her fingers together. "Well, I'm not sure it's up to me to tell you if they have decided not to."

I sat on the ottoman at her feet, leaning towards her. "I don't think they *decided* not to, I just think it's too upsetting for them to think about. I'm sure they'd be glad for you to do it," I pleaded.

Aunt Ruth tilted her head back and forth, considering. She took a deep breath and said, "Well, she hung herself."

The words lingered in the air, simple and ugly.

I felt sick. An image of Aunt Helen with a rope around her neck burned through my brain. I didn't say anything. Maybe the adults were right. Maybe I didn't want to know this stuff. But there was no getting the image out of my head now.

I took a deeper breath than Aunt Ruth had. "Why?"

The million dollar question.

Aunt Ruth shook her head, tears in her eyes. "I don't know," she whispered.

Duh, Jackie, this is painful for her too. Stop talking.

"Was she depressed?" I couldn't stop myself. I had to know.

Aunt Ruth nodded, wiping her eyes. "Yes, I mean, no one knew it was that bad, but she was . . . having a hard time."

"What was so hard?" I asked.

Aunt Ruth shrugged. "Well, it could have been any number of things. But they aren't the type of things that make most people, you know, that desperate."

"What things?"

Were they things Mom had too?

"Oh, she had some trouble with her job. Nothing out of the ordinary, slow to be promoted, that kind of thing. And she and Wes had some tension I think. But not that much. I think, uh, she had some disappointments in her life. . ."

What kind of disappointments?

Aunt Ruth looked like she was sorry she had started this conversation.

The door flew open and Mom stuck her head in. "There you are! Jock-leen, I need you to start on the dishes. Ruth, I wanted to show you what I've done to Davy's room."

What disappointments?

Sitting in the cold dark, thinking back to Aunt Ruth I wondered what she hadn't been saying. There were moments in the conversation I could tell she was holding something back. What was it? I felt as alone as Meg, in her attic room, the wind shaking the house. As alone as Beryl must have felt, out there in the dark woods, a dying dog in her arms. At least Beryl knew someone might try to find her. I had no such illusions. I could sit here for decades and no one was coming to help. I thought about Meg and Beryl and decided to add "Tough" to my list of Desired Personality Characteristics. I scribbled it down, straightened my shoulders, and repeated "Tough" to myself a couple of times until I felt strong enough to call Aunt Ruth. I needed more information.

I snuck downstairs, dug Mom's phone out of her purse and found Aunt Ruth's number. I scribbled it on a note pad and slipped back up to my room with my own phone.

Aunt Ruth was happy to hear from me but shut down the Aunt Helen conversation.

"Jackie, I really feel like I've said enough," Aunt Ruth said. "More than enough. You should talk to your parents about this. I don't want to go behind their backs."

"Okay, okay," I said. "But just one more question, not about Helen."

"Yes?"

"Have you ever, you know, been depressed?"

Does it run in the family?

"Hmm, nothing like that," Aunt Ruth said after a pause. "I've had the normal run-of-the-mill kind of blues, but everyone gets those. Nothing that would lead me to, uh, you know."

People really don't like to talk about suicide, do they?

"I can understand your curiosity, Jackie," said Aunt Ruth. "But it's not something you need to worry about. Probably better to just try to move on."

Easy for her to say.

After we hung up, I climbed in bed and pulled the blankets up around my neck. I thought about Beryl's courage. I thought about Claudia's confidence. I wondered what new trait Meg would bring me. I closed my eyes and imagined that my life was a book and I was the noble hero, even though no one knew it. After all, sometimes even the heroes don't know they are heroes. I would persist. I would figure out Aunt Helen, I would protect Mom, and I would vanquish Mean Girl Queen Bee Barbie. Whether I won the boy or not remained to be seen. Actually, I wasn't sure if I was even ready to win the boy. But I liked the idea of a little vanquishing.

Chapter Twenty

Not Quite a Thug

Melody came clumping into keyboarding on crutches after class had already started, followed by a brown-haired boy carrying her books. He never looked up from the ground and was so thin he reminded me of one of those fish that disappear when they turn sideways. I don't know how he managed the weight of even one book, let alone three. He dumped the books by the computer and slid away without a word.

Melody looked me and smiled and gave me a thumbs-up.

I smiled back and felt a flutter of excitement inside at the thought of my new friend. Quickly followed by a flutter of sadness when I thought about Emily.

Why does it feel disloyal to be happy for a new friend when Emily has eleven of them?

When the bell rang I offered to carry Melody's books to her next class. She said okay, and we waded into the babbling racket of three thousand students who had five minutes to talk before they were silenced again for fifty minutes. Clumps of kids swarmed by us, laughing and teasing each other. Melody giggled. "I still can't believe we caught Alex and Jennifer!"

"I know!" I said. "The look on her face! It was hysterical."

"Speaking of . . ." said Melody nodding her head to one side. Jennifer was headed in our direction.

At that moment Jennifer caught sight of Melody and me; her eyes widened and her face immediately turned red. She looked side to side like an escape hatch might suddenly appear, and slowed her steps. Then I noticed Cassidy at Jennifer's side.

"Hi, Jennifer!" Melody called out gaily as Jennifer and Cassidy got close to us. Melody elbowed me.

"Hi, Jennifer!" I called out in the same over-friendly voice.

"Uh, hey" mumbled Jennifer with a cringing glance at Cassidy.

Cassidy gave us the stink eye then whipped her head toward Jennifer and leaned in to whisper to her. Jennifer hung her head and shrunk away from Cassidy but kept walking with her.

Melody clumped along on her crutches laughing. "Now Miss High and Mighty Jennifer has to be nice to us!"

It should have felt good, but for some reason it didn't. Okay, so Jennifer was a vapid dancer and probably had as much character as a bag of rocks, but when it came down to it, I didn't have any real reason to dislike her. Being Tough didn't mean I had to be unkind. In fact, wasn't that what I hated about the bullies? The lack of kindness.

I was the noble hero in this story of my life. I was the one who held her head high, who bravely flew her airplane into the dark night, who stealthily discovered who sculpted the Angel statue, who boldly traveled through space to find her father. I could choose to be kind to people like Jennifer.

After I dropped off Melody and her books I hurried to chemistry pretending I was in a movie. The cameras were hidden but they were there and they were capturing my brave self. Even walking down these halls was filled with danger. And the whole audience was on my side, I could just feel it. I thought about one of the lines in *A Wrinkle in Time* that had caught my attention. *"We are asking you to do a difficult thing but we are confident that you can do it."* I could feel Meg's confidence streaming through me.

I took a seat on the Unnoticeables side of the room trying to put as much distance between MGQBB and myself. Not to mention Emily. Not to mention Alex. The image of him bent over Jennifer's chest was seared into my brain, and it made me feel all twitchy inside. It was one thing to hear rumors; it was another thing altogether to witness Alex in action. And to think Alex's mouth, the one that had been on a girl's breasts, was like, right there. Eeew. And yet, the adventuresome part of me, the part that seemed to be taking over my brain, wondered what that would feel like.

No! Stop thinking about that. It was too weird. Not to mention slutty.

I snuck a glance at Alex only to find him looking at me. I would have thought he'd be embarrassed, but he stared right back at me with a little smile on his face. Like he was glad I saw what I saw. Like I was next.

I was definitely going to flunk chemistry. I hadn't heard a word in a week.

Cassidy sauntered by my seat. "Hey Jackie, nice job finding yourself a *cripple* for a friend. And I thought you couldn't become even more of a *loser.*"

I mean really, who decides all this stuff? Who decides what makes a loser and what makes someone popular? Who decided blond hair is better than brown hair? Who decided straight hair is better than curly? Who decided thin is better than curvy? That Cassidy is better than Melody? I think one person has a strong opinion and then everyone just blindly follows that person. Cassidy is blond and thin and so her opinion matters more? That's bullshit. I was starting to really hate the person who came up with the Barbie. Maybe it all could be traced back to that.

I glanced back at Emily and my anger at her started morphing into pity. She was just a sheep. A scared, blind follower. She wasn't mean or evil, not yet. She was just scared. Scared she wasn't enough, scared of being alone, scared of being the target instead of the Pom. So she was vulnerable to Cassidy's attention. And I started getting really pissed at Cassidy for the way she was about to make Emily into a mean girl.

The more I thought about it, the worse I felt for Emily. Cassidy was a bitch.

I turned around in my seat and stared straight at Cassidy until she looked back at me. She turned the full force of her mean girl stare at me. I kept my eyes steadily on hers until she broke and looked away. It was all very gangster, this staring each other down. Pretty soon we'd be calling each other *mofo.* But if I was going to stand up for Melody, I could stand up for Emily too, right? Even if Emily didn't know that's what I was doing.

During class my mind wandered to *WWTN.* Maybe it was because I was reading one book right after the other, but it occurred to me that *West With the Night* and *A Wrinkle in Time* were kind of similar. Both Beryl and Meg had traveled through the sky, not knowing what would happen at the end of their journeys. Beryl had searched from the sky for elephants, she had flown from Africa to England, and then she was the first person to fly from Europe to North America alone. That's where the title of the book came from, she flew west with the night. I imagined what it must have felt like. To be the first person flying across the ocean in that direction! To be one of the first female pilots in the world. To do it without all the technology we have now. No radios or radar screens or anything. To take off across the ocean with no one knowing where she was until she landed. And Meg, not even planning a journey, all of a sudden finding herself on a distant planet, her guides seeming to be old ladies but turning out to be so much more. And I understood how Meg could soldier on, desperate to find her missing father.

Talk about courage! I tried to imagine I had some of that courage.

On the way out of class Cassidy walked quickly toward me and banged into my shoulder as she went by. I resisted the impulse to trip her. It is one thing to stand up for a friend, bravely. It is another thing to slip into thuggery. If I could call up Bravery, if I could summon Toughness, who's to say Thuggery wasn't hanging around in there too? I would not sink to Cassidy's level, even in the fight against Cassidy. *Especially* in the fight against Cassidy.

"Hey Cassidy," I called before I could stop myself. I wasn't going to trip her, but I could talk to her.

Cassidy turned around, eyebrows raised. Had I dared to speak to her?

"Don't touch me again." I said it strong and low, my eyes narrowed like Clint Eastwood staring down a no good, shifty outlaw. I walked slowly towards her. I felt all the power of Beryl and Claudia flowing through me.

Cassidy must have felt them too, because she took a step backward and then seemed to realize what she had done. She stood up straighter and stared boldly at me.

"And lay off Melody. She's cool," I said, working on my hard stare. "She actually has a brain instead of a head stuffed with pom poms."

Cassidy snorted. "Whatever." She spun around, grabbed Emily and marched out of the class.

I felt a wave of heat come close to my back. "Nice," Alex breathed in my ear. He eased alongside me, a whole different kind of bump than Cassidy's. If it's possible to feel someone up with your hip, he did it, sliding his hip along my hip and looking down at me with a seductive smile. And then he was gone.

I waited until Emily and Cassidy were far ahead of me after class and then took a shortcut to geometry. I waited inside the door and when Emily came through it I grabbed her arm.

"Hey, Emily," I said.

She sat down, looking at me with a confused-guilty-scared face.

"Look," I said in a low voice so no one else could hear us. "I can't believe Cassidy is putting you in this position. You don't have to listen to her!"

Emily looked left and right, as if afraid someone could see her talking to me. I had meant to tell her I understood, that I knew why she was giving in to Cassidy and that I was okay with Emily, but all of a sudden I was back to being mad at Emily too, not just Cassidy.

"You just don't understand," Emily whispered, agonized. She pulled away from me and scurried to her seat.

Mrs. Buttondale rapped on the front desk for attention and class started. Emily looked steadily ahead, never once glancing in my direction. I should have felt rejected and alone, not to mention scared. I did feel those things a little, but I mostly felt like I had finally found the courage to face what was right. What Cassidy was doing wasn't right. I wasn't going to pretend it was okay, even if Emily was.

And it occurred to me, with everything that was going on, that I couldn't wait for the noise in my head, all the swirling emotions, to calm down before I could concentrate on school. I had to listen in class despite those things. And I thought about Beryl in her plane, alone, and how she had to find a way to focus on the instruments and what she was doing *despite* her fear. How her plane engine cut off and she was diving toward the ocean while she tried to get the gas tanks switched over. *In the dark*. If she had given in to fear she would have crashed into the ocean. Beryl made herself focus *in the face of fear*. Meg was willing to travel through the Dark thing, the most evil energy in the universe. She acted despite fear too. I stared at Mrs. Buttondale's face, her wrinkles filled with foundation two shades too dark for her skin, and willed my brain to hear her words. And soon the swirling emotions were like party background noise, something you hear but aren't paying attention to.

Chapter Twenty-One

Brave, Breathless, Alone

That night, Dad didn't come home. I had been hoping to ask him some more about what Aunt Helen meant but no such luck. So I headed upstairs, did some homework and then got in bed with *A Wrinkle in Time*. Meg was another brave character but in a different way. Her bravery was the reluctant kind. She didn't set off looking for an adventure, she just went along because she wanted her father back so badly. And of course she was a genius, but as I well knew, that didn't guarantee anything a teenage girl wants. Meg was more like me, stuck in a hard situation, trying to save a parent. Maybe this book would give me some ideas about how to actually do that.

Mom came into my room at ten o'clock, then at ten thirty, then at eleven thirty. I guess Mom wasn't feeling very brave either. I pretended to be asleep every time, but I could feel her standing there looking at me. Finally at midnight she came in and made so much noise putting away my laundry that no one would have believed I was asleep. As soon as I moved, she jumped on me.

"Oh, are you awake Jock-leen?"

"No," I said, trying to sound sleepy.

"That's silly," said Mom. "You couldn't talk to me if you weren't awake. You must be worried about your father, he's not home yet."

"Daddy's late all the time," I said. "He probably had a meeting."

Mom sat down on the side of my bed. She got quiet and her shoulders drooped like she was really tired. I don't know if there are such things as auras, but *some* kind of darkness was flowing from Mom's body. I tried not to think about strangler figs. I tried not to think of her arms as creeping vines, sneaking around my body and slowly squeezing me to death.

Keep her calm. Keep her happy.

I didn't know what to do. I wished she would leave and let me go back to sleep, but she obviously was expecting something from me. I felt heavy with the pressure to fix something I couldn't even name.

The never-to-be-removed image of Aunt Helen flashed through my head.

"It'll be okay," I said. That was one of Mom's favorite lines. She didn't care if it was true, she just liked hearing me say it. It didn't used to bother me so much to lie like that. Maybe it was the way I was acting different at school, but I felt sick lying to Mom.

Because the truth was, there was a good chance that Dad wasn't coming home. Maybe she had pushed him too far. If I had the option to go somewhere else, I would have gone a long time ago. Who could blame him?

Then I thought of Aunt Helen, again, that ugly swinging image that cursed my brain now, and pushed any thoughts of truth out of my head.

Mom nudged me over on the bed and climbed in. "This is different. I don't think he's coming home," she said, her voice breaking at the end. "And he's not responding to my calls."

It was too much. Mom was too unhappy for me to fix.

Mom snuggled in against my body, and started crying. "Maybe we'll both feel better if I just lie here awhile, right Jackiebear?"

Oh yeah, that would feel super.

I didn't answer. I felt like I had forgotten how to breathe. Like The Black Thing from *A Wrinkle in Time* was pressing down on my chest, engulfing my whole room.

"Right?" Mom said again, and it occurred to me that maybe Mom was stuck in the Darkness, maybe the Black Thing had engulfed her too.

"Yeah," I said, trapped as only a girl with a crying mother can be.

I thought about Beryl, alone in the night with Buller, hearing the far off roar of a lion. I thought of her alone in her plane, the engine dying. I thought of all the times she had been brave, alone. Just like I was alone.

I thought about Aunt Helen again and imagined I was like Beryl, switching between gas tanks as my plane plummeted in the dark toward the ocean. Must act.

"Mom, I'm sure it's just a late dinner. And he's talking away, trying to convince someone of something and just forgot to call. That's all." I tried to keep my voice calm and reasonable. Like my explanation was truly reality. Like our lives weren't a total freaking mess right now. Like air was actually entering my lungs.

Mom squeezed tighter.

"You know Dad, especially with work stuff. He loses track of time."

Mom grunted. I squeezed her. I felt rigid inside. I felt my breath barely moving in and out, like my lungs had been compressed and held that way.

Mom gave a big sigh, "You may be right. Maybe he is just caught up in the moment."

I felt the barest breath squeeze into my lungs. Maybe I would live.

"Oh Jock-leen, you are just so wise," Mom said, her voice still tearful.

Yes, that is the very definition of me. Full of bullshit is more like it.

Mom snuggled around me, her arms like vines pinning me to the bed. "I think I'll just stay here a little longer, though," she said.

I could feel her tears falling on my arm, but eventually I heard Mom's breathing get deeper and more even and I knew she was asleep.

With my eyes wide open I started counting the flowers on the wallpaper border around the top of my walls beginning in the left upper corner of the wall in front of me. When I lost track I just started again. They were hard to see in the shadows, but there was enough of an outline to work with. I let myself get lost in the question of whether to only count the big ones, or if the little ones that linked the big ones, like an ivy trail, should count too.

Chapter Twenty-Two

Gutted

Mom slept through the night on the hope of my lie. Only it wasn't a lie because there Dad was at the breakfast table in the morning. I wanted to know when he got home but didn't want to ask in front of Mom.

Claudia didn't have to play marriage counselor to her parents. Neither did Beryl, as far as I knew. Meg's parents were separated by circumstances, not a lack of love. In fact, out of all the books I'd read recently (or maybe even historically), Meg's parents were the ones I'd want the most. Smart scientists, in love with each other, completely accepting of their eccentric children.

Davy slurped his cereal cheerfully, unaware of the drama around him. And there was some kind of drama, I just didn't know how much. Mom was silent and pale, and Dad was silent and there was a tension in the air.

Or maybe it was just my imagination.

Dad stood up, filled his coffee travel mug and said "see you" to no one in particular before disappearing through the garage door.

I had mistakenly grabbed *West With the Night* instead of *A Wrinkle in Time* when I came down to breakfast so I opened it up at random and dove back in. If I could just read enough I could escape, could feel myself back in Africa and far from Kentley Heights. I would keep Africa and Beryl alive in my brain and that would give me courage.

"Okay Davy, now go get dressed," Mom said, wiping Davy's mouth. "Your clothes are laid out on your bed."

Beryl was helping Arab Maina skin a reed-buck, and I had managed to get my brain more in Africa than Kentley Heights, so I wasn't paying much attention to Mom.

"Jock-leen," Mom said, grabbing my hand. I looked up. *Back to reality.*

"Jock-leen, what am I going to do about your Dad?"

Everything in my body went still. I thought I might have an idea of how Beryl felt when the lion landed on her back. I thought I might have an idea of how Meg felt when she traveled through Dark Thing.

"Jock-leen, what should I *do*?" Mom said again when I didn't answer. She squeezed my hand so tightly I wondered if any blood could get in there. "What if he hadn't come back last night? What would I do?"

"Umm…" I still couldn't answer. I looked down at my book, longing to be in there, really in there. I would gladly trade places with Beryl even though she was holding the reed-buck's intestines.

Be Tough.

"I'm sure he just, you know, forgot to call, right?" I said, trying to sound as matter-of-fact as Beryl seemed with those intestines in her hand.

"Maybe he wasn't going to come home," Mom said, eyes full of pain, gutted in a whole different way.

"But he did. And didn't you ask him?"

"He said exactly that," Mom admitted.

"So why doubt it?" I asked, regretting the words as soon as they were out of my mouth. I didn't want to be more involved.

"I don't know," Mom said, eyes tearing up. "It just seems so inconsiderate. And we . . . he . . . just has seemed distant lately."

I had a flash of Aunt Ruth talking about "tension" between Wes and Helen. Now it was my guts that felt torn out.

"Mom, he has, like, the hardest job in the world," I said. I had to make this right. "He is so stressed and he is working so hard and Mr. Dubroski is trying to get him in trouble all the time. No wonder he's gotten a little forgetful."

"Do you really think that's what it is?" Mom asked, desperately hanging on my words.

No! What do I know? I've never even had a boyfriend.

I nodded vigorously. "I totally believe it. He's just really stressed from work. That's all. And you're the one that said that men aren't very good with emotions."

"That's true! They are like little babies."

"So he's just stressed, and he'll get it under control and then it will all be fine."

Mom draped herself around me, and then I wasn't thinking about intestines or lions, I was thinking about strangling vines.

"Give me a hug," Mom said when my arms didn't move in response to her draping.

Feeling like I could barely breathe, I reached my arms up to hug Mom.

Chapter Twenty-Three

Exposed

Brave Beryl-me climbed down from the bus, pretending I had just flown far away from my pathetic home life. As if I had traveled several hundred miles in the journey to school and was master of my own fate.

Apparently I landed right in a pride of hungry lions.

Cassidy appeared out of nowhere and slammed me into my locker before my coat was even off.

"*You're* THAT Carson's daughter?! YOU?! YOU LITTLE BITCH!"

If Cassidy hadn't been so brainless she would have made the connection already, but I still wasn't fully ready for it. I was surrounded by Cassidy's Pom posse. All dressed identically in tight jeans, tight shirts, and Ugg boots. Empty brains, cold hearts, and warm feet. They were all staring at me and smirking as Cassidy poked her finger into my flat chest. I guess she felt more confident surrounded by her friends. Only Jennifer Walker looked scared.

"I should have known! You're just as much of a sneak as your dad. Well guess what? He's going down and so are you!" Cassidy gave me another shove with her hand.

Nothing like a locker handle jabbed into your back to start the day off right. As I edged sideways to at least relieve my back from the poking I noticed Emily standing at the back of the group, staring down at her brand new Uggs. What a waste of a good person. I thought about when Beryl met up with Kibii, her childhood friend now an adult. And how Kibii told her the lessons he had learned about being a man. ". . . of how a man should live his life, keeping his voice soft and his anger sheathed until there was just need for it – like this sword that hangs from my belt."

Maybe it was time for the sword. It was definitely time to show no fear. Cassidy was just showing her natural state, like a lion would show its natural state and nothing would make her happier than a scared victim.

I stared her straight in the eye. "What's it to you what my dad does?"

"He's a sneak and a loser and so are you!" Cassidy snarled.

"Looks to me like my dad is not the loser in this scenario," I said, as calm and cool as Cassidy was steaming.

There was a giggle from the back of the posse and Cassidy spun around to see who did it.

"Yeah, well you wait," Cassidy said, poking back at me. "He'll lose big time and so will you. Who needs an ugly flat-chested loser like you around? *Nobody!*" Cassidy looked back towards Emily who had never lifted her head. "Even your own *former* best friend can't stand you."

"I don't know, *Alex Madigan* seems to find me interesting."

There was a collective intake of breath from the group, like I had just thrown a grenade into the middle of a crowd and everyone was staring at it, waiting for the explosion.

Cassidy's nose flared and her eyes widened, and I thought steam might start coming out of her ears. "Uh!" she yelled. "He wouldn't be caught *dead* with you."

I shrugged. "Sure, whatever you say." I looked at her and around at her posse. "Maybe Alex likes girls who are, you know, *real,*" I said. "You know, real hair color, real fingernails . . . real brains."

Cassidy narrowed her eyes and snorted. She gave me one more hard shove then flipped her hair and turned to walk away, banging into Jeff Brice who came bursting through the group.

"Stop! Leave her alone!" Jeff spun around looking up at all the girls. Apparently no puberty hormones yet for him because he was boob level with all of them and didn't seem to notice at all.

Cassidy looked down her perfectly shaped nose at Jeff. "Oh look, Jacqueline, you *do* have a friend. Have fun with the rest of the *retards.* They'll be the only ones left who will talk to you. You wait and see."

Cassidy shoved Jeff aside with her shoulder and walked off. The rest of the Poms followed. In their matching Ugg boots they looked like a harness of Clydesdales. Jennifer shot me a pained look over her shoulder, probably afraid she'd be up against a locker next. Emily never made eye contact, just shuffled behind the group.

On the outside I think I managed to look Dignified or at least not totally freaked out. On the inside I felt like someone took an eggbeater to my abdomen.

Jeff was looking at me with big, hopeful eyes, like a trained seal waiting for his fish treat.

"Thanks Jeff," I said. "I don't know what I would have done without you."

Jeff smiled a big crooked-teeth smile and reached high to pat my shoulder. "No problem, Jackie!"

After keyboarding, I started to pick up Melody's books, but she waved me away with an embarrassed smile. "Doug Freedman is going to carry them for me," she said, looking down as she blushed.

The skinny-as-a-fish boy appeared and picked up Melody's books. She clumped off beside him, neither looking at the other or speaking. How did she even know he was coming? Hard to imagine they'd actually had a conversation.

Well wasn't that super? No Emily, and now Melody, my one shot at friendship, was hooking up.

And I thought I couldn't feel more like a loser.

See, those are the kind of thoughts you should *never* allow yourself, because you'll just prove yourself wrong. You'll find you can *always* feel like more of a loser.

Like for instance chemistry class. After walking alone to chemistry, I took my second class citizen seat beside Crazy Lucille and sat watching her peeling the skin off of her fingers. I looked away only to be exposed to Chuckie Miller's penis. Yep, you heard me. He was sitting there, zipper down, drool coming out of his Joker-wide mouth as he laughed at my expression. He had his textbook propped in his lap so Mr. Redmond couldn't see him wagging his wanger at me.

Gross!

Eew, eew, eew. I actually have never seen a penis that size. The only one I've ever seen is Davy's and it's five-year-old sized. Chuckie's thing was disgusting. I looked down at my lap and didn't

look up until Mr. Redmond was well into the lecture. And then
only because I heard him say my name.

"Jacqueline?"

I looked around. The entire class was staring at me. What
had I missed? Obviously Mr. Redmond had asked me a question.
The logical thing would have been to ask him to repeat himself.
But here's the thing: I had been attacked by Cassidy, dumped by
Emily, abandoned by Melody and visually molested by Chuckie.
There was nothing logical going on in my head. No sign of Claudia
or Beryl or any helpful literary character.

"Huh?" was all I could manage.

I heard giggles from the Cassidy section of the room.

"Can you answer the question?" Mr. Redmond said.

I felt like my face was on fire. I felt like the entire world was
staring at me, naked. I felt like getting up and running until I hit
Canada. Nothing came out of my mouth.

"Obviously you weren't paying attention. I said, in what
state do molecules bend or vibrate but still stay in close proximity?"
Mr. Redmond was staring at me, not exactly mean, but not his
normal friendly self either. I was usually his star student. That is,
until lately.

I couldn't get the image of Chuckie's penis out of my head.
My mind felt like a poltergeist had just slammed through. Random
thoughts were scattered around and tumbled together in
uncomfortable ways. Words like "bend" and "close proximity" and
"penis" flew around my head.

"Copulation?" I said. It came out a scientific word, but it
had nothing to do with the topic. The class lost it. Hoots and
laughs and yells filled the room. Mr. Redmond narrowed his eyes at
me. Was I making fun of him?

I was about a millisecond away from bursting into tears.
Time seemed to slow. The laughter went on and on. Mr. Redmond
kept staring. I fought the tears pushing toward the edges of my
eyes.

About five years later the laughter died down.

"Yes Cassidy?" said Mr. Redmond looking away from me.

"The answer is 'solid.'" Cassidy said in a smarmy voice.
Emily must have fed that one to her because Cassidy is dumber

than an earthworm. This was the first question she had ever answered in class.

"Correct," said Mr. Redmond. He moved on with class but periodically sent me puzzled looks.

"Okay, remember the quiz tomorrow," Mr. Redmond finally started wrapping up class. "Jacqueline, come see me before you leave."

Oh joy.

I made my way to the front of the classroom, but I couldn't look Mr. Redmond in the face. I stared down at his desk and listened to the snickers behind me as everyone made their way out of class.

"What was that?" Mr. Redmond said. "What is going on with you?"

I couldn't look him in the eye. I focused on his stapler. It was shiny and black and had blue tape along the back with his name written neatly in black marker. I shook my head in a don't-know move.

"Copulation? Are you trying to be some sort of comedienne? Because that wasn't funny."

There was no way I could tell him what Chuckie did. I barely could stand the image in my head let alone actually describe it using words. And if I did manage to squeak out something, Mr. Redmond would feel forced to do something about it, and then it would be a whole big thing and people would hate me even more.

"No sir," I said. Adults love it when you say sir or ma'am. "I'm sorry. It won't happen again." I was still staring at the desk. My gaze had moved on to the row of pens, all perfectly aligned from light to dark colors. Mr. Redmond was a little obsessive, I think.

"Don't let it," Mr. Redmond said. In my peripheral vision I saw him make a dismissed move with his hand.

"Thank you," I whispered and left.

I hated Pennsylvania. I hated ninth grade. I hated my parents for making me move here. Nothing like this ever happened in Michigan. Not to me.

Chapter Twenty-Four

The Path of Least Resistance

Not even Guitar Hero could clear that gross penis image from my head. All that happened was that my fingers just wouldn't work right and the screech of missing notes made my brain even more jagged inside. I dumped the guitar on the couch and headed to the library to work on the books.

In the library I left the overhead light off and switched on only one lamp. With the leaden sky outside the room felt dark and cavelike. Just what I needed. Maybe I'd never leave. I ran my hand along the books I had shelved, hoping the wisdom would absorb right through my fingertips. There were still eight or nine boxes I hadn't even opened yet. This project was going to take way longer than I had thought. I opened the closest box and started pulling out books. *How to Faux Paint Anything,* went onto the How To shelf. *Women's Bodies, Women's Wisdom* went in the Health section. Or should it be the Women's section? No, Health. *The Words of Peace* could have gone with the poetry stuff or inspirational or maybe non-fiction. Hmmm. The sorting decisions started to loosen the knots in my brain. Shrink the world down to where this book goes and it starts to feel more manageable. *What to Expect When You're Expecting.* Hadn't I already shelved that? Yep, sure enough, in the parenting section. I stuck the extra copy by the first one, maybe Mom would want to pass a copy along to someone. I didn't think she'd be using it again. What a random collection this box was.

I Hope You Dance, a little hardback, tumbled out of my hands. It landed cover open, and there I saw it.

Helen Charmot.

Aunt Helen. I picked up the book, staring at her handwriting. It was spooky to see her name, in her writing, and know she was gone. I flipped the pages. It was filled with stuff about hope, and faith and chance. There were a couple of pages with the corners turned down, and I imagined Aunt Helen reading this, trying to find her way out of a dark place. And one of the marked pages read, "Never give in to the path of least resistance."

Before I knew it, I was crying. What happened Aunt Helen? What was so painful? What let you give in to the path of least resistance?

Please don't let it happen to Mom.

Please don't let it happen to *me*.

It was now or never. I hid in my room and dialed Uncle Wes. I had to know more about Aunt Helen, I just had to. And still, I half hoped he wouldn't answer.

And when he did it took a couple of awkward moments for him to figure out who I was. Uncle Wes had fallen out of contact with the family, and it only just now occurred to me to wonder if that was his choice or ours.

I fumbled around a little with 'hello's' and 'how are you's' and finally said, "Uh, yeah, so uh, Uncle Wes, I just, well, I'm sorry to bother you but I just, you know, kind of want to know about Aunt Helen."

Silence. Then, "Well what is it you want to know?"

I couldn't say it. My heart was pounding. I was starting to sweat. I tried to pretend I was Beryl, or Nancy Drew. Anybody but me.

"I just, you know, kind of want to know about family, uh, about Aunt Helen." That didn't come out right. "I'm sorry to ask. I don't want to make you feel sad."

More silence. Then, "You know, Jackie, it does make me feel sad to talk about Helen. But it makes me even more sad not to. I don't want to pretend she was never alive. I loved her. I miss her."

Deep breath. "Why, um, why did she, do you think?" I couldn't say the actual words.

"You know she was the most creative person I ever met," Uncle Wes said, either not understanding me or intentionally ignoring my question. "The beautiful blankets she made, her paintings, the way she decorated our house. Even a little note asking me to get milk was so beautifully written, almost calligraphy really."

"I remember," I said, deciding to just let him talk the way
he wanted to. "I still have that woven picture thing she did of the
family. So cool."

"Hmm, mmm," he said. "That was from her photography
time, she was so into pictures for a while. But doing different
things with them, not just straight photos."

"Oh yeah, I think I remember," I said.

"But I'm sure that is not why you called," he said.

I just couldn't bring myself to ask about her death. And yet,
I thought of Mom in the bed when I couldn't wake her up. I never
wanted to go through that again.

Deep breath. "Well, I guess I just, you know, worry." I said
the rest in a rush, "like, what if my mom gets all depressed and . . ."

"Ahhh."

Uncle Wes's voice was quiet. "I don't know what to tell
you, Jackie. I didn't see it coming."

My heart sunk. I needed some information. I needed some
signs to look for, some red flags. Something that jumped out and
said "Hey! Pay attention! Woman in trouble!"

"I've asked myself the same thing over and over. I just
didn't see it. She was, how to put it, unhappy, and stressed about . .
. a lot. But not in a way that ever, not even once, made me think
that she could do something like that."

"Oh."

I could feel pain stretching through the phone wires. Maybe
five years hadn't lessened it much for Uncle Wes either.

His voice was almost a whisper. "Jackie, I better go. Best to
your family. I miss them too." And then there was a click and that
was it.

What was she so stressed over? His pause made me think
he had decided not to say something. What was it?

Well that was no help.

"How do you like the salad?" Mom asked. We were
gathered around the dining room table and had barely picked up
our forks.

Oh yeah, that is the important thing here.

Dad grunted.

"I think the toasted walnuts go great with the goat cheese. And the cranberries! Such a nice touch," Mom enthused. "This recipe is a keeper!"

Getting no response from Dad, she looked expectantly at me. It is an unwritten rule that all Mom's meals must be praised. Before the first bite of anything is completely chewed.

I can barely get it down. I hate goat cheese. I could live the rest of my life without a cranberry.

I looked at Mom's puffy eyes, and then at Davy's innocent little face. I looked at the wrinkles creasing Dad's forehead that I hadn't noticed before. Must keep the peace.

Bravery, whispered Claudia-me in my brain. And Beryl-me reminded me that she had probably eaten bugs and weird wild animals and stuff.

"It's good," I said, sliding the cranberries under a stray lettuce leaf. And then, afraid I was lacking enthusiasm, I added, "I *love* it!"

"And with the mustard vinaigrette, well, I just love this salad," Mom said closing her eyes in pleasure as she ate another bite.

Great, we'd get this salad every night for a month.

"Susan Fitzpatrick fell down the stairs today at school," I said, willing Chuckie images out of my head.

"And what about the swordfish? What do you think of the artichoke salsa on it?" Mom asked, looking around the table.

"I think her leg is broken," I said.

"Mike?" Mom prompted Dad.

"Oh, uh, is she going to be okay?" Dad asked.

"No!" said Mom. "What do you think of the *fish?*"

"It's fine," he said. He was almost done with it so he must not have hated it.

Dad pushed back his chair and stood up. "I'm going to go take a shower." He picked up his drink and walked out of the dining room.

Mom pressed her lips together.

"How come *he* doesn't have to ask to be 'scused?" asked Davy.

Huh, if you only knew.

"He's a grown-up. Now finish your fish," Mom said.

"I don't like fish," Davy said. "It's yucky."

Mom narrowed her eyes at Davy. "You will eat it! And that is not polite, to say something is yucky. How do you think that makes me feel?" Her voice was whiny and angry. What happened to the ecstatic salad eater of a bare few seconds ago?

"Don't make fish anymore. Make chicken nuggets," suggested Davy, pushing the fish around with his fork.

"You will sit here until you eat that!" Mom's voice got tighter. "And you will finish the potatoes and salad too."

"I hate salad!" whined Davy. "It's slimy. And the cheese is stinky."

Mom stood up quickly, slamming her chair across the floor behind her. "That's it! No dessert! And no TV tonight! Jackie, sit here with him until he finishes!" Then she stalked out, hitting the swinging door between the dining room and kitchen so hard it banged back and forth at least twenty times before coming to rest.

More Dialogue That Would Happen if People Spoke the Truth Around Here:
Me: Dad, don't you realize Mom is depressed and acting funny?
Dad: Oh she'll be fine.
Me: Really? Like Aunt Helen was fine? Maybe someone needs to get Mom to a therapist or something. You know, get an expert on board so it isn't me watching her like a hawk night and day.
Dad:

I had a hard time with that one. What would Dad say if I fronted him up about Mom? He had to know, in some part of his brain, that she was acting weird. And yet he wasn't even willing to talk about Aunt Helen, let alone Mom.

Me: Hey Dad, how come we aren't allowed to talk about Aunt Helen?

I thought about Mom and the things we weren't allowed to talk about. The list was really long. I thought about Dad and how he seemed to have agreed to the Forbidden List. I wondered if other families lived with off-limits areas. Like police tape over a crime scene, "don't go in here. Ever." Or maybe it was just my family that avoided the truth. Nobody saying "hey, mom's sister freaking *killed* herself, what happened? What's up with that? What was wrong? Is it still wrong?" Or no one saying "hey, Mom has never acted the same since." Or, "hey, Mom just overdosed on sleeping pills in the *middle of the afternoon.*" Instead, around here, it was all fakey fakey, nicey, nicey, "everything's fine." Oh sure, Mom and Dad still argued, but not about the real stuff.

I let these thoughts swirl for a while. I didn't like them, but even more, I didn't want to continue participating in the Great Carson Cover-Up. At least *I* would be one person in the family who didn't immediately run from the truth. Whatever that truth was.

After thinking about it long enough to feel like I wasn't avoiding it, whatever IT was, I grabbed *A Wrinkle in Time* and read to the end. In that book IT was evil, pure and huge. I finished the book and let if fall against my chest as I looked out the window into the dark night. I loved the science parts of the book and how my brain seemed to be getting a work out trying to understand them. But even more, I liked how flawed Meg was, how she got angry and resentful with people, how she felt like she didn't even fit with her own family, as much as they all loved each other. Some books seemed to try to make their main character so perfect that I couldn't even identify with them. But not this one. After all, Mrs Whatsit told Meg that going into the battle for her father her gift was her faults. Maybe the point here was that it was okay not to be perfect. To be different than other people. Meg was Tough but I think I'd also have to add "Flawed" as a Desired Personality Trait. You know, to remind myself not to get so upset when I messed up. And I like how it turned out that Meg's flaws helped save her dad. I wondered if my flaws could help save my mom. I wondered if I could actually know what my flaws were.

Thank you Meg. Now you'll be with me too, added to my silent but present group of literary friends.

I didn't want to be out of the world of a book for too long. It was like reality had reversed, like real life was the Dark Thing all around me and I could only escape it if I was in a book. Hmmm, what next?

I climbed down from the window seat and grabbed *The Secret of the Old Clock* thinking it might be time for a little Nancy

Drew. Then I picked up *A Little Princess*. Maybe I'd allow myself one more true escape before Nancy and I finished my investigation.

I climbed into bed, got out my little reading light and escaped into *A Little Princess*. It was one of my all time favorite books and re-reading it was like digging out my childhood blankie, resurrecting the comfort of a simpler time. Within minutes I was living in turn-of-the-century England with little Sara Crewe. Even though I knew bad luck was coming for her, I liked reading the beginning of the book when she was treated like royalty. It only took a couple of pages before *I* was the one with the loving father and the French maid and school friends who adored me. It felt soothing, even though there was a part of me that realized there must be something wrong with my life if I would rather be a seven-year-old who is about to become orphaned and penniless.

Chapter Twenty-Five

Delayed Copulation

In the morning I made my way downstairs, thinking about how Sara had befriended the much laughed-at Ermengarde. I wondered what it must have been like for the dullest girl in the school to have the attentions of the new, much talked about, student. Sara's papa's words echoed in my head. *"If Sara had been a boy and lived a few centuries ago," her father used to say, "she would have gone about the country with her sword drawn, rescuing and defending every one in distress."* I wondered if I could be like Sara, rescuing everyone in distress. I wondered if that might even include rescuing myself. I could be my own white knight. A Kind White Knight.

I found Davy sitting at the kitchen table in his Speed Racer pajamas, his hair sticking out in four different directions. He waved his fork at me. "Hi, Jackie!"

"Hi, Davy-wavy," I said going around the table and kissing him on the top of his head. I could smell baby shampoo in his hair and for a second my brain was happy. Thoughts of Sara even made me feel loving towards Davy.

"Davy! You're splashing syrup everywhere, don't do that!" grumped Mom.

"Where's Dad?" I asked, still not having had a chance to ask him any more about Aunt Helen.

"He left early," said Mom.

Davy waved his fork again. "He's going to go get that Damn Dubroski!"

"Davy!" Mom said. "No swearing. And *don't* wave the fork."

"But that's his name!" Davy said, puzzled. "Damn Dubroski."

I turned away to hide my smile.

"His name is *Mr.* Dubroski to you, little boy," Mom said.

"I'm not a little boy! I'm five!" Davy cried.

I wondered what Damn Dubroski Junior had planned for me.

The day was gray and frigid, and the forecast was for sleet. Just another day in paradise. I schlepped to my locker to dump my quilted ski jacket but stopped cold ten feet away.

"Jacqueline Loves to Copuleight!" was painted across the locker in sparkly blue, large, neat block letters.

Gee, think it was Cassidy? Only she could come up with that spelling for "copulate." What an idiot. A mean, underhanded, about-to-die idiot.

People around me watched my face and giggled.

I made my face stay still, like Beryl might have looked facing a lion. I would not be malicious and rude like Cassidy. I shrugged like "who cares?" and walked away. Maybe I'd keep my jacket on all day.

In history I asked for a pass to go to the bathroom. On my way back, I detoured to my locker to dump my jacket and pick up the books I'd need the rest of the day. I saw the janitor headed toward my locker as I was leaving it, and stopped him.

"Can you take that off?" I asked, gesturing to the painting.

"That's what I'm about to do." He was a skinny old guy whose hands shook all the time. He gave me a soft smile and nodded his head toward the locker, "Buncha assholes in this school."

"Tell me about it," I agreed. I could have hugged him, but I just hurried back to class. Sara would have liked that guy. The Little Princess was always befriending people no one else even noticed.

I seemed to hear the word "copulate" echoing through the halls all morning. I don't know if it was just my imagination or if people were really making fun of me. I pretended I was the noble Sara, misunderstood and mistreated but still a princess.

Then I heard the word for real, behind me, sexy and low. Before I could turn to see who said it, Alex Madigan's arm landed around my shoulder. I was walking from lunch to keyboarding, hopeful that I'd finally see a friendly face in Melody.

"So Jackie likes to copulate, huh?" Alex said, looking down into my face. My whole body was buzzing from his touch. The Kinetic Molecular Theory that Mr. Redmond had been trying to get out of me flooded back through my brain. *With a solid, molecules are held close together by their attractions of charge. They will bend and/or vibrate, but will stay in close proximity.* Oh sure, *now* I remembered it. I looked up at Alex. Talk about "attractions of charge."

I rolled my eyes.

"Actually, I thought that was pretty funny. Old Redmond about pissed himself," said Alex, keeping his arm firmly around my shoulder. "And Cassidy looked completely disgusted," he added, grinning.

The buzzy feeling in my body reminded me of turning into one of my fictional friends. I felt around in my brain for Beryl's Bravery and Claudia's Confidence. Not that Sara didn't have bravery, but I needed the flirt-with-a-boy kind of bravery right now.

"Do you think I offended Cassidy?" Claudia-Beryl-me asked. "You know, her being so *anti*-copulation and all."

Alex threw back his head and laughed. It was a beautiful sound, dark and rich and strong, like if mahogany could laugh. "Well, if you are, you know, *pro*-copulation, you just let me know."

Ooooh. I was in way over my head.

"Maybe later," Claudia-Beryl-me said. "I've got a lot going on right now."

Alex gave me a squeeze and dropped his arm away. "See ya," he said and ambled off.

I took my vibrating molecules off to keyboarding. Emily was not going to believe this! I actually pulled out my phone to text her before I remembered she was done with me. The buzz died down.

I whispered it to Melody, and her eyes opened wide.

"Alex Madigan?!"

I nodded.

"Ohmigod, stay away from him!" Melody warned. "He'll slip you rufies or something and before you know it . . ."

I agreed Alex was trouble, but somehow I couldn't see him as a guy who would feel like he had to trick you into anything. He'd just *smooth* you into it. And be smiling and proud the whole time. Anyway, not an issue for me because Chuckie cured me of any interest in *that* part of a teenage boy for a long time. Talk about an abstinence motivator. Cassidy should just print pictures of penises on her "WAIT Training" brochures because no reasonable girl would want anything to do with something that ugly.

In chemistry I sat in the front center seat, hoping that my proximity to Mr. Redmond would keep the class from hassling me. I fussed with my books until class started, thinking that the front row better work because I was almost out of options for where to sit once I avoided Cassidy, Emily, Alex, Crazy Lucille and Chuckie.

"Yes Jason?" Mr. Redmond said.

"Yeah, uh, Mr. Redmond, are we going to learn about *copulation* today?" Jason said.

The class burst out laughing. My blood vessels burst into a full body blush. Even my toes felt hot. Temperature-hot, not Alex-hot.

I thought about how Sara had to deal with Lavinia, her century's mean girl. Bullies have been around since the beginning of time, haven't they? I remembered how Dignified Sara was after her father died and everyone thought she was a pauper. How calm she remained, even when all the other girls were making fun of her, even when people in the street laughed at her worn-out clothes. I thought about Sara until I felt I *was* her, my eyes grey-green, my hair long and dark, until I could feel I was looking out of her intense little face. I straightened my back and held up my head and looked directly at Mr. Redmond. I raised my hand.

"Jacqueline?" said Mr. Redmond, nodding his head at me.

"Mr. Redmond, I know there are people in this room who would love to learn about this topic, seeing as they might not learn anything firsthand for *years*," I stared at Cassidy and then pointedly shifted to Chuckie, "if not *decades*," then shifted my stare back to Cassidy, "if not *ever*." I let my glance linger on Cassidy. "I know it's your job to educate, but maybe you better wait until some people are mature enough to handle it? Especially given that *some* people in this room are very against the whole concept."

The class started laughing again, but this time I felt them laughing with me. Cassidy was the one blushing now, and all I could see of Chuckie was the top of his greasy haired head.

"I see your point, Jacqueline," Mr. Redmond said when he could finally be heard. "This is chemistry, in case no one noticed. So we don't need to worry about discussing, ah, copulation, or any of the other biological sciences."

With a few lingering giggles still echoing around the room, Mr. Redmond launched into his lecture. My heart kept pounding for a good twenty minutes. It felt like it would never slow down but eventually it slowed from its rabbit pace and my skin cooled back to normal. I kept my back straight the whole class, which by the way is very tiring. I felt Sara and Beryl and Claudia around me the entire time. I couldn't believe I spoke out like that. I get nervous just answering a normal question.

When the bell rang Alex appeared instantly by my side.

"Good one," he said, knocking his shoulder against mine. Jimmy Valante nodded at Alex's words as he angled past us, as did Sharon Daugherty.

Alex walked out of the classroom with me, managing to bump into me at least five times before we even hit the door. Each bump sent a new buzz through me. I swear I could have lit up Times Square with the sizzling going on in my body.

I tried not to look in her direction, but I knew Cassidy was somewhere behind us.

"Hey Cassidy," I heard Chuckie say in his skeezy voice. "Want to know what copulate means?"

"Eff you!" I heard Cassidy hiss.

"Yes please!" oozed Chuckie.

In the hallway Alex gave me one more bump and a playful jab at my shoulder. "See you later, Princess," he said, and walked away.

How did he know I was trying to be a secret princess?

Emily ignored me in geometry and study hall, but in a way I was just sad for her. *She* was the one with the slumped-over shoulders and miserable looking face. *I* was the one standing tall, even though I was practically friendless and the object of school-wide ridicule. I would have predicted it would be the other way around. Newly popular Poms are usually full of confidence, aren't they?

I guess the Kentley High Poms don't have my secret weapon.

They don't read.

Chapter Twentuy-Six

A Royal Pain

"When do you start Jock-leen?" Mom asked. It was Sunday night and we were at the country club for dinner. "We are so pleased that you are going to volunteer at the hospital."

Even though we were in the supposedly casual Grill Room, Mom still had the tight face on that said she was afraid Davy would act like the little kid he is and embarrass her. She expected him to act like a forty-five-year-old, not a five-year-old.

"Davy!" Mom said in a low but tense voice, her eyes and mouth pinched inward. "Put both legs in the chair!"

Davy squirmed back into his seat.

"I didn't say I was going to do it," I said. *Must ease her into this.*

"Well you went to the meeting! You must be interested," said Mom. While she talked her face was animated, and she tossed her shiny dark hair around a lot. Totally an act for the dining room full of people who probably could give a shit. Nevertheless, Mom loved to play the part of the perky wife and mother. See? Wasn't she at this very moment having an interesting conversation with her daughter?

"I went to see what it was about, but then I remembered how much I hate hospitals," I said.

Mom shot a meaningful look at Dad. "I am disappointed to hear that."

Really? Were you hoping I'd be there next time you get admitted for taking a "nap?"

Mom continued. "We have been quite concerned about your lack of involvement with school or anything outside of school."

We?

I looked at Dad. His face was blank. He probably had no idea what she was talking about but was presenting the united parental front.

"What do you mean, 'concerned?'" I asked.

"You aren't involved with anything. We understood at first, it's hard when you move somewhere new. But we've been here long enough that you should have found your place by now."

My place? WTF?

"You don't want to do sports. You don't want to play an instrument. You don't belong to any clubs. You aren't interested in *fashion*. What are we supposed to do?" Mom said. She gave me a big fake smile and twisted her shoulders a bit playing the loving-but-firm mom role for the uninterested audience.

Way to pump up the self esteem there Mom.

"You are supposed to be proud of my grades and the fact that I never get in trouble. You are supposed to be happy that I like to read, and that I help you around the house whenever you ask me to, that I babysit Davy, like, all the time," I said.

Dad kept chewing.

"How are you going to make any friends?" Mom said. "How are you going to become part of anything this way?"

Great. It's not enough that I feel like a friendless loser, my Mom thinks I'm one too.

"I have friends," I fibbed. Actually only one at this point. I have lots of frenemies, though, do those count?

"Name one," said Mom.

"Melody," I said.

"I don't know Melody, do they belong to the club?" Mom asked.

"No."

"Hmmm, well guess what? You are going to volunteer at the hospital," said Mom.

She's going to make me? Yeah, right.

Dad's eyebrows went up a fraction. Mom seemed to sense it and said, "If she can't do this herself, I'll have to help her. It's decided."

"I don't want to," I whispered. I was trying so hard to keep Mom happy but this was too much. I looked down at my plate and pushed some mashed potatoes around with my fork. Then I flattened them. Then I drew some tracks with the tines of the fork. It looked like one of those Zen sand gardens. It didn't calm me down at all. Weren't those Zen gardens supposed to be calming?

"Well it's that or join the junior tennis team here at the club. Your choice."

This was unbelievable. Forced into a social life by my mother?

"You're the one who was interested in the hospital. That shouldn't be so hard," Mom added. "If I can do it, you can."

I flashed back to my conversation with Aunt Ruth and how she said Mom and Aunt Helen did everything together.

"Mom, how old were you when you were a candy striper?" I asked her.

"Hmm, I guess I started around your age," Mom said, nibbling on a salad leaf.

"What did you like about it the most?" I asked.

"I just felt so *useful,*" Mom said. "Like everything going on there was just so important and I was part of it."

"And did Aunt Helen do it too?" I asked, my heart beating faster. I had just broken one of the unwritten rules, but maybe she could talk about the younger days.

A shadow passed over Mom's face but she answered. "Yes, actually she did. She's the one who had the idea, to tell you the truth."

I tried not to seem too eager. "Did she like hospital stuff? Did she want to be a doctor or something?" I asked.

"She loved taking care of people. Just loved it." Mom smiled but her eyes looked sad. "Her favorite was the nursery, though, all those cute little babies." At that she dropped her head down, staring at her plate.

I felt a stab of fear, had I pushed too far?

Just then a big hand landed on Dad's shoulder.

"Mike!" boomed Tom Thornton III, father of Tommy Thornton IV, who was in my class. Tom III was a loud talker, confident that everyone around would want to hear what he had to say.

Mom jumped up from the table. "Excuse me," she said as she took off for the bathroom.

Oh crap. I couldn't decide whether I should follow her or not.

Dad and Mr. Thornton chatted about business and golf and the new layout of the sixth hole.

Davy spilled his ginger ale and burst into tears. Dad flicked him a look of annoyance and didn't stop talking so I grabbed Mom's napkin and my own and blotted at the ever widening wet spot. Two waiters appeared. One whisked away the mess, while the other placed two clean napkins over the spill. By the time Mom returned, Davy had a new ginger ale, a dish of ice cream, and a big smile. I wanted to take these waiters home. I wondered how good they were at whisking away hurt feelings.

Tommy IV came up behind his dad. "Excuse me," he said, the picture of a respectful child. Ha. Tommy's favorite activity at school was farting on his football buddies.

Mr. Thornton turned around.

"Mom said Grandma is tired and needs to go home."

"Yes, yes, well, good to see you all," said Mr. Thornton waving a hand around the table.

"Well hello, Tommy," Mom said in a sickly sweet voice as she slid back into her chair. She was looking at Tommy like he was Brad Pitt, not the blond-haired, red-faced, piggy-looking guy that he was.

"Hello ma'am," said Tommy. I had to give him credit, he knew how to suck up.

"Ma'am! Oh please don't call me ma'am, it makes me feel old," Mom giggled.

Well that was a relief, she wasn't crying.

Mom gave me a perky look. "Jock-leen, did you say hi to Tommy?"

Amazing how quickly she could turn on the fake.

I nodded in Tommy's direction and mumbled hello. I felt like a marionette with Mom pulling the strings. Like we were all just part of her little show and she would make us play the exact parts she wanted. I'm sure she believed if she could just pull all the strings the world would turn out fine. Too bad Dad had no strings.

"Hi Jackie," Tommy said. Score two for Tommy for not calling me Jock-leen.

"Tommy, you should come over to our house sometime!" Mom said. "A cute boy like you!"

I'm going to barf.

"Yes ma'am," Tommy said. "That would be lovely."

Tommy's mom must be a puppeteer too. What fourteen-year-old fart-happy boy with a borderline IQ says "lovely?"

Mom gave my arm a little push. "Jock-leen, wouldn't you love to have Tommy come over? Maybe even on a Friday night?"

Ohmigod. She didn't. She DIDN'T.

Tommy's eyes widened before his manners kicked in and his face went blank.

Was I so pathetic that my mom had to arrange dates for me? What I wouldn't give for Beryl's spear right now. I would plunge it into her forehead. How could she be doing this to me?

"Jock-leen doesn't have many friends yet, we're just trying to help," Mom said, nodding at Tommy.

I wanted to sink through the floor. Just disappear forever.

Tommy remained blank faced but nodded in a polite way. If Mom had said, "Isn't the veal delicious?" he would have given the same nod.

I needed some serious help here. Claudia, where are you? Beryl, what have you got for me? I didn't want Sara's Kindness, my mom didn't deserve it. Even the waiters were nowhere to be seen.

I just sat there, stewing in the juices of my embarrassment. Sara came into my head anyway, as I remembered the Little Princess's idea that "there's nothing so strong as rage, except what makes you hold it in – that's stronger." I wanted to feel stronger than my mother. Focusing as hard as I could, I imagined I was just like Sara, staring quietly but with confidence at the mean Mrs. Minchin.

"Actually, Mother, I think Tommy is busy on Friday nights, you know, playing football and all?" Sara-me said calmly. Sara-me smiled politely at Tommy. "I'll cheer for you!"

Tommy's whole body seemed to relax and he nodded. "Sounds good," he said and then waved goodbye to the table as he followed his dad away.

The car ride home was webbed with tension. How had Mom taken me so quickly from fear to hate? Because I hated her with every fiber of my being. How could she embarrass me that way? She was supposedly the queen of social graces. How could she not know what an idiot she just made me look like? I sat in the dark behind her seat seething, doing my best to make it home without attacking her.

"That young Tommy is just adorable, isn't he?" Mom said.

Ohmigod she never stops.

When I didn't answer she tried again. "Isn't he?"

Yeah, if you are into Porky the Linebacker.

I still didn't answer. I was afraid if I opened my mouth poison tipped arrows would fly out and embed themselves in her body. I kept reminding myself that holding in rage is stronger than letting it out, but I was having a hard time with it. Why couldn't mom just *shut up?*

"Mike, wouldn't Tommy be great for Jacqueline?"

"I don't know," Dad said. "That family is a little off if you ask me."

Thank you Dad.

"I mean, nice enough and all, but not the brightest bulbs on the tree. I give them one more generation to burn through their money."

"Will Tommy be your husband, Jackie?" Davy said.

"No," I snapped.

"Will *I* be your husband?" Davy asked.

"No."

"Why not?"

Okay, this was a parent question if I ever heard one. I looked out my window and wished for something to save me. *Think about books.*

I thought about Miss Minchin and how mean she was to Sara. I thought about how even the other servants had started out mean to her too, but when Sara continued to be kind and polite to them, they eventually started to like her. I was trying so hard to pull Sara's self-control into my body but I felt helpless. All I could do in the moment was admire Sara, not be her. I was feeling way more like the Flawed Meg.

When we pulled into the garage, I jumped out of the car; but before I could get away, Mom grabbed my arm.

"What's wrong with you? Why won't you answer me? Here I am trying to help you get some friends, and you are acting so spoiled."

I finally lost control.

"You just totally humiliated me! That's why!" I screamed. I couldn't hold it in anymore. "Who wants their freaking MOTHER trying to make dates for them? You made me look like an IDIOT!"

I tried to pull away, but she had my arm too firmly.

"I was just being nice, my goodness, how ungrateful can you be?"

"You want to be nice to me? Stop embarrassing me and *leave me alone!*" I said and finally managed to wrestle myself free. I ran up to my bedroom and threw myself on my bed. I guess my flaw, or one of them, was a temper. I didn't see how that was going to save Mom. Still, I was going to remember it is okay to not be perfect. It all worked out for Meg, didn't it?

I dove into *A Little Princess,* desperate to escape.

By the time I shut off my book light, I felt like I was living in the attic with Sara, pretending I was a prisoner in the Bastille and making friends with a rat and the sparrows outside my rooftop window. I was Sara, imagining I had warm blankets and a fire in the grate and food. I pretended I was a secret princess and behaved with way more dignity than the horrible Miss Minchin who ran the school. I was definitely adding Dignity to my list of Desired Personality Characteristics. And Kindness. Sara was so kind even when people were mean to her.

As I drifted towards sleep, the kindness and dignity of little Sara started to make me feel guilty inside. Hadn't I vowed to be the Perfect Daughter? Hadn't I decided to be nice to mom to keep her from getting depressed? The image of Aunt Helen, the one I so thoughtlessly badgered Aunt Ruth into providing, flashed through my brain.

What was I doing?

Chapter Twenty-Seven

Protector of the Pom

I threaded my way through the morning jumble of students in the school halls. I felt like one of those silly little ducks that bob along in a stream at the fair, waiting to be popped with a gun, not sure where the shot will come from. I made it to history without any popping. None of the players in my life were in that class, so I actually managed to listen to about five minutes of lecture before worries about my mom took over my brain. I was running out of brain space for all my problems: Emily not talking to me, Cassidy threatening me, Dad and Mom not getting along, Mom embarrassing me every time we ran into someone from school. Not to mention Mom pretending she was fine when she clearly wasn't. Cripes.

I hurried to PE, hoping to be dressed and out of the locker room before Emily arrived. Just too painful to be near her and not talk. Slamming through the door I almost hit Jennifer Walker. She wasn't in my class so she must have been late leaving the class before.

"Oh, sorry," I said, then noticed her face was red and her eyes wet. We were the only two people in the locker room. The smell of mildewy floors mopped with week-old water filled my nose. Just part of the full PE experience in all its nastiness.

Jennifer shrugged. "Who cares, my life sucks."

We were standing face to face. The spirit of Sara was strong in me, and I found myself asking her if she was okay.

"No, that creep Donovan just gave me detention *again*. He's a freaking perv."

I agreed with the perv part. "Yeah, that sucks."

"It *sucks* because he keeps making up reasons to give me detention when he is the supervisor. It *sucks* because I'm going to have to sit there and let him leer at me for an hour all by myself." She hiccupped back tears and wiped her eyes. How did she still look so pretty when she cried? I turn into an alien as soon as the first tears pop out. "I don't know how he does it but he always makes sure no one else is there. I hate him!"

Super creepy. Once again, happy to be an Unnoticeable.

I felt like patting her shoulder but held back. Who was I to comfort Jennifer Walker? "Sorry." I didn't know what else to say. The Little Princess would know *exactly* what to say. She'd comfort her and then tell her a fantastic story to distract her.

"Yeah, I better go. Now I'm late for history, and I'll probably be in even more trouble."

What was wrong with the adults in the world? Were *any* of them capable of mature behavior? I felt a rush of empathy for Jennifer. The thought of her sitting there under Donovan's leering eyes made me sick for her. Eew.

As I dressed, I tried to imagine what Sara would do. Or Beryl, she had a lot of spirit too. I had to do something. I took a deep breath and entered the gym. I sat down on the bleachers, and when Mr. Donovan blew the whistle I stayed there.

"Carson! In line," he barked.

I shook my head.

"Get out here!"

I shook my head again. Mr. Donovan walked over to me with a mix of anger and bewilderment on his face. How could a goody-two-shoes like me disobey him?

He stuck his face down in mine, and I could smell his nasty cologne and see the comb tracks in his over-gelled hair. "What are you doing?"

"I don't feel like participating today," I said in a smarmy voice.

"Excuse me?" he said.

I repeated myself and smiled a pleasant Sara smile.

"Are you sick?" he asked.

"Nope." I crossed my legs, straightened my spine and stared back at him.

"Get in line now or I'll have to give you detention," he said.

I nodded a yes motion but didn't move.

"Are you kidding me? What is your problem?" Mr. Donovan could not get it. The rest of the class was staring and giggling. I think it was the giggling that finally did it.

"Fine! Detention. Today. After school!" Mr. Donovan yelled dismissing me with a wave of his hand.

Mission accomplished. Anxiety flooded through me. What the heck was I doing? For *Jennifer Walker?* I shook my head at myself. Oh well, too late now. And I imagined Sara's papa might have been proud of me, just like he had been of Sara.

Somehow I suffered through PE and the irritated looks Mr. Donovan kept shooting me. I made it clear to English without a Cassidy sighting but felt a sense of dread because she was in my lunch period. Unless of course the Poms were practicing, Cassidy would be holding court, and Emily would be one of her newest jesters. Melody ate during a different period so forget sitting with her. Finally I dropped down at the end of a table by myself, feeling like a big neon light was shining down on me, flashing "Loser! Loser! Loser!" No one sits by themselves at lunch. Even *Jeff Brice* has people to sit with. I'm lower than a retarded boy.

But wait, Sara wouldn't have thought that way. Sara felt better or worse than no one. She imagined herself a princess, even without all the money and trappings and so would I. And she wouldn't call herself a loser by comparing herself to someone who was retarded. It wasn't Jeff's fault he came into the world with a simple brain.

I wasn't hungry at all, but eating gave me something to do so I shoved down yogurt and a banana. I pulled out *A Little Princess* (in a book cover from the latest superficial bitchy teenager series, no way would I let someone see me reading such a baby book) and prayed for time to accelerate. I had just managed to get absorbed in the book when someone punched my left shoulder, driving me hard against the back of my chair. Brilliant move, bruising my front and back all at once.

"Well if it isn't Miss Bitch!" Cassidy said glaring down at me. Here it was, death by dancer. She had five girls with her, all with identical hostile sneers on their faces. Did they line up in front of a mirror to practice?

I didn't say anything. I slid my book into my lap hoping to avoid Cassidy's ridicule. I resisted the urge to rub my shoulder, not wanting to give Cassidy any satisfaction.

Be Dignified, remember. Hold back rage.

Cassidy smirked. "Did you know your dad is headed to jail?" Cassidy raised her voice and gestured to the pack of girls with her. "Did you guys know that Jacqueline's dad is a pervert?"

"What?" That was so farfetched I couldn't help myself. "That's crazy."

"Oh yeah? Then why is he being charged with harassment at work? *Sexual* harassment? He's a loser just like you. And he's about to be fired!" Cassidy gave an evil laugh.

Kids at the tables surrounding me started to snicker. "I guess this sexual perversion stuff runs in the family!" Cassidy said loudly, cackling at the end. More laughter from the surrounding tables.

"Better move on, in case it's contagious," Cassidy howled, and slunk away with her posse.

I looked down at the table, trying to pretend my face and neck weren't red. Maybe nobody was looking at me. Yeah right, just like nobody noticed Melody's face and neck had been bright red in keyboarding.

Fear coursed through me. I hadn't heard anything about my dad being charged with harassment. Without stopping to think I pulled out my phone and texted him.

> Cassidy Dubroski said you were
> charged w harassment. Is that
> true? r u ok?

I hit send and then, thankfully, the bell rang ending the period.

I headed to keyboarding, eager to see Melody so that I would have at least one friendly face in my day. When I got there she was sitting on a different side of the classroom and wouldn't look at me.

What is going on? Did I fall into some parallel world where everything about my life is f-d up?

I walked over to her.

"Hi, Melody."

Melody flashed me an angry look and then looked back down at her desk.

"What's going on?" I said. Normally I would have just slipped away, but this was too much. I was down to my last friend.

"Oh, like you don't know!" Melody spat.

I was bewildered. "I *don't* know. What's going on?"

"Like it wasn't you saying all those mean things about me on FaceSpace!"

"What? I don't even use FaceSpace! I don't have an account or anything! My Dad is a Nazi about that stuff."

"Yeah, sure. Just leave me alone," Melody said, turning her back on me.

I stumbled to a seat and sat down. What was going on? Could my life get any worse?

My list of worries was getting longer, the brain space even more stuffed: My dad charged with harassment, someone impersonating me on the internet, Mom not turning into Aunt Helen. I wanted to go somewhere and cry for about a year. Instead I started "qwerty" exercises. I pretended that I was Sara and the mean Miss Minchin had put me to work helping the younger students. I was to show them how to type. I imagined them all lined up behind me, watching me. I spun so far off into the fantasy I almost forgot where I was. Comforting but a little worrisome. What if I got so lost in fantasy that I never came back? Come to think of it, that was more comforting than worrisome. Screw it. Whatever worked.

In my next class I snuck out *A Little Princess* and reread the part about being a princess, even if I were in rags and tatters. Boy did I need princess qualities right now.

The rest of the day I pretended to be the Dignified Sara. I was a secret princess and my royalty would be revealed in good time. The more dignified I behaved in reaction to the trials I was being subjected to the more it proved I was a real princess. And not only was I a princess, I was my own white knight, strong and brave and able to rescue myself. I tinkered with the idea that my life was a reality show, but I didn't know that there were cameras on me. The cameras were catching me behaving with grace and dignity and the viewers couldn't believe it, how could someone be so strong.

The make-believe worked well enough to get me to detention without any tears. Before Mr. Donovan settled into his desk in the front of the room, I snuck a look at my cell for the thousandth time. No answer from Dad.

Jennifer came into the classroom and stopped when she saw me.

"What the . . ?" she said.

I gave her a weak smile. "Hey, fellow delinquent."

Her face relaxed into a real smile. "What are you doing here?" she said as she made her way over to a desk beside me.

"Got in trouble in PE today."

"Girls, be quiet!" Mr. Donovan snapped from the front of the class.

Jennifer looked at me with her brow all furrowed. I could almost see smoke coming out of her ears as she worked hard to figure out how I'd ended up there. Okay, that's not nice, but the secrets of the universe were safe from Jennifer. It occurred to me that she was kind of like the slow-witted Ermengarde in *A Little Princess* and that made me feel even more protective of her.

Jennifer pulled a notebook out of her bag, scribbled a note and angled it toward me so I could see it.

"Did you get in trouble on purpose????" the note said in bright purple ink.

I nodded. No reason to hide it from her. I was in desperate need of a friend, any friend, and I couldn't afford to hide my good deeds.

Her eyes opened wide and she mouthed, "Thank you!"

After an hour of watching Donovan watch Jennifer we were released. Out of Donovan's earshot Jennifer started babbling.

"Why did you do that? That was so nice. No one ever did anything that nice for me!"

"I don't know," I said, checking my phone again. Nothing. "It just seemed too creepy to think of you stuck in there with Donovan by yourself."

"I know, but still, you are so nice! And he didn't stare at me all weird! At least, mostly. Thank you." Jennifer impulsively threw her arms around me and hugged me. "And I can't believe you never even told anyone about, you know, the Alex thing. Cassidy would freak out and give me a big lecture about not Doing It. Not to mention that she is so hot for Alex she'd probably give up her

140

vow for him. Anyway, I don't know why Cassidy says such mean stuff about you."

I shrugged. "Yeah, well, I think it has to do with our dads, more than anything."

Jennifer shook her head. "That is so wrong."

Jennifer could afford to be nice to me right now, the halls were vacant. Wait 'til tomorrow, she'd go back to obeying the Great Cassidy.

Jennifer and I stepped through the front doors.

"Thanks again!" said Jennifer skipping off to a waiting car.

"Yeah, sure," I answered. "Anytime." Then I realized I had another problem. How was I going to get home? I had missed the bus by staying for detention.

I pulled out my phone to call home, but before I dialed, I saw a text from Dad.

> It's true, been charged w
> harassment but it never happened.
> Dubroski prob
> behind it. Don't worry, truth always
> wins out. Don't tell mom.

Before I could really think about what Dad had written, Jennifer popped out of the car.

"Hey, Jackie," she called. "Do you need a ride?"

"Sure," I yelled back, shoving my phone back in my bag and hustling over to the waiting SUV.

Jennifer's mom was tapping on the steering wheel as I climbed in the back seat. I'll bet the last thing she wanted to do was give me a ride home.

"Mom, this is Jackie, she was so nice to me today," Jennifer said, buckling herself into the front seat. "I mean, like, she saved my life!"

The frown on her mother's face softened into a smile. "Nice to meet you Jackie."

I knew what Jennifer would look like in thirty years or so because her mother was an exact replica. Same long blond hair, same long eye-lashes, same tanning salon dark skin. I would have thought it would look stupid on an older woman, but she looked kind of good, like the Hogan family looks good. You know, if you like that bleached blond look regardless of some age lines on the face underneath. Something told me that men found Mrs. Walker attractive but that women, at least Kentley Heights women, would whisper about her behind her back.

I couldn't get Dad's text out of my mind. He was charged with harassment! I knew he hadn't done anything wrong. My dad was the last great Boy Scout. He never broke rules, not even when no one was looking. Sounded like Dubroski senior and Dubroski junior were working out of the same playbook.

He didn't need to tell me not to tell mom. That was a no-brainer.

Chapter Twenty-Eight

Housewife Barbie

At home I found Davy in a Spiderman suit lying on the kitchen floor, Power Rangers scattered all around him. And scattered all around the Power Rangers were crackers and chips and candy wrappers.

"Where's Mom?" I said.

"In bed," Spiderman answered, slamming a red Power Ranger into my foot. "Bam! You are crushed! You have been vaporized!"

I hurried up to Mom's room, heart pounding, hating the déjà vu feeling it gave me.

Why had I yelled at her last night? What was wrong with me? Why didn't I hide those stupid pills?

I whipped open her door and ran to the bed.

"Mom!" I yelled at the huddled figure.

This was getting old.

Mom rolled over from her face down position, hand thrown up to cover her eyes. "What do you want?" she snarled. "I was *sleeping!*"

She was alive.

The adrenaline that had flooded my body turned my muscles into pudding. I could barely stand up.

"Go away!" Mom barked at me and flipped herself back into a cocoon.

Shaky with relief I tiptoed to the side of the bed with the pill bottle, slipped it into my pocket and left the room.

Relief turned to anger. Why was she making life so hard? And what was she doing sleeping so much? This was completely unlike her. People called her the Energizer Bunny. People told her she should do energy drink ads. She was usually the perkiest (even if it was fake perky) mom around.

I made my way downstairs, only then noticing the trail of crushed crackers on the stairs. The family room was even worse. A big blue sports drink stain greeted me by the door with even more crumbs ground into it. Toys littered every surface. If Mom saw all this she'd be beyond furious.

I found Davy back in the kitchen. "What were you doing all afternoon? Were you playing Hansel and Gretel and leaving trails?" I asked him.

"No, I was protecting the earth!" he said.

Whatever.

"This place is a mess," I said looking around the kitchen. "Come on, help me clean this up."

As I started picking up I found Davy's Batman costume with underwear inside under the kitchen table.

"What is this?"

"I kind of got pee-pee on myself," he said. "I couldn't get the suit down to pee and Mom wouldn't wake up to help me. So I kind of peed myself. But then I got it off, and I got new clothes!" I flipped the Batman suit over and sure enough, the button holding the top together at the back of the neck was popped off. "Look! No underwear though," he added proudly.

I felt sick. The poor kid peed his freaking pants because Mom didn't help him. I flashed back to yelling at Mom last night and felt awful. This was my fault. I *knew* she was sensitive these days. And I knew what had happened to Aunt Helen. What was wrong with me? I couldn't upset her anymore.

I renewed my cleaning efforts. Mom always kept the house immaculate, which seemed like a lot of wasted effort to me, but there it was. We had cleaners that came every other week and sometimes I wondered why. She always had the house spotless, even on the days the cleaners came. I found ants crawling on food crusted plates in the sink.

Gross.

I drowned the ants with sprays of water and then filled the sink to soak the dried food off of the plates. I gave Davy a bottle of Windex and let him spray the counters and wipe them with paper towels while I piled other miscellaneous plates and cups into the sink as well. The acrid smell of the Windex felt good in my nose. It was too strong to be pleasant, but it left a feeling of something made right. Or at least clean.

And FYI, if you want to make a little kid happy, give him a spray bottle. Davy went to *town*. I think he used at least half of the bottle.

After the kitchen we straightened the family room and then the hall and stairs. Davy wouldn't leave my side so we made a game out of picking up. I don't love cleaning, but I found a sort of satisfaction in returning the house to its normal state. I wished it were as easy to do that to a family.

Davy and I did a quick tour of the bedrooms and shoved a bunch of dirty clothes down the chute, following them to the laundry room. There were piles of laundry everywhere.

I felt like Housewife Barbie.

She sorts! She washes! She folds! She cleans dishes!

Bo-o-oring.

"Jackie! I'm a snowman!" Davy said, curled into a ball and covered with the pile of whites.

And yet necessary. I'd have to be Housewife Barbie if that is what it took to keep Mom from getting stressed.

I started a load of laundry as Davy rolled out of the whites.

Davy saw me with the Batman costume.

"I want that!" he said, grabbing for it.

"I need to wash it," I said. I held it to my nose. "It smells like pee! You can have it back as soon as it's clean," I said, tossing it in the washing machine. "And anyway, you're Spiderman right now, he's awesome."

"Batman's better. He's got the BatCave."

He had me there.

"Jackie, what's "sexy" mean?"

I stopped my loading and stared at him. "What do you mean? Where did you hear that word?"

"On TV. There was this man with his shirt off, and he said it to this lady. They were wrestling on a bed, in their underwear!"

Christ, Davy was probably watching soaps all afternoon. Great.

"Oh it just means someone, uh, looks nice. But it is a grown-up word, okay?"

"Were they married? Is that what mommies and daddies do?"

"Yes, they were married. But you don't need to worry about that. Let's go color, okay?"

Back in the kitchen I got a stack of colored paper out and added some markers. The Windex smell lingered, giving me courage. "Here Davy, make me a picture of Batman. I'll be right back."

I knew I needed to get back to working on the library books at some point, but I had something else I needed to do first. I locked myself in Dad's office and turned on his laptop. My heart pounding I Googled "Suicide."

Part of my brain said this was ridiculous, a waste of time, something that Mom would never do. The other part of my brain said that if Aunt Helen could do it, so could Mom. Maybe I needed to know some more about it.

I scanned through the risk factors and felt better that Mom wasn't a young male who had a substance abuse problem. Then again, she did seem to be depressed and although her marriage hadn't broken up there were lots of fights. I couldn't tell if that counted, I would think it had to.

Then I read that people who try to do . . . that . . . often do it impulsively and it is a good idea to hide things like pills or guns.

I felt sick inside just reading this stuff. It was hard to believe it was something I had to think about. I felt a very strong urge to dive back into *A Little Princess* and pretend I was nine years old again and nothing could ever happen to my family. No wonder the adults liked living in denial. Reality sucked.

While I had the computer on, I thought I might as well check this FaceSpace thing. It didn't take long to find Melody's FaceSpace page, and as I read I felt sicker and sicker. "JackieC" wrote:

> Hey Melody, what's up with the dump you live in? And why don't you do something with that lame hair? Like dye it or stick it under a hat! Otherwise, I can't be seen with you anymore at school. I have a reputation to think about. I know you don't have a rich dad like me, but I'm sure you could find a way to be less of a loser.

How could Melody ever think I'd say that kind of stuff? And what kind of vicious bitch went out of her way to do that? The second question was easy. It could only be Mean Girl Queen Bee Barbie, trying to ruin Melody's life and mine at the same time.

I tried to post a real comment, but the site was blocked. Oh sure, *now* she blocks it, after the damage has been done.

I grabbed my phone and texted Melody, trying one more time to explain.

> I SWEAR I didn't say
> anything mean about u.
> Why would I? U know
> that Cassidy is trying to ruin
> me – you know it must be
> her, right?

School mean girls would have to wait. I closed the laptop and snuck back into Mom's room. I collected all the pill bottles that looked even remotely toxic and took them back to my room. After circling the room a couple of times I came up with the idea of hiding them in my old dollhouse. I didn't use it anymore and doubted anyone would think to look in there for the pills. I shoved the little bag I had filled into the back second floor bedroom and closed the front of the dollhouse.

That truly was enough reality and instead of sorting and shelving, instead of homework, instead of paying attention to poor Davy, I disappeared back into turn-of-the-century London.

It was amazing to me that Sara could spin such fascinating stories that Ermengarde, in sneaking up to visit her, found the attic exotic and exciting. For Sara it was cold and depressing, with its hard bed and thin walls, but so powerful was Sara's vision and storytelling that the attic became a warm and happy place for Ermengarde. In making the attic bearable for herself, Sara made a haven for Ermengarde. Ermengarde was so transfixed by Sara's stories that it didn't even occur to her that Sara might be hungry, might be cold, might stumble from one miserable day to the next.

I didn't have a person like Sara in front of me, but I had story and that was enough.

Chapter Twenty-Nine

Beggars Can't Be Choosers

In the morning I walked into the kitchen, determined to be the Perfect Daughter. I pretended I was Sara. I told myself the same thing Sara told herself, *"To be kind is worth a great deal to other people. . ."* I told myself no matter how unfair or crazy mom acted I would be kind. Just like Sara refused to cry in front of Miss Minchin when told her father had died, I would keep my calm in front of Mom. If a little penniless orphan could be that strong, so could I.

I pulled the egg carton out of the refrigerator. "Would anyone like some eggs?" I asked. Mom and Davy were seated at the kitchen table, Mom with her face buried in her coffee mug, Dave slurping cereal out of his Spiderman bowl.

"I want eggs!" Davy said, pushing away his cereal bowl. Milk and Cheerios slopped out over the side.

"Eat your cereal," Mom said to Davy in a tired voice.

"I'll make extra, you can have both," I said to Davy. "Mom, do you want some too?" I added.

"No thanks," Mom mumbled.

I looked at Davy. The back of his hair was sticking straight up. His Pooh bear was sitting beside him on his chair, wrapped in a tattered blue blankie. He didn't know about bullies yet, or having the right haircut, or abstinence programs. He didn't know that parents could divorce or that people could decide to end their own lives.

Sara would see that this family, particularly Davy, needed a functioning mother. Sara would find some way to connect with Mom, to help her feel happy again. How could I do that? I looked at her rumpled hair and pinched face.

Sara, help me out here.

"Hey, um, Mom," I started. "I'm really sorry I yelled at you the other night. I don't know what got into me. It was very disrespectful. I know you were trying to help me."

Mom raised her head and stared at me with dull eyes.

Okay, going to need more.

"I guess I just get nervous, you know, around boys," I flashed back to porky Tommy thinking that he wasn't one of those boys who affected me one way or the other.

Mom tilted her head a millimeter, as if agreeing.

I took a deep breath. Might as well go whole hog. "So, maybe, you know, I *do* need to spiff up my clothes a bit. Maybe that would help. And, you know, you're a genius with fashion and all." PATT PATT PATT. Praise. All. The. Time. How could I have forgotten?

That got an actual smile. "Well, I suppose we could find some time to go shopping," Mom said. She was still quieter than usual, but her eyes had a bit more life in them.

Gee, I can't wait.

As the bus bumped over pot-holed roads, I leaned my head against the cool, wet window. The heater in the bus clanked and blasted out air that smelled like wet dog. Kids on the bus were mostly subdued, half asleep and half depressed to be facing a whole day of imprisonment.

I ran through my classes in my mind. Was there anyone in any of the classes I could try to be friends with now that Melody was ignoring me? Let's see, I needed to find a Loser like myself. Someone with no other friends who would be thrilled to have even a pariah like me talk to her. Because I was pretty sure it had to be a her. It was going to be complicated enough without taking the whole gender divide into account. Although come to think of it, boys didn't seem to have that viciously mean streak that girls could have. No, I'd think of a girl first. If that didn't work, maybe a boy. Heck, maybe Jeff Brice. He'd be happy to have me as a friend.

By the time I got to English, I had settled on Lisa Wilson. She was short and potato shaped with a forgettable face. Not ugly, not pretty. Long, dark hair and who knew on her voice because I had never heard her speak. Maybe she was schizo or maybe she was just shy. Maybe she was a fabulous person just waiting for a chance to be friends. Or maybe she was nuttier than a peanut butter cup. I'd have to chance it.

Sara-me sat down beside Lisa before English got started. I imagined myself with Sara's green eyes, straightened my back into the posture I always imagined her in, felt her bubbling around in me.

"Hi," I said, all Sara-friendly. "Did you finish your thesis proof?"

Lisa stared down at her notebook and didn't move her head. Her eyes cut sideways to me. I think she couldn't believe someone was talking to her.

"I had a hard time with it," I continued, as if we were actually having a conversation.

"Unh," Lisa grunted, still looking down, her dark, stringy hair hanging over her face.

"I don't even know what a freaking thesis proof is," said a voice from the other side of me. I turned to the right and saw Tommy Thornton sitting in a seat beside me.

I nodded. Was porky the linebacker talking to me? I flashed back to the country club and Mom inviting him over to our house. I felt a blush coming on and pushed the thought aside.

"I mean, what's that got to do with freaking English?" Tommy said, shaking his head at me with an easy smile. I think Tommy felt easy talking to anyone. What would *that* be like? Tommy was leaning back in his chair, his legs stuck out into the aisle between us. He had on a faded blue Pitt T-shirt and baggy warm-up pants. His beat-up running shoes were untied. The clothes looked homeless, but the careful haircut and thick sports watch said money.

I actually thought the thesis proof was easy, but maybe playing dumb was the strategy here. "Yeah, what's the point?" I said.

"Just a bunch of busy work if you ask me," said Tommy. He gave a chin raise at me. "But you're so smart, it should be cake for you."

I shook my head, trying to look puzzled. "Yeah, I don't know about those things."

Tommy waved a pudgy hand at me. "Ahh, I'll bet you finished it in, like, five minutes." His voice was friendly, like the way you might tease a buddy.

I glanced back at Lisa who seemed to be trying to merge herself into the desk. Not much hope there. I looked over at Tommy and his flushed wide face.

Beggars can't be choosers. Tommy it is.

When English ended I worked it so that we walked out of class at the same time and then casually said, "So are you going to do thesis proof, persuasive, or problem-solution for your essay?"

"Man, they all suck, don't they?" Tommy said, falling into step beside me.

Maybe boys were easier to make friends with. Who knew?

"Yeah, it's like the teacher just has to make stuff up for us to do," I said. "Like we're ever going to use this stuff."

"No kidding!" said Tommy. "I guarantee that I'm not going to need one thing I'm learning this whole year. Except maybe the football stuff. Teamwork, now that's helpful."

A familiar blond head appeared down the hall. My heart started to race, here came Cassidy. With Jennifer Walker and Melinda Barnes. They must have hair bleaching parties. They all had the exact the same shade of neon yellow.

Cassidy saw me and narrowed her eyes into the death stare that was so effective on 98 percent of the population. Guess she didn't know I was Tough and Brave today. She angled across the hall toward me. She must have noticed Tommy because the death stare disappeared, and a big seductive smile spread across her face. I guess anything male got that look. "Hey Tommy," she said in a super sweet, super sexy voice. Jennifer stopped on the other side of the hall and gave me a wincing smile, then turned to talk to Melinda.

I didn't know whether to stop or keep walking. Were Tommy and I just talking because we happened to be walking at the same speed or had we been walking *together*? I didn't want Tommy to think I was presuming anything. I kept moving forward. Cassidy slid her foot near mine and gave a swipe. I tripped, tried to miss falling onto the girl in front of me, and landed on the ground. It was enough to make everyone around me laugh.

"Hey Jackie," Tommy called, coming to my side. "You okay?

"Yeah," I said popping back up, and refusing his outstretched hand.

Nothing bruised but my ego.

Cassidy pulled on Tommy from behind, stopping him from walking with me.

"See ya," he said as I moved away.

That Tommy wasn't all bad.

At lunch I found a chair in the very back corner and hunched down over my book trying to ignore the "Loser!" lights over me. Back in Sara's world the fear of being a loser faded away. Instead, as Sara, it was the fear of starving or freezing to death. I went up to the attic and grabbed a glimpse of the setting sun, feeling one of the few real pleasures Sara ever got. And it was still a better world than my own.

The bell rang ending lunch. I grabbed my bag and books, thinking that Sara was not only brave, she was also super creative. I was working on Brave, and school work had always been easy for me. Maybe I could use my supposedly great brain to also think creatively in hard situations, like Sara. In keyboarding, pretending to be Sara, I walked straight up to Melody and using a calm and friendly voice said, "Melody, I didn't write that stuff on FaceSpace. Honestly, why would I?"

Melody didn't answer. She stared at me like she was considering my words. Then she looked around the room.

I kept at it. "Only a mean and stuck up person would say those things, and if you know me at all, you'd know I'm not like that. I was *happy* that we started being friends."

Melody looked back at my face. I could tell she wanted to believe me.

"Yeah, I don't know . . ." said Melody. I didn't want to push her too hard.

"What would be my motive? How could it possibly be good for me to say that stuff?" Then I walked to the other side of the room and sat down. Let Melody work it out.

Throughout class I could see Melody looking over at me once in a while. She was definitely thinking about it. Every time she saw me looking back she flipped her ponytail in her haste to look away. Why would I criticize her hair? It was pretty, all red and curly. Although red never sounded like an accurate word for that color hair. It looked more apricot to me. Who wouldn't want apricot hair?

Chapter Thirty

Soldier On

I was sitting on a wickedly cold stone bench outside of school waiting for Mom to pick me up for the "spiffing up" trip. *Oh joy.*

I unwrapped my dark blue scarf from around my neck and folded it into a pillow to sit on. A little better, but it was still brutally cold out here. I guess a Pennsylvania fall is no warmer than a Michigan one. Alex slid onto the bench beside me, nudging up against me. Suddenly I wasn't so cold anymore.

"Why're you sitting out here?" Alex asked. "It's freezing. Need a ride somewhere?"

Gee, let me see. Would I rather go buy stupid looking clothes with Mom or go for a ride with Alex? Such a hard call.

I slid a look sideways at him. His skin was so perfect and beautiful. Almost kind of golden and completely without any kind of zit or blemish. He gave me a bump. "So?"

"Just waiting for my mom. We're going *shopping.*" I rolled my eyes.

"What's wrong with that? Doesn't every chick like shopping?" Alex asked.

I shrugged. "Not my mom's version. She thinks she should still get to pick what I wear."

"If I remember, your mom is pretty hot, so what's the problem?"

Eeww. Yuck. I didn't want Alex thinking Mom was hot.

Just then Mom pulled up, the passenger window sliding down. "Jock-leen!" Mom yelled, as if I hadn't seen her, as if I hadn't leapt up to get away from Alex while she was looking.

"See ya," I called backwards, almost at the car by the time Mom came to a full stop.

I scrambled into the front seat and closed the door.

"*Who* is *that?*" Mom asked craning her head around me to stare at Alex.

Crap.

"No one, let's go," I said, sneaking a quick glance out the window. Alex was smiling and staring into the car. He gave a little wave.

"Go!" I begged.

Go! Drive away. Now.

I just knew I needed to get Mom away from Alex. She refused to move.

"Who is that boy? You were talking to him. He is very cute!" Mom said still trying to look around me. I put the window up, she put it back down.

"Just go, please," I begged again.

Mom unbuckled her seat belt and slid across the seat. She pushed me backwards, opened the window again and yelled, "Yoo hoo! Hello?" at Alex.

I'm going to kill her. I'm going to melt into a puddle of shame.

Alex gave another wave accompanied by a huge grin. He was laughing at me, enjoying my pain.

Mom waved back. "What's your name?" Mom yelled.

Just kill me now.

"Alex," called Alex, clearly entertained by Mom.

"You have a great day Alex!" yelled Mom and then she leaned back in and slid back into the driver's seat.

"Wave goodbye Jock-leen," Mom said.

"Just *go*," I said through clenched teeth.

"Jock-leen, wave at that cute boy! Don't you know anything? Don't be so rude or he'll never talk to you again."

Ha. Look who is talking about rude.

"Go!" I practically yelled.

Mom put the car in gear, finally, and eased away from the curb. "No wonder you don't have a boyfriend," she said shaking her head. "You are so unfriendly."

Keep Mom happy, keep Mom happy, keep Mom happy.

Maybe if I repeated it often enough I wouldn't start pummeling her.

I pulled out *A Little Princess* and flipped through it to find some help. *"I don't like it, papa," she said. "But then I dare say soldiers-*

even brave ones-don't really like *going into battle."* Yes, that was better. I would be a soldier going into battle.

*****

I swear Mom dragged me through every store in the mall. I'm quite sure I tried on every pair of jeans in the tri-state area. We lumbered toward the car with about sixteen shopping bags, most of them full of clothes for me.

The clothes were perfect. Perfect for a cougar, that is. Because Mom picked them to look hip and young, but it was a forty-two-year-old woman's version of hip and young, which is not the same thing as actual hip and young. Teenagers don't even use the word "hip." Not unless they are referring to the bones on either side of their stomach.

We climbed into the car in the dark, cold parking lot.

"Oooh, I just can't wait to see you in these clothes!" Mom enthused. "I don't know which I like more! Maybe the green shirt? No, no, the magenta one, no, the bright yellow striped one!"

Mom seemed to think I looked best in "jewel tones." AKA clown colors.

"Jockleen, as my mother used to say, you've been hiding your light under a barrel!"

Mission accomplished. Mom was out of bed and happy.

Great. But what about me?

Why did I have to be so not-myself for her to be happy?

*****

Davy jumped up from the Lego castle he was playing with and scooted over to Dad, who had barely sat down with a drink and the TV remote.

"Daddy, come play with me!" Davy pleaded, trying to climb into Dad's lap.

Dad held his drink out to the side so it wouldn't spill and tilted his head around Davy's to better see the TV. "Not right now, Sport. I just need a moment to relax, okay?"

157

I looked at the slump of Dad's shoulders, the pale sag of his face. I thought about the harassment charge. "Hey Davy, I'll play with you," I said.

With a last disappointed look at Dad, Davy dragged himself back to me.

"Where should we put the soldiers?" I said. "Up here on top?"

"No! Over here by the gate," said Davy, grabbing the soldier from me.

"Mike, could you take the garbage cans down to the road before we eat?" Mom called to Dad from the kitchen.

Dad flicked his eyes in her direction and didn't answer.

"Did you hear me, Mike?" Mom called again. "Mike?"

A snort of air came from Dad. "I *heard* you. I'll get them later."

Mom appeared in the doorway. "You always say that, and then it gets late and you don't want to do it, and then you forget in the morning. I don't want to be stuck with a week's worth of trash!"

"We have never, not once, been stuck with a week's worth of trash," Dad said, eyes on the TV as channels flashed by.

That was true. Although it was also true that at times I have seen Dad tear out of the house in his pajamas when the rumble of the garbage truck woke him at five thirty in the morning. But he always managed to get the cans down in time.

"I don't see what the big deal is," said Mom, rubbing her hands on a dish towel. "I ask so little of you around here! I do *everything* and all you have to do is move the cans. That's it! I'm making the whole dinner. You don't do dishes, you don't give baths, you don't do laundry. Should I go on?"

Actually, I do the dishes, Mom.

Dad chugged the rest of his drink and poured himself another one.

Mom does everything? What about Dad being the only wage earner? Who does she think bought this house?

"Marion, I can't even begin to tell you how exhausted I am. I won't bother you with the details of my day, but please understand it was rough. All I want to do is sit down for a few minutes. Is that too much to ask?"

Yes.

Mom rolled her eyes. "You don't think *I'm* tired? You don't think *I* work hard?"

Dad turned up the volume on the TV.

"Well?" Mom prompted when Dad didn't answer.

"I didn't say that. Jesus Christ, I had to deal with Dubroski's lies all day. Can't I have a moment's peace?"

"What about Dubroski's lies?" Mom said, momentarily distracted from the garbage.

My ears pricked up too. Dubroski being, of course, Cassidy's dad.

Dad paused. I could almost see the information flashing through his head, the editing process as he figured out how much to tell her. "I told you before; he's out to get me. He told Sam Baggins I sold material non-public information about the company. He told Marv Johnson I falsified reports. And those are just the lies I know about. I'm sure there are people less loyal than Sam and Marv who aren't telling me what Dubroski is saying. He is undermining me at every turn."

Not to mention the sexual harassment charge.

"Oh surely people know he is lying," said Mom. "Everyone knows what a Boy Scout you are."

"Not necessarily," said Dad, finishing his second drink. "Even if he can't prove anything eventually people start to think where there is smoke, there is fire. And I *do* know Tom Beckett, even though I'm not the one who gave him that information. Great. All I need is to be called at his trial. I'm having to spend so much energy on his bullshit that I'm not getting my real work done."

"Daddy said a bad word!" Davy said eyes opened wide, mouth opened wider.

Dad's shoulders were bunched up, and he had lines across his forehead that I had never noticed before.

"I should be at work right now, but I couldn't take one more minute of it," Dad said.

I hated to see Dad like this. What if he had a heart attack or something?

"Put Daddy on the Naughty Stool!" yelled Davy.

Dad got a third drink. He drank half of it before he even sat down again.

"Fine!" Mom said, spinning around and heading back to the kitchen.

Way to be supportive Mom.

I heard the garage door go up and the scraping of cans being dragged out of the garage.

Dad stood up and slammed his glass down on the coffee table so hard that ice flew out. He stalked out of the family room toward the garage.

A few minutes later Mom and Dad came back into the kitchen arguing.

"It just has to be exactly what you want, when you want it!" Dad yelled.

"What is the big *deal?*" Mom yelled back. "I said fine, and I took the cans out myself."

"Goddamn it, Marion! You know and I know fine does not mean fine! It means you're going to be a goddamn martyr all night. Jesus! I do not need this right now!"

Davy was sitting frozen in the middle of his Legos, eyes scared.

"Davy, let's go upstairs," I said, grabbing him under his arms to get him to stand up.

Davy wouldn't move, so I hauled him up and dragged him to the stairs. By the time we got to the playroom Mom and Dad's voices were muffled enough that we couldn't make out any words.

But even without words it sounded like a family falling apart. Great, all my "spiffing up" efforts down the drain.

"Why are they yelling?" Davy asked as I settled him into a chair at his little table.

I pushed the basket of crayons toward him and opened a coloring book.

"They're just a little upset, they'll be fine," I said. What was wrong with them, scaring Davy like this?

I opened a second coloring book for myself. "Let me see, I think I will color Pooh bear purple."

"Coloring is for babies. I don't want to color," said Davy. He popped out of his chair and rummaged in the big toy bin against the wall. He found a kiddie basketball and started shooting at the four foot plastic hoop next to the bin.

"Besides, Pooh bear isn't purple," Davy said, chucking the ball at the hoop with one hand.

"Oh, right, I forgot," I said. "Hmmm, I can't remember, what color is Pooh?"

"Poo-poo is brown!" Davy laughed, delighted with his play on words. And delighted to say poo-poo. Must be a boy thing - he was obsessed with poop.

"Poo-poo head!" Davy screamed, laughing. "Pee-pee head! You are a poo-poo head."

Mom would have stopped him and given a lecture on manners. Me, I was willing to be a poo-poo head to see Davy laugh.

I felt like Sara, playing mommy to little Lottie when she was acting particularly immature. Although I wasn't orphaned and penniless (well, I was kind of penniless) it struck me that Sara and I had a lot in common. You know, seeing as how we were both way more mature than any of the grownups around us. You know, the people who should have known better.

The doorbell rang and not hearing any footsteps in the front hall I zipped down the stairs. It was Aunt Ruth, returning Dad's laptop. She breezed in the door, stamping her feet.

"Whew, it's getting cold out there!" Aunt Ruth laughed, brushing past me and heading towards the kitchen. "Where're your parents?"

Could she not feel the fight hanging in the air? It seemed so obvious to me that this was an unhappy house. I would think you could smell it when you walked in.

I trailed along behind her, trying to give warning to Mom and Dad. "Mom" I yelled, "Aunt Ruth is here!"

I went through the kitchen door a second behind her to find Mom and Dad squared off, each leaning against a different counter, glaring, but silent.

Mom's face lit up with all the warmth of a cold LED light. "Ruth," she smiled all fakey fakey, the face version of the fake phone cheer.

Aunt Ruth held the laptop out towards Dad, who, while not smiling had at least put away the glare. "Thanks Mike, you're a life saver. Mine is finally fixed, at least I hope!"

Dad waved a hand at Ruth, "You should just keep it, you know, as a backup. I don't need it anymore."

"Isn't he *generous?!*" Mom said, so sarcastically over the top that Aunt Ruth stared at her, finally aware something was going on.

"Uh, yes, but no thanks Mike," Aunt Ruth said, eyeing her sister. "Keep it around for the kids, I'm sure Jacqueline could use it."

"Oh but then he couldn't be the *big* man," Mom said, and shoved the computer back at Ruth.

Ruth looked at dad and then Mom and then back at Dad. Caught between a rock and a crazy lady. She set the computer gently down on the counter and backed away. "You know what? Talk about it a while. I need to run, many hours of reading left tonight."

I walked out to the front door with her, wishing she didn't have to go. Uncomfortable at the scene she just walked into but glad to have a witness. Because when someone else saw them get all mean and snarky I didn't feel so crazy. And desperate to keep an apparently sane adult in the house. She gave me a big long hug and I said, "You should come over more often," but that sounded stupid. Who would want to be around that mess?

Aunt Ruth gave me an extra squeeze and then was gone in a whoosh of cold air as the door closed behind her. It was like a gray cold day when the sun bursts through the clouds and everything seems okay, but then the clouds close over again and you are left wondering if the sun will ever win that battle, ever again.

Chapter Thirty-One

Warm, or Hot?

In the morning the streets were a wet mush of slush and salt, the ground patchy with old snow. It seemed that the only color was our bus. And of course my "jewel tone" shirt although that was hidden under a sweatshirt. The monochromatic scene was oddly calming to my brain and my plan for the school day started to form.

Step one: Talk some more to Tommy. He seemed approachable and nice enough, and there were no other immediate candidates for friendship.

Step two: Maybe try one more time to talk to Melody? It was still killing me that she thought I could say something so mean.

Step three: Avoid Cassidy.

Step four: Make life easy for Mom.

And oh yeah, Step five: Investigate more about Aunt Helen.

I was sure there was more to do, but that seemed enough for one day. Although step one promised to be a little tricky in that I didn't want Tommy to think I was, you know, *romantically* interested in him. I just wanted a friend.

I liked having a plan. A plan took the worries that were whirling around in my head and kind of lined them up into rows. They were still there, but they felt a little more under control.

Nothing dramatic happened in my first class. And believe me, I could live the rest of my life with no drama. Then, after I stepped into the locker room to change for gym, I ran into Jennifer Walker again. She said hi and looked back and forth, I guess to see if anyone saw her talking to me. She leaned in to me getting close enough that I could smell her fruity hairspray and gave me an intense stare with a little smile. As if she had something exciting to tell me but couldn't open her mouth. She slid a note into my hand without looking down then slid away like she was James Bond and these were the codes to all the nuclear bombs around the world.

I set my bag on a bench and opened the scrap of paper.

Jacqueline,

I'm sorry that Cassidy is being so mean to you. I don't know why she does that except that she is a really mean person to everyone. Personally, I don't think she is very happy. And I'm sorry I haven't talked to you more but she would kill me. Anyway, I thought you should know that she was laughing the other day about how her dad is getting your dad into trouble at work. She said her dad got your dad charged with some crime or something even though he didn't do anything. She thinks it's hysterical.

You were so nice to me I just wanted to let you know. Whatever is going on, it's her dad's fault.

The note wasn't signed, and I could see why. If Cassidy knew what Jennifer had written she would rip out Jennifer's long fingernails and use them to tear her into tiny pieces. I sat down on the bench to let the note sink in. Wow! I had proof for Dad! Although I really didn't have proof because no way Jennifer would admit writing the note, and no way Cassidy would admit to saying those things and that was that. But still. It was something. I knew I'd be late for PE, but I ignored the seagull-like shrieking of a locker room full of girls and texted my dad to let him know what I'd found out.

Clues were falling right into my lap. Maybe I really *was* like Nancy Drew. She was definitely next on the book list.

I hovered near the door to English until I saw Tommy coming down the hall. I gave him time to walk in the room, and then I casually walked in behind him and sat down next to him. I felt anxious – what if he thought I was interested in him? But I had to keep to the Plan or else the mush inside my body would take over.

I fussed with my books hoping he would talk to me first.

"Hey, Jackie," Tommy said.

"Hi, Tommy," I answered, reminding myself that I was Brave and Confident.

"Man, what'd you ever do to Cassidy?" Tommy shook his head, laughing.

"Huh?" I said, caught off guard.

"Dude, she can't stand you," Tommy laughed, like it was no big deal. Like it is hysterical to be on the receiving end of Cassidy's wrath. "She told me not to even talk to you."

"Oh," I said, "I think it is mostly my dad getting the promotion her dad wanted."

I looked down at my books. So much for making a new friend out of Tommy.

As if he knew what I was thinking Tommy waved his hand and laughed again. "What do I care what Miss Priss says to do?" He leaned over to me. "Like Alex says, she's just a big tease."

I had forgotten he was friends with Alex. Maybe because they seemed like such an unlikely pair. Talk, dark, and trouble versus short, pink and harmless. I guess football made strange friends.

Just then Mark Miller slid into a seat on the other side of Tommy.

"Hey, Mark, your girlfriend said to give you this," said Tommy and he leaned to the side and farted toward Mark.

"Yeah, and your mom said to give you this," said Mark, flipping Tommy his middle finger. Then they both laughed.

Boys are so odd.

I found my now-normal spot alone for lunch. I dove into *A Little Princess* managing to shut out the lunchroom roar of laughter and taunts and gossipy whispers. I barely noticed the taste of my bologna sandwich, lost on the muddy cold streets of London. So I was completely out of it when Alex sat down across from me.

"What's up?" Alex said, leaning forward, arms resting on the table.

I had book-to-life whiplash and couldn't speak. I looked around, it was just him. And it was just me.

"Uh, nothing," I said.

"What are you reading?" he asked.

Darn it.

"Mmmmm, a mystery," I lied, sliding the book into my lap.

"Cool."

What did he want? Why was he sitting here?

I flashed on his face above Jennifer's chest and then on our long stare at each other. My face got hot.

Pull it together. Be someone else.

Somehow I couldn't be Sara with Alex. He was too sexy, too cool for the young, sweet Sara. It would have to be Beryl or Claudia. Maybe some combination.

"What's up with you?" Beryl-Claudia-me said.

Alex shrugged. "Nothing much. Little of this, little of that."

"So what do you want with me?" Beryl-Claudia-me said, kind of flippant, a smidge flirty.

Did I just say that???

Alex threw his head back and laughed. It was a beautiful sight. White teeth against golden skin and that slight curl in his hair swishing around.

"You crack me up, you know that?" he said. "Maybe I just wanted to say hi."

"Okay, hi," I said, smiling at him. It wasn't anywhere in the range of a seductive smile, but it wasn't completely innocent either.

"You know what I think?" Alex said, leaning in close to me.

"Huh uh," I said forcing myself to keep eye contact with him. I felt a buzz from my eyes clear down the center of my body. Like Alex's hormones were being streamed from his eyes to mine and down into my body. I didn't want to think about where the buzz ended up.

"I think you are the opposite of Cassidy Dubroski. Cassidy's all show but nothing inside. *You* got that kind of quiet on the outside thing going, but I think on the inside you are *hot,* you know what I mean? Like, wild kind of hot."

Yikes.

I shrugged like "maybe I am, maybe I'm not."

This is completely over my head.

I broke eye contact, afraid the buzz inside might come through and light my skin on fire.

I pushed my empty baggies back into my lunch bag just to have something to do.

"And you know what else?" Alex asked.

"I'm afraid to ask," Beryl-Claudia-me said in a completely calm voice.

How was I doing that?

"I think Cassidy hates you because she knows that. And she's jealous."

I burst out laughing. No need to pretend. That was just ridiculous.

Alex leaned back in his chair again and looked sideways at me. "Laugh if you want to. I'm right."

"Whatever," I said, waving a hand at him. This was just too silly. Playboy body Barbie jealous of me. Please.

Alex stood up and gave me another intense stare. That one went straight to my toes, lighting up everything else along the way.

"I'm going to spend some time with that hot side of you someday," he said, eyes flashing.

Then he walked away.

It must have been pure muscle memory that got me to keyboarding because my brain was not working at all. My brain was stuck in a continuous loop video of Alex's stare and his words and his super-fine butt walking away from me. So I didn't even notice when Melody clumped up alongside me on her crutches until she almost tripped me. We were right outside the door to keyboarding.

"Really, it wasn't me," I tried, one more time.

Melody wouldn't even look at me, just slid her crutches and self past me.

I seem to be breaking barely even. Make a friend, lose a friend. That is, assuming I could count Tommy as a friend. One of these days it would tip in the wrong direction and I'd have no one. I couldn't really count Alex as a friend. He was more of a dark spirit that landed in my path every once in a while.

Chapter Thirty-Two

Martyrs and Mysteries

Mom and I were standing in her "dream kitchen." At least that's what she called it when we first moved in. The first couple of weeks we lived here she couldn't stop talking about the marble counter tops and high ceiling and custom ivory colored cabinets. How light it all was. How much she loved the butler's pantry and the wine cellar and the Sub Zero refrigerator. Now she just complained that our old breakfast table didn't look right here. Maybe when you get your dream it doesn't really change your life as much as you thought it would.

"Why hasn't Emily been over lately?" Mom asked, plopping a bag of potatoes in front of me to peel.

I shrugged a don't know.

Because she's gone over to the dark side. Because she's an effing Pom now, and she's got to practice waving her ass around and then saying no when boys want to do something with that ass.

Mom pulled out a potato to show me what to do. Like I hadn't done it a million times already. "Here, rinse it off after you've peeled it, then cut it into pieces about this big." She cut one of the potatoes into quarters and pointed at it. "Then put them in some water in this pan."

Mom pulled out a package of chicken breasts and started pounding them with a meat hammer. "You be nice to that poor girl."

Me be nice? I don't think that is the issue here.

"CeCe said Emily's parents had the wildest divorce," Mom continued. "I mean talk about a reason to try to make your marriage work!"

I didn't say anything, but I put a pleasant expression on my face, like I cared what she was talking about.

"CeCe told me Emily's mother followed her father to a motel and then beat down the door and found him with the checkout girl from the Stop and Shop! I mean, apparently he was one of those guys who just can't keep it in their pants, but still, a common *shop girl.*"

Like it would be better if he cheated with an heiress?

A shred of chicken shot into Mom's face as she pounded, and she wiped it off with the back of her hand. "And the girl was *fat.* How embarrassing. Emily's mother took a tire iron to the motel room door!"

I looked intently at the potatoes I was cutting, trying to use my entire brain to make perfectly equal sized pieces. Wouldn't it be great if you could turn off certain portions of your brain while leaving others on? Like right now, I needed the move-your-hands section, but I could do without the hearing language portion. I flashed back to Sara and the way she coped with painful situations. *"What you have to do with your mind, when your body is miserable, is to make it think of something else."* Perfectly square potato piece. Another perfectly square potato piece. And another.

"Men can be such pigs, can you imagine if your father did that? I'd cut off his balls, that's what I'd do." Mom slammed the meat hammer down, breaking my concentration. "Oops, just pounded straight through the chicken." She flipped the chicken onto a plate, pulled out another boneless breast and started flattening it.

Was this my sex talk?

"That mother of Emily's though, she's not blameless," Mom continued. "Maybe if she'd taken a little more care with her looks, he wouldn't have needed to look elsewhere. Now look at me," she gestured up and down her body. "I wouldn't think of letting your father see me in sweatpants or without makeup when he gets home. Jackie, the way you look shows whether you have any self-respect, and a man can tell in a second if you don't."

Mom finished the pounding and moved to the sink beside me. She started washing the meat hammer. "Just remember that, okay?"

Keep Mom happy. Keep Mom happy.

"Oh, I will," I said, nodding furiously, as if she just gave me the key to life.

Mom couldn't stop. "I mean, it is okay for a girl your age to not always be dolled up, but once you get older, you can't expect attention from men if you let yourself look like a boy." Mom scrubbed her hands hard, shaking her head at the same time. "Why, they could think you were one of those *lesbians*! No, makeup and hair and the right clothes are very important. Very important."

I finished the potatoes.

"Put that pot on the stove and turn it up to high," Mom said as she shook flour over the chicken. "Speaking of which, pull your hair back out of your eyes. Why are you always covering up your face? And look at your clothes. Where are the cute shirts I bought you?"

I looked down at my purple shirt and Hilfiger jeans. I had changed out of the "jewel toned" shirt when I got home. Whoops, should have left it on.

"There's not much about that outfit that's feminine," Mom said. "And after all that money I spent on you!"

"Oh, I spilled something on it," I lied. "And I didn't want to waste another nice one, you know, save the good ones for school."

Mom stopped her work on the chicken and looked at me with a soft smile. "I used to dress you so cute! You had the prettiest clothes of anyone your age. And always a matching bow!"

Puke.

Mom put the flour away. "Oh well, those were the days."

Like I had died or something.

Those were the days when she could completely control every aspect of my life. No wonder she loved those days. The Control Freak.

"Am I done?" I asked, fighting to keep my voice pleasant. Must keep her calm. She was grumpy today but at least she wasn't comatose in her bed. I never knew what version of Mom I'd find when I got home. Very unsettling.

"No, get out the lettuce and wash it and start making the salad." Mom said as she chopped an onion.

I tried one more time. "I was kind of in the middle of some homework."

"Oh there's only a little time left before dinner, I don't think you'd get much done in twenty minutes," Mom said, scraping the chopped onion into a saucepan. It sizzled in the melted butter and the kitchen filled with a warm dinner-is-coming kind of smell. Funny how raw onion smelled so awful and sautéing onion made my mouth water.

"And I need your help," Mom continued. "You are plenty old enough to have some responsibilities around here. In fact, it's about time you started making dinner for the family once a week."

I bit back a comment about being the family's slave. I thought about poor little Sara and how she was forced out in the cold to do errands, holes in her boots, no real coat. How she was fed so little and driven so hard and how she would tell herself that whenever her body was miserable she had to make her mind think of something else. How she would pretend she had a feast when she was hungry, how she would weave hypnotic stories for her servant friend Becky to make them both forget. If Sara could "soldier on" as she often put it, so could I.

I opened the refrigerator to get out the lettuce.

"So where is Emily these days?" Mom asked. "You still haven't told me."

"Busy," I said.

"Busy with what? Does she have a boyfriend?"

"No! I mean, I don't know," I said.

"Did the two of you have a fight? Because you seemed thick-as-thieves, and now she's not around. Did you say something mean to her?"

"No, she's just busy, with, uh, dancing and stuff. You know, the spirit squad dance thing at school. They're called Poms."

"*Dancing!* Why, that's fantastic!" Mom's eyes went wide and her face lit up like she'd just won the Powerball. "Why didn't you try out?"

How stupid can my Mom get? Has she ever noticed what a complete klutz I am? Has she ever noticed I have zero interest in being a dancer? How could this woman be biologically related to me? Maybe I am adopted. I just shrugged.

"My goodness, it's just like being a cheerleader, and I LOVED being a cheerleader! That is just so fantastic for Emily. *That* will help her forget her parents' divorce." Mom was vibrating with excitement. She actually twirled around the kitchen.

I've been bringing home straight A's for years now, and never once has it made Mom dance around the kitchen. Plus that was the dumbest thing I ever heard. How could something like being a Pom come close to helping you feel better about your parents' divorce? On the other hand, dancing around the kitchen, for any reason, was better than swallowing too many sleeping pills. I guess I had Emily to thank for that one.

"You should try out next year!" Mom said. "Emily can help you get on the squad, I'm sure she can."

Okay, now *that* was the dumbest thing I ever heard. Emily wasn't even speaking to me anymore. Not to mention my complete inability to dance.

Mom stopped flipping her arms around in ancient cheers and stared at the onions with a smile on her face. "Ahh, cheerleading, now that was fun. Cheering for your dad on the football team, going to dances. Life was so easy then. So fun." She turned to look at me. "You really should enjoy school, you know that? You're never going to have it this good again!"

"Actually, I think school is kind of hard." *Understatement of the year.*

Mom laughed bitterly. "Hah! You think you know hard?" Mom was arranging the chicken pieces in the frying pan and shook her spatula at me. "Try living without love! Now THAT's hard."

> *Dialogue that Would Happen If People Spoke the Truth Around Here:*
> *Mom: Try living without love! That's hard!*
> *Me: Uh, hello? Already am. You don't show me any love.*
> *Mom: I was talking about me, why did you change the subject? We must always talk about ME.*

I had made it through dinner and was lying on my bed, propped on my elbows writing.

> *Mom: Emily's father cheated on her mother! Isn't it awful? I'd cut your dad's balls off if he did that.*
> *Me: Oh yes, that's a nice image to give your daughter. Her father's balls and a violent mother. Lovely.*
> *Mom: Jock-leen, you need to know the realities of the world!*

I felt a mean kind of pleasure at the words. Then I felt a
rush of guilt. Sara would never have been this mean. People were
awful to her but she never let herself be awful back. My back was
hurting from lying in one position for too long so I picked up the
diary and moved to my window seat.

I thought back to Meg and how different she was from her
family, how much I admired her for being flawed. Maybe my flaw
was an unwillingness to play the stupid family game of pretending
not to know the truth.

But how much truth did I know? My brain drifted back to
Aunt Helen. Oh yes, depressive thoughts were way better than
feeling mean. I still didn't understand what happened with her.
Detectives in books always seem to write down all their clues and
information. Maybe I should try that. What did I know about Aunt
Helen? I flipped to a blank page:

*Identical twin with my mother. Apparently inseparable growing up,
which changed at some point. Loved taking care of people, especially
kids. Very artistic, very creative. Like Mom but Helen actually made
art, Mom made houses look good.*

I stared out the darkened window. What else did I know
about Helen? I searched my memory.

*Married to Wes, who works in a company that has something to do
with computers. Went to same college as mom, majored in art.
Worked as a Human Resources manager for a bank, whatever that
means. Didn't come see us that much in Michigan, maybe once? I
don't remember much about that. Saw her at family things in
Norwick, at Grandma and Grandpa's house. Good cook, like Mom,
like all the women of their family.*

There had to be more. That all just didn't add up. I stared at the facts I had written down. It seemed like so little. And then the part about loving to take care of kids jumped out at me. What had mom said? That as a Candy Striper Aunt Helen's favorite part was the nursery. And how she loved kids. So why did she never have any of her own?????

Chapter Thirty-Three

WAIT Training

In the morning I sorted through the piles of my new clothes until I found a pair of jeans and a shirt that weren't too ridiculous. The shirt was, of course, jewel toned, but at least it was a sort of pretty green, if a little bright for my taste. I dug around my closet and found an off white sweatshirt that didn't look too bad with it, and shoved the sweatshirt into the bottom of my backpack planning to cover the green shirt as soon as I left the house. I picked up the spiked boots that were a clone of Mom's, no way I was wearing those. I'm not sure I could even walk in them, let alone take on mean girls and get from class to class.

I went downstairs in the jeans and shirt and the Uggs Mom had insisted on buying me. It made me feel sick to think I was wearing the Poms' uniform, but at least the Uggs were warm. And they didn't make me tower over half the school.

On the way to school I kept thinking about Aunt Helen. The more I thought about her the more questions I had. Like why she never had kids. And why did she and Mom seem to drift apart? And what was going on in her life right before she ended it? Climbing off the bus I shook my head, as if motion could push all the Aunt Helen thoughts away.

The halls were filled with giggles because Cassidy had blanketed the school with a new round of WAIT Training pamphlets. It was her third round of them since school started. The pamphlets were the same as before, an attractive teenage couple on the front looking so lovingly at each other you would think they just *had* sex, not that they were promising to wait years for that big event. Yeah, *that's* realistic.

I was in the locker room changing for PE and heard some girls over in the next alcove tittering about the pamphlet.

"That boy is *cute*. I'd have sex with him right now," I heard one say.

"Maybe not the whole way sex, but definitely some other stuff," answered another. "Like, I'd freak with him."

"*I'm* waiting," said a third in a prissy voice.

"Whatever," said the first and they laughed and ran off to the gym.

Walking to English I swear several guys looked at me and kind of smiled. Guys who have never noticed me before. What was up with that? Ugg boots aren't that sexy. And the green shirt was well hidden. Maybe the WAIT Training pamphlets were making people think about sex *more,* not less. That would be kind of funny. Or maybe everyone but me was sex-crazed. I mean, think of gross Chuckie.

Tommy and Mark were laughing in their seats and waving the pamphlet around when I got to English. As I slid into my seat, I heard Tommy say, "Yeah, right. Dude, if he's waiting it's because he's *gay.*"

"No doubt," said Mark. Then Mark looked at me and smiled. It was a weird smile. It had something more than friendliness in it. It was kind of a smile with a leer underneath.

"Hey, Jackie," Tommy said and he smiled at me too, but in his regular friendly way. He waved the pamphlet at me. "What do you think of this stuff?"

I shrugged. "I don't know."

No boyfriend = no worry about sex.

Mark snickered. "Maybe you know more than you're saying."

Tommy smacked him across the aisle. "Shut up."

What was going on?

I didn't hear a word of class (again). My heart pounded the entire time with the fear that Cassidy had been spreading more rumors about me. Maybe that would explain the looks from boys and the comment from Mark. Then again, maybe I was totally paranoid. I needed to find out more.

Nancy Drew would take action, and Claudia would make that action bold. As soon as class ended, I slid in between Mark's and Tommy's desks. "Wait a second!" I said holding up my hands. "Before you leave you have to tell me what's going on."

Tommy and Mark looked at each other.

"Now!" I said in my best commanding voice.

"Word is, you uh, moved here from your old school because you *had* to," said Mark.

"Had to why?" I demanded leaning my face into his. I'd beat it out of him if I had to, and he must have seen that on my face.

"Uh, because you were, uh . . ." Mark looked to Tommy for help.

"Pregnant," said Tommy. "But no one believes it. Forget about it."

"What?" I said, dumbfounded. Then I burst out laughing. It was almost as silly as the idea of Cassidy being jealous of me.

Mark got up to leave, and I grabbed his shirt. "Where did you hear that?"

I knew what he was going to say before he said it.

"Cassidy. She was handing the pamphlets out to a bunch of girls and telling them they could end up like you. Run out of school because they had sex."

I looked at Tommy. "Yeah, she told me the same thing," he said. "But she's full of it. She just doesn't like you. No one believes it, don't worry."

I let go of Mark's shirt. The wave of laughter had passed. It wasn't funny. It was awful. People thought I had been pregnant! First the copulate thing and now this. Boys were smiling at me because they thought I was easy! I was going to kill her. I really was.

Cassidy usually walked past me after this class. I stomped out of class and scanned the hall for her. Within a minute I saw her coming.

My life had gone so crazy that new parts of my brain were opening up. The one that was pouring out commands right now was the Anger Department. "Welcome to Jacqueline's brain" the rest of my brain seem to be saying. I think I heard applause. I walked straight at Cassidy, and before she could even register that I was in front of her, I shoved her past her posse and into a bank of lockers.

"What is your *problem*?!" I said pushing her shoulders back into the locker until I heard a banging sound. I let go, then grabbed her brown wooly sweater and did it again. *Very satisfying sound.*

Surprisingly, Cassidy didn't fight back. She kind of shrunk into something small and helpless. Then again, I was taller than her and way more juiced on adrenaline. I pushed again and held her there. I put my face close to hers.

"You are full of shit, and you've gone too far." I narrowed my eyes and stared into hers, encouraged by the fear escaping out of them. "I know you are telling people I left my school because I got pregnant. And I know you pretended to be me on FaceSpace."

I could sense a crowd behind me. I pulled back my head raised my voice. "For the record, I was never pregnant. The reason we moved here is because my Dad got the promotion *your dad* wanted. The Dubroskis lost out to the Carsons, and you can't stand it."

Cassidy struggled a little, but I held firm. Mostly she looked scared, like she thought I was about to start really beating on her. I thought about all the trouble her family had caused my family, how her dad was making my dad's life hell, how Cassidy was making my life hell, and I felt like I could pound her against that locker for hours.

Where was this superhuman strength coming from?

I heard someone behind me yelling "Girl fight! Girl fight!"

I looked around without letting go of her. I focused on several of the girls standing near me. "Did Cassidy tell you I moved here because I was pregnant?"

Several nodded yes.

"Thank you!" I said. "I have witnesses."

I turned back to Cassidy and gave her one more satisfying shove before I let her go.

"Cassidy, if you say that one more time, I am suing you for slander. That's S-L-A-N-D-E-R, go look it up you Airheaded, Barbie-*tease*."

I heard laughing behind me as I walked away. I felt like I was walking in a hazy tunnel, not able to focus on anything around me. Somehow I made it to the lunchroom.

I found a new seat, one up against a wall so I could see if Cassidy was coming for me.

Where were these survival instincts coming from?

I opened my book and a carton of yogurt to try to appear normal, but it took a good twenty minutes before my brain and heart rate calmed down enough to actually focus on anything. Who was that back there? Not Nancy-me. Not Sara-me. I'm not even sure it was Claudia or Beryl. Maybe that was pure Jacqueline. What had I just done? I couldn't decide how I felt about it. Part of me was appalled. What happened to the nice Sara-me? The one who thought it was stronger to hold back rage? Part of me was proud. I finally stood up for myself! Part of me still felt really powerful. No wonder people enjoyed being aggressive, it felt great. Was I going to turn into Rambo? I didn't think so. I didn't think I enjoyed the pushing itself. It was that I enjoyed pushing *Cassidy*.

As I was thinking about this, I watched Cassidy pass out more pamphlets to the lunchroom. She hit every table but mine, which was fine by me. A lot of the pamphlets ended up on the floor. The janitorial staff must love her as much as I do.

Then Alex slid into a seat in front of me. Again. Ahh, no wonder he thought I was so hot inside. Cassidy must have gotten to him yesterday. What a jerk.

"Hi, Jock-leen," he said smiling like he thought he was adorable.

"Go flash your brighty-whiteys at someone else," I said. *I guess the polite, scaredy-cat Jacqueline was gone.*

"In a bad mood, huh?"

"What's it to you?"

He shrugged. "Just thought I'd come by and say hi."

"Okay, you said it. Bye."

Alex stood up. The I'm-so-adorable look was replaced by concern. "Just so you know, a lot of people think Cassidy is full of shit."

I hadn't expected him to be *nice*. I looked down, afraid I might start crying.

"And I'm one of them," Alex added before he walked away.

Chapter Thirty-Four

A Familiar Loneliness

I guess Mom didn't have my power to resist crying. When I walked in from school she was sitting in the unlit kitchen, staring out at the dead backyard. The day was so gray and the sun seemed so far away that light hardly penetrated the windows. Her face was wet and her eyes were as dead as the bare trees outside the window.

So it was going to be one of those *days. Crap.*

"Hey, Mom," I said, trying for a normal greeting. Pretending she didn't look like a zombie.

Mom grunted.

Wow, what a welcome home!

Mom slowly rubbed the back of her hand across her face and finally turned towards me.

I dropped my backpack on the floor and wondered if foraging for food would be rude in the face of Mom's mood.

More tears started flowing from Mom's eyes.

Okay, no food.

Maybe if I kept thinking about food, I wouldn't have to think about how helpless I felt. How dark the room seemed. How dark the world seemed.

"Come here," Mom whispered.

I floated over towards her, drawn like I had none of my own will.

"Give me a hug," Mom ordered in the same creepy whisper.

I slid onto the bench and gathered my arms around her. She felt bony and small and fragile under my touch. Like a wounded bird.

"Ummm, what's going on?" I asked, not wanting an answer, wishing I was anywhere but here. Even at school with Cassidy.

Mom breathed in and out deeply, like she was trying to calm herself. She let her head fall against my shoulder and did some more deep breathing.

We sat in silence for what felt like hours but was probably about two minutes before she finally spoke.

"I don't know," she whispered. "It just all seems so hard."

Ain't that the truth.

I patted her back awkwardly, just wanting my arms back but feeling like I was the only thing keeping her from falling off of a cliff.

"It is, it is," I said, just to be saying something. "It is, and then eventually, somehow it isn't. You know? Somehow things always seem to get better."

What a line of bullshit.

Mom raised her head at me and gave a little smile through her tears. "You have always been so wise, Jock-leen. Such an old soul."

Wise?

Well, whatever it was, it was working so I kept on. "Things will be fine, I just know it."

Wait for the lightning strike. Such preposterous lies surely can't go unnoticed by God.

God. Now there's a thought. Where was he or she in all this? Why isn't God helping out here?

"I know we don't go to church much these days," I said to Mom, inspired by the God thoughts. "But maybe praying would help. You know, ask God to guide you, us, ask for his help." No use referring to God as a 'she' around Mom, nothing irritated her more. Myself, I think God is bigger than gender, so why not rotate using 'he' and 'she'?

Mom snaked her arms around my waist and put her head back on my shoulder. "Good idea, I'm going to do that right now," and then got silent. I guess she was praying. Thank you God for having her do it in silence.

I was torn. On the one hand I really didn't want to know what was going on with Mom, didn't want to know the enormity of the problem that I would be unable to fix. And on the other hand, I desperately wanted to know what was going on so that I could understand, predict, prevent . . .

Mom finally released me, sitting back against the cushions on the bench.

"Oh, Jockleen, sometimes I feel like I just work so hard and try so hard and nothing seems right." She gestured around the kitchen.

"I mean, look at this. It is all beautiful and who cares? Who cares about tennis or decorating or cooking a great dinner? Just a waste of time."

Huh? She just described her own life. The stuff she usually got ecstatic over. The stuff she was always after Aunt Ruth to do.

"Your dad doesn't appreciate it. You and Davy don't appreciate it. Why do I bother?"

"I do appreciate it!" I protested. "I mean, I probably don't say it enough, but I do."

Mom shook her head.

"I do! I'm proud of how you've done our house and I love your meals. And everyone knows you are so great at putting fashion together."

Mom kept shaking her head but she was looking at me. She was listening.

Oh crap, might as well give it all to her. "And every one thinks you are so pretty. Even boys at my school think you are hot."

I cringed, thinking of Alex talking about Mom.

Mom's eyes lit up at that one. "Really?"

Eeww. Eeww.

Anything to make her feel better.

"Yes. Not telling you who, though." I had a flash of her flirting with Alex. Uber-eeww.

"They think I'm hot?" Mom asked again.

I nodded. "I'm sure everyone else is jealous that I've got you for a mother."

Yeah, who wouldn't want a moody, overdosing, perfectionist for a mother?

Mom gave a weak smile. "You're too much, Jockleen, you know that? Too much."

Mom stood up. "Well, I guess I'd better get up, I have a million things to do. You should go finish putting the books in the library away. That is taking forever."

"Umm, are you okay? Do you want help with dinner?"

"I'm okay. I feel better." She smiled, "hot mom, huh?"

I barely managed to keep from rolling my eyes. Why undo all that good work?

The library was dark and cold and the couple of reading lights were not enough to fight off the leaden sky outside the window. I fiddled with the fireplace and managed to turn on the gas. I usually preferred a real fire but wouldn't have had the energy to bring in wood, so I was glad for this gas-in-fake-wood set up. At least the flames were real and they did cheer up the room. I grabbed a handful of books from the closest box and found it was a mix of almost everything. First a book of baby names. I couldn't resist, I flipped through the pages until I found "Jacqueline." From the French for "supplanter." What did that mean? I wandered around until I found the dictionary I had put on the reference shelf. Supplant meaning "1. to take the place (of another), as through force, 2. to replace one thing by something else."

Interesting. Here I was pretending to be these fictional characters and my name meant kind of that. Hmmm. As I considered the idea of "supplanter" I kept working on the box.

A gardening book, a financial advice book, two paperback mysteries and then one of my all time favorites, *The Little Prince*. I shelved the rest of the handful then sat down in front of the fire with *The Little Prince*. It wasn't a long book and I couldn't resist a quick read. I had to laugh at myself, I was in the middle of *A Little Princess*, and now was adding to my royal book club with a prince.

An hour later, far off in the Sahara, I felt well and truly quiet in my soul for the first time in a long long time. It wasn't that I felt far away from my life, the little prince's story made me feel *okay* in my life. Made me realize all the school stuff was silly, and not the kind of thing that was important about life. I stared into the fire, thinking of how many people across the centuries have stared into fire while their minds sorted out their problems. I thought of the pilot and the little prince, sitting by their fire, looking up at the stars. I thought of the how the little prince saw the silliness of the grown ups and how he learned the secrets of friendship. How he came to understand his rose and his love for her. I thought about my parents and the kids at school, and I wondered how we all had managed to make life seem so complicated.

I flipped back to page 83 and re-read one of the best parts. The fox has taught the little prince about taming each other.

> But you have hair the color of gold. So it will be wonderful once you've tamed me! The wheat, which is golden, will remind me of you. And I'll love the sound of the wind in the wheat . . .

The loneliness of the little prince felt so familiar. Maybe we all wish for someone to tame us, for someone to miss us, for someone to care to know our hearts. How did he do it, Antoine de Saint Exupéry? How could he capture my exact kind of sadness? I felt quiet inside, but with a comforting kind of melancholy because someone knew how I felt. Someone else had felt it, and found meaning in it. It was the sadness of anyone who's ever been lonely. And in this calm quiet place I felt a stirring of pain for my mother. How she must miss her sister. How many wheat fields did *she* see every day? How often did something remind her of Aunt Helen, something that no one else would even notice?

And maybe *it is okay* to feel sad, to feel lonely, to miss someone. Maybe the sadness is a worthy price to pay for having loved someone, and maybe eventually you will hear a little boy laughing among the stars.

Mom did everything she could to avoid talking about Aunt Helen, but I was starting to wonder if that was the most helpful thing. It would be like the fox pretending he had never met the little prince, instead of enjoying the golden color of the wheat fields. It would be like the pilot never looking at the stars, never listening for the tinkling laughter of the little prince.

In this unnaturally peaceful moment it seemed clear to me that Mom would never be okay as long as she pretended Aunt Helen away.

Now what was I supposed to do?

Chapter Thirty-Five
Friends and Frenemies

I stepped on the bus Friday morning to lots of stares. People who had never seemed to notice me looked right at my face, then looked away really fast. "It's not contagious," I wanted to yell. "And it never happened!" The silver lining was that no one sat beside me. I dove back into *A Little Princess* and made it to school without dying of shame.

Same thing at school. Lots of interested stares and quick look-aways. Even pervy Donovan gave me extra time with his eyes. Eeew. And I swear I heard a couple of whispered "slut" comments in the halls. Great.

After PE, Emily lingered in the locker room and sat down beside me once it had mostly cleared out.

"Ohmigod," Emily said. "I can't believe Cassidy is telling people, you know, the lies about you."

Now she talks to me?

I shrugged. "Yeah, it sucks."

"It is so rude! So lame!" said Emily. "I'm sorry. I know it's not true. I *know* you. Cassidy is such a bee-yatch."

My eyes got hot with tears, and I fought them back. One word of kindness could undo me. I worked back to anger – much easier to handle. "Well, do you mind letting people know?"

Emily looked uncomfortable. I guess it was one thing to feel sorry for someone, another to actually put yourself on the line to fix the problem.

I stood up. "You know, one of these days you're going to have to decide who you are going to be. Right now you are letting circumstances decide for you and by circumstances I mean Cassidy."

Emily kept her eyes towards the ground.

"Whatever," I said and walked away.

As I walked I noticed a piece of paper sticking out of my bag and pulled out another note from Jennifer Walker.

I guess that was something. But here's the thing that kept bugging me: A lot of people seemed to dislike Cassidy, so why was everyone so afraid of her?

In the hall on the way to English, Tommy fell into step with me.

"Hey, Jackie," he said. "How's it hanging?"

I had to smile. Tommy treated me the same as his buddies, and I liked the simplicity of that. He seemed to have one rule for everyone. Not a separate persona for Poms versus Unnoticeables or football players versus math geeks or even girls versus boys.

"It's all hanging *out*, that's what," I said.

"Yeah, it'll all blow over. In a day or two Cassidy will make up a lie about someone else and everyone will forget you."

"Gee that's comforting. I don't know which part is better, that she'll make someone else miserable, or that I'll be forgotten."

Tommy slung his arm around my shoulder. "I meant that they'll forget the lies. They won't forget *you*."

Tommy must have been pushing back from the table early these days because he was starting to look less porky and a little more, I don't know, cute. Okay, cute was stretching it, but definitely not ugly. And he smelled good. Not hot-good like Alex, more clean-good. Like he had a nice soap and had just used it.

Tommy dropped his arm and slowed up to let me go through the door to English first. He did have good manners, I'd give him that. Aside from the farting and all.

After English, Tommy walked out the door with me.

"You going to lunch now, right?" he said.

"Yeah. That should be a joy," I said, dreading the stares and whispers of an entire lunchroom. I had been trying not to think about the eternity it would take to get to the bell at the end.

"I have history or I'd come sit with you," Tommy said. He said it casually, but we both knew what it meant. Of all people, Tommy Thornton as my protector? Go figure. I was reminded of

Sara and her loneliness and how she realized that maybe kindness reaches people somehow, and that you feel comforted without knowing exactly why.

Tommy peeled off, and I trudged into the cafeteria. Headed toward my usual solo spot in the back, I stopped when I saw Alex sitting there with a couple of his buddies, immediately turning it from a Loser Table to a Hottie Table. I started to turn around when Alex called out.

"Hey, Jackie, come here, we saved a seat for you."

I was standing twenty or so feet from him but still felt his buzz. It pulled me toward the table like I was a little paperclip and the table was a huge magnet. It barely registered that Alex had called me Jackie instead of the mocking "Jock-leen."

Alex slid over a seat leaving me a spot in between Ben Parker and himself. Crap! Ben was Cassidy's boyfriend. I hadn't seen him when I started over. Across the table were Nick Stuart and Andy Primanti. I was torn, on the one hand thrilled not to be sitting alone, on the other hand feeling like I might have just entered an alligator pit. Were these guys interested in sitting with me to be nice, like Tommy would have done, or were they interested in sitting with me to get close to a slutty girl? My bet would be on slutty girl.

I racked my brain for the right character to be. I needed Confidence, Bravery, Dignity. Definitely Thick Skin. I took a deep breath as I sat down.

It was a tight enough fit that I was pressed against both boys on either side. I'm never this close to boys, and now here I was wedged between two hotties. It felt like I was conducting an electrical current between the two. My brain waves were scrambled, and it was all I could do to say hello.

"Hi."

So far so good.

"You guys know Jackie, right?" said Alex looking around the table.

Who didn't know me now?

A chorus of yeah's.

"Whatd'ya have for lunch?" asked Andy.

"Uh, sandwich, yogurt, you know, stuff," I said, forcing myself to concentrate.

"Cool," Andy said.

Silence.

I couldn't even look at Ben. If there was one person there who had been told all the lies it was him. Plus he was on the older side for his year and just seemed so mature to me. Maybe it was his deep voice or the facial stubble or maybe it was just that he seemed totally calm all the time. Like he was quiet out of choice, not because he was shy or anything.

Alex nodded at Ben. "I guess you and Jackie have something in common, eh?"

Huh?

"You know, being trashed by Cassidy."

What?

I must have looked puzzled.

"Cassidy and Ben broke up and Cassidy's been trashing him all over school. Saying that he tried to force her to, you know, do stuff," Alex said.

I looked at Ben, eyes wide. He nodded. "I didn't! I mean, the whole abstinence thing is you know, whatever, but I respected it. Honest."

"You don't have to convince me," I said. "Hey, maybe you were the one that got me pregnant!"

Did I just say that? Ohmigod.

They all burst out laughing. Ben shot soda out of his mouth and Andy pounded the table. People at tables around us looked over interested in what was so funny. I still wasn't used to the stares and couldn't figure out if people were staring at me because of the pregnancy rumor or because I was sitting with four hot boys or because I had just made those boys laugh.

I felt an intense stare from across the room and saw Cassidy glaring at me, flames of rage shooting out of her eyes.

Hey, this is all your doing Cassidy! Thanks for setting me up with these guys.

I was scared though. Now she had even more reason to hate me. Her plan hadn't exactly worked the way she thought it would. Yeah, lots of people were making fun of me, but here I was sitting with the coolest guys in school. She couldn't have meant for that to happen.

"I told you guys she was funny," Alex said.

"Who're you going out with?" Nick asked. Nick was a full on skate-boarder dude with long bangs swept across his forehead, low slung tight jeans and a shirt that looked like it had been silk screened by a drunk maniac. Andy's thick neck and big shoulders screamed football. Ben played all the sports but at six foot three was the obvious basketball player. Kind of an odd collection of guys.

"No one," I said, feeling the insecure Jacqueline returning.

"Huh," said Nick. Not like he was thinking of asking me out. More like he was filing me away for a match up with someone else.

"You're new this year, right?" said Andy.

"Yeah, we moved from Michigan at the beginning of last summer."

They were all staring at me. I felt a blush starting to rise. "My Dad got a *promotion*. That's why we moved."

They nodded.

"He got the promotion that Cassidy's dad thought he was getting. That's why she hates me."

Ben's head was still going up and down in agreement. "Yeah, she was pissed about that. I mean, talk about taking something *personally*."

"What's her dad like?" I asked, realizing I had a great source of information on the Dubroskis right in front of me.

"I don't really know," Ben said. "She never wanted me to come to her house. Always met me somewhere else or made me wait outside in the car 'til she came out."

"No offense dude," Nick said to Ben, "but she's one weird chick. Hot, but weird."

"I know," said Ben.

"So you never met her dad?" I couldn't believe it. How was that possible? My dad would interrogate the crap out of someone before he took me out. Not that it had happened yet.

"I mean, what's up with all that virgin 'til marriage stuff?" asked Andy. "She dresses like a stripper and then says 'don't touch.'"

Ben looked mad. "Hey, she's kind of messed up, but she was my girlfriend, you know? Chill."

190

"Did you ever meet her dad?" I asked again.

"Nah," said Ben.

"What about her mom?" I asked. Surely there was some kind of good dirt here.

"Yeah, I met her."

"And?" I was curious what he thought of her.

"I don't know. Kind of one of those ladies who likes to think she is younger than she is. You know, wearing mini skirts and stuff. Probably calls herself a cougar."

My impression exactly. The kind of woman who would refuse to be called Grandma when the time came. She'd be "Nana" or "Mimsy" or something like that.

"Did Cassidy ever tell you her dad got my dad in trouble?" I asked. I didn't want to give Jennifer Walker away, but it would help to have another source for that information.

"Hmmm," Ben considered the question. "She said her dad was going to 'take Carson down' and stuff like that. But I don't remember anything more specific."

Shoot.

The bell rang ending lunch period.

Wow. Can't believe I made it through. Can't believe I just sat here talking to the hotties.

Alex hopped up. "Later," he said and then faded into the crowd.

"Where do you go next?" asked Andy-with-the-big-shoulders.

Was he talking to me?

"Keyboarding," I said.

"Cool, I'm walking that way." Andy stood still while I got out of my seat then followed me out of the cafeteria.

In the hall I tried to ignore the stares. It helped that I felt like I was walking with a bodyguard since Andy's shoulders took up half the width of the hallway. Still, I felt jumpy inside, uncertain about Andy's motives for walking with me. "Nice" was not the first word that came to mind for a guy with a neck that thick.

"Are you sure you want to be seen with me?" I said. "Cause now you're going to be the next rumor."

Where was this stuff coming from? I should be curled up in a ball on the floor crying.

"Maybe I wouldn't mind being the next rumor." Andy looked sideways at me with a smile.

I felt SuperBitch rise up inside of me. "What does *that* mean?"

Andy rolled his eyes. "I don't know. It was just something to say."

"You do understand it really was a lie? I really wasn't pregnant. I really haven't even ever had a boyfriend."

Why did I just say that? Why not just tattoo "Loser!" on my forehead?

"So you're into the abstinence thing too?"

"Yeah, involuntary abstinence."

"Oh really?" he said all suggestively. Like I meant that I didn't want to be a virgin.

"No! That came out wrong. I just meant it hasn't been an issue yet. You know, no boyfriend, no big sex decision."

I couldn't believe I was having a discussion about sex with a guy I'd just met. A big-football-playing-hot-popular guy who might have been talking to me just because he thought he could get some.

Keyboarding was a blur. My brain had too much stuff floating around to concentrate on anything. I walked by myself to chemistry in enough of a trance to not notice people staring at me. I headed to my normal seat in the Unnoticeable section and only came out of my fog when Alex slid into a chair next to me.

"What are you doing?" I asked, unable to censor my thoughts any more. The first I was aware of a thought was when it was coming out of my mouth. Who was this girl?

"What do you mean?"

"Why aren't you in the back with Cassidy?"

"Maybe I wanted to sit here. Cassidy is the one who sits down by me, not the other way around."

"You didn't know I existed most of the year, and now all of a sudden you want to talk to me and sit with me. Why now?"

Alex shrugged. "I've known you existed ever since last summer."

"And?"

"Maybe I'm shy."

I burst out laughing which got me dirty looks from Cassidy and the teacher. Emily was staring at me in a longing sort of way. I couldn't tell if it was that she missed me or wished she were the one talking to Alex.

"Okay, well I thought you were kind of cute when I first saw you but, you know, thought you were probably just another rich girl."

He thought I was cute?!

"Meaning?"

"Meaning you'd only want to talk about clothes and your latest trips and how much better you are than other girls."

I had to smile at that. That was *so* not me.

"But now I see you're interesting."

"Oh."

"Worth getting to know," Alex added with a devilish look in his eye.

Gulp.

He thought I was cute.

Chapter Thirty-Six

Intrepid

It seemed like I would never get home, and then finally, finally, I was up in my room, cocooned in my window seat. I was wrapped in the fuzzy peach blanket, and I had *A Little Princess* in my lap. I needed to be far far away from my life right now. Far away from Mean Girl Poms and pregnancy rumors and sexual harassment suits and crazy mothers.

But first I allowed myself the tears that I had managed to hold back at school. I leaned my head against the cold window and felt the hot, salty stream flow out. People thought I had been pregnant! They thought I was slutty. That's why boys were smiling at me that way all over school. That's why girls had been looking at me with such contempt. Cassidy was the meanest, most awful person I knew.

Why was my life so hard? Why couldn't *something* work out? Everything was a mess.

"I know, I know" a kind voice said in my head. "So mean. You are not that way. At least you can take pride in that." I knew that voice. It was Sara. The Little Princess, the one who had been treated cruelly by everyone, the one who was almost living in the street with old clothes and not enough food. And it was true. I could take pride in not being mean like Cassidy.

I wiped my face with an edge of the blanket and the tears slowed to a stop.

"Ah, forget 'em" another voice said. Beryl. Being Tough and Self-sufficient.

Enough with the tears. I pulled the blanket tighter around me and disappeared into Sara's world. My misery seemed to match Sara's misery, only hers was about to come to an end. After being made into a servant and hardly fed and treated so horribly by Miss Minchin, Sara finds out that she is actually wildly rich and the neighbor is actually her father's partner, and he wants her to live with him. When Miss Minchin starts to grovel and act like she has been nice to Sara all along, Sara stares her right in the face and says, "You know why I will not go home with you, Miss Minchin. . . you know quite well." Take that you bee-atch Miss Minchin!

Love it.

I love any kind of happy ending and I needed happy endings right now. I tried to imagine I was like Sara and that my happy ending was right around the corner. Sara didn't know she would have a happy ending. She was ready to endure a lifetime of misery and then, boom, it all worked out fine. Maybe if I could just pretend hard enough that could happen to me.

I didn't want to leave Sara's world so I re-read the ending three times. Finally, I let the book fall into my lap and stared out the window.

What had I gained from Sara? Well now my list of Desired Personality Characteristics was: Confident, Planful, Brave, Self-sufficient, Endurance, Tough, Flawed, Stealthy, Kind and Dignified. I definitely wanted to hold onto Sara's Kindness. And I thought some more about the little prince. What did I want to take from him? He was so wise, in a simple, cut-through-the-bullshit way. Wise. I could add that and know it meant his kind of wisdom. Confident, Planful, Brave, Self-sufficient, Endurance, Tough, Flawed, Stealthy, Kind, Dignified and Wise.

Ah yes, little Sara had served me well. And finally, it was time to dive into a Nancy Drew.

When things seem completely out of control I turn to Nancy. Nothing like solving a mystery to make the world seem manageable. And I like that out-of-this-era simplicity in Nancy's stories. In Nancy Drew stories there are bad guys and good guys. No complicated in-between kind of characters. Nancy always wins and does it with grace and style and without sacrificing her popularity. There was bravery and triumphing in Nancy's stories. I could use a little triumphing.

I sat down in front of the Nancy Drew section of my bookshelves. I ran my hand along the yellow spines. For a few seconds I convinced myself that the answers to my life might be hidden in one of them.

Might as well start at the beginning. I wondered if I should read my copies or Mom's. Too lazy to go down to the library, I pulled out *The Secret of the Old Clock* and climbed up onto the window seat and sailed away to River Heights.

All through dinner (shrimp risotto and the dreaded goat cheese, cranberry salad) I thought about Nancy Drew and wondered how she would be handling this whole Aunt Helen thing. I just had to know what happened to her. And I had to get Mom to stop pretending Helen never existed. I wished Nancy was my big sister. How awesome would that have been?

After doing the dishes, with no real plan in mind, but Sara's Kindness at the front of my brain along with Nancy's investigative impulses, I wandered towards Dad's office. I knocked on the open door frame and went in as he looked up.

"Hey, pumpkin," Dad said, pulling off his reading glasses and leaning back in the big leather chair behind the even bigger desk. Everything in this house was big. Dad was the only one that really fit, since he was big too. Tall and broad shouldered he still looked like he could play football, even though it had been years since his college football glory days.

I jumped in before I could think about it too much. "So here's the thing, Dad," I said, plopping myself on the leather couch on the side of the room. "I want to understand what happened to Aunt Helen. I don't know why nobody in this family talks about her."

There. I said it. I got it out. Then I remembered Sara's Kindness and gave Dad a warm smile. Like, no hard feelings, but can we just talk about this?

Dad pressed his lips together and tilted his head. Then he let out a big sigh.

"What's this recent interest in her?" he asked.

Duh. Mom overdosed? Hello?

"Well she *killed* herself. And Mom just, you know, took sleeping pills," I couldn't believe I was actually saying it. The thing I had been obsessed with every waking moment was now, finally, coming out of my mouth. My heart was racing but I had done it.

When Dad didn't say anything I continued. "You don't think those two things might be related?"

Dad let his head fall against the high back of his chair. Like he was just too tired to even support the weight of his own head.

"Jackie, your mom is okay," he said softly.

"How do you know?" I asked.

"She is not going to do what Helen did," Dad said.

"How do you know?" I asked again. "I mean, really, *how do you know?*"

"I just do."

"But everyone said they were exactly alike, inseparable, did everything the same," I said, all of a sudden feeling close to tears.

"Not exactly alike," said Dad. "Helen had some other . . . issues, that's all."

"What were they? Why won't anyone *tell* me?" I said.

"Look, it really upsets your mom to think about Helen, so do not talk to her about this," Dad said.

"Then tell me what Helen's issues were," I said.

Dad stared at me without speaking, narrowing and then widening his eyes like he was having an internal debate.

"Come on, I'm old enough," I begged, hoping I was right, flashing back to the image I now wished I hadn't weaseled out of Aunt Ruth.

"If I tell you this, you have to promise not to bring it up with your mother," Dad said leaning forward in the chair, energy back in his body, eyes intent on my eyes.

Ooh. Hard one. I flashed back to that calm, quiet moment in front of the fire with the wisdom of the little prince still echoing through my head. I had felt so sure that Mom couldn't keep pretending nothing had happened with Aunt Helen and when I felt around for it, the certainty was still there.

"Just tell me," I said.

"Promise," Dad countered. He was too expert at negotiating for my tastes.

"Fine," I said, desperate to know whatever he was about to share. I'd figure out later how to get Mom talking about Helen.

"Okay, well, we don't know for sure, and I've never even discussed it with your mother, but it seemed pretty clear to me that Helen was depressed over not having a baby."

Ahh. I thought of the extra copies of *What to Expect When You're Expecting*. I thought about the baby names book. I thought about how mom said Aunt Helen had loved kids and how I wondered why she didn't have any.

"She and Wes had hoped for years, and it just didn't happen. And she took lots of fertility drugs and explored every option, but it just never happened for them." Dad's face was sad. "And I can see how hard that would be. We were so blessed to have you and then . . . Davy." His faced darkened.

"And?" I asked. He had looked like he was about to say more.

"And that's it," he said. "At least, that is what I think happened."

"But why won't Mom even talk about her?" I asked.

"Jackie, just let it go," Dad said. "Your mom didn't have that same issue, so you don't have to worry about her . . . doing that."

"But what if it runs in families?" I asked.

"Jackie," Dad sounded annoyed, "she's not going to do that. It was a special circumstance."

I wished I could be as sure as Dad. He wasn't the one coming home to find Mom in bed in the middle of the day. He didn't see her sitting alone in the kitchen crying. And maybe he didn't want to believe it could happen to her. Maybe he was in denial too. Was there anyone who could face the truth?

"I really need to get back to work here," Dad said. "And remember, do not bring this up to your mother. She's ah, she's not strong."

So she's "not strong" but he's sure she won't try to kill herself?

It didn't all add up.

In my room I pulled open my diary.

<u>*More Dialogues That Would Happen if I Could Speak the Truth Around Here*</u>*:*

Me: Dad, aren't you worried about mom killing herself?
Dad: No. She's weak, but she won't do that.
Me: Why not?
Dad: It just wouldn't happen. Too inconvenient.
Me: Oh, you mean it is too inconvenient for you to face it.

I stopped writing, feeling guilty. Dad was a good guy, really. Why was I criticizing him? But maybe good people live in denial too. Uncle Wes was a good person and look how that ended. What was wrong with me that I couldn't just let this go? Maybe this need for the truth really was a flaw. It was bothering everyone.

I was too tired to think. Too tired to do anything but climb in bed and shut out the world.

I was wakened in the middle of the night by a yank on my bed sheet and the sound of Davy crying.

"Hmm, huh? What's wrong" I said, fighting to wake up.

Davy just kept crying.

"Davy, what's wrong?"

"My bed is wet!" Davy cried.

I sat up in bed and leaned down to hug Davy. I could feel that the front of his Batman suit was wet. "Oh, did you have an accident?"

"Mmm mmm," Davy said and cried harder.

"It's okay, it's okay," I said. "I'll go fix it."

"No!" Davy cried. "Want in your bed."

"Okay, okay, let me just get you some clean pajamas, okay?"

"No-o-o! I want my Batman suit!"

I took Davy into my bathroom, stripped off his costume and wiped him off with a washcloth. I told him to sit down on the rug by the bath tub and ran to his room to find some pajamas. I got him in his pajamas, put him in my bed and told him I'd be right back.

I went to the linen closet and found clean sheets and took them to Davy's room. Then I switched them with the wet ones on his bed. I took the dirty sheets and the Batman suit down to the laundry room and threw them in the washing machine, vowing to myself I'd get down here early and switch them over to the dryer. Mom doesn't handle wet beds well, and I didn't want her to know it had happened. The last thing Davy needed was to get yelled at. And the last thing Mom needed was more stress.

I let Davy sleep in my bed the rest of the night. Davy was a snuggler, curling up against me while he slept, rearranging himself in his sleep to get as much physical contact as he could. It wasn't quite the same as having Nancy Drew-the-big-sister there, but it was kind of comforting to have Batman nearby. Even if Batman was a bed-wetting five-year-old.

In the morning I stopped at my desk and wrote "Intrepid" on my List of Desired Personality Characteristics. I'd have to look it up to be sure, but Intrepid to me meant being brave and smart in hard situations. If Nancy could be Intrepid, so could I.

Chapter Thirty-Seven

Little Jack(lin) Horner

At school I found both Tommy and Melody hovering around my locker.

"Hi, Jackie," said Tommy and Melody at the same time. They looked at each other, probably unaware they were both waiting for me. I doubted they knew each other.

I stared at Melody, surprised by the friendly face. Had she finally realized I had nothing to do with the FaceSpace trashing?

"Hey, uh, so can I talk to you?" Melody asked in a rushy kind of voice.

"Yeah," I said.

Tommy gave me a friendly jab in the arm. "I'll leave you guys to it. See ya later," he said and sauntered off.

"I'm so sorry," Melody said looking briefly at me and then glancing away. "I should have known you'd never say those things. Yesterday when I heard Cassidy saying all those lies about you I realized she really does hate you and she really would do something like that to make you look bad. I mean if you'd tell people someone was *pregnant* . . ."

Melody shook her head. "Evil. The girl is just plain *evil.*"

No argument with that.

Melody shifted her crutches to move away from my locker so I could get into it.

"Can you believe someone would say that stuff? I mean, really," I said, swapping some books between my backpack and locker.

"Evil," Melody said again.

"T'sup?" growled a voice from behind us.

I turned around to see a mean looking girl standing by Melody. She had heavily lined eyes and one of those ponytails that look like they took about an hour to arrange. Her dark hair was smooth along the sides and puffed out in back, with long bangs flattened alongside her face. Her size 8 jeans didn't quite cover her size 12 body and her short shirt showed off about three inches of the muffin-top spilling out of the waistband.

"Hey, Tricia," said Melody giving me an anxious look.

"Why're you talking to her?" barked Tricia, narrowing her eyes at me.

Another fan.

"Uh, Jackie, this is Tricia," stuttered Melody. "She's my neighbor. She's in eleventh grade, and used to kind of watch out for me while my mom was working but now we just hang out."

"Yeah, I told Melody she doesn't need to be hanging around with a *Heights chick.* Especially one like you," Tricia said.

"Tricia!" Melody exclaimed. "Jackie's my friend and I'm telling you, she didn't write that stuff. I know it." Melody looked pleadingly at me. "Tricia is like my big sister and she gets really protective of me. Sorry."

"Yeah, us ghetto girls have to stick together," said Tricia.

Like Kentley had a ghetto. Please.

I was saved from more angry glares when a tall pimply faced boy came up to Tricia, wrapped his hands around her and stuck them in her back pockets. Tricia leaned over almost backward and started sucking at his face like she was trying to inhale him.

"That's Jason, her boyfriend," Melody explained as we slipped away.

I was hoping it wasn't a stranger.

"Don't worry about Tricia, she just likes to sound tough. She's been really good to me and she'll come around," said Melody as she clomped along.

"She's like the eleventh grade mafia," I said, doubting that Tricia would ever come around to liking me.

Nancy Drew didn't have to deal with Goth-looking protective girls from the 'hood.

After school Mom was waiting for my bus.

"Climb in! We are going to La Luminesse," Mom said, full of smiles.

I guessed if it kept her happy, I would go hang around and watch her get her hair done.

"Where's Davy?" I said, looking into the back seat.

"Playdate at Charlie's," said Mom. "It's just us girls! I'm treating us both to mani's and pedi's."

The quest to girlie me up was still on. Actually, I didn't mind the idea of mani's and pedi's. I'm no good at putting on my own nail polish, but I'm not philosophically against it. Okay, this would be an easy one. Go along, keep Mom happy, get a professional job on my nails.

Mom peered over at me. "Where's that adorable shirt I bought you?"

Crap. Forgot to take the hoodie off.

"I have it on. I was just cold after school, so I stuck this on under my jacket." I said, unzipping the hoodie and showing her the puke green shirt I had worn this morning to please her.

Mom shot a look at my feet, encased in the Uggs. "Those boots are just adorable on you." She ran her eyes up to my head. "But you know what? You need some accessorizing with that shirt. A necklace or some great earrings."

Just shut up and take it.

I gave a golden retriever happy nod.

Mom smiled to herself. "Well, Christmas is coming! I know what to get you!"

Oh joy.

Mom angled the car into a space on Kentley's main street, three buildings away from the day spa. La Luminesse fit right in with the chic village look the downtown planners seemed to have mandated. It had dark awnings over leaded glass windows and was fronted by deep planters flowing with ivy and, in the summer, flowers. The warm light streaming through the windows was particularly welcoming, outshining the weak December sun. I pushed open the massive carved wood door and stepped into the land of money and beauty. The large front room was devoted to hair and nails and was decorated in a French-Zen kind of style with acres of pale hardwood floors, big bunches of lavender scattered everywhere in tall vases, and simple but soothing colors on the stylist's stations. At the back of the room a ten foot tall door shrouded by thick velvet curtains led to a labyrinth of treatment rooms for body wraps, massages and anything else wealthy women could be made to believe would make them beautiful.

I headed toward the huge lavender velvet chairs in the waiting area to hang out while Mom got her hair done. Then we'd get the mani's and pedi's together.

Mom grabbed my arm. "No! I have a surprise for you! Tony is going to do your hair too!" She guided me to Tony's station, pumped on beauty salon adrenaline. Must be all the estrogen swirling around.

Tony wore a black shirt, tight black pants and looked like someone Granddad Carson would call a "Fruit." Women loved Tony because he could not get enough details on every romance, every business deal, every tennis match. He swooned over decorating particulars and dissected parties down to each he said, she said and she wore, she wore. Women felt exciting and attractive in Tony's chair.

Too bad for me it turned out that kids don't.

Mom pushed me into a chair and then sat in one beside me.

"I don't need a haircut," I said.

Mr. Tony appeared behind me and ran his fingers through my shoulder length hair before even saying hello. He fluffed hair around my face and then pulled it down straight, all the while pursing his lips and frowning, concentrating like a neurosurgeon about to make his first cut. He pulled the hair back from my face and tilted his head sideways.

I started to speak and Mom shushed me, watching Mr. Tony intently.

Finally he spoke. "Hello, my dears!" He stepped to Mom and kissed her on both cheeks. "Darling!" Mr. Tony said staring at Mom's face. "You look fantastic!

I rolled my eyes, and Mom glared at me.

Mr. Tony came back behind me and touched my hair again. "Lovely bone structure, just lovely. She's going to be a beauty."

What did that mean I was now? A beast? An embryo? And why was he talking about me as if I weren't even here?

"And lovely color to her hair," he added.

What color? I wondered. My hair was mouse brown as far as I could tell.

"See these gold highlights? You can't pay for that! That's God's work."

I peered into the mirror, where were the highlights?

Mr. Tony stared at me in the mirror then shook his head up and down like he just made a big decision. "Definitely a Pob!" he proclaimed.

What the hell was a "Pob?"

"What's a Pob?" asked Mom.

"A Posh bob!" said Mr. Tony. "You know, Posh Spice, a-k-a Victoria Beckham?"

He actually said a-k-a.

"*Very* chic, very flattering. Especially with this bone structure!"

I wouldn't mind being chic.

After an involved wash and condition by his assistant Mary (pronounced "Mair-AY," emphasis on the "ay") Mr. Tony went to work, gold scissors flashing. He hummed as he snipped and talked to himself. At least I think it was himself. "A little tip inward here. Hm mm, oh just lovely. And a bit of an angle here. No, make that more angled. And more tipped in I think. Yes! Yes!"

Then he turned the chair away from the mirror and went crazy with a blow dryer and a round brush. Then he snipped a bit more with the scissors and finally swung the chair back around to face the mirror.

I was not looking at Posh Spice. I was looking at Scary Spice. At Mushroom-head Spice. At Frumpy Housefrau Spice. "Tipped in" my ass! My hair was like a big bowl sitting on my head, the sides puffing out at least two inches before they "tipped" back under right at my ear level. I looked awful, ugly, beastly. I looked like I got the *Dumb and Dumber* special.

Well it was settled now. I could never go back to school. I hated Mom with every fiber in my ugly head. I hated Tony even more. I thought I might sneak back later tonight and blow up the salon.

"It's darling!" Mom said. "Sort of an updated Dorothy Hamill."

Dorothy Hamill? Are you kidding me? She was from, like, 100 years ago.

What kind of power did Tony have over her?

Tony smiled triumphantly.

I momentarily forgot the plan to keep Mom happy, and the assertive me that had been popping out at school came through. "It doesn't look like Posh Spice at all. And besides, she hasn't had a bob in forever. Or a Pob, or whatever."

Forget Pob, I had a POS, as in Piece Of Shit.

Mom gave me a dagger look. "Jock-*leen*! That isn't nice."

"It doesn't look like Posh," I said. "It's *puffy*."

Mr. Tony waved his hand. "You can straighten that out next time you dry it." He fluffed the sides a bit, making them stick out even more. "*Look* at that bone structure! This cut totally highlights those cheekbones."

*F*** the cheekbones.*

I couldn't wait to get out of there.

"My turn!" Mom said, popping out of her chair and into mine as I stood up.

I went to the waiting area and found a seat facing into a corner.

Rage bubbled up inside me. My life wasn't bad enough? Now I looked like an *idiot*. So much for being cute. What the heck was I going to do with my hair? I had no hope that washing and drying it again would help that much. I was staring into a wall of hair products, shelf after shelf of pomades and shampoos and conditioners. I walked over and started looking for something like "Mushroom-Be-Gone." I finally settled on a product that promised to smooth and straighten. I took it to the front desk and told them to put the forty-five dollar item on my Mom's bill.

I was sitting brooding when Mom came back to find me for our pedicures. She, of course, looked fantastic. No deranged Pob for her. Same classic shoulder-length with body and bounce.

Aside from "Mystique Pink" I didn't say a word during my pedicure. I was trying really hard not to spoil Mom's good mood, trying really hard not to lose sight of the whole Plan I had going. Too bad I had to look like such an idiot for her to be happy.

As I breathed shallowly to avoid inhaling the toxic smell of nail polish, I tried to remember that this was all Stealth, that I was strong inside and was acting weak just to get her happy again and back with Dad for real. And up until the *Dumb and Dumber* special it was kind of working, but right now I felt the force of the strangler fig all over again. I didn't feel strong at all. I felt weak. And angry. Not to mention *ugly*.

Sara spoke in my brain and reminded me of how she had sacrificed and about all the ways she maintained her dignity.

Claudia said that anyone who made fun of my hair was just a superficial idiot.

I could almost hear Nancy saying "Pshaw!"

Beryl laughed at the idea of a fancy haircut. Just throw a cap on and go do what you really love, like flying a plane. Being as we weren't allowed to wear hats in class, the cap wouldn't work for long. And I couldn't just go fly a plane or ride a racehorse. Come to think of it, what did I love like Beryl loved flying?

Reading.

Always back to that.

"Oh Jock-leen, that color is lovely on you!" Mom enthused.

I didn't answer. We walked back to the car, me in silence, her babbling on and on. I was barely listening until I heard the word "divorce."

"What was that?" I said, momentarily distracted from my awful haircut.

"I *said*, Mr. Tony was telling me all about Fern Libowitz. How she is divorced and has no money anymore! Can't even come for highlights. She is living in an *apartment.*"

Mom said "apartment" like it was a four letter word. She actually even whispered it, like it was a diagnosis of cancer or something.

"She is *working*. As a *house cleaner*!" Mom's eyes were wide and her head was shaking back and forth. "I could never. NEVER."

Mom got quiet until we were in the car. I knew exactly what she was thinking. She was thinking about how much she and Dad were fighting. She was thinking she would never live in an apartment and work cleaning houses. I didn't point out that she cleans our house for free. What would be so bad about getting paid for that???

I flipped down the mirror on the sun visor and was traumatized all over again by my hair. It made my face look fat and boring. Not that it had been so interesting before, but now I looked like the boy who pulled a plum out of the pie.

Little Jack(lin) Horner.

Mom looked over at me staring at myself. "It's cute! You're going to end up liking it."

How could she begin to think that? Her of the exquisite taste, at least when it came to herself.

At home I went straight to my room and worked on my hair. Washing it, conditioning it, blow drying it, using the new product on it, nothing made a difference. I tried a headband, barrettes, twisties, to no good end. It was too short for a pony tail and too puffy for words.

In frustration I flung myself down on the bed and failed at fighting off tears. Great, now I'd have alien eyes to match my ugly hair. Not that it mattered. It was Friday night, so I had all weekend to cry before people at school saw my alien eyes.

Time for Nancy Drew number two, *The Hidden Staircase.* It took longer than usual, but eventually I was driving my blue car around, exploring the mystery of Miss Flora and Aunt Rosemary's haunted house. I imagined tapping walls, looking for secret doors and poking around in a dusty attic. I imagined going to sleep in a house where strange noises came at odd times. I imagined that my only worry in life was trying to help Aunt Rosemary and her mother stay in their house. For a short, blessed time, hair didn't matter so much.

Chapter Thirty-Eight

Muffinhead

My haircut really really really stunk. I conditioned and straightened and did everything I could to flatten it, but here it was Monday morning, and I still looked like I had a big mushroom cap on my head. The best I could manage was to stick on a headband to hold some of it down. I cursed the person who decided hats "weren't acceptable in the classroom." *Must* have been a man, 'cause every girl knows there are days when a hat is the only sane way to leave the house.

I stared out the bus window at the brown slush being flung up by the churning wheels. Lovely. Take a beautiful thing like snow, trample it around, mix it with dirt and salt and it turns into something you can't wait to scrape off your boot. Kind of like life. I thought about pulling out *The Hidden Staircase* but couldn't even get excited about that.

A conversation in the seat behind me caught my attention.

"You tell her," a girl giggled.

"No, *you* tell her," another girl answered.

Oh great. Probably another rumor circulating about me. I turned around to look at them.

"Uh, hey," a girl in a purple knit cap said looking at me and then looking away and then back at me.

"Yes?" I said. I was trying not to be Superbitch, but I could feel her moving around inside my brain.

"Yeah, well, we just wanted to say that we think you are awesome," Purple Hat finally choked out.

The other girl had pale brown hair wisping around pudgy cheeks that were bright pink, either from the cold or excitement. "For sure! I can't believe you beat up Cassidy Dubroski!"

What? Now people think I am a bully?

"I didn't beat her up!"

"No, you did! We heard! I think it's even on YouTube! And it's *awe*some," said Purple Hat. "She is such a bee-yatch. She *totally* deserved it."

"I just pushed her, that's all."

Pink Cheeks looked at me adoringly. "Even if you just pushed her, that's amazing. How could you be so brave?"

"Yeah, I wish I could have been there," said Purple Hat. She punched at the air. "Pow! Cassidy goes down."

"Yeah only I didn't actually punch her," I said again. "Honestly, I just pushed her."

"Well whatever, it's time *someone* stood up to her," said Pink Cheeks. "You rock."

There didn't seem to be much to say after that. I turned around and stared unseeing ahead of me. I didn't know how to feel about this. On the one hand, it felt good to stand up to Cassidy, and apparently lots of people wished they could do the same. On the other hand, well maybe there wasn't another hand. Maybe it was just all good.

No, no, said Sara floating around my brain, gently insisting that there were more dignified ways of handling Cassidy. Nancy suggested the same thing. Yeah well Nancy and Sara both lived in a different time. Like the freaking 1900s. The *early* 1900s. Maybe these days a girl had to be more aggressive.

Maybe there came a time when fighting was the right thing to do.

That thought was confirmed when I arrived at my locker to find a pregnancy test box taped to the outside. It had my name written on it in big Sharpie black marker. I ripped it down and shoved it into my backpack as I heard giggles and whispers around me. Maybe they were laughing at the pregnancy test. Or maybe they were laughing at my hair. Amazing how many ways I could provide entertainment for this school.

Changing for gym, I decided to take charge of the whole hair thing. I had to have control over *something*, right?

"Hey Emily," I said in a loud voice. "What's up?"

Emily looked at me in surprise. I had broken the "don't talk to me" rule.

"Look at what that goofy Mr. Tony did to my hair!" I said, loud enough that it echoed off the lockers. I wanted the world to know that I wasn't deluded enough to think it looked good. "It's ruined!"

Two girls near me looked at me and nodded. It was the good kind of nod, a friendly agreement kind of nod.

"That sucks," said Emily, a little uncertainly.

"I mean, look how puffy it is!" I added.

One of the nodders said, "You should use a flat iron. You could *totally* straighten it."

The other nodder agreed. "Yeah, it wouldn't look that bad if it was just straight."

A flat iron? Probably everyone but me had one of those. Hmmmmmmm.

*****

"Jesus, what did you do to your hair?" Alex said staring at me.

It was lunch time and it had only been half a day, but I was really tired of the whole hair thing. I was once again sitting with Alex, Ben, Andy and Nick. They were all staring at my head. I rolled my eyes at Alex. "Don't *even*. It was my Mom's idea."

"Does she hate you?"

"Ha ha," I said but wondered for a second if he was right. Did she do this on purpose? As many things as I hated about Mom these days, I didn't think she'd make me look bad on purpose. Seeing as how I reflected on her and everything.

Alex stared at my hair some more, craning his head to look around the sides. "I guess it will grow again, right?"

Insecure Jacqueline went to war with New Tough Jacqueline inside my head. Part of me wanted to crumple up into a pile on the floor and just lay there until school was over and it was dark enough to crawl out without anyone seeing me. Part of me wanted to smack Alex and tell him how superficial it was to care so much how someone's hair looked.

"What's it to you?" I said. "It's just freaking *hair*."

Nick laughed. "Dude, most girls would stay home until it grew out."

"Jeez, what can I come up with for tomorrow?" I said, sarcasm flooding my entire being. "First it was my fake pregnancy, now my hair. What in the world can I give people to talk about tomorrow?"

"How about your new boyfriend?" said Andy, staring intently at me. He was leaning forward, his massive forearms making the table they rested on look flimsy. Didn't he realize I had a hair disaster of great proportion here? No one could possibly think I looked good. Or maybe the hint of sex, even made-up sex, kept a girl attractive.

New Tough Jackie disappeared. I was in over my head here. Luckily, I was saved by Melinda Barnes, Cassidy's latest Pom sidekick.

Melinda slipped between Nick and Ben and leaned over toward me. "Hey, Jackie, did you get the double blue lines? Are you pregnant, *again?*"

"Hey, Melinda, how do you know that the positive test is double blue lines?" I said back without missing a beat.

Melinda blushed. "I, I, I just heard, that's all," she stammered. The boys turned their laughter toward Melinda.

"Yeah, how *do* you know that?" said Nick.

Melinda flipped her hair in an attempt at bravado. "Uh, *hello?* Because I took the Pledge. All the Poms do." She gave me a smarmy wrinkled nose glare and stalked away.

I scurried after her and caught her arm. "Wait," I whispered looking around. I didn't need people listening in.

"What?"

"You don't need to be this way," I said, thinking of Nancy and how she talked to the prisoners in jail who had kidnapped her father. She had told them she knew sometimes people did things they shouldn't and convinced them to help her find her father. "I'll bet that wasn't like you at all to say that. I'll bet Cassidy put you up to it."

Melinda looked down.

I talked fast before she could pull away. "I don't know you, but I've seen what she does. She makes other people act mean, act mean in a way that isn't really them at all. Don't let her do that to you."

Melinda flashed me an uncertain look, and I walked back to my table.

Why did I care what happened to Melinda? Maybe I didn't. Maybe I cared what happened to me. Even if it was in response to bitchiness, I was *becoming* a bitch and didn't want to keep going. It felt good in the moment, but that was not who I wanted to be.

Once again Andy walked me to keyboarding.

"Are you sure you want to be seen with the Muffinhead?" I said.

Andy laughed and leaned in against my shoulder briefly. "Like you said, it's just freaking hair."

I wish he'd said it didn't look bad, but I guess I wouldn't have believed him anyway.

"So about this boyfriend thing. . ." Andy said and his voice lost its joking tone.

Ohmigod.

My insides were so stirred up by everything going on I couldn't think straight. But I was pretty sure I wasn't interested in Andy as a boyfriend. Which took me by surprise because he was cute, in a Neanderthal kind of way. And he was popular. But the jury was still out on his motives.

Who *was* I interested in? I almost couldn't let my mind go there. There was that buzzing down the middle of my body when I was around Alex. And there was also that easy comfort around Tommy. And . . .

"Earth to Jackie," Andy said.

"Oh, what? Sorry," I said. "I think Mr. Tony cut out part of my brain too. Hey, here we are!" I scuttled to the keyboarding class door. "See ya!"

Walking through the door I saw Kelly Munson and Sandra Bonita look at me, put their heads together and start giggling.

"I *know*," I said loudly to the class. "My hair looks like crap. Get over it."

"It looks fine," said a voice behind me.

I turned around to see Melody smiling broadly at me.

"Hey," I said.

We found seats together. "Hey, do you have a flat iron?" I asked as the teacher started rapping on her desk for attention.

"No, but Tricia does. She's *great* at doing hair."

"Hmm, you know, Tricia doesn't seem to like me," I said. "Maybe you could just borrow the flat iron, not really tell her who it's for?"

"Don't worry," Melody assured me. "I got it."

Chapter Thirty-Nine

Cinderella

Mom vetoed my idea of going to Melody's after school. She needed me to watch Davy while she went to play tennis. On the one hand, it sucked that I was the constant babysitter whenever she needed one. On the other hand, I was glad she was playing tennis instead of lying around the house like a sack of sand. Depressed people don't play tennis, right?

Melody said she could come to my house instead of me coming to hers. Once again, a two hand issue. On the one hand, I was happy to have her back as a friend, and she was going to try to fix my hair. On the other hand, I was embarrassed for her to see our big house. Kentley didn't really have a ghetto, but I knew that Melody lived in the less affluent part of town. "Sure," I agreed, hair and friendship winning out. Melody said she'd find Tricia, get her flat iron and then get a ride over.

I checked on Davy in the playroom and then went to my room to write in my diary.

Yikes! I had left it lying in full view on my desk. If Mom ever read this, the solar system would implode from her anger.

The doorbell rang, and when I opened the front door, I was surprised to see Tricia with Melody.

"Hey," said Tricia as she brushed past me. *Miss Manners.*

"Hi," said Melody, holding back before coming in. "Tricia drove me over and . . ."

"Come on in," I said to Melody. "Hi, Tricia."

Tricia was already peering around the foyer, looking up the big staircase and down the long hall to the kitchen. This time she had paired the painted on jeans with high black biker boots and a maroon down jacket. Her long dark hair stuck out of a green knit Rasta hat.

Melody awkwardly tried to brush snow off the bottom of her crutches and feet.

"Don't worry about it," I said.

Tricia held up a black bag. "Where do you want to do this?"

"What?" I said.

"You know, the flat iron."

"Oh, right!" I said. I was trying not to let myself believe it might actually work. It would be too disappointing when it didn't. "Uh, maybe the bathroom down here?"

I peeked into the powder room. "No, no room for Melody to sit down."

"We can go to your room," said Melody looking up the stairs with interest. "I can go upstairs okay."

I carried Melody's crutches, and she hopped her way up, leaning against the railing for stability. I motioned them to my room. "I'm going to check on my brother real quick. I'll be right back."

Davy was absorbed in coloring, all ninety-six colors scattered around him on the table. I made my way back toward my room, and as I neared my door, I slowed down and listened in.

"Must be nice," I heard Tricia say in a sarcastic voice. "Did you see that bathroom? Christ, it's all hers."

"I know, and look at this bed! It is so pretty," said Melody.

Should I pretend I didn't hear them? Or say something? The old Jacqueline would have lived in denial.

I walked in my room. "I know!" I said to Melody. "I love my bed too. It's crazy, though, this house, isn't it?"

"You're telling me it's crazy," said Tricia, pulling open my closets and peeking in.

What if I just said what was crazy before someone else could?

"It's kind of embarrassing," I said. "I mean, I didn't do anything to earn this place.

"Melody, we must have been criminals in our past lives," said Tricia. "That's why we don't get to live in a crib like this."

Melody shrugged. "Whatever."

"I think I must have murdered people," said Tricia, getting into the whole past life idea. "Maybe I was Ivan the Terrible."

From the amount of makeup on her face, I'd say she'd been Bobo the clown.

"I think I was Calamity Jane," said Melody, gesturing to her leg.

"You know what I always wondered?" I said. "How come everyone with a past life was someone famous? I mean, if there is such a thing, there had to be peasants and workers and all that, you know?"

"Yeah, well, I guess *you* put in your time," said Tricia. "Because now you get to live in Nirvana."

Yeah, my life is totally Nirvana.

"Let's try this flat iron thing," I said. Enough about my great life.

I sat on a stool in the bathroom while Tricia unpacked her bag. Out came a flat iron, two brushes and a collection of hair products. Tricia was clearly running the show, and that was fine with me. If I tried to flat iron my hair myself, I'd probably burn it all off. Or inadvertently brand myself.

Tricia sprayed something all over my head, then clipped my hair back in sections and went to work. She took one small section at a time and ran the iron over it, pulling tightly the whole way down. The smell of burnt hair made me nervous, but what could be worse than mushroom head?

Tricia spun me around, facing away from the mirror. "Don't worry," she snapped.

Melody nodded from her spot on the floor of my room. She was lying down facing the bathroom with her leg propped on a pillow. She had on pink velour sweatpants and a matching sweatshirt that she kept tugging down over her stomach. "Don't worry is right. Tricia is a master. She can do anything with hair."

"I'm going to cosmetology school next year," said Tricia. "I'm going to open my own salon."

"Well don't give anyone a Pob," I said.

"What's a Pob?" asked Melody.

"A Posh Spice bob," answered Tricia. Point for Tricia knowing what a Pob was. "Not that she's had that style in eons. It's a cool look, but I never would have tried it on your hair Jackie. Too thick. Plus he didn't cut the layers right. Posh had more angle to her cut. He gave you the suburban mom version."

Maybe Tricia did know something about hair.

"What would *you* do with my hair?" I asked her.

Tricia stepped in front of me, narrowed her eyes, and stared at me for like two minutes. I felt like a virus under a microscope because it wasn't exactly a kind stare. Finally she spoke. "Well I wouldn't do an outdated cut. The Pob is so over. I'd let it grow maybe two more inches, cut it straight across the bottom, then I'd do some long bangs, just a fringe really. I'd add a few honey highlights, not blond really, just a couple shades lighter than your hair color now. A sort of Jennifer Lopez-like color. Then, if I had all the money in the world . ." She glanced around the room and opened her eyes wide to point out that maybe I did. "I'd get the Japanese straightening. Or the Brazilian, it's good too."

Just then, Davy came running into my room, Batman cape flowing. He wore the suit every day and it was starting to fray, not to mention smell bad.

"Hey dude," said Tricia. "Whassup?"

People responded to Batman, I'll tell you.

"Jackie, I had an accident," Davy said. He pulled to a stop and stared at Tricia and Melody. I guess he didn't hear them come in. He ran back out of the room.

"I need to help him a second," I said and ran after him, hair half pinned up on my head.

Poor Davy. Five years old and suddenly he was having accidents. He was wetting the bed two or three times a week now. I didn't want to tell Mom, but I was starting to wonder if this was a problem that wasn't going to go away. It didn't take a genius to figure out the tension around the house must be affecting him. I helped him into some new clothes and threw the Batman suit in the washing machine. That thing was not going to survive many more washings.

I gave him a handful of M&M's and stuck in a video with six *Go, Diego, Go!* episodes on it hoping he wouldn't complain about me going back to Tricia and Melody.

"No, no, I want SpongeBob," Davy said.

"Fine," I said, switching back to the TV.

I slid back onto the stool in my bathroom. "What's Japanese straightening?" I had to know. It sounded intriguing.

"It's this six hour process where they put all this shit on your hair and, in the end, your hair is silky and straight. No matter how often you shampoo and everything. You don't have to straighten it yourself at all. And it lasts like six months. But it costs the bomb."

Tricia stepped back in front of me and looked at me. "Yeah, you'd look great in it. Who am I kidding? We all would. But *you* could probably afford it."

"How much does it cost?"

"Like eight hundred dollars."

Melody sucked in air. "Holy cow! That's like, a *car*."

My hopes fell. No way could I talk my parents into that.

"So, you popped Cassidy Dubroski, huh?" said Tricia, yanking so hard on the hair on the back of my head I was pulled almost horizontal.

"No! Why does everyone think I hit her? I just pushed her."

"Cool. She had it coming," said Tricia.

Melody nodded. "I can't believe how mean she is."

"Someone should pop her one every day, if you ask me," said Tricia. She picked up a pair of small scissors. "That man totally butchered you. Let me shape it a little."

"No!" I squealed. "It's short enough."

"I just want to angle it, you know, shorter to longer around your face. It'll look good." Tricia seemed so confident that when she started snipping I didn't stop her.

"You know, she's the kind that if you heard her boyfriend hit her, you'd almost understand," said Melody.

"No one deserves that," I protested. Then I thought of Ben and how Cassidy was telling everyone he forced her to do sexual stuff. I could understand if he wanted to hit her. Not that he would.

Tricia worked her way from the left side of my hair, around the back, finishing on the right. Then she stood back, stared, and nodded to herself. Finally, she picked up a tube of something, squirted some in her hands, rubbed her hands together and then smoothed it through my hair.

"Okay, I'm done," said Tricia, spinning me back around toward the mirror.

I was speechless. This time out of joy.

The mushroom was gone. My hair was straight and sleek looking. I flipped my head around and the hair slid back and forth and then fell back into place. I couldn't understand how shortening the back helped, but it did make the front look longer and kind of edgy. It felt light and airy and, for the first time ever, stylish.

"Wow." I didn't know what else to say. I kept staring at myself because I had morphed from *Dumb and Dumber* into something almost cute. Who knew what hair could do to a face?

"That's kind of what Japanese straightening would do, except that it would be shinier and last a lot longer. This will only last until you wash it again," said Tricia.

"You're a genius!" I said, forgetting how prickly Tricia was, how judgmental, how much she seemed to dislike me. Right now I loved her to death.

Tricia smiled in a sheepish way and, before her normal scowl came back, I had a glimpse of the person who cared so much about Melody.

"Ooh, you look awesome," said Melody, then she turned toward Tricia. "Can I be next?"

"Sure," said Tricia. "I've been telling you forever that you should let me flat iron your hair."

"I was scared," Melody said to me. "I was afraid she'd burn it off. But look at you!"

I thought you said Tricia was a master?

While Tricia worked on Melody, I looked at myself in the mirror from every angle. Tricia slid me a bag of makeup. "Come into the twenty-first century and put a little of this on."

I pulled open a drawer. "Oh, I have some makeup. My mom bought it for me, I just never really tried it." I hadn't tried it because Mom wanted me to so badly. I hadn't wanted to be a miniature version of her. Plus, I really wasn't sure how to use it.

"Mine, yours, whatever, put some on," commanded Tricia.

I tried a little lip gloss, which looked nice. I added some mascara, managing to smear it on the top of my eyelid and near my nose. I brushed on a little pink to my cheeks. Wow. I looked like an actual girl.

I stared in the mirror and ran my hand over my hair. It was so sleek and shiny. Then, panic. "How will I do this myself?"

Tricia gave me a "you are an idiot" look. "Buy a freaking flat iron."

"I know, but I mean, I don't know how to use it, and I don't have one yet, and I don't know when I can get to the mall to buy one."

Tricia rolled her eyes. "I can lend you mine for two days. TWO days, then I need it back. Capeesh?"

Even after Tricia and Melody left I kept wandering into bathrooms to look in the mirror. It's an odd feeling to look different, and yet staring at the new me felt familiar too. Like maybe my outside was starting to match up with all the new stuff that had been happening inside.

Chapter Forty

Paradise Lost

Tucked away in my reading nook, I felt the hot Florida sun on my shoulders. I smelled the fresh pine forest and felt the churning of my legs as I ran through the Florida scrubland. For the moment I was Jody, a twelve-year-old boy living in rural Florida and now I was lying face down by the stream in the Glen, waking up to a light rain on my back.

Mom was out at dinner celebrating her tennis group's win, Dad was working late, Davy was fed and pajama'ed, and I let myself fall deeper and deeper into the world of my new book. I was taking a break from Nancy Drew to read a book assignment for school. And I hated to admit that I kind of was glad to take that break. I still liked the Nancy Drew stories, but they weren't giving me as much inspiration as they had in the past. Maybe things worked out a little too easily for Nancy. Nothing was working out easily for me. And I could already tell I was going to like *The Yearling*.

It had taken a few chapters to get used to the cornpone language, but now I didn't even notice it. Jody's world was so completely different than mine that it was like traveling to a distant country, or even another planet. As I read, I felt my bunched-up muscles slowly ease apart. I felt anxiety draining away like dirty dishwater and without losing the thread of the story had the thought that this must be how drug addicts feel.

Jody's runty, uneducated father would be the target of total ridicule at my school, and yet I could tell he makes Jody feel so completely loved and protected. I couldn't believe it, but I was jealous of Jody! Jealous of an ugly, poor kid who lives miles from anyone but his mother and father. Jody can count on his dad. There was no doubt about that.

And I was jealous of Jody's ability to find such pleasure in the world around him. He loves the sun through the fir trees, the nuzzling of his pet fawn Flag and the chance to lie down by the sinkhole instead of hoeing the corn. I wished I lived somewhere as beautiful as Jody, and then it hit me that Jody is someone who would find beauty anywhere. Jody would probably be crazy about the snow outside my window, and as delighted with the bare trees in winter as he is at their full leafiness in summer. Jody carries around an ability to find pleasure in the world around him, wherever that world might be.

Maybe I could do more of that. Here was another Desired Characteristic for sure. What should I call it? Nature lover? Not quite. Pleasure in the small things – too long. Gratitude? Closer but not exactly it. An Eye for Pleasure? Maybe. Appreciation. Maybe that was closest. I wondered how much I had missed from lack of looking. Okay, I was adding Appreciation, meaning noticing the good stuff. No better time than now to notice pleasure, I can tell you that.

As I felt myself slipping into sleep, I imagined how Jody might feel in my place, snuggled down under warm, soft blankets, secure in my spacious room. He would probably be amazed at the smoothness of the pillow, and the cozy heavy quilt piled over me. Seeing through Jody's eyes I felt so pleased with my little cocoon, I could have stayed in it forever. Mean Girl Barbies and pregnancy rumors and unstable parents seemed far away.

I was torn out of sleep by Mom shaking me. "Jock-leen, wake up this instant!"

"Hmm, what?" I said. I could barely open my eyes but finally noticed that the clock said eleven fifty-four and my little lamp had been turned on. Then I noticed Dad standing next to Mom. Then I noticed both of them looking at me like I had committed a major crime and the police were waiting for me downstairs.

"What?" I said, sitting up.

Mom turned on the overhead lights in my room and stood in front of me holding out the pregnancy test kit box. "What is *this*!?"

Dad looked sad, uncomfortable and irritated all at the same time. Like this was one of those parenting moments that had to be faced, but why did it have to be right now?

I felt like Cinderella after midnight. I went to sleep feeling beautiful and was woken up to ugly reality.

"Oh that," I said, forcing a laugh. "That was a joke."

"You expect us to believe that?" Mom said. She sat down on the bed. "What kind of *joke* is a pregnancy test? What is going on? Do you have a boyfriend? Or are you just having random sex with people?"

"Oh please," I said. Did she know me at all? How could she begin to think those things? "I told you, it was a mean joke. Cassidy Dubroski did it."

Dad's eyes opened wide. Maybe I had a chance at him believing me.

"Cassidy Dubroski? Why would she do such a thing?" Mom said, sounding like she didn't believe a word.

"Because she hates me. Because her dad hates Dad. Because she's a bitch. Take your pick," I said.

"Don't get flippant with me, missy," barked Mom. "You really expect me to believe that?"

"Cassidy is a big abstinence promoter. She was handing out pamphlets and telling people I had to leave my last school because I was pregnant and that they better be careful or it will happen to them. Then she taped this on my locker."

Mom stared at me. Dad made a sad grimace. He could believe it only too well, I could see it in his face.

"That's ridiculous," said Mom.

"No, it's not," said Dad, unexpectedly weighting in. "It's exactly what a Dubroski would do."

Mom spun her head toward him. "You're taking her side?"

"Well, I can see how it might have happened that way," said Dad.

"Mom, just look at the box. It has my name on it. Why in the world would I write my own name on the box?"

Mom looked down at the box. Then she looked back at me. "Okay, Jock-leen," she said in a measured voice. "I'm going to give you one more chance to be honest with us. Are you sexually active?"

I burst out laughing. Partly because it was so silly, partly out of nervousness. For someone who had never even been kissed, I was doing a lot of talking about my sex life.

"Do you think that it's funny?" Mom demanded.

"No. Yes. It's just crazy," I said. "I can't believe we're talking about this. I am not sexually active. I don't have a boyfriend. I never have."

Mom gasped and covered her mouth with her hand. "Don't tell me you have a girlfriend! Don't tell me you are like *that*."

"Mom, listen to yourself. On one hand you think I'm taking pregnancy tests, on the other hand you're asking if I'm lesbian. Make up your mind."

Dad gave a snort of laughter, which he cut short when Mom shot him a glare.

I flopped back against my pillows. Defending yourself is draining.

"You know, instead of yelling at me, maybe you could feel sorry for me. You know, show a little compassion for how crappy I get treated at school."

Dad nodded. "Jackie," he started and then stopped. He shook his head. "Jackie, I'm sorry. I really am. This is all my fault."

"What?!" Mom looked at Dad incredulously. "How is this *your* fault?"

"Because Dubroski is mad at me, and he must be passing that on to his daughter. Poor Jackie here is the innocent victim."

"Huh, how you can call someone with a pregnancy test in her backpack innocent is beyond me," said Mom.

"Yeah, and by the way, why were you in my backpack anyway?"

"Your phone was ringing."

"And? You were going to answer it or some other intrusive thing?"

"I was going to turn it off. And don't speak to me that way." Mom turned to Dad again. "Tell her not to speak to me that way."

Dad looked stuck. Like he wanted to defend me but knew he should present a united front with Mom. I thought about Jody from *The Yearling* and how he and his dad were so close and how he had to be respectful to his mother even when he didn't want to.

"I'm sorry I spoke to you that way, Mom," I said. I couldn't let them get any more divided. As much as I liked having Dad's support. Come to think of it, Dad and I were a little like Jody and his dad. Facing common enemies, tolerating a difficult mother. That made me feel secretly better.

"You better be sorry." Mom stood up. "And don't think this is over. Your father and I are going to discuss this, and we will talk about it more in the morning."

Something to look forward to.

In the morning to please Mom, I put on another ridiculous looking shirt. This one was bright red with ruffles along its crisscrossed front. I wore a plain white T-shirt under it, and stuck the gray hoodie in my bag. First thing at school I'd take off the crisscrossing, ruffly thing and just wear the hoodie and t-shirt. I grabbed the necklace mom had bought to go with the shirt, a silver chain with several discs of translucent colors hanging from it. Dark red, pink, and silver. Not too "matchy" as she had put it, but it picked up the red.

I look like a teenage version of my mother.

To take my mind off of the stupid shirt, I reminded myself to be like Jody and notice the beauty and pleasures of the world around me. Maybe that would distract me from the hell that was my life. And getting into the spirit of Appreciation, my hair still looked awesome. And Melody was back as a friend. And the hottie boys at school seemed to have taken me under their wing. So now I just had to get my Mom over her depression, save Dad's job, and deflect Cassidy's hatred toward something else. Hey, maybe I could get her to picket abortion clinics or something. Those people seemed to be obsessed and have little time for other things.

"Jock-leen, you have an appointment next month with Dr. Lewis." Mom was serving Davy pancakes while I stared into my bowl of cereal. The kitchen smelled pleasantly of the vanilla scent of the pancakes cooking.

"Who is Dr. Lewis?"

"My gynecologist. I don't like it, but you're going to have to be examined if you are going to be doing. . . these things."

Eewww.

"Jeez! Mom, I'm not doing anything! I really don't need an exam. I really don't *want* an exam."

"What's a gynorologist?" asked Davy.

"Nothing," Mom said to Davy and then turned to me. "Too bad. If we are at the point where I can't even believe you, then we better do the safe thing. I just wish she had an opening sooner."

Mom looked at me more closely. "Do you have on makeup?"

"Just a little," I said.

She raised her eyes. "It looks nice. I've been telling you to show off those eyes!"

Dad walked into the kitchen.

"Hi, dear," Mom said in a sweet voice. How could she do that? Change her whole personality so fast? "Your coffee is already in the mug."

"Thank-you," Dad said, giving Mom a brief smile. He leaned over the counter and snagged the newspaper.

"I told Jock-leen about the appointment," Mom said to Dad.

Dad gave me an uncomfortable look. He and I both knew Mom was acting crazy. But they seemed to have some sort of teamwork vibe going, and I guessed I could sacrifice for that. I kept my mouth shut. When Dad wasn't around I'd find some way out of it.

"Daddy, can you come home early tonight?" Davy said, syrup dripping down his chin.

"We'll have to see," said Dad.

"You never play with me," said Davy.

"Yes, I do," said Dad, flipping through the newspaper, not even looking at Davy.

"No you don't!" yelled Davy, all of a sudden in a rage. "You say you will but then you don't!" He jumped up and ran at Dad full tilt, Batman cape flying out behind him. Before Dad could react Davy buried his syrupy face in Dad's pants and dug his buttery hands around his waist.

"No, no! Wait!" said Mom, but it was too late. Davy pulled back to look up at Dad and we all could see the shiny syrup clinging to Dad's dark pants.

"Davy, you ruined Dad's pants!" said Mom. And we are back to Bitchy Barbie.

Davy burst into tears. "I'm sorry Dada," he wailed, lapsing into his baby version of Dad's name.

"Shit," said Dad looking down. Mom ran at him with a wet dishtowel and wiped at his pants.

"I can get it out, don't worry. It's fine," said Mom.

"Daddy said a bad word," Davy said, still crying.

Mom patted Dad with a dry towel. "Look you can't see a thing."

Dad ran his hand over the spots then looked at his watch. "I better change," he said, sprinting out of the kitchen.

Davy started after him crying, "I'm sorry! I'm sorry!" Mom grabbed Davy and pulled him back into the kitchen. "Don't bother him!"

Davy was still crying when I left for the bus.

Just another peaceful start to the day for the Carson family.

Chapter Forty-One

Double Exposure

For once, the sun was actually out as I walked to the bus stop. It was a weak December sun that gave off no heat, but at least my hair wouldn't get snowed on.

I tried to use my Appreciation while riding to school. I noticed that the arch of the bare branches of the trees lining the road was kind of graceful. And most of the houses had their Christmas decorations up, I always loved seeing those. We passed a church with stained glass windows that looked like they came from Europe. I hadn't paid attention to those in a while. I loved the intricate patterns and the fact that you could make art with glass. And at least the bus was warm, and I had sleek hair. By the time I reached school I wasn't exactly Suzy Sunshine, but I wasn't Stressy Samantha either. Amazing how much good stuff I ignore every day.

I headed toward my locker feeling anxious. What new horror awaited me there? Imagine my relief when I saw it unadorned by pregnancy kits or slurs. Definitely could Appreciate a blank locker. As I got closer, I noticed Tommy leaning against the wall nearby.

"Hey," I said, whizzing through my combination and opening up the locker. I dumped my coat and backpack and pulled out a notebook.

"Hi," said Tommy, standing up. "What's going on?"

"What are you doing? Guarding my locker?" I asked.

Tommy shrugged. I had been joking, but the look on his face made me think maybe that was exactly what he was doing. Then I remembered how he'd been waiting here for me yesterday morning too.

"Nah, just waiting for you. Thought you might have something interesting to tell me about. You know, stuff always seems to be happening to you."

"Yeah, well, my parents found the pregnancy test and my Mom doesn't believe it was a joke."

Tommy fell into step with me and shook his head. "Moms don't get anything."

"Tell me about it."

He looked at me again. "Hey, your hair looks good. What'd you do?"

"Thanks. I flat ironed it."

We passed Jennifer Walker, and she stopped in her tracks then zipped over to me.

"Jacqueline, your hair looks so amazing! You look adorable!" Jennifer bubbled.

Was she speaking to me in public?

"Thanks," I said. I ran my hand around the back and sides as I turned my head. "I can't believe what a flat iron can do."

Jennifer nodded vigorously. "Totally!"

"What's going on?!" a loud voice said behind Jennifer. Cassidy popped over Jennifer's shoulder. "Are you talking to *her?!*"

Jennifer jumped, like a spider had landed on her back. "Uh, yeah, no." Then Jennifer looked straight at Cassidy. "Actually, yeah, I am."

Cassidy looked at me like she was about to spit in my face. Tommy stepped a little closer to me. "What's up, Cassidy?" he said easily.

"Stay out of this!" Cassidy snapped at him. She turned to Jennifer. "What are you doing?"

Jennifer shrugged. "I was just telling Jacqueline that she looks good."

Wow. Jennifer taking a stand. Who would have thought it?

"Huh!" breathed Cassidy huffily as she whirled around and stomped off.

"Welcome to the dark side," I said to Jennifer and we both giggled. Nervously.

Tommy threw his arm around my shoulder. "Dude, she totally hates you!" he said laughing.

Yeah, what a joke.

On the other hand, Tommy was not a joke. He headed down a different hall to make it to class, and as I watched him go I thought about what a good guy he was. He had waited at my locker and maybe even prevented more vandalism. And then he had stood protectively by me when Cassidy came up. Pink and wide was kind of growing on me. Not in the Alex category of looks, but still. Not bad.

"Hey, you flat ironed!" said girl number one from the locker room as I changed for PE.

"Yeah, it looks great," said girl number two.

"Thanks," I said. "And thanks for suggesting it."

Emily wandered closer to me. "It does look good! How did you figure out how to do it?"

"Melody and her friend Tricia came over. Tricia's a genius at hair."

Emily dropped her eyes to the floor. "Oh."

Funny that I felt disloyal to Emily saying that. Like she hadn't totally ignored me and followed Miss Priss around like a little lap dog. I pushed the feeling aside and went into the gym.

Mr. Donovan stared at me, then smiled. "Looking good, Carson!" he said, his voice as greasy as his hair.

Gross. Maybe I'll lose the makeup.

You know what that made me wonder about? How creepy it would be to be one of those girls in Playboy. Not that I have that kind of body, but think about all the weirdos and creeps who stare at them and have sicko fantasies. I didn't even like Donovan looking at my *hair* for crying out loud. How did those girls handle millions of strangers looking at their bodies? Not enough money in the world, if you ask me.

On my way to lunch, I heard a voice behind me.

"Hey, Jacqueline." I looked back to see Sandra Bonita, from keyboarding, smiling at me. "You look awesome," Sandra said.

"Uh, thanks," I said. Was she just waiting for me to look good to talk to me?

"I hear you're dating Andy Primanti. He's *so* cute!" Sandra tilted her head to the side and sighed. "I've had a crush on him forever. How did you do it?"

How did I do what?

"I didn't do anything," I said. "I'm not dating him. I walked with him like two times in the hall."

Sandra's eyes lit up. "Really? You're not? So he's available?"

I shrugged. "He's not with me. I don't know about anyone else."

But maybe he'll walk with you if he thinks you're easy.

I headed toward the lunchroom, hoping I wouldn't see Andy. Then again, Alex would be there too. I got a warm little rush just thinking about Alex. Wait a minute, hadn't I been feeling kind of something for Tommy earlier? What was wrong with me? Maybe I was boy crazy. Maybe the whole sex in the air thing was affecting me too.

The last three classes of the day used to be my favorites because Emily was in all of them. Chemistry, geometry then study hall. Now they were miserable for the same reason. I got to chemistry too late to get a front seat. I sat on the opposite side of the class from the Cassidy-Emily-Alex club and felt a stab of horror as Chuckie slimed his way into a seat next to me with a sick leer on his face. I had managed to avoid him all this time since the . . . exposure. How had I let this happen?

Crap. Chuckie was on my left, meaning I had to look sort of his direction to watch Mr. Redmond in the front.

I kept my eyes focused on Mr. Redmond like a laser. I could feel Chuckie's perverted energy beside me, but I refused to look at him. And then it happened. I let my eyes drop somehow, and there was Chuckie, book propped in his lap, zipper down again with his unmentionable hanging out. Again.

"Put that thing away," I heard a cool, calm voice say.

It was me!

Mr. Redmond stopped talking and looked at me. I pointed at Chuckie who was fumbling with his zipper and the gesture of swinging my hand out to point bumped into Chuckie's book. The book fell to the floor and there was the worst of Chuckie hanging out for the whole class to see.

"Eeeewwww!" Tanya Martin screamed from the other side of Chuckie.

The rest of the girls seemed to have the same reaction. Lots of screams and yelling. Lots of laughter from the boys. Within seconds everyone who couldn't see what was going on was standing and peering over the shoulders and backs of those around Chuckie.

Mr. Redmond was at Chuckie's desk in a blink. Chuckie had managed to shove his penis back in his pants but couldn't get the zipper up. It was pretty obvious what was going on.

"What the hell are you doing?" Mr. Redmond yelled at Chuckie.

"He had his *thing* out!" screamed Tanya. "It was disgusting! Get him out of here!"

Mr. Redmond grabbed Chuckie by the back of the shirt and hauled him up out of his seat. "What are you doing?" he demanded again.

"Nothin," mumbled Chuckie.

Mr. R. looked at me. "Did he really . . . ? Is that what you saw?"

I nodded. "Unfortunately, yes," I said, as calm under pressure as Sara or Beryl might have been. "And it's not the first time."

Mr. Redmond yanked Chuckie up the aisle and out the door. The class burst into loud discussion. People sitting near Chuckie repeated what they saw over and over. Girls screamed every time. Cassidy looked like she might throw up.

Alex slid into the seat vacated by Chuckie. "So Chuckie really had his pecker out?"

I nodded. "Yeah, second time he's done that to me. What a little jerk."

"Man, that's bold," said Alex shaking his head with a smile.

"It's gross!" I said. "It's not funny."

"I know, I know," said Alex. "And you were so calm! 'Put that thing away.' How'd you think of that?" Alex's eyes were staring straight into mine. There was genuine admiration there. My stomach fluttered. How could I be so calm and cool with Chuckie and feel so hot and bothered by Alex?

I looked away and shrugged, not trusting my voice. Then my eyes found their way back to Alex's. More fluttering but I held my stare as my insides got hot and melty.

He smiled again.

I smiled back.

It was a good moment.

I felt a friendly punch against my shoulder while I waited for the bus. I turned around to see Tommy, bundled into a down ski jacket, cheeks even pinker than usual from the cold.
"Did you really say 'put that thing away' to Chuckie?" Tommy asked, a big grin on his face.
I nodded. I was enjoying the fact that for once I actually had the right words at the right time and *said* them. On the other hand, I was still super-skeezed out by the thought of Chuckie.
Tommy playfully punched my shoulder again. "Way to go. What a perv."
"Tell me about it. He can't seem to keep his zipper up."
"And Cassidy was in there?" Tommy said, laughing. "Man I wish I could have seen *her* face. Miss Priss."
"Yeah, she looked kind of sick."
"I think she's allergic to those things," Tommy added.
I snorted with laughter, but truth was, I thought I was too.
"And to you," he finished.
"Yeah, I know," I said as I saw my bus move up in the line. "Gotta go."
"Catch you later," Tommy laughed.
I'll give him this, the boy was way cheerful.

Chapter Forty-Two

A Different Kind of Wilderness

At home in the library my hands were shelving books, but my brain couldn't stop going over the scene with Chuckie. I couldn't believe I had finally opened my mouth! I finally said one of the things that seemed so witty in my head and let it fly. And it had worked! Maybe I *was* a secret hero of some sort. Maybe I really was a princess. Maybe I was strong like Jody and his father Penny, someone who could survive and take care of myself.

Then Queen Gloomy came in and dropped into one of the leather chairs.

Mom gave a deep sigh and let her head fall back against the top of the chair. "I'm just so tired," she said, closing her eyes.

Maybe it was the Chuckie triumph still coursing through my body, maybe it was the surrounding comfort of the books and the cavelike feeling of the library, but I found myself unable to agree with her little lie. I knew it was more than being tired.

"You must miss Aunt Helen so much," I said.

Mom's eyes popped open. "What?"

I took a deep breath. "I said, you must miss Aunt Helen so much."

"This is not about Aunt Helen!" Mom screeched. "I said I was tired! I can't even get a little sympathy for how hard I work?"

"I know you do, I know you get tired," I said. "I just thought, you know, you probably miss her and we never talk about her and sometimes I just wonder, about it all."

Mom jumped up. "Why does everything always have to be about *her!?* Isn't it possible that this is just about *me?*"

"I was trying to be supportive, sorry," I said. "I just figured you must get sad but you never say. . ."

Mom rolled her eyes. "Thanks, Miss Psychologist. How about you let *me* tell you what I feel?"

The topic was out there, and I couldn't let it go.

"It's just that I *wonder*," I said. "I want to know about Aunt Helen, I really do."

"Stop it!" Mom screamed. "Stop it!" She put her hands over her ears like a four-year-old and stormed out of the room.

That went well.

A few minutes later the door flew open again.

"What the hell did you just say to your mother?" Dad asked, his voice tight and high, his tall frame filling the doorway.

"Nothing," I said. "I mean, she said she was tired and I just asked her if she missed Aunt Helen.

Dad came in, shutting the door behind him. Deep sigh. "What is it with you and Aunt Helen? Just leave it alone!"

"Why? Why can't we talk about her?"

Dad sunk into the same chair mom had been in. "Look, Jackie, I'm stretched to my limit with work, okay? It is taking every waking moment, every bit of my energy. And I'm sorry, and that will get better, but for right now I can't fight a war on two fronts, okay? Please just keep things calm around here until I get through this work stuff. I can't deal with your mother being this upset too."

I looked down at the book in my hands. Betty Crocker's cookbook. Oh, if life were really that simple. How to make the perfect pie crust.

Every bit of my life with my parents told me to agree with him. Agree. Go along. Keep the peace. But I kept thinking of sitting in this very room, feeling a connection across time and space and reality to the Little Prince, knowing so deep in my bones that we couldn't just ignore the whole Aunt Helen thing. It felt like a festering wound, deep in the bones of the family, like the venom that almost killed Jody's father. Only Penny's quick thinking at using the deer liver to suck out the venom managed to save his life. I need some way to get the venom out of the family.

"I know Dad, I know work is tough. But I think Mom needs to talk about Aunt Helen. It can't be right to just pretend she didn't live, to pretend it all didn't happen. That just doesn't seem right."

"We're not pretending all that," said Dad, running his hand through his hair.

Yes you are.

"This is just not a good time. Okay?" Dad leaned forward, towards me on my spot on the floor. "Just for now, please don't bother your mother with this, please?"

What could I say? When a reasonable, loving Dad, a Dad in charge of thousands of people, a Dad who could convince anyone of anything, looked at you like that you had no chance.

My turn to sigh. "Fine," I said, feeling torn up inside. How could this be going so wrong? It was the opposite of how things turned out with Chuckie. When I ignored it, things just got worse. When I spoke up, better. How come that principle wasn't working at home?

Dad left, but I couldn't keep working on the books. They'd have to wait even longer. I went up to my room, grabbed *The Yearling* and disappeared.

I was deep in the woods of Florida at the part of the book where wolves attack the animals in Jody's barnyard. His dad has to leave to go meet other men to decide how to get rid of the wolves, leaving Jody home to protect his mother. I couldn't imagine ever protecting someone from wolves, and Jody is doing it at age *twelve*. Then again, maybe that was exactly what I needed to do, considering how the adults in my house were behaving. Maybe it was just my time to grow up, like Jody had to grow up.

This thought was confirmed when I heard doors slamming and Mom and Dad yelling. Then Davy appeared in my room, clutching his Pooh bear, his face wrinkled in fear.

"Can I sleep in your bed, Jackie?" he said, his eyes squinting at the bright light in my room.

Another door slam.

"Sure," I said, quickly closing my own door and turning out the overhead lights. I helped him up into my bed and tucked the blankets around him. "I'm going to get my pajamas on too, and then I'll read in bed, okay?" I said.

"Wait, don't leave," Davy begged, grabbing at my hand.

I sat beside him and rubbed his head a few times.

He laid back and pulled the bear up to his cheek.

I heard Mom and Dad go past my room in the hall.

"Where are they?!" Mom shrieked. "Why would you take them?!"

"I didn't do anything," I could hear Dad say before his voice disappeared down the stairs.

I heard Mom stomping after him, still yelling at him.

How could they be so mean to each other? Even if I couldn't have made out the words the sound of their voices was poison, like hate. Talk about venom.

I stayed by Davy, rubbing his head and face. He turned on his side, and I rubbed his back.

A few minutes later I heard the heavy stomping up the stairs again, and then my door flew open.

"Where are they!" Mom yelled at me. "I'll be it was you, such a little sneak. Where are the sleeping pills?"

Ahh.

Mom's eyes were wild and mean as she descended on me. I flashed on the wildly hungry wolves that Jody's family had to fend off. I reflexively stuck my hand up as if she were going to hit me. She stopped and then turned towards my dresser and started flinging open drawers. Davy squirmed down under the covers. I kept my hand on his back.

Where was Dad? I needed him. I didn't want to give her the pills, but I didn't know if I could hold out against her anger.

Mom slammed a drawer shut and turned towards me, tears streaming down her face. "I just want to go to *sleep!*" she cried. "Please, just let me go to sleep."

She sunk down to the floor, propped against the dresser. Her face dropped into her hands and she continued crying. And not just little whimpering kind of crying but big, ugly, gulping sobs, her chest heaving like the air coming in was fighting with the air coming out.

I could feel Davy, his body rolled into a tight ball, his back tense, fear coming out of every cell.

Why did I have to open my big fat mouth and ask about Aunt Helen? Maybe the adults were right, maybe Mom just couldn't handle it. No maybe about it, clearly she couldn't handle it.

What have I done?

It seemed like time expanded, like we were going to stay frozen in this moment forever. Davy tense and scared, Mom sobbing on the floor, me paralyzed.

Finally Sara-me seemed to surface. I got up and went and sat down beside Mom. I had a feeling if I touched her right away she might disintegrate. After a few minutes (hours?) the gulping kinds of sobs subsided into a steady but softer cry. Her head stayed in her hands, propped on her knees, but her chest stopped heaving. I was reminded of Sara, sitting patiently by Lottie as she cried, the way she just waited out the tears until Lottie was calm enough to talk.

Finally the time seemed right to touch her. I reached out a hand and put it on Mom's back. She didn't push it away or explode so I left it there. I could feel her rib cage expanding and contracting, her breathing still faster than normal. Then it turned into sighs, big inhale, bigger exhale. Definitely slowing down. I was worried about Davy, over there hidden under the covers, probably feeling completely scared and alone, but I didn't think I could leave Mom. How could Dad be downstairs so unaware of all this? Or was he ignoring it?

I didn't know what to do next. I waited for an idea.

"I'm sorry," Sara-me said softly. "I'm sorry" covered a lot of possibilities.

It seemed to set off a new round of crying, but now Mom leaned in against my shoulder, her head still down. I slid my hand from her back up around her shoulders.

"I can't stand it," she whispered so low I wasn't completely sure that's what she said. She stayed against my shoulder for another ten minutes or so. I couldn't see her face but it seemed the crying had stopped.

Mom slowly pulled herself up to sitting. Her face was slack and wet, her eyes had lost their craziness and just looked tired, like she hadn't slept for weeks.

She stood up and said, "I'm going to bed," seeming to forget the search for her sleeping pills. Maybe power crying wears you out so much you don't need any help getting to sleep.

Mom zombie-walked out of my room. I crept back to my bed and pulled the covers down to see Davy, his eyes screwed tight, his body rolled tightly around Pooh bear.

I rubbed his back and leaned in. "Davy," I said softly, "it is okay. I know it is scary to hear your mommy cry but it is okay.

She's just tired. You know, sometimes you cry and then you are completely okay later, right?"

It took me forty-five minutes of soft rubbing on his back to get him to sleep.

It took a lot longer to get me there.

Chapter Forty-Three

A Turning Tide

It turned out I had coined a new phrase. Or made some regular words famous. All over school the next day I heard people saying "Put that thing away!" and then busting out into laughter.

"Did you really *say* that?" Jennifer Walker stopped me in the halls between geometry and study hall.

I nodded yes.

"Omigod, that is so great! That guy is a loser-pervert! He did that to me once too," said Jennifer as she fell in beside me, walking.

Hold on, publicly walking with me? What would Cassidy say?

I wrinkled my nose in disgust. "Super gross. Mega gross. Uber-gross."

Jennifer nodded. "I wish I had said what you did. I just sat there, nothing coming out of my mouth."

In the lunchroom, Courtney Brizzet sat down beside me with her lunch tray.

"Hey," she said. "Nice work on Chuckie."

I nodded and tried for some modesty, "Anyone could have done it."

Courtney shook her head. "No way. Chuckie did the same thing to me in social studies and I totally froze. It was *sick*. I had nightmares for months."

Wow, turned out Chuckie had a hard time keeping his zipper up. What was his problem? Not that I really cared to know.

"I mean, what you said, it was just awesome! Like, you didn't freak and scream or anything. Just 'put that thing away.' So great!"

Two more lunch trays landed beside us. Samantha something and Ally Smythe dropped into seats, dumping their purses on the floor below us.

"Hi, Jackie," said Samantha, all bright faced and smiley.

"Yeah, hi," echoed Ally.

I mumbled a "hi" back.

"So, like, how did you even think to say that?" asked Samantha as she forked at her salad.

I shrugged. "Well, he had done it to me before, and the first time, I was just totally paralyzed. And pissed because then I ended up being embarrassed in class. So I guess I just had kinda had enough, you know?"

They all nodded. "Enough!" said Ally. "What's wrong with boys?"

"Yeah, well, I don't think all boys are like that," I said.

"Oh, they totally are. If they could get away with it, they'd all have them hanging out all the time," said Ally. "Believe me, I have three brothers and their thingies are their pride and joy."

The other girls giggled.

"So I hear Chuckie did that to, like, two or three other girls too!" said Ally leaning in with the excitement of good gossip.

"Yeah, like me," said Samantha raising her hand.

"No way!" gasped the others.

"Way."

"Eeeewwww," cried Ally.

I shook my head in silent support. It was just too gross. But as I looked around, I realized Chuckie had done me a big favor. All of a sudden I had people sitting with me at lunch, and not losers either. And other people in the lunchroom and halls were giving me congratulatory smiles. Maybe this was my fifteen minutes of fame. All thanks to a disgusting penis.

Life is strange.

Chapter Forty-Four

Burning with the Truth

What is a lie, exactly? The failure to tell the truth. It seems so clear when you first consider it. Even Davy could tell you very clearly what a lie is and isn't. Black and white. True or false. I ate the cookie. I took Jill's new pencil. I spilled the juice on the living room carpet. From the start, what do our parents tell us about lying? It is wrong. Don't do it. You will be punished. Even, as we get a bit older, the truth is paramount, "I won't punish you if you just tell the truth." The truth is supposed to be the all-important, never-broken, rule.

At what point do adults slip away from the absolute? Is it a well-intentioned side step at first, "your hair cut looks great!"? And then perhaps, a convenience, "my husband and I adore each other!"? And then maybe truth has become just another *concept*, not a rule at all.

I was walking up the driveway, the sky already darkening even though it was barely 4:00 in the afternoon. The thick gray clouds had a weight that seemed to press down into my very body, making it an effort to move. I was thinking about Jody in *The Yearling* and how confused he was when Grandma Hutto lied and said it was her fault her house burned down. Shocked, Jody started to say it was the Forresters, angry at Oliver for stealing Lem's girl, but his father silenced him. Grandma knew that her lie could prevent a lot of damage, a lot of pain, years worth of feuding. That seemed like a good kind of lie, a clean kind of lie. It seemed nothing like the lies that were going on in my house. The lies in my house felt poisonous, like they were draining the life force from everyone in it.

I flashed back to Mom, slumped against my dresser sobbing. How could I make that worse? How could I keep asking about Aunt Helen at the risk of sending Mom into an even darker place? And yet it seemed so clear to me, so absolutely clear, that these were the wrong kinds of lies. To pretend your twin sister didn't even live, to pretend it isn't ripping your heart apart that she died, to pretend everything is fine, those didn't seem like ways to save a life.

Inside the house was even darker than outside. If I hadn't seen Mom's car as I came through the garage I would have thought no one was home. Not one light was on. No sound. A stab of fear hit me.

I dropped my backpack and raced through the house looking for Mom.

No one downstairs.

I shot up the stairs and ran to her room. Flung open the door and hit the light switch and there she was, again, in bed.

I was at her side in a split second, not breathing. Ripped back her covers and stuck my head near hers to see if at least *she* was breathing.

"What the . . .?" Mom mumbled.

I sank to the floor in relief.

This was *really* getting old.

"What're you doing?" Mom mumbled again. Then her voice got louder, "I'm *sleeping!* Go away! Jesus Christ, can't a person take a *nap?*"

I breathed in and out trying to recover. My heart was racing and suddenly I was so angry that she kept doing this to me. I staggered up to standing.

"Why are you sleeping all the time?!" I demanded.

Mom rolled away from me and threw her hand up over her face. "Leave me alone."

"No. I'm not going to leave you alone," I said. "I am SO not going to leave you alone!" Rage overtook my body. "I'm not going to leave you ALONE because when I do I'm afraid you are going to KILL YOURSELF!" My voice was a scream by the end and I was shaking.

I had said it.

The truth.

"Don't be crazy," Mom said, but her voice was tired and not at all convincing.

"I'm sick of it, Mom!" I said. I grabbed her shoulders and pulled her back over to face me. "You are not yourself anymore.

You are always sleeping or sad or angry. And I get it. You *deserve* to be all those things. You deserve to be sad that your sister died. You deserve to be angry. I know it is an awful awful thing. So stop pretending it didn't happen!"

My heart was pounding and my whole body was shaking, but there was a purity of purpose in me, a deep knowing that someone had to say these things to her. And that someone, apparently, was me.

Mom's eyes flickered open and shut and then stayed open. She stared at me, and I saw her let the knowledge flow into her consciousness and her brown eyes become a bottomless pit of pain. I thought of Beryl, sitting with her dying dog. I thought of Jody, sitting by his dead friend's body. I felt defiant as I stared back into her eyes.

I would not be the one to run away from the pain.

Mom continued to stare as tears streamed into her hair.

"I know," I said. "*I know.*"

A stranger could have walked into the room and looked into Mom's eyes and read the whole story. The raw pain, the sickness, the grief, the loss, all shone out at me and the tears kept flowing. No sound. Just tears.

It seemed that we stared at each other for a million years, and then the sound came. First a gasp, like she had forgotten to breathe, then choking sobs.

I sunk down on the bed and pulled her towards me. She crawled her head up onto my lap and curled around me and cried.

It seemed to go on for hours. Or more, I lost track. She cried and cried, then her body shook and then did the whole thing over again. Crying, then shaking, crying then shaking. I should have been scared. Mom was more miserable than I'd ever seen a person be. I should have been scared but I wasn't. *This* was better than the lies. This was better than waiting for the crash, waiting for the fall, waiting for the worst to happen. This seemed to me to be something that should have happened a long time ago.

Finally Dad appeared in the doorway.

"What's going on?"

Mom didn't answer, didn't move from my lap.

Dad walked towards us. "What have you done?" he said, a fierce stare at me.

"Dad, she's *sad*. She has a reason to be, she's *allowed*," I said.

Dad rolled his eyes and bunched his lips up. "Why are you upsetting her?! Did we not *discuss* this?"

I kept my hand on Mom's back. She showed no signs of hearing us talk about her. "You know Dad, you can't *time* something like this! You can't say, 'oh, I'll deal with that later, when it fits my schedule.' Everyone around here is acting like everything is fine and it's NOT."

Dad stood on the other side of the bed, arms crossed, shaking his head at me. Still angry. Still *inconvenienced*.

"Jackie, I know you are sensitive," Dad started.

"It's not THAT! Don't blame ME!" I said, my voice getting hot. "Why won't anyone in this house say the TRUTH! Mom has been a mess. She took PILLS." I stood up, unable to sit still. "She might have been trying to KILL HERSELF! Sorry if the timing is *inconvenient*."

Dad threw his head back and looked at the ceiling and then me again. "Hey, don't talk to me that way."

"Dad, *you don't get it*. I come home from school every day, and I don't know if I'm going to find her alive. Do you know what that is like?"

We were standing across the bed from each other, glaring. Mom was a curled up lump between us.

"Aunt Helen killed herself. Can we just SAY that? Can we just TALK about it? What is the big secret here? And Mom acts like everything is fine. It is NOT FINE."

"Okay, okay," Dad said, slipping into his 'manage the crisis' voice. "Let's just calm down here. Yes, there has been, uh, trauma, in our family. Yes, I'm sure we are not all over that yet . . ."

Mom unfolded herself and twisted her head up at Dad. "She's right," she said in a low voice. "She's right, Mike." Then she curled herself up again.

Dad stared at me for a long second then sat on the other side of the bed and leaned elbows onto his knees and his head onto his hands.

"Christ," he muttered. "Jesus Christ."

We could have sat like that forever, unsure of the next words or action, but the doorbell rang. Dad didn't move so I slid away from Mom and went down to get it.

As I opened the door Davy shot past me and I found myself staring into the puzzled face of Mrs. Herrington. "I think I must have gotten my signals crossed with your mom, she was going to pick him up at 6:00?" Mrs. Herrington said. "I tried to call but no one answered so I thought I'd just, you know, shoot on by."

"Oh, ah, yeah, no problem. Mom, uh, got a headache, and I was supposed to answer the phone, must have not heard it," I fibbed. How quickly I was back to lying. But maybe this was the okay kind? I was so confused. "Sorry," I added. "Really sorry. I'm sure Mom will call you."

Mrs. Herrington's face relaxed. "Oh, I'm just glad there's no problem, I had to run out to the store anyway. Glad everything is okay."

Yeah, everything is completely okay. Ha ha.

I made Davy a sandwich and then Dad appeared in the kitchen.

"She's a mess," Dad said, scowling at me. "*Why* did you do this?"

"Mommy made a mess?" Davy said.

I looked at Davy and then pointedly back at Dad, trying to alert him to shut up while Davy was around.

"No, Mommy just is sick, doesn't feel well, so leave her alone to sleep tonight, okay?" I said to Davy.

I was starting to get a feel for the difference between a Grandma Hutto kind of lie and a rattlesnake venom kind of lie.

Dad stared at me some more.

"Here Davy, I'm going to let you eat your sandwich in front of the TV!" I said, grabbing his plate and shepherding him into the family room.

Back in the kitchen Dad hadn't moved.

"Dad, she IS a mess. That's what I've been trying to tell you. I can't take it anymore. She needs help."

"Well thanks to you she's not even speaking!" Dad said. "If she is such a mess why in the world would you try to upset her *more?*" He slammed his fist onto the counter.

"Because everyone in this family is pretending like nothing bad happened! Like Aunt Helen didn't *kill* herself. You can't just make stuff go away by ignoring it!"

Dad shook his head, took a deep breath and then walked around the counter and slid onto the kitchen table bench. His shoulders slumped and his face was gray and lined. "Christ," he said again. He looked up, like the answers might be written on the ceiling, and then looked down again, staring at the tabletop.

"I just don't have it to deal with this," Dad said softly.

Even though I knew, in my heart of hearts, I was right, I got scared. What if this was too much for Dad? What if the stress from work and now Mom made him have a heart attack or something? And it would be all my fault. Well, partly my fault.

I stared at Dad's bent head and felt more and more alone. He was kind of marginal to our every day life in many ways, but I just now realized how much I counted on his steadiness, his ability to handle any crisis. I had never seen him look small and, well, weak. Dad had always been the rock. Like Penny, Jody's dad, had always been the rock.

Rock, don't fail me now.

"Well we need to do *something*," I said. "She needs help. Like, expert kind of help, not family kind of help."

Dad shrugged. "I guess you're right."

I was starting to get angry at him too. What was wrong with these people? It seemed so obvious to me. Get the woman some help.

"Of course I'm right," I said. "Find her a therapist or something."

"And until I do?" Dad said. "I mean, what do we do tonight? Tomorrow?"

"I don't know," I said. I was tired of being in charge of this whole intervention.

Dad snapped his head towards me, the first sign of energy returning. "You don't know? I thought you knew everything about what should be done. I thought you were so sure."

"I'm sure we shouldn't be pretending Aunt Helen didn't die, I'm not sure how to best help mom."

In the silence I traced the pattern of black specks in the gray and black granite countertop. Connect the dots, only nothing was emerging as a pattern.

"Well," I said, kind of thinking out loud, "she seemed to appreciate me just sitting there with her. And I think it was good for her to cry. I mean, cry for real. Like about the real thing that upsets her. So maybe, I don't know, just sit with her until she falls asleep."

"I did that," said Dad. "She was asleep when I came down."

"Okay, well, tomorrow, find a professional. And, I don't know, see what she's like in the morning."

Dad gave me one more stare that showed he was still angry. Fine. I was still angry too.

It was an uneasy bunch that fell asleep that night in our house. Mom sad and worn-out, Dad angry and worn-out, me just angry. Well kind of worn-out too I guess. Only Davy seemed oblivious, but the tension must have seeped into his consciousness because he appeared by my bed a little after 3:00. I let him climb in and got back to sleep by imagining I was Jody playing by the spring hole.

Chapter Forty-Five

An Unexpected Entente

In the morning I found Mom sitting in the kitchen, pale and puffy eyed. She didn't notice I had layered the bright blue blouse she had picked out for me over a white t-shirt, but at least she was up and out of bed.

"Hey," I said by way of good morning.

"Hey," she said softly.

"Um, how are you?" I asked, scared.

Deep sigh. "I'm not sure yet. Kind of numb right now."

I nodded. That made sense. When you cry for that long it might be hard to feel things again for a while. Or not, what did I know.

I fixed myself a bowl of cereal and sat down across from her. Something told me to just eat in silence, not badger her with words.

As I slurped the last of the milk out of the bowl, Dad walked in.

He shot a look at Mom and then me, raising his eyebrows. I shrugged.

He pulled the coffee pot out and stared at it. I guess no one thought to load the automatic feature last night. He dumped the old cold coffee and set about making new.

"Anyone want coffee?" he asked.

I guess that was his way to try to engage Mom, unless he thought I was drinking coffee these days.

No answer.

"How much do I put in?" he asked.

Really? Was he that clueless? Had he really never made coffee?

Mom stood up and walked to the freezer, removed a bag of coffee, then moved to the coffee maker, grabbed a filter from a drawer and began filling and hitting buttons. She returned to her seat without saying a word.

I guess if my Dad didn't even know how to make coffee, he wasn't going to be the one to open up any kind of emotional conversation.

"So, what's happening next?" I ventured.

Mom remained silent.

"Dad?" I prompted.

"Huh?" Dad said. "I think the water runs through the maker, then the coffee is ready."

The man could be way concrete.

"No, I mean with *Mom*," I said. "You know, the whole grief thing? The whole, needs to talk about Aunt Helen thing?"

Dad shot a look at Mom, maybe afraid she would disintegrate on the spot.

No answer.

I was getting really annoyed with these people.

"Like, Mom, do you need someone home with you today? You have to tell us! You have to tell us what you need."

Mom frowned. "I don't know. I just feel tired and numb."

"So will you be okay? Do you need someone to take care of Davy after school?"

Mom shrugged.

"I say we call Jenny," I said, praying the babysitter would be available. "Or I can just stay home . . ."

"No, you don't need to do that," Mom said.

The more I thought of it, the more I thought I should stay home. Otherwise, I was going to spend the whole day worrying.

Mom seemed to pick up on my thoughts. "I won't do, you know, anything. I know I won't." She gave me a wan smile. "I feel like shit, but I also feel, I don't know, a little more calm inside."

So we were probably okay for today. Once I called Jenny, who turned out to be available, I felt like I could actually go to school.

I followed Dad to the garage as he was leaving. "So you're going to get on that counselor thing, right?"

"Fine, fine!" Dad said, clearly annoyed. "I'll ask around."

So sorry to keep bugging you about my potentially *suicidal* mom.

Okay then, off to my other battleground.

I barely concentrated on any of my morning classes. I kept replaying the scene with Mom. I kept hearing her sobs and feeling her head in my lap. Kept thinking about how, even now, Dad didn't seem to get the urgency of the whole thing. Or maybe he got the urgency but just didn't want to have to deal with it all.

I was wondering what Mom was doing at home as I moved slowly through the hot lunch line. Yum, fake pizza, my favorite. How hard is it to make pizza? You'd think that would be an easy one. But no, they loaded stale crust with overly sweetened sauce, then covered it with fake cheese, the kind that doesn't even really melt, and then baked the crap out of it. Whatever. I grabbed a slice and stuck it on my tray.

I hesitated at the front of the lunchroom. Where to sit?

Bam! All of a sudden I was flying toward the floor. The tray dropped and I landed on it, smashing the pizza into my chest. Utensils clattered away and my water bottle flew off to the side.

"Oops, *sorry*," said Cassidy standing over me with an evil stepmother type grin. "I must not have seen you." Kids at nearby tables laughed and pointed as I pulled myself to my knees.

"Sweet move!" hooted a boy at the closest table.

"Isn't she graceful?" laughed Cassidy poking the girl beside her. It was only then I realized that the girl beside her was Emily, frozen stiff with a horrified expression on her face. "Good thing you dumped that loser! What a klutz," Cassidy added, sneering at me. "Let's go," said Cassidy, nudging Emily's shoulder.

Emily stood frozen, her eyes moving frantically between Cassidy and me. She wanted to stay with me. I could see it on her face. Time stretched out, like we were in slow motion. Emily's moment of choice, follow the Pom dream or stay with your old friend.

From nowhere a hand grabbed my arm to pull me up. I looked up to see Tanya Martin at the end of the arm. She helped me off the floor and gave Cassidy the stink eye.

"What's your problem?" Tanya spat at Cassidy. Tanya, the girl so squeamish about Chuckie's penis, was facing Cassidy with no fear.

"What's it to you, pizza face?" Cassidy said to Tanya.

Someone else handed me my books and another person was picking up the tray. Sandra Bonita? Samantha? What were *they* doing helping me?

Sandra and Samantha stood next to Tanya facing Cassidy. They were like a shield in front of me. "What did Jackie ever do to you?" Sandra said to Cassidy. "You go around telling lies about her and she's done nothing wrong."

"Yeah!" echoed Tanya sticking her face right up to Cassidy's. "You ask me, you're the slut! Acting all prissy. I'll bet you lost your cherry when you were ten. Bee-*atch*."

A crowd had gathered around and were laughing and yelling. It was hard to tell for whom. I noticed Melinda Barnes standing to the side, not helping her fellow Pom Cassidy out at all. Just staring at us with no expression on her face.

Emily was still standing frozen.

"Screw you all! Bunch of losers!" huffed Cassidy. She spun around and grabbed Emily's arm and dragged her out of the circle with her. She saw Melinda and barked, "Come on!"

Cassidy and Emily disappeared. Melinda didn't move. *Wow.*

Samantha and Sandra patted my shoulder. I mumbled, "Thanks."

"Bout time someone knocked that bee-atch off her throne," laughed Tanya, pumped on her own bravery. "Hey, if you can call out Pervy Chuckie, I can tell Cassidy she's a bitch!"

I still couldn't make my brain work to understand that they had all just stood up for me. While Emily stood unmoving.

"Thanks," I said again, this time with more strength. "I can't believe it."

They all nodded and high-fived each other. They were buzzed with excitement and nerves and who knows what else.

Tanya walked to the bathroom with me to wash off my shirt. I stared in the mirror at the stains covering the blue crisscross and the shirt underneath. I laughed, for the first time since Cassidy knocked me down. Tanya laughed too. I got more and more hysterical.

Thanks Cassidy! I hate this shirt! And now I know how many other people hate you too!

We laughed until I almost couldn't even remember what I was laughing about, until the laughter itself took over with its own momentum. My stomach muscles started to hurt I was laughing so hard. The little bit of mascara I had put on trailed down my face.

We managed to stop, and then Tanya said, "bee-atch" and we started all over again.

Finally I got myself under control and took off the blue blouse and threw it in the garbage. I scrubbed the sauce off the shirt underneath and covered it all with my sweatshirt. I wiped off the streaks of mascara just as the bell rang for class change.

Walking through the halls I swear I felt a different energy from the school. Like it was a welcoming place. Like I wasn't battling through a stream of bullies and critics, but maybe floating along with more of a mix. Some bee-atches, yes, but also some nice people and some shy people and some friendly people.

A definite improvement.

Chapter Forty-Six

Aching and Vacant

When I got home I found Davy in the family room playing Chutes and Ladders with Jenny.

"Jackie, come play with us!" Davy yelled as I poked my head through the door.

No thanks, I've got enough chutes coming at me these days. I don't need the reminder.

"Hi Jackie," smiled Jenny. Jenny was an uncomplicated twenty-four-year-old community college student putting herself through school. She worked three jobs and was cheerful all the time. She had shoulder-length blond hair pulled back into a ponytail with wisps falling around her face. Her eyebrows were plucked into a thin crescent, and she had on just enough makeup to look like an ad for something natural, like ocean breeze air freshener.

"Hey," I said, almost afraid of the answer, "where's Mom?"

"In her workroom," Jenny answered, flicking the spinner and counting out her moves. "Oh no! Down again I go."

Davy chortled. "Ha ha. You're gonna lose."

I had homework to do, books to put away, *The Yearling* to disappear into. "How long are you supposed to stay?" I asked Jenny.

"Just until you got home," she said, confirming my fears.

Why should Mom pay a babysitter when she has me for free?

"Don't go!" begged Davy, launching himself onto Jenny's lap.

My thoughts exactly.

"I'll finish this game, okay?" said Jenny, ruffling his hair.

"And one more, one more game!" Davy insisted.

"We'll see," laughed Jenny.

I wished she lived with us. When she was here, life seemed more manageable. Like there might actually be happiness in the world.

What a thought.

I knocked quietly on the workroom door and then opened it. Mom was sitting on the pale couch, some sort of sewing project in her hands, her head slumped against the back of the couch in sleep. Somehow this sleep looked just like someone who was tired, not like someone trying to escape life. Like she had just nodded off while sewing.

I was okay with that.

I gently removed the swatch of material from her lap and slipped a light blanket over her. I'd check back on her in a little while.

Thus released, I headed to my room. Ignoring the calls of my backpack I flopped onto my bed with *The Yearling*. Jody and his father discover that the wild animals had contracted the "black tongue" after a flood hit their area, and Jody was worried about his fawn Flag contracting the disease. Jody couldn't stand the thought of losing Flag, ". . . Flag lived in a secret place in his heart that had been long aching and vacant."

My chest contracted like I'd been hit by an arrow. Like the arrow had landed right on my vacant spot, only I hadn't had a name for that spot until this very moment. My vacant spot was mom shaped and it had been vacant for a long time. Like five years. Tears spilled down my cheeks and sadness pinned me to my bed.

Jody's emptiness had been filled but mine hadn't. The vacant spot, named, opened up and up until it felt like I wasn't anything but vacant. I rolled over and bit my pillow to try to keep from sobbing out loud, but it didn't work. My throat was tight and the tears wouldn't stop, and I couldn't hold the sound of my crying back. It spilled out into the pillow and I felt like I would never be okay again.

I cried.

And cried.

My mother was gone, I couldn't ignore it anymore. I guess I had been lying to myself as much as Mom had been lying to herself. The mother I remembered, the laughing mom, the kind mom, the mom who actually *saw* me, she hadn't been around since Aunt Helen died. And I missed her. The mom I kept trying to resurrect might never come back.

I cried.

And cried.

It felt like I cried for days. It was completely dark by the time I could let go of the pillow. It felt like it might stay dark until the end of time.

A thought floated into my tear soaked brain. A thought that this must be how Mom felt. This darkness, this deep loneliness, *this* is what she had been running from.

And I had sent her straight into this darkness.

My eyes fluttered open to gray morning light. My eyelids felt like thick pillows sliding over gritty sand. Close, open, close, open, nothing improved.

So. I had slept all night. In my clothes. Clutching the pillow.

I wondered why no one had come to get me for dinner. I wondered if they even noticed I hadn't come out of my room. And then I couldn't summon any energy to really care. Back to sleep.

When I woke again the light was bright, the gray gone. It felt late and when I looked at the clock, it read 10:13. Yep. Missed the school bus. And then some.

I could have stayed in bed all day, but my bladder was having none of that so I eased myself up, looked out through slitty puffy eyes and stumbled to the bathroom.

Refused to look in the mirror, just peed and went back to my bed.

I was starting to appreciate Mom's afternoon nap idea. Maybe I'd do the same. Maybe I'd start right now. I pulled a pillow over my face to block the sun and floated like that for a while.

I felt numb and unable to move. It was like I was floating in a sensory deprivation chamber. Suspended animation.

So this was the sadness Mom had been fighting against. It felt like I had opened up Pandora's box and every ugly, mean, or sad specter ever created in the history of the world had flown out. And grown and filled the room and the sky and the world with their dark heaviness. And they were never getting back in that box again, no way.

Bang, my door flew open and Davy jumped on the bed.

"Jackie! What are you doing home? Are you sick!" Davy said, ripping the pillow off my head.

Ooh, too too bright. I flung my arm up over my face.

"Yeah, I'm sick, you should go away so you don't get it," I said.

"Well mom is sick too! And no one is making me any breakfast!" Davy said.

Shit.

"Where's Dad?"

"Duh! Work!" Davy said in the "you must be a moron" voice. "He had to go extra early."

Ahh. So mom was comatose, and I was too. Poor Davy. Some small part of me stirred with sympathy, but it wasn't enough to get my muscles to work. Not getting up.

"Get some cereal," I said.

"Don't want it," he said. "Come make me eggs."

I just wanted him to go away. Or maybe I could drag him into the underworld with me and Mom, that would be festive. Then I could be three for three. Ruin us all.

"Have a popsicle," I said, hoping to just get him to go away.

"Really?! Okay!" Davy said, hopping down and running away before I could change my mind.

Ahh. Back to lala land. Pillow back over head, I drifted off. Not quite asleep but not really here either.

Davy came back, slurping at his popsicle.

"Wake up, Jackie!" he said, hopping up on my bed.

I didn't answer.

"Come on, I'm bored. Nobody took me to school today."

I searched around my brain for feelings. I still felt numb. The darkness whispered that it just didn't matter. Nothing mattered. So what if I didn't go to school? So what if Davy didn't go to school? It was all a farce anyway. Bad things happen and people don't recover, and I had been fooling myself that I actually had a mother. It was like she was dead and I had only just realized it.

Davy shook my arm. "Come on! Come watch TV with me at least."

His soft brown eyes pleaded with me.

Gee, Davy was without a mother too. Then again, he never knew the real Mom. He just got what he got. Which was a paper cut out of a mom.

Stab.

The pain was back, full force. Poor Davy. Never really had Mom. At least I had had the real her at one point. I wondered which was worse. Having her and losing her or never having her.

Poor Davy.

He poked at me again. "Come on!"

And I thought my heart couldn't break any more, but there it went. Davy didn't deserve any of this. Maybe none of us did, but he was the most innocent, the most vulnerable.

I dragged myself up on my elbow, "Okay, I'll come watch TV with you."

"Your eyes look funny," said Davy, hopping down from the bed, grape popsicle juice dripping onto my carpet.

"Yeah, I know," I said, swinging my legs over the side, trying to find the energy to actually stand up.

"Let's watch Batman!" Davy said.

Well. I had a reason to try to live, I guess. Someone had to watch out for Davy. Someone had to pay attention to him and love him and *see* him. I felt around inside my head for Jody. Tried to imagine I was looking out of his eyes, moving his thin little body around. Felt a rush of appreciation for Davy.

I grabbed Davy and pulled him close and gave him a kiss. "You got it," I said. "Batman it is."

Chapter Forty-Seven

Taking it for my share

After four Batman episodes I had had enough. Mom was still in bed (breathing, pills well hidden still), and I couldn't be bothered to do anything productive. I told Davy I'd be back in a little while and grabbed *The Yearling* and went into the library. I turned on only the little reading light angled over one of the leather chairs, wrapped up in a blanket and tried to disappear from my life. Although why I was still in this book I didn't know. This book had ripped open my little mom fantasy (you know, that I still actually had one) and poured darkness all over my world. But what the heck.

And then, the magic of reading worked again, and I was more in Florida than Pennsylvania. Emotions still swirled because Penny decided that Flag had to be killed. And even worse, he expected Jody to do it. Jody is so hurt and angry that he runs away and almost starves to death. And the starvation helps him to finally understand that his dad isn't betraying him by making him shoot Flag. That his dad knows that their worst enemy is starvation and that Flag eating all the corn shoots might cause them to actually starve to death.

I could feel Jody's relief in my own body, his joy that he doesn't have to hate his dad. That he gets to love and admire him again. The whole experience makes Jody grow up and take on the bulk of the work since his dad is injured and can't do it so well anymore.

By the end of the book I was crying when I read about how Jody was ready to take on the responsibilities of life. Ready to take his share.

It was like the words had been written just for me. Maybe it is natural to want life to be fun and easy, but it is also natural that life won't always be that way. That there will be hard parts to life and you just have to take it for your share and go on. Maybe I just had to let go of the Mom I used to know and accept whoever she was now. Maybe my share was to take care of Davy. Maybe it was time for me to grow up, like Jody had to grow up.

I closed my eyes and sent up a little prayer of thanks to God for giving those words to Marjorie Kinnan Rawlings. Under all the sadness there was a little flicker of comfort in the idea that someone else had felt this way. How was it possible that a story written in a different place and a different time could reach inside me, see my loneliness, and by seeing it, somehow lessen it? How was it possible that this story was able to beat back the darkness, if only a little?

Okay then. Time to take it for my share.

I went upstairs, washed my face, and got dressed. I went back downstairs and made Davy lunch. Mom appeared while he was eating his tomato soup and I offered her a bowl. She nodded and sat down next to Davy.

Okay then. I could take care of both of them.

After Davy finished the last of his soup, I sent him upstairs to the playroom to play with his Legos. I sat across from Mom.

"If you want to go sleep some more, it is okay," I said. "I understand, I really do."

Mom stared at me with half-dead eyes. A tear slipped out. "I don't know what to do. I can't sleep all day. But, I don't know, I don't feel like doing much else."

"It's okay, I said again. "Really. I can watch Davy. You just do what you need to do. Maybe that thing you were sewing yesterday?"

Mom shrugged. "It's as good as anything, I guess."

I did yesterday's homework, made dinner, cleaned the kitchen and put Davy to bed. Dad came home around 9:30, when I was still putting books away in the library.

He stood in the doorway without speaking. It was like everyone in this house was half dead. Maybe the house was built on top of a strangler fig, and it was invisibly winding its tendrils around all of our throats. I kept shelving but said "hey."

Big sigh from Dad. Big tired sigh.

"I put some feelers out for a name," he finally said.

"Good."

"I don't know if she'll go," he said.

I shrugged. "You have to try."

"Mm-hmm," he agreed.

"Maybe we should all go," I said, surprising myself. Where did that come from?

Dad cocked an eyebrow. He was still standing in the door, still in his overcoat, still holding his briefcase.

"I don't think any of us are doing that great," I said.

"Yeah, I don't know," Dad said.

"Well, talk to Mom first, I guess," I said, squeezing my hands together to hold onto the stack of books I was trying to slide onto a shelf. The middle books squirted out and the whole stack clattered to the floor.

Dad walked in, dropped his briefcase, shrugged out of his coat and leaned down to help pick up the books. We got them back up onto the shelf and then he looked around. "You're doing a good job in here. Who knew we had this many books?"

"A bunch are from Grandma's basement."

"Hmm- mm" Dad said, walking slowly around the room, scanning the shelves. He pulled out *The Woman in White* and smiled. "I liked this one. I did a good paper on this one. Did you know it was one of the first mystery books? Wilkie Collins, he was an interesting guy."

"Really?" I said. "I haven't gotten to him yet."

"Hmm," Dad said. "He had two families, went back and forth living with them."

"Huh?" I was confused.

"He divided his time between two, uh, women and the kids he had with each. Not married to either but, you know," Dad didn't finish but had a little smile on his face.

I shook my head, "Probably more interesting than his made up stuff."

Dad laughed. "For sure."

"I could live in here," I said, looking around. "Surrounded by books. What could be better?"

Well, a functioning mother, that could be better.

Dad followed my glance. "Yes, this is a good room. Kind of cool to have a real library, huh?" He sunk into one of the leather chairs, leaned his head back and closed his eyes. The lamp beside him lit up one side of his face and left the other in shadow, but what stood out even more was the depth of the lines on his forehead and around his eyes, even, I saw, around his mouth. I had forgotten to worry about Dad too, in all this. The Wilkie Collins smile was gone.

"Hey, um, what's going on at work?" I asked, not wanting to come right out and mention the harassment thing.

Dad sighed and answered without opening his eyes. "Nothing. Everything."

"What about, you know, Dubroski's lies?" I said.

Another sigh. "Still under 'investigation.'"

"I can't believe someone could just make up lies and they'd believe it!" I said, but even as the words left my mouth I thought about all the leering looks I got at school when Cassidy told people I had left my last school because I was pregnant. Actually, I could believe it only too well.

Dad's eyes flickered open. "Really? You can't?"

"No, you're right," I said. "I totally believe that can happen. It happened to me."

Dad gave a half smile. "What are we going to do about those Dubroskis?"

I smiled back and then felt a tightness in the back of my throat. He had said "we." Someone else was actually in this with me. I had a flash of what Jody must have felt like, always having his dad on his side.

Dad's eyes closed again and I continued to shelve. Within a couple of minutes he dragged himself out of the chair. "Well, still got some work to do, better get to it before I fall asleep."

There were only a few boxes left and I was determined to finish the job. I worked for another hour, surrounded by silence. The lamps gave off a soft light and inside I felt a matching glow that I was "taking it for my share."

In the last box I found a battered paperback titled *My Friend Flicka*. It had a picture of a horse and a boy on the front, and it seemed vaguely familiar although I was sure I hadn't read it. I put it aside to take upstairs.

It was almost 10:30, and I looked around the library with satisfaction as I placed the last book on a shelf. The colorful, neatly arranged shelves tingled the organizational region of my brain. For a moment I felt like I had brought order to my whole chaotic life, not just these books that started out so randomly tossed into boxes. I walked from one side of the library to the other, trailing my hand along the spines of the books, feeling their energy and power. Touching all the help I would probably ever need, or at least it felt like it this moment. If I could just take the time, the answers were in one of these worlds, or maybe more than one.

I felt a sense of pride that comes from finishing a big project, imagining I was like Jody, keeping their little patch of land planted and harvested, keeping his family fed and protected. I was taking my share.

I took a deep breath, picked up *My Friend Flicka,* and floated upstairs.

Chapter Forty-Eight

Welcome to Wyoming

In the morning I threw the as yet unread *My Friend Flicka* into my backpack. I had fallen asleep before my sheets had even settled around me so would have to start it today. I was getting quicker at the flat ironing and was pleased with my work on my hair. Downstairs I found a pale but awake Mom. She was drinking coffee and gave me a tired smile when I came in.

Relief. She was up and giving appropriate social reactions.

I got myself a bowl of cereal and sat down across from her.

"So, ah, what do you have going today?" I asked.

Mom rolled her eyes. "Supposed to go to Garden Club but really don't feel like it."

"You should go, just get out," I said.

"I'm going to have to, Cece is coming by to get me. Won't take no for an answer."

Hard to believe it, but for once I was grateful for Cece.

"It is some marathon meeting and work thing," Mom said. "Most of the day. Jenny will be here when you get home."

Whew. Mom supervised, Jenny here. Good news. But looking at Mom I couldn't imagine how she'd summon the energy to get dressed, let alone actually leave the house. She was folded up against the back of the breakfast table bench as if she had no bones in her body.

Davy ran in and grabbed Mom's arm, begging her to come find his Paul Frank T-shirt and managed to get her into a standing position.

By the time I left for school, I half believed she might make it out of the house, but still carried a feeling of unease on the ride to school.

Too bad for the uneasy feeling about Mom because Cassidy was missing for the second day in a row. It would be nice to have one day where the good things at school lined up with good things at home. Oh well. Emily was spreading the word that Cassidy had hurt her leg practicing a cheer. It didn't matter if it was true, no one believed it. Queen Bee Mean Girl Cassidy had lost control of her hive and she couldn't face it. I knew this only second hand, because Emily wouldn't look at me. Not in PE, not in geometry, chemistry or study hall. Not anywhere.

Emily had made her choice.

There was a small part of me that could admire her loyalty because Cassidy's star was fading. Since she wasn't at school to force everyone to pay attention to her, the tide of Cassidy's popularity was turning. I could hear it in the halls. All the people who had been scared of her or just plain didn't like her were starting to talk.

And I couldn't walk between any classes without at least three or four people saying hello to me. I don't know why the attention was now focused on me. Aside from the Chuckie thing. And also having the reputation of having stood up to Cassidy. Although I really hadn't done much, I guess what I did was enough. I was the pebble at the bottom of the pile that moved, bringing the whole thing down.

It was too much, my brain felt like the holding cage for a pack of rabid squirrels. In study hall I pulled out *My Friend Flicka* and sunk into a different world.

Bliss.

By the time the bell rang I could smell the open Wyoming fields, hear the clopping of the horses, feel the fresh breeze on my face. I was Ken, dreaming of a colt of my very own. Ken, freed from the endless classes of school, finally home on his ranch for the summer. Ken tense and uncomfortable every time he was in his dad's presence. Ken who could not seem to please his dad. The bell jarred me back, and I wished, tough dad and all, that I could trade places with Ken.

On the bus home I wasted no time slipping away again to the ranch. Feeling like I was a boy, in a distant place, in a distant time, was such a relief. Being me just gets too tiring, and I needed a rest before facing whatever dramas were waiting at home.

I lingered over the descriptions of life in Wyoming, on a ranch. I loved the day-to-day details, the way Ken's mom hummed as she made bread and cheerfully did her chores. I liked how happy

O'Hara made the mom in the little tasks of her life. She seemed so real and yet so unlike my mother. I felt a wave of nostalgia, both for Ken's mom and the way my mom used to be. I could remember a time when she seemed happy enough to be a mother, happy enough to be in her life with us.

Chapter Forty-Nine

All Stirred Up

Being forced to be around people all day seemed to have helped Mom. She moved easily around the kitchen making dinner, her face more animated than I had seen in a while.

"Jock-leen, grab an onion for me please," Mom said, sliding chopped celery off a cutting board into a frying pan.

"How was Garden Club?" I asked, hoping to keep the not-depressed mood going. I grabbed an onion from the refrigerator and handed it to her.

"Fine," Mom said, slicing off the top of the onion. "That Meredith though, I don't know if I can stand to be around her one more minute. Now she's president and you'd think she was president of the United States. Drunk with power."

"Hmm," I said.

Mom's hands were a blur, chopping the onion into small bits. "It's like she thinks she should change everything, just because she can. And that husband of hers, he gives me the creeps. Get out some more butter."

I rifled around the refrigerator looking for more butter. "Yeah, I've seen their son at school, but I don't really know him," I said.

"I can't imagine being married to him! All tall and ugly and just, ew, creepy. Makes me think of Ichabod Crane."

Later, sitting at dinner staring at Dad, I thought about Mom's comments about Meredith's husband. I hoped Mom was grateful for Dad. I knew they were fighting more these days but didn't he look good in comparison?

"Do we have Christmas figured out?" Dad asked, scraping up the remaining bits of his Mediterranean chicken and licking them off the fork.

Mom blew out air, "I told everyone, we can have it *here!*" She shook her head. "Obviously, we have the room. Why should we all pack into my parents' house? I mean, for crying out loud."

Dad nodded. "Fine with me, just curious."

Ah hello? The chances of getting Mom to go to Norwick were zero point zero.

It made me think, though. I mean, it seemed obvious she didn't like to go to Norwick because that was where Helen, uh, died. But was there any other reason? We had been back there exactly once as a family since we moved back to Pittsburgh and Mom couldn't wait to leave. Then again, that once was for the funeral. Then again, she went to pick up the books recently. Hmm. Seemed to set off this latest downward spiral. Must investigate further.

"Well if they are mad about it, too bad. We have the space and the big kitchen for cooking and the room to spread out while I'm cooking. I mean, you'd think everyone would be grateful that I'm willing to do all the work!"

Dad just nodded. Not the hill he wanted to die on, even though I'm sure his parents wouldn't have minded hosting either.

Mom excused Davy to go watch TV and stood up to clear the plates.

"Uh, could you hold on for a moment Marion?" Dad said.

"What?" Mom said, holding her plate and Davy's.

"Just uh, sit down, please?" Dad said.

Mom sank down and clanked one plate on top of the other.

"So, I have a couple of names, you know, someone you can call."

Mom's face went still.

So much for the good mood. I guess I shouldn't have expected it to last.

Mom remained silent but her eyebrows drifted just the slightest bit up.

Dad made an embarrassed little smile. "Just, you know, what we were talking about before, might help to have someone to talk to. You know, about, uh, things."

My insides were completely still. Like a deer freezing into the landscape. Not moving, not wanting to be part of any of this and yet desperately wanting Mom to agree. Which Mom was he talking to – the long-term denial Mom or the recently aware of the need to grieve Mom?

Mom tossed her head. "I'm fine. I don't know why you even bothered. I don't need to 'talk to' anyone."

Yeah, one good day at Garden Club and you're fine.

Dad pressed his lips together and sighed.

I stared at the painting on the wall across from me, focused intently on the color blue. Was it more of a royal blue? Navy? Something more exotic, like peacock.

"Well, I think maybe you do," Dad said. "You have not been yourself lately."

Lately? Like for about five years?

"I'm *fine!*" Mom said forcefully standing up and grabbing the plates. "You act like I'm crazy or something. *Crazy* people go to therapists, not me." She stomped out of the room.

Finally I stopped staring at the painting and looked at Dad. He shook his head.

"Well, I tried," he said. As if that was it. He tried, she said no, story over.

"That's it? You aren't going to say more?'

Before he could answer the swinging door flew open and Mom was back.

 "I'm not crazy! How dare you even suggest it?!" Mom was wound up now. Like she went into the kitchen and thought about it some more and got herself really worked up. "You think I'm some kind of *nut?* I'm not one of those people! I'll tell you who is crazy. YOU!" she said, pointing at my dad. "You work insane hours, you are always tense, you have no hobbies, no friends, no NOTHING. If there is anything wrong with me it is YOU!"

Mom whirled around and stormed back through the swinging doors.

"Well, that went well," Dad said, raising his eyebrows. I think it was his attempt at humor.

I heard pots clanging in the kitchen. Like she was still yelling at him with the pots.

Was angry better than depressed?

The door swung open yet again.

"And YOU!" Mom screamed, pointing at me. "This is all YOUR fault! Stop asking your stupid questions. Stop stirring things up!"

Once more, she whirled around and banged through the doors.

So much for being camouflaged.

Dad stared at me, and I could swear he was thinking the same thing. Why had I stirred it all up? I'm not sure I knew myself.

Dad stood up, picked up his plate and glass and went to the kitchen.

"Get away from me!" I heard Mom yell. "Just *go away.*"

Dear Diary,

I've heard the phrase "walking on eggshells" but tonight my house felt even worse. Like walking a tightrope over an alligator pit. Blindfolded. One wrong move and we'll all be devoured. I really thought Mom understood, that for a moment there she agreed with me about letting herself feel sad about Helen. But no, she is a mess. She thinks she is okay but she is far from okay. Help!

Once I made sure Davy was in bed and the pills still well hidden, I climbed into my own bed with *My Friend Flicka*. Too bad I couldn't crawl into the book and stay there forever. Even though it kept getting him in trouble, I loved Ken's ability to completely lose himself in an imaginary world. Just like me.

For an hour or so I lived someone else's problems. By the time I fell asleep, I was pleasantly sick with the longing for my own colt.

Chapter Fifty

Wonder Girl

I woke at 5:30 half listening for the whinny of horses and the wind brushing across the wide Wyoming spaces. With no need to get up right away and wanting to stay in Wyoming, I reached a hand out into the cold morning air, grabbed *My Friend Flicka* off the nightstand and pulled it under the covers with me. Ken loses himself in staring into his mother's duck painting and then rushes to breakfast, waiting for his father's disappointment with him, yet again. He gets it but then, my heart racing right along with Ken's, his dad surprises him by telling him he can have a colt after all.

Ken's father sends him to get the Stud book so they can look over the choices and Ken dances and skips and jumps the whole way to the stables. Even though I sort of figured he would get a colt, given the name of the book and the picture on the front and all, I was just as excited as Ken. Maybe if good things were happening for Ken, they could happen for me.

Which made me think about my list of Desired Personality Characteristics. Things seem to be going okay at school but what about home? Maybe it was time for a review. Plus, I didn't know yet what Ken was going to offer me, but I could feel something floating around when I read that book, and I wanted to be ready for his addition. I pulled my diary out from under my pillow and wrote down each one, considering where I was with it.

Confident – well this one was certainly taking root in me.

Planful – I had kind of lost track of this one, but maybe that was okay. Maybe Planful is important to get something going, but then it all starts to feel kind of natural. Then I remembered my plan to solve the mystery of Helen's death and make sure it didn't happen to Mom. Needed to get back to that one. Although maybe I kind of already knew. Helen was depressed because she couldn't have a baby. And Mom had kids, so that couldn't be a problem for her. Right? But what was this aversion to Norwick? Was it just that it reminded her of Helen? Still some investigating to do.

Brave – I was definitely showing some brave behavior. The feeling couldn't be far behind.

Self-sufficient – If it meant not needing Mom, then definitely. If it meant not caring what happens to Mom, then way off track. I decided it meant the first more than the second.

Endurance – I had to say I was hanging in there. I could be like Santiago. I *would* be like Santiago.

Tough – I felt good about this one. I was still standing, wasn't I? What is that if not Tough?

Flawed – Well there would never be a problem with this one. Although it helped to remember that my flaws might just be my strength someday.

Stealthy – hmm, don't think I'd call my behavior lately Stealthy. Not at home or at school. Would have to work on it at home for sure.

Kind – Good reminder to keep Kindness around. Reacting to all the mean stuff at school could make girl, well, mean. I wasn't trying to *replace* Cassidy, just survive Cassidy.

Dignity – I'm holding my head up high, right? That is, when I'm not getting knocked face down in my pizza.

Wise – ooh, tough one. Sometimes I felt the wisdom of the Little Prince, sometimes it drifted away from me. Must remember what is essential.

Intrepid – Again, a reminder. Stay with the Aunt Helen thing until Mom was okay.

Appreciation – Well, no time like the present. I thought about how much I loved *My Friend Flicka*, already. And how comfortable my bed was. And how I could just walk downstairs and always find food. Not everyone in the world could say that. And how I seem to be gaining friends every day. Or at least, pleasant acquaintances. And my hair, that was looking good. Never underestimate the value of good hair.

I didn't want to forget these things. I needed something to remind me, but what? I wrote out the letters: C-P-B-S-E-T-F-S-K-D-W-I-A. I played with arranging them into some sort of word. KISSED plus something else.

Hmmm. KISSED PAT WBCF. I liked the "KISSED" part but the rest didn't make any sense.

As I wrote down strings of letters, it occurred to me it would be easier if I could move them around. And then I had a brilliant idea. I ran to Mom's work room, and started opening cupboards until I found the box of letter beads I thought might still be there. Leftover from some craft stuff we did when I was younger, they were the little blocks, some silver, some white, with letters on them and a hole in the middle for stringing into necklaces and bracelets. There was some stretchy cord left in the box and I brought the whole thing back to my room. I found all the letters in silver and laid them out, moving them back and forth.

I would make a bracelet to remind myself of my Desired Personality Characteristics.

As I came up with even more odd combinations (FEW BAD KISS TPC), I realized I didn't want anyone to know what this was about. Maybe just a random order was better anyway. I strung them onto the stretchy cord in their original order, tied a knot and slipped it over my wrist.

All day at school I felt protected, reminded, empowered by my bracelet. Like I had a secret. Like I had on Wonder Woman's powerful cuffs.

I looked across the room in chemistry, enjoying my secret power, and my eyes fell on Emily. She looked small and alone without Cassidy, who had missed school for a third day in a row. Talk about shrinking into a desk. Her head stayed down for the whole class and afterwards she slipped out like a wisp of smoke. Of course she never looked in my direction.

I followed her to math and then study hall, feeling like I could see the loneliness trailing behind her. Meanwhile, people chatted with me in both classes, and the hallways in between. It felt like watching the old me, lonely and scared, while at the same time living the new me. I tried to catch Emily's eye, let her know I wasn't mad at her, but she never looked up. Funny how that works, when you are so sure you won't find a friend, you don't even look for one.

Chapter Fifty-One

Sea Change

Even though Christmas was still a couple of weeks away, Mom was in full preparation mode. She was sending Dad out almost constantly for something or other. It was Monday and for once he got home by 6:00 only to have Mom send him back out to the store.

"Jacqueline, you better go with him. You know the kind of pie shells I get. And don't forget the whipping cream! And here, here's the rest of the list."

Mom handed me list, the printing so perfect it could have come from a computer. Depressed or not she still managed to do a lot of things perfectly.

"Oh, and I need cognac from the State store, just a cheap bottle for cooking," Mom added.

Dad hadn't even taken off his coat, so I grabbed mine and we headed to the garage.

I loved riding in Dad's car. First of all, because it was with Dad and he was always just so calm. Even a drive felt different than with Mom's wound up energy. And there were no Davy toys rolling around on the floor. And it was low and sleek, not like riding up high in Mom's SUV. I felt like an adult when I rode in Dad's car, especially when I was in the front seat like I was right now.

An hour later, groceries stowed in the trunk we headed down the main street towards the liquor store. The frenzy of Christmas shopping had clearly begun because every parking spot was taken. Finally, we found something in a lot on one of the back streets.

Cognac bought and bundled into a paper bag, we were sliding along the poorly shoveled Second street sidewalk towards our car.

"Oh shoot, I meant to get deodorant at the grocery store," said Dad, pulling his heavy coat sleeve up to see his watch. "I'm just going to run into the drugstore and grab some."

"Go ahead. I'll wait for you in the car," I said.

Dad handed me the keys and the bag. "Watch out, it's pretty dark and drivers might not see you so well."

"Aye aye captain," I said.

I picked my way carefully through the slush and ice and crossed into the parking lot.

As I stepped between two parked cars, I heard a man's voice, loud and angry, coming from the next line of parked cars.

"Get in the car now, or I'm going to whack you one," yelled the ugly, contemptuous voice. "Hurry up you little whore, just like your whore mother."

I felt sick at hearing that and was afraid to even look toward the voice. What if he saw me looking and turned that wrath on me? I hoped it was dark enough he wouldn't even notice me, but there was a glare from the lights arching over the parking lot. I sneaked a glance around the car I was standing by and saw a large man roughly grab a girl's arm and push her toward the open door of the car they were standing beside. With his other hand he whacked at her head, and even though she ducked he connected with her cheek. As the girl half fell, half climbed into the car I saw her face for a split second, and I realized that it was Cassidy.

I stood frozen, horrified. That was Cassidy's dad. Her dad calling her and her mother whores. Her dad hitting her! It was like the entire world stopped, like in movies where they pause action and show one character step out of it and do something while everything else remains frozen. As I stood there not even breathing for fear he'd see me, it all clicked into place. *Cassidy's dad abused her.* Cassidy lived in an awful home, with awful secrets.

Perfect Cassidy didn't have such a perfect life after all. I would have thought I might feel some secret gladness at Cassidy's misfortune, but instead all I felt was a huge aching sadness. Was nothing as it seemed?

Now like a fast-frame movie it all ran through my head. Her unwillingness to have Ben pick her up at home. Mr. Dubroski's vicious attacks on Dad, of course those happened at home too. The bruises I'd seen on her legs and arms that she chalked up to dancing injuries – and how no other Poms had so many. The need to control everyone and everything around her. The Mom who desperately tried to stay pretty. Everyone in the house trying for perfection to prevent abuse. And probably eventually always failing. And oh my god, the abstinence program. I couldn't even let myself think about that.

"Stay in there you little bitch!" Dubroski growled jabbing at her shoulder one more time and then slamming the door. I heard him crunch around the car to the driver's side and then heard another door slam. The engine caught and the car shot backward and then pulled out of the lot.

I didn't move for at least another minute, somehow fearful he'd come back and see me. Finally, I moved away from between the two cars and found our car, two rows over. I beeped it open, climbed in, locked the doors and slumped down on the seat.

Cassidy's dad beat her. I almost felt stupid for not putting it together before. There was an abundance of evidence from Dad of how evil and vicious Mr. Dubroski was. And Cassidy's out of control behavior at school. Duh.

I was shaking and freezing. I stuck the key in the ignition and turned the heater on, but that wasn't enough. I turned the seat heater up to high and pulled my feet up under me, making myself a small ball.

I didn't know a lot about psychology, but anyone could figure out that if someone treated you badly at home, you might end up treating other people badly somewhere else like school. Not only because that is what you learned at home, but also because it would be a way to feel some element of control in your life. I knew only too well that when your parents are messing up everything about your family's life, you have to find something in your life that feels under your control. For me it had turned out to be pretending to be fictional characters and writing in my diary. But Cassidy must not have found those kinds of things. Cassidy found abstinence programs and bullying the Unnoticeables as her way to cope.

Dad pulled on the door handle then peered in at me. I unlocked the doors and wondered how to tell him what I just saw.

"The deodorant fairy has arrived!" Dad laughed, tossing a drug store bag in the back seat. "Wow, it's baking in here."

"Yeah, I was cold," I said. I couldn't find the words to describe what just happened.

Dad sensed something was up. Or maybe it was the stiff body and blank face I had. And the way I was curled into the fetal position.

"Are you all right?" Dad asked.

"Yes, well, no, I mean, I'm fine, but I just saw something awful," I said and I burst into tears.

"Jackie! What's going on?" Dad asked.

I shook my head side-to-side. "I just can't believe it. I was walking back to the car, and I heard this man yelling awful things, and then I looked and it was Mr. Dubroski and he hit Cassidy! And he called her a whore!"

Dad shut his eyes absorbing the image, like he could believe it and not believe it at the same time. Then he opened them up and grabbed my hand. "I'm so sorry you saw that. How terrible."

I was sobbing as I told him all the rest of the details. It felt like I was describing the end of childhood. All the stuff that had happened up until now paled in comparison. They were worries, they were dilemmas, they were hardships. This was evil. I really had always believed that deep down, people were good. That things worked out and people did the right thing. That someone that mean could exist and even look outwardly successful made me want to throw up.

Dad slid over and put his arm around me. Finally my crying slowed down.

"That guy is truly an asshole, isn't he?" I said.

"Truly," agreed Dad. "The definition of."

"Now I see what you are up against," I said, feeling even more scared for Dad. "That guy would do anything. If he would hit his daughter! What if he hurts you?"

Dad squeezed me. "Don't worry about me. I may not have his level of assholeness, but I can be just as tough in my own way."

"What should we do?" I said. Part of me felt like we should drive straight to the police station and report him, part of me wanted to pretend nothing had happened.

"Right now there's probably nothing we can do. It would just be your word against his, and then he'd probably go home and beat her again."

"But there must be something!"

"I suppose you could approach Cassidy at school, tell her you know and offer to help her."

"Cassidy *hates* me. Her dad must talk all the time about hating you, and she passes it on to me. I'm the last person she'd want to talk to." Even as I said it I flashed to the image of Cassidy cowering against the locker when I pushed her. No wonder she had been scared. She was waiting to be beaten. I felt awful. Here I was thinking she had it all, and she was probably thinking the same thing about me.

"Um, Dad, just for now could we not tell anyone?" Mom would never keep this quiet and this might just send the Dubroski-Carson war nuclear.

Dad nodded. "Of course."

Every couple of minutes on the way home Dad shook his head. Like even he was surprised at how deep Dubroski's wickedness went.

I couldn't get that harsh voice out of my head, a father calling his daughter a whore! And so rough with her too. I kept thinking about how incomplete my ideas about Cassidy had been. It still wasn't nice to be mean to people, but it made a huge difference to know that Cassidy had such an awful dad. Why did that matter? I wasn't sure, but it did. What if I was making the same kind of mistakes about other people? You could never really know what was going on in someone else's life. I hadn't known about Cassidy's family, I knew other people didn't know about my family. What if *everyone* was trying to cope with hard stuff? What if all those kids at school who seemed to have everything actually didn't? Maybe they were more like me than I had ever thought possible.

It was almost completely dark by the time we wove up the narrow hill road toward our neighborhood. Every once in a while we passed a weak streetlight, and I wondered why anyone even bothered to put them in. They illuminated almost nothing, just gave a little circle of light every half mile or so.

I knew the feeling would probably pass, but driving through that dark night I felt a strong connection to everyone at school. I felt a kinship with them all, with the jocks and stoners and nerds and the Unnoticeables. Even with the Poms. I knew that when I went back to school people would still do stupid stuff and mean stuff, but I also realized that I had a whole new perspective on *why* they might be doing that kind of stuff. I felt like I could see right through to everyone's vulnerable insides, like I was Superman or someone with special vision. It made everything different. We were all in this together.

Chapter Fifty-Two

"Anything Essential is Invisible to the Eyes"

I was actually eager to get to school the next day. I couldn't wait to see if the feeling of connection to the world would continue. I felt like Ken, when he felt like he had turned into someone new. Nothing new on my locker, that was a plus. I slipped into homeroom and walked toward my seat.

Scott Cooper, a boy who I had never heard say a word, stopped me. "Hey, um, Jacqueline, nice hair."

I looked at Scott with my new eyes, and realized that while I had always thought of him as practically mute with shyness, maybe that wasn't accurate at all. Maybe he was just uninterested in school or people, maybe he was depressed. Who knew, maybe his dad had cancer and he could barely keep his mind on anything else.

I smiled at Scott. "Thanks." Then, because he didn't seem to know what to do next, I kept going. "At first it was such a mess, you know? And then I found out about flat irons." I was starting to realize that sometimes it wasn't actually what you said, it was just that you said *something*. Like Scott probably didn't really care about flat irons, but he was trying to connect, so hey, I was going to help him. Maybe that's why people talk about the weather so much. Just a way to connect.

Scott nodded vigorously. "Yeah, that's good," he said, his voice changing from little boy to man between words. That must suck, the whole voice change thing. He blushed and turned away and slid into his seat.

I had never really paid any attention to Scott. I guess lots of people were Unnoticeable, even to me. Now I really looked at him. He was tall and skinny with blond hair flopping over one eye. He was bent over his desk, shoulders hunched up to his ears, scratching intently at a sticker embedded into the desk top, as if it was the most vital thing in the world to get it off immediately. He's embarrassed, I thought. But in a good way, that he talked to someone when he wasn't used to it.

I looked around the homeroom, feeling like I was seeing everyone in there for the first time. I systematically ran my eyes up and down the rows, starting at the front left corner. I looked at each person, wondering what was going on in that person's life. This boy could have an alcoholic dad, that girl could have parents who hit each other. That girl might have a family that threw things, that boy might have a mother who was blind. Come to think of it, that boy right there, Chris Connelly, didn't he have a sister with Down syndrome? For the first time I really thought about what that might be like for him. What was Chris's life like at home? Did he have to help with her? Did his sister get all the attention? How did his parents handle it? Was he embarrassed about it? Did he think about it during school? And then I remembered that another girl in the class, Amy Donahue, had lost her dad in a car accident.

I knew that it was unlikely that everyone in the class had big dramas in their lives, but then again, maybe they did. It made every single person seem so human, so vulnerable that I wanted to hug every one. Even the boy whose BO practically knocked me back against the wall. Even the mean Goth girl who always seemed to be sneering at my conformity. I especially wanted to hug that girl because now I was convinced that the mean people were the ones with the most pain in their lives. If she was being mean to me, it was a good bet that someone was being mean to her.

The bell rang and I walked to my classes in a haze of goodwill. I had ordinary conversations with people that seemed extraordinary. I felt like I could see below the skin of everyone around me. I felt soft and yet strong inside. Fearful it would disappear, I thought about how to remember this feeling, this ability to see people for the collection of imperfections that they were.

As I walked toward history my letter bead bracelet clinked against my watch. I looked down at it. Maybe everyone was wishing they could be those things. Maybe everyone would like bullet-deflecting bracelets.

I sat in history unable to listen to the lecture. It was weird, like I was living in two different dimensions. The worries and problems weren't completely gone. Dad's job was still at risk,

Cassidy still hated me, Mom was not herself. And yet I had this sense of seeing through to the middle of things, of understanding why people do what they do.

Aha!

That's what the Little Prince was referring to when he talked about "anything essential is invisible to the eyes." This feeling of seeing through to what is inside people, that's what he meant. I wanted to stand up and sing it to the class, but I didn't. I hadn't lost all touch with reality. I still cared if people thought I was a nut.

And then I thought about Sara and her Kindness, and I had another aha! go off in my brain. This connected feeling, this seeing to the inside of people was *empathy*. And that is what allows you to be kind to other people. It's understanding that they are probably going through something hard. It's understanding that if you lived in their skin, in their brain, you'd know why they do what they do.

Which made me even more sure than ever that there was more to the Mom-Helen story. And I needed to find out what it was.

As I changed clothes for PE and saw Emily come in, I knew why I hadn't stayed mad at her for her behavior. Disappointed, yes. Sad, definitely. But I *knew* Emily. I knew her well enough to understand what was going on in her brain. I knew how roughed up she felt from her parents' divorce. I knew how badly she wanted to be a Pom. I knew that it was costing her to keep at it and that she couldn't find the strength to stand up to Cassidy. A wave of compassion hit me, and I gave her a big, warm smile as she walked by me.

"Hey, Em," I called.

"Uh, hi, Jackie," Emily said, slowing down but not fully stopping. She went around to the next alcove.

It was okay. I couldn't control her behavior, just my own. I said hi, I felt my empathy, it was up to Emily to figure out her side.

I was late to English, but Tommy had saved me a seat. I slid in and we exchanged friendly smiles. I wondered what it was like to be Tommy. To come from generations of money. To be kind of chubby and short and pink. To have a loud-talker dad. I tried to imagine I was in his head, looking out of his eyes. How would people respond to me? I immediately felt the disappointment of not attracting attention from girls. He seemed to deal with that pretty well. I felt the insecurity of not being as tall as some other guys. He dealt with that well too. I was thinking that Tommy was a pretty solid guy, and not just in the literal sense.

It was almost too much, this new ability to see the world through other people's eyes. I tried to focus on class. Especially since we were talking about *The Yearling*.

After English, Tommy and I walked out together

"Good weekend?" Tommy asked.

Wow. How to answer that one? "Okay in some ways, weird in others," I finally said.

Then I saw Cassidy coming down the hall. My heart overflowed with a whole stew of emotions - sadness, sympathy, compassion. Cassidy was flipping her hair and shaking her chest just like she always did, but now I saw it for what it was. A brave attempt at making something in life hers. She ignored me, which I kind of regretted. I wanted to smile at her, let her know with my eyes that I empathized with her.

I was sitting in my now regular lunch spot with the hottie boys. Alex picked up my hand and slid my letter bracelet off. He held it up in front of his face.

"What's this?" he asked.

"Just a bracelet," I said, trying to sound like it was no big deal. Trying to sound like his hand touching mine didn't just set off a series of shocks through my body.

"What do the letters mean?"

Just my whole life plan.

"Stuff I want to remember," I said.

Nick took the bracelet from Alex and slid it on his own wrist where it landed against two leather bands and a woven red and purple string thing. He held his arm out, twisting it around as he looked at it. "It's cool. Did you make it?"

I nodded.

"I think it's the initials of all the hearts you've broken," said Alex, giving me one of his soul penetrating looks.

I have to say Alex's stare still made me feel kind of buzzy, but I also could see something new about him. Alex was no different than everyone else with their secret dramas. I knew he

came from a rundown section of town. I had heard his dad had
disappeared and his mother was around but not much of a parent.
Alex was trying to control his world every bit as much as Cassidy.
His method was just way more fun.

I gave him a huge, genuine smile. "I *wish*."

Alex moved his head back slightly. I don't even think he
was aware of it. I think *my* Mojo was now affecting *him*.

Andy glanced back and forth between us. Was something
going on here? I wasn't flirting with Alex, I was just feeling
particularly connected to the universe at this moment.

"How come you guys don't sit with other girls? I mean,
why me?" I said. Apparently nothing was too bold for me these
days.

They guys all looked at each other and no one answered.

I gave a palms up gesture to Alex, he seemed like the
ringleader.

He shrugged. "Too much drama."

"Me or other girls?" I asked.

"Other girls," said Nick, finally slipping off my bracelet and
handing it back.

Ben nodded in agreement. I looked at him and wondered if
he had any idea of Cassidy's drama. Any clue at all about his former
girlfriend's family. I didn't think he did. It's not where your brain
goes unless you've had some kind of hell in your own life.

That gave me an idea. If I told anyone, maybe Ben would
be the one to tell about Cassidy's dad and his abuse. I didn't want it
getting around school, but Ben seemed like a decent guy. Cassidy
needed someone on her side.

"*I'm* not drama? With the pregnancy rumors, bad haircuts
and all that?"

Ben looked at Andy who looked at Nick. "Yeah, that's
entertainment," said Nick. "You don't make it a drama." Nick
launched into falsetto valley girl talk. "Like 'Oh my god?! Look at
my hair! Look at my extra ounce of fat! Oh my god, what will I
do?'"

The other boys laughed. Even three days ago I would have
too, but now I felt a kinship with those girls. Maybe they were
agonizing about hair because they were too anxious to talk about
something else, like the weirdness of getting your period or the boy

who you totally crushed on who liked your best friend or not
growing breasts fast enough or growing them too fast.

Chapter Fifty-Three

Better to be an Orphan

Isn't it funny how life doesn't let you feel happy for very long? Like today all day at school I had felt connected to the world, and all warm and happy and feeling compassion even for Mom. And Melody and I had a good laugh in keyboarding when we noticed that the keyboarding teacher's skirt was stuck up in her pantyhose in the back. Like, I had actually had a good day. And I hadn't needed to pretend to be anyone fictional at all. Of *course* it couldn't last.

When I got home, Mom told me Davy was sick and asked me to sit on the couch with him while she made dinner. Davy's face was so pale it was almost green, and every once in a while he would lean over and retch into the garbage can Mom had set beside him.

I went out to the kitchen for more gingerale for Davy right as Dad came home.

"Could you run by the drugstore? I need some stuff for Davy," Mom said to Dad.

Uh, maybe a hello first? She didn't even realize how rude she was these days.

"Sure. You should have called me on my way home," said Dad.

"I tried, you didn't answer," said Mom.

I was tired of listening to puking. "Let me come," I said. "I need some poster board."

After the drugstore run, Dad and I walked into the kitchen, laughing about the goofy clerk who'd helped us. Before I even saw Mom, I could tell something was wrong. There was an ugly energy in the room, and then I saw Mom sitting deathly still at the table. I looked down and saw my diary in front of her. I went as still inside as my frozen mother.

Uh oh.

Dad had no clue anything was wrong.

"Here's the medicine, the new thermometer and some more gingerale," he said, setting the bag on the counter. "How is he?"

Dad finally looked at Mom.

"What's wrong? Is Davy okay?" he asked in a panicked voice.

"Davy is fine," said Mom in a monotone, her face unmoving, her eyes staring straight at me.

"Your daughter, however is NOT FINE!" and with that Mom jumped up and started yelling.

"Apparently, I am just a big crazy NUT!" Mom was shaking and sobbing and almost exploding with rage. She looked crazy, like a lab rat injected with a triple dose of methamphetamines. Like there was an alien inside her body scratching to get out. Like she could start clawing my face off at any moment.

Mom shook my diary high in the air.

"Do you know what this is? It is Jacqueline's DIARY. It is the most vile, mean thing you have ever seen!"

How dare she look in my diary!

Dad still didn't have his coat off. "What are you talking about?"

"What an ungrateful, mean, little SHIT she is!" Mom was crying so hard and yelling so intensely she stuttered the words out. "I haven't gotten the whole way through, but here's a sample: She thinks we are all liars around here. She thinks I am the most egocentric, CRAZY person alive. She calls me a 'soul eating virus!' My daughter apparently HATES me." Spit and rage spewed out with the words that Mom couldn't scream fast enough.

How STUPID am I to write all that down?! I'm an idiot.

Dad shrugged out of his coat. "Hold on, calm down."

"Calm down?! My daughter thinks I'm psycho and apparently you do too!" Mom's wild eyes made her look exactly psycho as she stabbed her finger at dad. "Don't bother your mom, she's not strong." You think I'm "weak"! I'll give you weak!

Mom threw the diary across the room and charged towards me.

Dad stepped in front of her and grabbed her shoulders. "Marion, just calm down. No one thinks you are crazy."

I shrunk behind Dad, wanting to run out of the room but afraid to leave.

"Of course you think I'm crazy!" Mom wailed, her face screwed up into a million wrinkles, her eyes bare slits. She poked her finger at Dad. "*You're* the one talking about sending me to a therapist. You do think I'm crazy. You all are in it together!"

Dad had Mom by the shoulders by this time. "Marion, calm down. Let's just calm down everyone, okay?"

"Everyone hates me! You all can just live together in your happy little family WITHOUT ME. All you *perfect* people!" With that Mom wrenched free from Dad, and ran towards the garage grabbing her car keys off the mom desk on her way.

"Marion wait!" Dad called, hurrying after her. The garage door was already going up and I heard the SUV squeal out of the garage.

I heard the sound of vomiting from the family room. Great. A puking kid and a crazy Mom.

Dad came back in and paced up and down in front of the island. "Should I go after her? Should I call someone? She's really upset. She shouldn't be driving."

I felt like I could vomit too. This was all my fault.

What was wrong with me?

I started to cry, silent at first, and then I couldn't stop it, big hulking sobs erupting from my chest, fighting with the tears to get out. Like my insides couldn't stand me either and were trying to escape.

I felt Dad's arms around me, and I melted into his big chest, his coat scratching my face but I didn't care. I just wanted to crawl inside his coat and cry forever.

How had it all gone so wrong?

Eventually, I heard Davy crying. I didn't know how long I had stood there, melted into Dad. I pulled back. "You better go help him," I whispered, and staggered over to the bench in the breakfast nook.

I laid my head down on the table on top of my folded arms. My nose was so stuffed from crying I had to breathe through my mouth, but the tears kept coming.

I felt Dad come back and sit down beside me, and his arm go around my shoulders.

"It's going to be okay," he said, unconvincingly.

I pulled my head up and looked at him. "That's bullshit and you know it." I was shocked to hear myself talking to Dad that way but all he did was tilt his head, as if in agreement.

"Okay, well, things are a bit of a mess," he amended.

I sat further up, back against the cushions. There was a battle going on inside me, half of me in deep shame that I had caused all this, the other half outraged at Mom's behavior. How could she read my diary? How could she be so crazy? Why did I ever have to start all this Aunt Helen business? Why did I have to *write* about it for crying out loud? Why was I pushing an already fragile person over the edge?

Dad sat back against the cushions beside me and pulled out his phone. He hit a button and a few seconds later I heard muffled sound of Mom's phone ringing. We both looked over toward the mom desk and sure enough, there was her purse. Dad walked over and pulled out the phone.

"Well, so much for calling her." He turned off the ringing and set it down, then picked it back up. "At least we have the phone numbers of her friends. He brought the phone back over to the nook and sat down. One after the other he called Mom's friends to let them know to call us if she showed up. As an afterthought he called Aunt Ruth and Grandma too.

Davy called out again and this time I dragged myself up to go help him. I felt stuck in some kind of horror movie, time seemed to warp and life felt like it would never feel right again.

The night dragged on with no word from Mom. No sound of the garage door going back up. No phone calls, no texts.

It didn't feel right to go to bed and Davy was still periodically throwing up so I made him a bed on one couch and laid down on the other one with a blanket. At some point Dad must have come in and turned off the TV because when I woke in the morning, the only light was the barely gray haze of a Pennsylvania winter sunrise.

I stumbled into the kitchen and found Dad fumbling with the coffee maker.

"I talked to Ruth, your Mom is in Norwick," Dad said, poking at the buttons on the coffee maker. "How does this thing work?"

Relief, followed by confusion and fear. "Norwick?" What could that mean? Was it good, her heading towards her parents and sister? Or was it bad, heading towards the place where Helen . . .?

Dad shrugged. "Ruth called a little after two. Sounds like Mom was, ah, still quite upset, but she's at least with someone."

Both of us knew what kind of relief that brought. Only now, as he said it, could I really let myself admit the dark thoughts that had haunted my dreams all night. Mom, crazed with anger and depressed, off doing . . . something . . . to herself. I started crying all over again.

Dad pulled me into a hug. "We are going to work this out, I promise. You were right. She needs help, help that we can't give her."

At least Dad finally got it. But had Mom gone too far to come back?

Chapter Fifty-Four

Something Lost, Something Gained

No way I was going to school. I was too worried and Davy was sick and Dad kept sneaking glances at the clock on the microwave.

"It's okay, you can go to work," I said.

"Well, I don't know what to do. There's stuff I really can't miss, but things are kind of a mess here," Dad said.

"Go. Nothing you can do here," I said, but I'm sure we were both wondering what would happen if Mom came home.

"I'll call you or text you if I hear from Mom, or if she comes home," I said.

Dad stared at me, then gave a nod. He pulled me into a big hug. "I'm sorry you have to go through this, honey, I really am."

My face was buried in the faded gray Steeler shirt he wore over his pajama pants. I just nodded. It sucked.

I pulled away. "I'll make coffee. I think I know what to do."

Dad patted my shoulders, "Thanks. I'll check on Davy, take a shower and be right down."

With Dad gone and Davy still sleeping, I wandered into the library looking for relief. The pull of books was stronger than ever. If I could just figure out how to disappear completely. The relief of knowing Mom was with Ruth started to fade. What if Ruth didn't stay with her? What if Ruth had to go to school and Mom was all alone? I went back to the kitchen, found my phone and texted Aunt Ruth.

Is Mom ok?
Is she with you?

While I waited to hear back I got *My Friend Flicka* from my room and came back to the library. The phone buzzed and I opened up Ruth's text.

Hanging in.
Can stay w her all day.

My shoulders released themselves from up around my ears, and I pulled a blanket over me and burrowed into the leather chair with only one little lamp over my shoulder. The light illuminated the book but not much else, leaving the library in shadows. The day outside had never lightened into more than a dull gray, and I felt like I was the only person alive in the world.

I let myself drift into Ken's world, became a Wyoming rancher's wife when he described how his mother broke her horse, Rumba. It was slow, calm, an easing up to the horse not a violent breaking of its spirit. So different than the way the men did it. I could hear her quiet voice, my voice now, slow, slow, letting horse smell me, see me, get used to me. Leaning into the horse once it nuzzled my shoulder. Every once in a while lifting my knee as if about to mount but then lowering my leg. Slowly preparing the horse for what was to come, with a long, easy, patience. I felt my insides relax, as calm as the horse, as calm as Ken's mother. Patiently waiting for whatever was to come.

Finally, reluctantly, I came back into my world and took a break. I peeked in at Davy but he was still asleep. I filled a cup with gingerale, stuck on a lid and a straw and set it beside him, Nell's patience still swirling in my brain. I thought about my mother compared to Nell and then realized my mother was more like the unbroken horse, scared and wild, than the calm mom. I wondered if Nell's kind of patience, her calm presence, would do anything for mom. If she ever came home I'd have to pretend to be Nell. Pretend mom was Rumba and ease up to her. See if that quiet calm could spread to her.

As I eased back into the chair and tucked the blanket around me I thought about how there were mother themes all over this book. Ken wonders if Flicka will be crazy like *her* mother, Rocket, or strong and brave like her sire Banner. He constantly monitors Flicka for signs of Rocket's craziness.

How much does a mother matter?

I realized I wouldn't know until the end of the book. And in my own life, I might never know. I thought about Beryl Markham and how she seemed to grow up just fine without a mother. And about the Little Princess with no mother. And even Nancy Drew, for crying out loud. She had no mother either. It suddenly struck me that in most (all?) of the books I liked, the mother was just not important. Or maybe "important" wasn't the right word. Maybe the thing I liked so much was how all these characters seem to figure life out without a mother. Claudia had a mother but didn't seem to need her. And same with Jody. For Ken it was a bit different. His mother was what I dreamed a mother would be. But Flicka, Flicka's mother was just crazy enough that Flicka might never make it.

Ken's dad is sure that Flicka will be crazy like her mother Rocket, but Ken won't give up on her and it leads to a long test of wills between Ken and his dad. I found myself siding with Ken, almost begging Flicka to behave, to prove Ken right. Score one for the dreamer, please.

I couldn't put the book down. Such a relief to live other people's dramas. And Flicka herself represents the untamed heart, the wild force of nature, uncaught, untethered. As they try to catch Flicka, even Ken has mixed feelings watching her, half hoping for her to escape, half wanting to catch her. I was right beside him, admiring Flicka's untamed nature, her wild freedom. And yet, wanting her for Ken, wanting him to have his dream, wanting him to prove his father wrong.

I stopped a couple of times to check on Davy, once making him some chicken noodle soup, but for the rest of the day (no word from Mom), I read the book.

Through the attempts to break Flicka, through her injuries and then recuperation, through Ken's long illness and his grief at thinking that Flicka is dead.

And once Ken starts to get better the doctor says not to tell him Flicka made it because even good news can be a shock and Ken is still very weak. Says he will leave it up to Ken's mother to know when the right time is. By the time she tells Ken he seems to have no interest, he's still cut off from life, weary and listless. Then, out driving with his dad Ken sees a stag, noble and proud and unmoving and asks his dad why the stag doesn't run away and his dad says he is watching over his doe. And Ken stares and thinks about it and says "Because *she's his responsibility?*" and his dad says yes and Ken thinks about Flicka:

> When he could no longer see the stag, his eyes roved over the hills and woods. He did not know what had ended the cold, weary detachment and united him to the world again, he only knew that it was his own once more, that it was beautiful and alive, that he wanted to see Flicka. And he pressed his face against his father's sleeve and wept.

Ken goes to find Flicka, who had looked for him every day, and she hears him calling as he comes to her and lets out a neigh she had never made before. Boy and horse finding each other again. My lonely dark room felt warmer, lighter, even hopeful.

I sat in the small glow of the side lamp, looking out into the dark room. Ken's joy swirled through me but it had a weight to it, a gravity. It wasn't the joy of a child, it was the joy of an adult, an understanding of the difficulties of the world and a discovery, in the middle of them, of something good. It wasn't something that came easily, in fact it almost didn't come at all. I thought about Mom. She was in the middle of the hard part, and I wondered if she was more like Flicka or Ken. Both of them near death, both had to find the way back to life. Both tamed, in a way, Flicka of her wild Albino blood, Ken of his daydreaming. And what about Mom? Did she have the loco blood like Rocket or was it just a growing up kind of thing like Flicka? I knew that battle for her was going on right now and felt helpless, like Ken's mother sitting next to him in his fevers, or Ken lying in the stream with Flicka. No, not even that because I wasn't with her.

I thought about Cassidy, and the pain she was going through that nobody even knew about. If you could know, really know, what went on in a person's heart, wouldn't you always feel some sort of sympathy? What if I really knew Mom's pain. Would I understand her more? If I could feel compassion for Cassidy, surely I could feel it for Mom. Maybe I could help Mom, gentle up to her like Nell did to Rumba. But then I thought about how long it took Flicka to recover, how long it took Ken. I didn't know if I could stand for things to last that long with Mom. And yet, when things looked the darkest, when there seemed no hope for anyone, it all still turned out okay. That was the part I needed to remember.

I sat with Davy, giving him sips of broth alternated with sips of gingerale. His face was less pale, but his eyes were still missing his usual impish boy energy. It was 6:00 and Dad had texted that he'd be home close to 7:00. No word from Mom.

"Why isn't Mommy here? I want Mommy," Davy whined. "She always takes care of me when I'm sick."

"She had to take care of Aunt Ruth, she's really sick too," I said, amazed at how easily the lie slipped out. No need to worry Davy. Enough bullshit around this house that I couldn't shield him from, might as well protect him when I could.

"I'm bored! There's nothing on TV," Davy said.

I guess bored was a good sign, meant he was feeling better. Nothing on a TV with 900 channels? That didn't seem possible. Then again, he couldn't watch a lot of those channels.

"Let's stick in a movie, how about Puss in Boots?" I said, knowing it was a favorite.

"I guess. And I'm hungry. I want some chips. And a corn dog."

Amazing. Puked all night, slept all day, asking for crap food tonight. He was ready for college.

I started the movie, gave him a sleeve of saltines, and settled back on the couch beside him. I played with my letter bracelet wondering what I should add from *My Friend Flicka*. How did I feel after reading the book? A very pleasant kind of melancholy. Relief that both Flicka and Ken survived, joy that they found each other again, but a kind of sadness of the price they both paid. Flicka lost her wild, untamed nature. Ken had to give up his daydreams, face the responsibilities of adulthood. Both things seemed unavoidable, and yet, somehow it made me sad. Maybe it captured my life too well. I didn't want to worry about my mother, didn't want to have to protect Davy, didn't want to know what I knew about Cassidy. But once you know, there is not going back to unknowing.

No wonder the adults get so crabby sometimes.

And it made me remember Jody and taking my share. Thinking about Jody and Ken made me realize that both books were really about growing up. They were about the things you have to give up to grow up, and how sometimes you are forced into giving those things up before you are ready. And maybe the real sign of growing up was not fighting that.

So, what characteristic to take away from the book? Well, they all survived. And they found some measure of joy. And I hoped that could happen for me too. So, "Hope" it was.

Chapter Fifty-Five

A Strange World

In the morning there was still no Mom, but Dad said he had spoken briefly to Aunt Ruth and she was going to stick with her. Whatever that meant. He said he had arranged with Jenny to come stay after school until he could get home. Davy felt better so we all headed off to our daytime places, Dad to work, Davy and me to school.

From the moment I walked through the front door at school, I felt a different kind of hum in the halls. Like people were talking more than normal, which seemed impossible. Melody was waiting at my locker, vibrating with excitement.

"Omigod, have you heard?" Melody asked, hopping up and down on her crutches.

"Heard what?" I asked, confused because the big news in my life was my parents, and I couldn't imagine other people would have already heard about that.

"Cassidy. Naked. On the *internet!*" breathed Melody.

"What?" That couldn't be. Miss Abstinence? "Must be a mistake. Must be someone who looks like Cassidy."

"Nope, it's her. I saw it! Tricia drove me to school today and showed me on her phone."

"How did she know?"

"I don't know. It's just going around. It's gone viral! *Everyone's* talking about it."

"What is she, you know, doing?"

"That's the best part! She's having SEX!"

"With who?"

"You can't see the guy. It looks like maybe he took the pictures and made sure you couldn't see his face."

There was a time this might have been funny to me, or at least interesting in a silly way. But right now all I could think was, *Poor Cassidy.*

Now that I had a glimpse into her home life, now that I saw her attempts at coping, now that my own life was trashed again, all I could feel was sorry for her.

"Poor Cassidy," I said without thinking.

"Poor Cassidy?!!!!" shrieked Melody. "What are you saying? She's made your life hell! She's made *everyone's* life hell."

It was the talk of every free moment at school. The word "hypocrite" echoed through the halls the way "copulate" and "pregnant" had. I hadn't seen Cassidy yet, but I'd heard she was at school. Probably didn't even find out until she got here because no way she would have come had she known she was today's Hot Topic.

And then, after English, there she was in the hall. No posse, only Emily at her side. Emily looked as haunted as Cassidy, but I had to give Emily credit for not abandoning her friend. Cassidy's face looked almost frozen into a small smile. Like she stuck that look on and forgot about it, just trying to survive the day.

I knew the feeling.

I tried to give her a smile that said, "it's okay, not everyone is judging you," but she wasn't making eye contact with anyone. She looked like a zombie.

And then in the lunchroom. Now instead of me it was Cassidy shrunk into a corner trying to survive the period. Oh boy, I knew that feeling too. I felt so bad for her. The one place she had felt some dominance in her life, school, had completely turned on her. Brutally.

The buzz had reached a higher frequency, like the mild zzzzz of flies had turned into the drone of a couple hundred hives of killer bees. You could tell everyone was talking about the same thing because their mouths moved and then they looked at Cassidy and then their mouths moved again. Lots of snickering. Lots of abstinence flyers being waved around. And not one Pom sitting with her. Where was Emily now?

I was sitting with the boys and wishing I wasn't. I didn't want to hear them talk about it.

"Unbelievable," said Nick. "Ben, you holding out on us?"

Ben shook his head. "I swear. It's not me. And I never, you know, saw . . . I mean, we never did anything. . .I don't even know if it's her. I haven't looked." He gave up.

"It's her," said Alex. "I'm not so shy. I looked and it's her and don't be mad at me for saying this, but she's got one smoking body."

This is why I didn't want to sit with them today. I don't need to hear how boys talk about girls.

Ben shot Alex the stink eye. "Cool it man."

Alex shrugged. "I'm not the only one saying it."

"Yeah, well you don't have to say it around me."

Alex stared at Ben for a second. "True," he said. "Sorry."

Andy punched playfully at my shoulder. "Well you must be happy, mean old Cassidy off your case now, huh?"

"Yeah, actually I feel bad for her," I said. I couldn't tell them all why. She didn't need any more grief at school

"You are a way bigger person than me," said Andy. "Cause I'd be doing a dance. I'd be forwarding that shit to everyone I know."

I didn't even answer. I stared across the tables to Cassidy, sitting by herself.

"Nice pics!" a chubby kid yelled at Cassidy as he lumbered by her table. He stuck out his tongue and whirled it around at her.

Kindness. Sara was talking in my brain. Reminding me.

I stood up and grabbed my lunch and books and walked out from behind my table.

"Where're you going?" asked Alex.

I ignored him. I walked over to Cassidy's table. As I got closer people around us got silent, and I felt like the eyes of the entire school were on me. Probably expecting me to do some kind of gloating dance or something.

I sat down facing her, trying to block at least a slender slice of the view.

"Hey, Cassidy," I said in a soft voice. I didn't smile because I didn't want her to think I was laughing at her like everyone else.

Cassidy flicked her eyes at me but didn't answer. Her face was pale and vulnerable. Her normal sneering kind of expression was nowhere to be seen. Of course, it made her prettier than ever.

"I'm sorry for all this crap," I said. "Buncha assholes in this school," I added, repeating what the janitor had said to me. It had been so helpful.

Cassidy looked at me again, puzzled. Was I being nice to her? I'm sure she didn't expect that.

"It wasn't me," she said dully.

"Hey, guess what?" I said. "I don't care if it was you or wasn't. I don't know why people make such a big deal about this stuff."

Then I thought about how when things are really bad, it feels better to just admit it. Thought about Mom pretending her sister hadn't died, Dad pretending Mom wasn't depressed. "But I get it," I said. "This sucks. No way around that."

Cassidy nodded. "No *kidding* it sucks."

I almost could feel like I was seeing it all through Cassidy's eyes. At home I'm getting punched around and now at school everyone is laughing at me. And calling me a hypocrite. And it will never end, and I will have no safe place to go. The circumstances were different, but the feelings were pretty similar to what I'd been through recently. Except of course her situation was worse. But when you are feeling that awful, degrees of worse probably don't matter as much as you think they would.

"Why are you sitting here?" asked Cassidy. "Is this some kind of joke?"

"No," I said. "I'm sitting here because I know how it feels to have everyone laughing at you. I'm sitting here because," and I knew I had to be careful with how I worded this, "everyone has their own troubles, you know? We don't always know what they are, but everyone has crap at home they have to deal with and crap at school."

Cassidy nodded vigorously.

"I don't know what to do," she said.

Yeah, that was a tough one.

"I don't know what to do," she repeated.

If it were me, I would have gotten a "stomachache" immediately and got sent home. Cassidy wouldn't be thinking of home as fondly.

"Where's your next class?" I asked her, noticing the time was almost up.

Cassidy took a deep breath, as if she dreaded walking through the halls again.

"History."

"I'll walk with you," I said.

When the bell rang, Cassidy and I stood up together. There was lots of pointing and giggling as we walked out of the lunchroom.

"Just ignore it," I whispered.

Cassidy was still in a daze and seemed ready to do whatever I told her. Her gaze was on the floor about three feet in front of her.

I felt all my characters with me. Like they were walking shoulder to shoulder with Cassidy and me. Claudia and Beryl and the Little Prince and Sara and Nancy and Jody and Ken and even old Santiago. I felt surrounded by everyone who's ever been kicked down and found something inside that made them stand back up. By everyone who has ever had to figure out the true meaning of dignity. Had to find endurance. I held my back straight, and I looked casually side-to-side, actually trying to make eye contact with the people we passed. Daring them to laugh when they looked right at us.

It was scary, and it felt like the exact right thing to do.

We made it out of the lunchroom and both of us exhaled.

As we headed toward the history room, Plaid Shirt jumped in front of us.

"Hey, these are the *fun* girls!" he said. He grabbed at his crotch. "How 'bout some action?" A couple of boys near him laughed and looked at us.

Sometimes dignity is not enough.

I squinted my eyes and stared at his crotch. "I'm sorry. I don't see anything in there. Are you sure you're not a girl?"

The boys near him yelled with laughter. "I got plenty for you," he said, red faced.

I put my hand on his shoulder and moved him aside. As we walked away I looked back over my shoulder and said, "Sorry, I didn't bring my tweezers." The crowd laughed harder and one boy poked at Plaid Shirt's shoulder, almost knocking him down.

No one ever said you couldn't mix a little Assertiveness with Kindness, right?

We got to history and I patted Cassidy's shoulder. "Hang in there," I said, feeling like it was a completely inadequate thing to say. Then I had a great idea.

I slipped my letter bead bracelet off and slid it onto her wrist. "Wear this. It makes you strong and brave and all that good stuff. It really does."

Cassidy rubbed her fingers along it. "Okay. Thanks." She turned to walk into the room and then turned back around. "I don't deserve this. I mean, you, of all people, being nice to me." Her eyes filled up with tears. "But thank-you."

"Sure. See you in chemistry. Right after this, okay? You can make it."

I was late to keyboarding and snuck into the seat Melody had saved for me, pretending I didn't see the teacher's irritated look.

Melody looked at me wide eyed. "What were you *doing*!?" she whispered. "I heard about lunch."

"Tell you later," I whispered back.

It would have to be way later because after class I jetted to chemistry as fast as I could to meet Cassidy. Suddenly, protecting her was my obsession.

Go figure.

I caught up to Cassidy right before she went through the chemistry room door.

"Hey, here I am," I said, breathing heavily. I had actually almost run to get there.

Cassidy shook her head. "I don't know why you are doing this," she said, her eyes still looking dazed.

I shrugged. "No one deserves this."

Signs of life flickered through Cassidy's eyes, and I had the feeling she was recalling how she had been on the other end of this scenario. Many times. She shook her head. "I didn't know. I just didn't know."

I gave her a little push through the door. "Come on, let's get it done."

I steered her to her normal seat and glared at Alex who was already lounging in the back of the room. I leaned down close to him and said, "Be nice!"

He gave me the palms up gesture to say why wouldn't I be? Haha.

Emily came in and I gave her a wave. "Hey, Em, come on back."

Emily looked confused, but I had discovered that telling people what to do actually works. Of course, you had to sound like you knew what you were talking about. I had gotten so good at faking it that I almost believed I did.

I sat next to Alex and put Cassidy next to me with Emily on her other side. As other people straggled into the room staring at Cassidy, I stared back at all of them with a "what're you looking at?" stare.

Cassidy was rubbing the bracelet, taking it off and playing with it, putting it back on, rubbing it some more like a genie might just pop out and grant her three wishes.

I could guess what at least two of those wishes would be.

After class, Emily and I walked with her as far as we could before we had to turn off for geometry.

Cassidy clutched my arm. "Hey, um, could you wait for me by my locker after school? Can I talk to you again before I go home?"

"Sure," I said. "See you there."

Going home. What a viper pit that must seem to her. What if her dad knew? I had heard that voice of his, the hatred and ugliness it revealed in him. I couldn't imagine the fear.

Cassidy's problems did the one thing I thought was impossible. Pushed the scene with Mom to the back of my head.

Emily and I walked as quickly as we could toward geometry.

"What are you doing?" Emily asked as we dodged around a slow moving trio of girls. "Cassidy has been awful to you! Why are you being so nice?"

"I guess I understand how it feels," I said.

"Yeah, but jeez!" Emily said. "I just can't believe she *did* that. Eeww. Eeww. Eeww. Have you seen the pictures?"

"No," I said. "I don't want to."

"I mean she went on and on about abstinence and she was doing *that*! I don't get it."

I shook my head. "I don't know. I guess there is a lot of stuff I don't know. But I do know it feels awful to have the whole school laughing at you. And I don't wish that on anyone."

Emily looked shamefaced. "I'm so sorry, Jackie," she said. "So sorry."

We pushed through the geometry door and found our seats.

"It's okay," I said. "Really."

"How did you get so, so, I don't know, so *strong*?" said Emily.

It sounded funny to me, but she was right. Somewhere along the way I had gotten strong.

Yet again a class where I heard next to nothing. I was feeling so sad for Cassidy and yet pleased to have Emily back as a friend. Cassidy was no longer an issue between us. And my new eyes applied to Emily too. Who knew how hard her life had been when her parents were divorcing? Who knew what arguments she lived through, what fears? Emily kept looking at me and smiling, so I got the feeling she was as happy as me about our reconnection.

Cassidy was late to her locker after school. I kept checking my watch, worried I was going to miss my bus. Emily had been waiting with me but finally peeled off to catch *her* bus.

Cassidy was desperate for support so there's no way she would have blown me off. I was getting more and more worried. Just as I was about to leave I saw her come running down the hall.

As she got closer, I could see that Cassidy had been crying, tears streaking her mascara down her face. "Jackie! "

She threw herself into my arms, sobbing. "Omigod, omigod, omigod," she said over and over.

"What happened?" I said but got no answer for the longest time.

Finally Cassidy pulled her head up and looked at me with wild eyes. "I can't go home! *I can't*!"

"It's okay, calm down," I said, bus forgotten. By now the halls were empty so at least we didn't have to tolerate all the looks and laughs.

"It's NOT okay!" Cassidy sobbed. "If he finds out, my dad will kill me."

A cold shiver went through me. That may not have been an exaggeration.

"Maybe he won't find out," I said.

I squeezed her shoulders. So inadequate but the only comfort I could come up with.

Cassidy looked at me with grief. "You don't understand . . ."

"Actually, I think I do," I said softly. "I saw you and your dad on Saturday, in the parking lot behind Wally's."

Cassidy stared at me, probably so brain beaten by the day she couldn't process what I just said.

"I saw him hit you," I said.

Cassidy fell against my shoulder again and started crying all over. "*That's* why you were so nice to me. You know. *You know.*"

Her whole body sagged into mine as she cried. "You know," she sobbed again. I knew a little bit about the loneliness of pain. Cassidy knew a lot.

I kept wanting to say it's okay, but it wasn't. Nothing about her life was okay right now.

Finally Cassidy pulled herself back. She rubbed her eyes and then leaned back against the bank of lockers behind her and slid down to a sitting position. Her knees were bent up and she rested her arms on them, leaning her head on her arms.

"What am I going to do?"

"You're coming home with me," I said.

It's a strange world.

Chapter Fifty-Six

Breaking Free

Cassidy stared up at me with shock. "*Your* house?"

"Do you have a better idea?" I said. "We'd better hurry, we may have already missed the bus."

Jenny was in the family room with Davy when we came in. She was crouching behind the couch, pretending to fire a finger gun at Davy, whose was holed up in a fort made of couch pillows. "Pow, pow!" Davy yelled, sticking his own finger out of a space between pillows. Jenny gave me a wave and dropped down again.

Cassidy and I went to the kitchen and grabbed a bag of chips, a bag of mini-cookies, and some diet sodas, then headed up to my room.

"This is so bizarre," said Cassidy, "being here, at your house."

"Yeah, kind of weird," I said. I would never have imagined Cassidy Dubroski and I talking. In my house. In my room. Ever.

Cassidy stood up and walked around my room, stopping at one of the window seats. "This is pretty. I would like something like this."

"It's my favorite spot," I said, popping open a soda. I had tossed some pillows against the wall by my desk and was sitting on the floor, leaning back on them.

Cassidy turned around to look at me. "Why are you being so nice to me?" She repeated. "I mean, I know you know about my dad and all, but still."

I shrugged. "I guess I just know how 'life can go back on you'" I said.

"Huh?"

"That's a line from *The Yearling*. You know, the idea that life can fall apart, can get really sucky. That's happened to me."

I thought about Mom. "That's happened to me a bunch, like just this week."

Cassidy's eyes widened.

I decided to tell her. Maybe it would make her feel less like a fake if she knew about my life. I thought about that feeling of connection to everyone, and how it was still in me, and how it *helps* to know other people's troubles. Not to judge them, but to realize you aren't alone.

"My Mom freaked out and left. Like, I think, left the family," I said. Tears sprang up from nowhere.

"Oh wow, I'm sorry," said Cassidy, sitting down on the edge of my bed.

"Yeah, well, it was kind of my fault," I said, stopping because I was too choked up to talk. I took a couple of deep breaths and continued, "she read my diary, and I wrote some mean stuff about her and she just lost it."

Cassidy rolled her eyes. "No *way* could I write in a diary. I think my Dad would actually kill me if he read something like that." She turned around and flopped down onto my bed.

I nodded, managing to stop the tears. "What's wrong with them? I thought the adults in the world were supposed to be, I don't know, together. Mature, responsible . . . ."

"*Grown up*," finished Cassidy.

We gave each other little smiles. Laughing at the idiot adults around us.

"My dad is such an ass," Cassidy said, her voice getting thick like she was crying again. She dabbed at the sides of her eyes.

I couldn't imagine what it must be like to have a dad like that.

"He's been so horrible to your dad. You have no idea."

Maybe I do.

"He set your dad up for that harassment thing," she said. "I heard him talking about it. He's having an affair with Cynthia Burnham." Cassidy was full out crying now. "What a jerk. He doesn't even try to hide it from my mom. He brought her to our *house*. And my mom is such a wimp, sticking around."

Yeah, I'll definitely stick with my own problems.

Cassidy rolled onto her stomach and rested her head on her arms sobbing.

A lot of crying has happened on this bed.

"I don't know if I can go home," she said, her voice muffled by the bed. "What if my dad found out about the pictures? You have no idea what he'd do to me."

I didn't know what to say. Cassidy had a really screwed up life.

"I do everything perfect, I really do!" she cried. "I do everything I can to please him and to not make him mad, and he still hits me." She picked her head up again and looked at me. "He would kill me if he knew I was telling you." She hiccupped out another sob. "I've never told anyone. I can't believe I'm saying this to you." Her eyes got scared. "You can't ever tell anyone! Please."

I shook my head. "Of course not! I won't."

Except my Dad. Whoops.

Cassidy rolled onto her side and propped her head on a bent arm. "Do you know why he was mad at me on Saturday, when you saw me? Because I forgot to pick up his watch at the jewelers! He was getting a new battery. I just forgot."

I felt small compared to her problems. I felt way in over my head.

"That sucks. I mean, just because you forgot something?"

She looked down at the bed and picked at the seam in the comforter. No answer.

I thought about Cassidy and her criticisms of people at school. It was all about looking and acting just the right way. One person was not pretty enough, another had nerdy clothes. No wonder she was so obsessed with perfection. At her house, imperfection got you clobbered.

"Cassidy, I just don't think it is up to you. If your dad is that mean, then there's nothing you could do to stop him. Nothing. Even if you were perfect."

Cassidy rolled onto her back, sniffling. I handed her some Kleenex. "I don't know. There were times when everything seemed fine at home. And it always seems like he starts hitting when me or my mom do something wrong."

"Hitting for forgetting to pick up a watch? It's just human to forget something. You don't deserve to get hit for that."

"And not to make you feel bad or anything, but it got a lot worse after your dad came to town," Cassidy added. "He *hates* your dad. Your dad is one of the only people he can't control and it drives him insane."

I felt so sad for Cassidy. What a scary home to live in. How awful to be always walking on eggshells, always trying to be perfect to prevent getting hit.

My brain went very still.

What was that?

I didn't even want to go back to that thought.

I stayed still for longer, not even hearing Cassidy's crying.

Finally, I let my brain ease up against that thought again. Always walking on eggshells, always trying to be perfect.

That applied to *me,* too.

That was *exactly* me. Doing everything I could to make Mom happy, keep her happy, anticipate her unhappiness and head it off.

And ultimately, failing.

Of course I failed. I had as much chance of success with Mom as Cassidy had with her dad. As much chance of Sara changing the horrible Miss Minchin, or the Little Prince changing his rose.

I stood up and walked around the room, mulling that over.

Ohmigod. Ohmigod. Ohmigod.

It wasn't up to me.

It wasn't under my control.

It never had been.

I felt my heart growing, like the Grinch's at the end of *The Grinch Who Stole Christmas.* I felt strength flowing through my veins, like when Popeye eats a can of spinach. I felt the strangler fig vines withering away.

It wasn't up to me!

"Cassidy! It's not our fault!" I said, moving back to the bed. The excitement was buzzing in me, and I wanted to share it.

"Huh?"

"My Mom, she doesn't hit me, but she is, I don't know, kind of crazy. There, I said it, the secret is out. She's been so depressed and nothing I do pleases her, not really. I've been cleaning the house and taking care of my brother and praising her." I tugged at my hair. "I even got this ridiculous haircut just to make her happy. I have worn stupid looking clothes. I have done all that and she *still* went freakazoid on me the other night." I grabbed Cassidy's hand. "It's not our fault! I've been thinking it was all along, but hearing about your dad, well that's just easier to see. Maybe because it isn't in my family."

Cassidy frowned at me. "*I* know he shouldn't hit me! I *know* that! I'm not an idiot. I don't believe I *deserve* it."

"Yeah, but you believe you can behave well enough to prevent it, don't you?"

"Well, I don't know, I guess so," she said.

"That's the thing that's wrong," I said. "I thought if I just did everything to keep my Mom happy that it would all work out, and it didn't. I thought if I could just figure out why my aunt killed herself I could prevent it from happening to my mom."

"Your aunt killed herself?" Cassidy stared at me in shock.

"Yeah, my mom's twin sister. And no one will talk about it and my mom's been so depressed and no one seems to believe she could, you know, do the same thing. And I've been trying so hard to keep her happy."

"Wow." For a moment Cassidy seemed to forget her own problems.

"She read MY freaking diary. I have a right to keep that private! That was MINE. It didn't matter how many loads of laundry I did or how often I put my brother to bed, she's still crazy."

"She shouldn't have read your diary," agreed Cassidy.

"Exactly," I said. "I mean, I'm sorry she's so depressed and all. I wish someone would help her, but does that mean it is all my fault she left?" Even as I said it, I had my doubts. It seemed clear that Cassidy wasn't responsible for her problems, but maybe I was for ours. Maybe I *should* have left it all alone.

"You can't help it if she's depressed," said Cassidy. "And everyone writes in a diary. Moms aren't supposed to read them."

"I had it hidden between some extra pillows in my closet," I said. "It wasn't even like I wasn't careful. But she still found it."

Cassidy nodded. "I can see your point about your mom, but I don't know if it's the same thing with my Dad."

In Cassidy's case I was sure. It was not her fault. It was not her fault her dad acted like a psycho.

"Oh, why did I take those pictures," Cassidy moaned. She had moved to the window seat and was staring out at the cold, darkening yard.

Good question.

I could guess, with no psychology background at all, I could guess. Maybe she wanted to please a different man? Maybe the way she acted around her dad was the way she would act with a boyfriend, or someone she wanted to please.

"I should have stayed with Ben," Cassidy's voice was muffled. "*He* was the nice guy. He was the one."

I had to agree with her there.

"Yeah, you know, it might not be too late with Ben," I said.

Cassidy lifted her head and looked at me. "Are you kidding? After all this?"

"Yeah, well I've been sitting with him at lunch, and he still seems to like you. And he defended you today too."

Was that just today? Seemed like years ago.

Cassidy shook her head and stared back out the window.

We sat in silence for a few minutes.

"I'm going to need a ride home, I guess," said Cassidy. "If I don't get home soon . . . ."

Her dad would be mad. And mad had a whole different meaning in her house.

"My dad could give you a ride," I said. "He'll be home any minute."

"Huh! No way could I drive up to my house with your dad! That would get me killed." Cassidy stopped and thought. "And I can't call my Mom. She might tell my Dad where I've been."

Cassidy got up and grabbed her backpack, pulling her phone out of it.

"Well, here goes," she said, punching in some numbers.

"Hey, uh, hi, it's me," she said into the phone, her voice soft and contrite. "Umm, first of all, I'm sorry, you know, for everything. Really. I'm such an idiot."

I couldn't hear the other person, but I had a guess as to who it was. Even though she could have said those words to a lot of people. Cassidy looked at me and all of a sudden I felt like I was invading her privacy or something.

"I'll be right back," I whispered and slipped out of my room.

Sure enough, Ben came to pick up Cassidy. Standing at the front door she hugged me. "Thank-you," she started to say and then choked back tears. "I'm so sorry for, uh, before. I had no idea . . . anyway, thank-you."

I hugged her back. "It's okay. Call me. And remember, it's not your fault. Never was."

Cassidy shrugged that one off. She'd have to come to that on her own.

She stepped out into the cold night, and I gave a wave to Ben in the car. He smiled back and flashed me a quick thumbs-up.

Chapter Fifty-Seven

An Uneasy Quiet

I sat down in the family room with Dad. He was off the phone and piling his papers into a stack.

"How in the world did Cassidy end up here?" he asked. I had made a quick introduction before she left with Ben. My dad had kept a straight face, but I could see the questions in his eyes.

I told him the whole thing. At first it felt weird to talk about sex stuff with my dad, but he stayed calm and focused on the point of the story.

"That poor girl," Dad said, echoing my own thoughts. He got up and made himself a drink. Some nasty looking caramel colored stuff.

"Oh, and I forgot! She said something about her dad having an affair with the lady who is suing you."

Dad's eyebrows went way up. "Really?" He took a long drink. "Hmmm. That would explain it. Why didn't I think of that?"

"Because your brain isn't as evil as his?" I said.

"Cynthia Burnham and Dubroski. Wow. Would *not* have put those two together."

"Well, does that help you?" I asked.

Dad rocked his head back and forth. "It might. We'll have to see."

I looked around the room. "Where's Davy?"

Dad gave a little smile. "Must be upstairs. Jenny already left." He looked at his watch. "Have you eaten?"

"Just some chips."

"Maybe a pizza?" Dad said.

"Sure." It felt weird to have Mom gone. Although she had not been herself lately (well, five years or so), she still imposed some kind of routine on the house. So even though it was calmer, it was an uneasy quiet.

Dad had way fewer rules than Mom so we ate the pizza at the coffee table. I was surprised by how hungry I was. It was like my stomach operated completely independently from my brain.

Davy was asleep inside his couch fort.

"Should we wake him?" asked Dad.

"No, when he falls asleep this late Mom just lets him sleep, then puts him right into bed." It felt funny to even say "Mom."

Dad must have picked up on my unease. "It's not your fault she left."

I nodded. "I know."

I mostly did. By looking in on Cassidy's life, I was able to see that it might be the same for me.

"I'm sorry for all this. Sorry I've been so, uh, unavailable." Dad took another huge bite and chomped for a while. "I've been thinking about how little I've been around you, how little I've been home." He blew out a big breath. "I'm sorry. Really sorry."

Dad looked tired, but, true to form, still calm and in charge. "I've blown it with your mother too. I haven't really wanted to see that she's been struggling."

I nodded.

"It's just, well, I never put her in the same category as Helen. Your mom didn't have Helen's issues.

"You mean being able to have kids."

Dad agreed. "It seemed so clear that Helen's depression came from that. They tried so hard for so long and she just, I guess, never got over it."

Made sense to me, but I guess not to Mom.

"And then, sure, your mom was really down right after Davy was born, but that was right after Helen's, you know, death, and I also thought maybe she had some post-partum stuff, baby blues kind of thing." Dad nibbled on the end of a piece of pizza.

"Well whatever it is, she's not over it," I said feeling emboldened. Anxious, but glad to be talking about it. "I don't think you realize it. I come home from school and she's in bed. And she barely pays attention to Davy. And she cries a lot."

Deep sigh from Dad. "No, you're right. I've been oblivious. I'm sorry."

I felt myself tearing up. The relief of having Dad finally get it was too much.

"Jackie, I know you probably don't believe this, but part of this is my fault. Sometimes I'm too unemotional. Sometimes I forget what she needs, what you guys need. I'm trying so hard to do a good job at work and I know there's a cost at home for that."

"Dad, you're great, she's the one who's a mess."

He shook his head. "I don't expect you to understand, but honestly, marriage takes two people." He paused. "I've been selfish, too worried about work to really be there for her. Willing to believe it when she said everything was fine."

I wandered around my bedroom, unable to sleep. Unable even to read. I thought about Cassidy and wondered if she got home all right. I wondered about her and Ben and if they would get back together, I really hoped they did. I thought about Mom and worked up some fresh anger at her for abandoning Davy the way she did. Forget about me or Dad, how could she just take off and leave Davy? Then I thought about Dad. How calm he was, even with the big messes around him at work and at home. I thought about how he really looked at me when we talked. How his attention didn't seem to be on anything but me. That when he was talking with me that moment was *mine*. With Mom it was like her eyes were directed toward me but always looking beyond me, to the next event, to the next person, to the new wallpaper selection. I felt closer to Dad right now than I had to Mom in years. Maybe ever.

Then I thought about what a relief it was to have Dad really seem to get it that Mom was not okay. To not be alone in trying to save her. To realize it wasn't even really my job to save her. I had felt so certain of that when Cassidy was here. It had seemed so clear, she didn't cause her dad to hit her, I didn't cause my mom to be depressed. And yet, I could feel how fragile that new belief was. It could disappear in a second. Part of my brain was already protesting, saying that was selfish and of course I needed to make sure Mom was okay. What daughter would just let her mother flounder in a depression? No, no, the new strong me said. Dad is on the case. Mom is an adult. I can't be the one to fix it all. My brain was getting too crowded. Time for a new book

I put on my nightshirt and looked for something comforting. Something old-fashioned and outside of my reality.

I picked *Anne of Green Gables*. A beloved classic. I knew exactly what I was getting into with Anne. Sweet, wholesome, optimistic. Everything my life wasn't. On the very first page of the book, I was reminded that the whole story starts with the fact that Anne is orphaned. I was starting to see the value in that.

The noisy voices my brain were gradually quieted by the descriptions of the town of Avonlea on Prince Edward Island and of the characters, even nosy Mrs. Lynde. Reading about Anne was like rediscovering an old friend. In no time at all I was rooting for her to get to stay at Green Gables when Marilla discovers that her brother Matthew has brought back a girl orphan instead of the boy orphan he set out to get. I read, "And upstairs, in the east gable, a lonely, heart-hungry, friendless child cried herself to sleep."

Tears slipped out of my eyes. I knew just how Anne felt, I was also lying in a lonely bed. And that made me think of the vacant spot in Jody's heart, and how mine was vacant too. How long I'd been missing a mother. Maybe you miss something more when you think you have it but really don't.

I forced myself back to the book and thinking about how Jody and Anne would have gotten along. I'm sure they would be, in Anne words, "kindred spirits" because Anne has Appreciation too.

As I read on, I was reminded of how imaginative Anne is. She gives things names like "Violet Vale" and "The Lake of Shining Waters" and notices everything and appreciates everything. Even when Anne is in the "depths of despair" she is able to appreciate the beauty around her.

Although I had been feeling pretty sorry for myself, I had to admit that Anne had a more difficult life than me. For one thing she is an orphan. No parents! And for another, she had been forced to live with families who made her work all day long. And then she comes to beautiful Green Gables only to discover Marilla doesn't mean to keep her. I was amazed that a person could still find joy on the day that she is to be sent away. ("Don't you feel as if you just loved the world on a morning like this?" Anne asks.)

When I read those words, feeling fully as if I were Anne and not Jacqueline, I was sure everything could work out fine. I stayed in Prince Edward Island until I drifted off to sleep.

Chapter Fifty-Eight

Super J

The next thing I knew, the gray morning light was coming in the window. Before my eyes even opened fully, I remembered it all. Mom gone, Cassidy here, Dad and I talking it out.

One day. I had gotten one freaking happy day out of this whole time in Kentley Heights. One day to float around school, warm and connected and happy. And then Mom had to complicate it all again. With the warmth of *Anne of Green Gables* still drifting around in my head, and my conversation with Cassidy still echoing, I felt closer to the connected feeling than to despairing ones, but it still felt fragile. I needed a way to keep reminding myself that Mom's problems were not my fault, not my responsibility. And to keep reminding myself that everyone is connected, everyone has challenges. I wanted to be like Anne today, seeing the beauty and wonder in everything. I reached for my wrist to touch my bracelet and then remembered I had given it to Cassidy.

Wear it well Cassidy. Wear it well.

I scrambled to make myself another bracelet and took a moment to look at each letter and imagine myself living that trait. I took three deep breaths and headed downstairs.

Between the two of us, Dad and I got Davy ready for school. Dad took off with Davy, promising Jenny would be here when he got home.

The rumors about Cassidy had intensified over night, especially with the news that the pervy gym teacher Donovan had been fired. The story going around was that *he* was the one in the pictures with Cassidy. Eeew, eew, eeww. By the end of the day the frenzy of gossip had grown to ridiculous proportions. Cassidy had slept with all the male teachers. Cassidy was carrying Donovan's baby. Cassidy made a sex tape with Donovan. Couldn't all be true, I'm sure.

Cassidy, of course, was not at school. Neither was Ben.

In English, we finished talking about *The Yearling*. And thinking about that book made me realize that it turns out I am not so bad at protecting against wolves after all. I felt a kinship with Jody that stretched across generations and states and the fiction/non-fiction divide.

Tommy walked out of class with me. "Yeah, that book ended up being pretty good," he said, shuffling along in beat-up running shoes and dragging warm-up pants. "You were right."

I nodded. "I loved the ending. That line about being lonely but how you can take your part and continue on."

Tommy agreed, his whole face lighting up. "I know! Awesome. And I like how the book talks about how life 'goes back on you sometimes.' Ain't that the truth!" There was admiration in his blue eyes. He didn't look at all like I imagined Jody, but there was a Jody spirit in him.

"For sure," I agreed. It made me wonder about Tommy, what had gone on in his life to make him identify with that line so much? Then I thought about Cassidy. And about my parents, Davy, Emily and everyone around me. Life goes back on everyone, at times. And we all just have to take it for our share and find a way to go on. Even Cassidy, dealt the awful family she had, had to find a way to go on. She had no choice.

I love books that show people with hard lives and how those people find their way out. Sure, the superficial books can be entertaining, but the books like *The Yearling*, they offer a road map for life. The main character doesn't even have to be like you, because in the end, we all have hard stuff happen, it is finding your way through and even out that is the crucial part. And Jody showed me that. And Sara. And Claudia. And Ken. And now Anne.

I felt for my bracelet and thought again about Cassidy, hoping the bracelet I gave her was giving her some kind of strength. Since she didn't know what the letters stood for, I could only hope that the bracelet would be some sort of reminder that someone stood up for her. For me, the bracelet stood for everything I had been growing inside myself. Looking at the letters, touching them, was just a reminder of what lies inside.

"So, uh, are you going to the Christmas dance?" Tommy asked.

"What? Oh, I don't know," I said, flustered.

"Do you want to?"

Was he asking me to go with him? Boys can be so thick sometimes. I didn't answer right away, trying to analyze his tone and the look on his face.

"I mean, if someone already asked you . . ." Tommy's face got even pinker than normal.

He was asking me!

How did I feel about that?

"Whoops, gonna be late, catch you later," Tommy said and took off down the hall.

I didn't even have a chance to answer him. I didn't have an answer. Did I want to go with him?

I caught up to Melody on my way to keyboarding. "Hey, Melody, what's up?" I said. "Here, let me take that stuff from you." I took the backpack that was banging off her crutches and carried it.

"So what was with you and Cassidy yesterday?" Melody said, swinging along. She had gotten fast on those crutches.

"I felt sorry for her," I said. "I know what it feels like when everyone is laughing at you."

"Yeah, you know that because *she* did it to *you*!" said Melody.

"I know, but I also think maybe she doesn't have the greatest home life," I said. That was as close as I could come to that story.

Melody shook her head. "Who does?"

"Exactly!" I said. "I think everyone's got tough stuff to deal with. And I refuse to be the kind of person who makes it worse."

"The new Mother Teresa," Melody teased. "With super cool hair."

"Oh yeah, that's me," I said.

Sandra Bonita and Kelly Munson rushed up to me as we walked into keyboarding. "What were you doing with Cassidy yesterday?!" panted Sandra. "She hates you! She's such a skank."

"She's not a skank," I said. "She's not so bad, after all."

"She's a nympho! And a hypocrite!" said Kelly.

"And you are so perfect?" I said.

Kelly gasped. "What are you saying?"

"I'm just saying we're all human. We all make mistakes. Get over it." I said it in as mild of a voice as I could. I wasn't judging Kelly or Sandra. I just didn't want to have these mean gossipy conversations.

Melody stared at me as Kelly and Sandra sank into their seats, silenced. "Where is this all coming from?"

I shrugged.

Melody smiled. "I love it. I think you're my new hero. Super J."

On the way to lunch, an arm landed around my shoulders. I could tell by the explosion of nerve endings throughout my body it must be Alex.

"Hi, Jackie," Alex said in his ultra-cool flirty voice.

"Hey," I said.

"So now you are like Superman, swooping in to save anyone who's in trouble?" Alex said as we jostled along in the crowd. I think he was adding some extra jostling of his own, banging his hip against mine repeatedly.

"Super*woman*."

"Good, because I'm in trouble. Can you save me?"

"Sure, what'll it be? Pick up a burning car? Stretch myself into a piece of bridge to allow the train to go over?"

Alex gave an extra squeeze and leaned into whisper in my ear. "I need a date for the dance on Friday. Save me and go with me."

I have lived over fourteen years with no date. No boyfriends. Not a kiss. And now I get asked out twice in one day. What was going on?

Before I could answer Nick jumped along my other side. "Hey kids," he said, throwing his arm around me too so that we were walking three across.

Saved. Because I had no answer.

Alex dropped his arm and we turned into the cafeteria.

I ate and joked with the boys and avoided Alex's intense looks.

"No doubt it was Donovan. You can see him flexing even during the deed," said Andy.

I was already tired of the Cassidy sex scandal. Too bad. It was going to go on and on.

"And that girl's. . ." Nick started before I cut him off.

"Are you guys going to say disgustingly sexist, objectifying kinds of piggy things? Because if you are, I'm out of here."

Lots of eye rolls.

"Okay, see ya," I said, gathering up my stuff and moving. "No hard feelings, just don't need to hear what you guys can't stop yourselves from saying."

I could feel Alex's eyes boring into my back. At least I hope it was my back.

Frankly, I was just glad to get away from Alex and think about the whole dance thing. What did I really want? Or whom?

Chapter Fifty-Nine

"Stars Upon Thars"

Dad stepped up. There's no other way to put it. For the next couple of days he juggled work, Davy and me. Not that I needed so much, but he was there. He did that same thing where he really stopped and listened when I was talking. And I saw him doing it with Davy too. Davy cried for mom a couple of times, but Dad told him she was on a trip with Aunt Ruth. Davy seemed satisfied with that answer, and I saw him find a whole new life with Dad. They rode Big Wheels in the hall every night. Dad figured out how to give him a bath without soaking the entire bathroom. And they started a game Dad called "let's get rough!" where they wrestled all over the floor. And the couches. And the stairs for crying out loud. Mom would have had a heart attack.

I could see it in Davy's eyes. He had a new hero. He added one of Dad's ties to his Batman costume.

I stepped up too. I tried to cook dinner by myself (with mixed results), and I already knew how to do laundry and stuff. Dad chipped in when he could. The house wasn't decorator perfect, but I kind of liked it that way.

It all made me think that being motherless wasn't so bad. Not that I wished Mom wouldn't come back, but the house was way calmer without her. Plus, I could see that a lot of people have made it through life without a mother. Look at Beryl and Sara and Anne. Even Nancy Drew was motherless. It actually seemed to help all them. They grew up faster and they got plenty Self-sufficient, and Brave and all my other Desired Personality Characteristics.

Living on Prince Edward Island with Anne helped me notice all the 'kindred spirits' in the world. There were people like me and we could find each other and that gave me some comfort in my upside-down life.

I didn't know what would happen with Mom, but I was assuming she'd come back at some point. Even *I* didn't think she was that crazy. So how to handle her when she did? I guess it depended on which Mom came back. If it was the recent Mom, the one who tried to pretend away huge chunks of her life, we'd be right back where we started. If it was the Mom who was willing to *deal* then maybe things would work out. Or maybe she was too far gone to be either one. Maybe she opened it all up and now was just a quivering mess. Maybe she'd hate me forever, blame me for setting loose the Dementors.

Whatever happened, someone had to be here for Davy. I could live without Mom's love (I think, I mean, I had when I really looked at it) but that was too cruel to ask of a five-year-old. Everyone believes you have to have a mother's love. But maybe that love can come in all sorts of packages. Maybe it can come in a dad. Maybe it can come in a sister, even a loving babysitter. Davy was actually looking okay these days.

And although Dad was working extra hard on every front, the tension on his face had lessened. And that stress had been removed courtesy of Cassidy, of all people. When Dad's lawyer confronted Cynthia Burnham about the affair, she broke down and confessed it all. Mr. Dubroski was in for some hell of his own. Couldn't happen to a better person, if you ask me.

Dad talked to Mom a couple of times but all he told me was that she and Aunt Ruth were "working on it." I was glad to have someone else take over as Mom's babysitter and didn't ask more.

Cassidy hadn't come back to school, and it kind of reminded me of the end of *The Little Prince*. Some days the pilot is happy, knowing that there is laughter in the stars from the Little Prince, and some days the pilot is sad, knowing that the lamb he drew for the Little Prince might have gotten loose and eaten the rose. Some days I was sure Cassidy was fine and better off gone, other days I thought she might just have ruined her life. And Ben's, because he hadn't shown up at school either. And then finally I got a text from her. She said that Ben drove her to Florida to her grandmother's house, and she was hoping to convince her mother to come there too. She wanted to know what the letters on the bracelet stood for. I texted her back.

> there is a way to
> get strong. mine
> was borrowing
> personality characteristics
> from book characters.
> yours might be
> something else. but
> i guarantee you, the
> something else is out there.

With Queen Bee Cassidy gone the Poms reorganized, in fact the whole school hive reorganized. It reminded me of *The Sneetches* from Dr. Suess. I *love* that book, the whole "stars upon 'thars'" bit. How the Sneetches with stars on their stomachs think they are better than those with none, and then how that guy comes along with a machine to add stars and then take them off. And how the Sneetches are putting stars on and taking them off so fast that in the end no one knows who was supposed to be superior. I'll tell you who was superior: the guy making all the money from putting on and taking off stars. At school the whole "stars upon 'thars'" thing got so complicated that I forgot who was supposed to be popular and who wasn't. I didn't care. I had my friends, and I was happy with them. Emily and Melody and Jennifer Barnes, who it turned out was as real and nice on the inside as she was fake, tanned and bleach haired on the outside.

I went to the dance with Tommy. I still felt a tingle inside around Alex, but dating him would be like learning to drive in a Maserati. A Volvo station wagon like Tommy was more my speed for now. Alex kind of said as much when I caught him after school and told him no.

"Okay, Carson. I'm going to take that as a no *for now*."

He pulled me toward him and before I knew what was happening, his mouth was on mine. And it stayed there a while, warm and wet and amazing. I completely melted against him, locked in his force field, all brain functioning gone haywire. He gave a last little swirly movement with his lips and then leaned back. He gave me a devil smile, one more squeezy hug and walked away.

My first kiss. And it was an *awesome* one.

I got my second one Friday night. It wasn't bad either.

Chapter Sixty

The Return

I spent all weekend replaying the dance in my head. I couldn't believe I ever thought Tommy looked piggy. He was cute and nice and just my speed. And then, Mom came back Sunday night. Dad told us at dinner she'd be coming back, keeping his tone light for Davy.

"How, uh, was her trip?" I asked, my eyes meeting Dad's to ask the real question of "how is she?"

Dad glanced at Davy, "Fine, I'm sure it was fine."

That was no help.

I heard the garage door going up around 7:00. Davy leaped off the couch and ran for the kitchen. I slipped out of the family room and went up to my room. I wanted to give Davy some time for pure joy, in case it all went bad again around me.

I knew Dad had talked to Mom on the phone several times while she was gone, but I didn't listen in. I was trying to reform those instincts to control and manipulate their world. I didn't talk to her at all, so I had no idea how she was feeling about me.

After fifteen minutes, I headed downstairs, repeating to myself "Kindness, Dignity, Kindness, Dignity." I rubbed the new letter bracelet.

I found them in the family room, Davy tucked securely into Mom's lap. Dad was standing near the TV, looking at me with eyes that said, "You can do this."

"Hello, Jackie," Mom said in a stiff voice.

She said "Jackie." She is trying.

"Hi, Mom," I said, trying for a kind voice.

Mom glanced down at Davy, squeezing him so hard he yelped.

In that glance, in just a millisecond, I saw pain, and fear in Mom's eyes. It reminded me of Cassidy, way back when, when I slammed her against the locker.

Mom is scared of me.

I burst into tears and ran to the couch, kneeling at her feet and wrapping my arms around her legs. "Mommy, I'm so sorry! I'm so sorry!"

It wasn't out of fear that I said it, and I wasn't trying to manipulate or hoping for a particular reaction. It was pure emotion, and it was driven by compassion for Mom, for all the pain she had been living in. And I felt genuinely sorry that I caused her additional pain. I knew I wasn't responsible for the big hurt, but I also knew my diary had added to that hurt. I think my words were just echoing what she already felt inside, what she was already saying to herself. She shouldn't have read my diary, but what she read had truly hurt her. And I was sorry about that.

Mom slid Davy to the side of her and bent down and hugged me. I felt her tears dropping on my head. "I'm sorry too," she whispered.

We clung to each other for a couple of minutes, and then I finally looked up at her. She gave me a pained little smile. I returned it.

"My smart girl," Mom said softly. "My smart, smart girl."

"Mama, did you bring me a present?" Davy asked, poking at Mom's arm.

"No, not this time. Next time maybe," Mom said. "Okay, mister, time to get you up to bed."

Mom stood up, grabbing Davy's hand and walking him towards the door. She turned around, "And Jackie, we have more to talk about. You deserve it."

Whatever that meant.

After the Davy bedtime routine, Mom came back and sat down next to me on the couch. She glanced at Dad and told him to go give Davy a little extra snuggle time. After he left Mom took a deep breath and blew it out. Did it again, then started crying. Swiping at her eyes and seeing my concern she smiled through the tears. "It's okay. I mean, it's not okay, but I am on the road to okay. You were right. You were the only one."

I realized my insides were tense and had been since she got home.

Mom went on, her voice shaky. "You were right," she repeated. "No one in my family ever talked about Helen, no one really grieved her." Mom broke down again, unable to speak.

"Mom, I'm sorry," I said, starting to cry myself, sorry for everything. Sorry about Aunt Helen, sorry Mom was crying so hard right now, sorry for my part in it all.

"No, it's okay," Mom said through the sobs "I need to do this. I *need* to cry. I need to talk about it."

I nodded. That had been my instinct all along.

"I thought I could just, I don't know, put it in the past. Make it go away, but it was always a big, no *huge*, dark shadow following me. It wouldn't go away."

Mom wiped her eyes, a losing battle if you asked me.

"And the worst, darkest shadow," Mom's crying got so hard she couldn't speak again, and then she got some control. "And the worst was, I knew Helen wanted a baby, and I here I had *two*. With no problems. I felt so guilty. So so guilty."

Mom looked down at her lap and let the tears fall. She stared at her thumbs, rubbing them together.

"And so Davy was born, and I had my boy and my girl and for a day I was so happy and then, Helen, I guess she couldn't take it and, you know, killed herself. And I felt so awful, like I had been the one to do it to her. *Why* did I have another baby? It was," she stopped and her voice went up about a couple of octaves. "It was *Davy* that pushed her over the edge."

More racking sobs.

Choking out the words, Mom continued. "And how could I love him when I felt like it had killed my sister for me to have him? And I *know* that is what it was! I just know it."

By now I was sobbing just as hard as Mom. How hard it must have been for Mom, feeling like the most joyous thing, the birth of her baby, killed her sister. I felt like I was in her skin, the way I feel when I am inhabiting a book character. I felt the dark shadows and the bitter, ripping pain. I literally felt like I was looking out through her eyes, that I felt like I had killed my sister.

I hugged mom, and we clung together, crying. I didn't have words, just pain.

Finally, when we both had used up what felt like our lifetime supply of tears, Mom pulled back a little so she could look

at me. "I'm telling you this because I have felt so crazy for so long
and you deserve to know why. I have felt so wrong for so long. I
have been afraid to love you, to love Davy." More sobs, but quieter
now.

"I have been an awful mother, just like all this time I felt
like an awful sister."

I protested, "No! No you haven't," but we both knew she
hadn't been a great mother.

Mom held up her hand, "No, I was, but Ruth and I have
been talking about this for days, and I am finally starting to think
maybe it is not my fault that Helen did that. If the positions were
reversed, I would *never* have wished her not to have kids. I don't
think she wished that on me. She just wanted some for her own.
She was very troubled."

Mom gave a wan little smile. "It was good to talk to Ruth.
No one in my family *talks* about this stuff and I think we both
needed to. Of course my mother and father wanted nothing of it.
They still live in denial-land."

Mom patted my arm. "They don't have someone like you to
force them out."

She gave me a smile and then turned, put both hands on
my shoulders and stared into my eyes. "This isn't over. I've just
started but it feels right. And you were right. And I'm sorry for all I
put you through." By the end she was in tears again.

I pulled her towards me into another hug. "It's okay,
mommy," I said, feeling like a little girl.

Mom gave a strong squeeze, holding me tightly. And for
the first time in a long time, the hug didn't feel like a strangler fig. It
felt like a mother, a tender little shoot of a tree that could someday
be a strong mother. "And I *love* you," she said fiercely.

"It's okay mom" I said again, through my own tears. How
many times had I said the words "it's okay" and not meant them?
For the first time, those words felt true. It was okay. I understood
her.

"You were right," mom repeated, head buried in my
shoulder. "You were right. You were the only one who was right.
You knew that the truth was the thing. It hurts so much, but it is
the thing."

We pulled apart a couple of inches and mom wiped her face. "I know there are a lot more tears in my future. But I see what needs to be done. I'm willing to take on the dark shadow. I've walked right into it, and I'm not stopping 'til it is gone. And yes, I will get help with it. Ruth and I are going to go see a therapist together. I don't think we'll ever get Mom and Dad there, but that is their journey I guess.

I guess we were both ready to take it for our share and move on.

Chapter Sixty-One

Reverse Strangler Fig

I was up in my window seat, wrapped in the fuzzy peach blanket, staring out the dark window at the new snow lighting up the lawn. I let *Anne of Green Gables* fall into my lap and looked out at the Christmas lights in the distance. I had forgotten even that the season was here. How many little kids would stare up at this sky, straining to hear the jingle of Santa's reindeer? Wishing and hoping that Santa would land on their roof soon, and that their life's dream of toys would appear in their living rooms. I knew life didn't work that way. The real good stuff doesn't just drop down from the sky. You had to work for it. You had to build it, bit by bit, from whatever materials you had. You had to fight your way through grasping vines and lonely darkness to get to the good stuff.

I looked down and ran my fingers over the passage in *Anne of Green Gables* that had stopped me. "*. . . in brief, the beautiful world of blossom and love and friendship had lost none of its power to please her fancy and thrill her heart, that life still called to her with many insistent voices.*" I thought about how lucky I was to have all my book friends. They were the insistent voices that called to me. I had a tribe. Even when I had no real friends, I was surrounded by the courage and example of Claudia and Beryl and Ken and all the rest. I knew I would not have made it through without them. I thought back to the passage in *West with the Night*, the one about loneliness and avoiding yourself. I thought about how I had worried that I was avoiding myself by taking Claudia and Beryl and the rest into my head. Now I knew I needn't have worried. Claudia and Beryl and all the rest of my book friends had helped me *find* myself, not lose myself. My heart was swollen with gratitude for them all, Claudia, Beryl, Meg, Sara, Nancy, Jody, Anne, even old Santiago. All those things I admired in Claudia and Beryl and Sara, it turned out, were parts of me. I didn't start out Brave or Confident or Self-sufficient, but I had the seeds of those things in me. And those characters helped me give water and light to the seeds, growing me big and strong. Strong enough that the strangler fig couldn't suffocate me. I was too big and too strong to be encircled by that pain. I felt so solid, so firmly *me*, that I honestly believed I could defend myself against any kind of wolf or Queen Bee or strangler fig that came my way.

My heart felt big enough to consider something else, too. All along I had thought of Mom as the strangler fig, but I realized now that she was just as much a victim of the strangler fig as me. Her heart had been encircled by the killing vines even more than mine. And I had a new understanding of the strangler fig. It was just a plant, just doing what it was designed to do, just trying to stay alive in the only way it knew how. It isn't evil that feeds the strangler fig, it is darkness.

And we had stepped into the light.

The End.

Acknowledgments

This book grew from my life long love of reading, so the first people I'd like to thank are all the authors who have come before me, lighting the way. As Franz Kafka said, "A book should serve as the axe for the frozen sea within us." I'm not sure I would have made it to adulthood intact without books and I'm certain I would still be a frozen block of ice had I not learned to read. Thank you to my parents for encouraging my love of reading and for buying me as many books as I wanted.

There is no way this book could have been written without the love and support of my husband Dave, who never hesitated when I told him what I wanted to do. He believed even during the times I doubted and he even provided me with an "Esquer grant" so that I could take time off from paid work. He is a rock star masquerading as a baseball coach.

My first reader, Alicia Rowell, gave invaluable advice (along the lines of "cut it in half! At least") and helped me believe it was possible to finish (again). Subsequent readers, especially my teen team, were also very helpful in identifying mistakes, plot holes, and the betraying signs of a middle aged woman writing as a teenager. Special thanks to Emily Sher and Hannah Sher.

Alison Hubbs has been an extraordinary editor, bearing the tedium of correcting my many mistakes with good humor and reading and re-reading the many drafts this book required without complaint. Any mistakes that remain are mine.

Kristin Abbott did an *amazing* job on the cover art for the book, giving so much of her time and exquisite skill. She completely captured Jacqueline.

Finally, this is for my children, Elle and Xavier, who show all the signs of being life long readers themselves. As I tell them every night, I'm the luckiest mom in the world.

Contact Information:
Lynn Rankin-Esquer
lynn@lynnrankinesquer.com